SALTY
MISS
TENDERLOIN

by
JACKI LYON

SALTY
MISS
TENDERLOIN

SALTY
MISS
TENDERLOIN

JACKI LYON

LITERARY LEGENDS, LLC
CINCINNATI, OHIO

Salty Miss Tenderloin

Literary Legends, LLC, Cincinnati, Ohio

Publication Date: March 4, 2013

Printed in the United States of America. For information, contact Jacki Lyon at jacqeulinemlyon@gmail.com.

This is a work of fiction. Names, characters, places and incidents either are a product of the author's imagination or are used factiously. Any resemblance to actual persons, living or dead, events or locales is entirely coincidental.

Cover Illustration:
(shutterstock.com/stock-photo-image 20343223):
© Guy Shapira | Shutterstock.com
Title: Cup of black coffee on the black background.

ISBN-13: 978-1480152946
ISBN-10: 1480152943
Library of Congress Card Catalog Number is: 2012921466
CreateSpace Independent Publishing Platform
North Charleston, South Carolina

Summary: Raised on the streets of San Francisco's Tenderloin District, Starlight Nox is adopted by wealthy grandparents after her father dies and mother disappears. She moves to Cincinnati and must navigate a different set of evils imbedded in high society and the entitled.

In loving memory of
NANCY CASTELLINI HECHT,
A HERO TO MANY

PROLOGUE

Oreo Cookies and a Snickers Bar . . .

Tenderloin District, San Francisco 1974

The hour before dawn was Tony Martinelli's favorite time of night. Most of the guns would be sleeping by then. He could relax. If something was going to happen, it usually went down by 4 a.m. The dealers and pimps had parked their Cadillacs in front of their one room efficiencies, and the drunks and addicts had found their own piss-stained stairwells hours before. Even these people had a routine, Tony thought.

But that was before the Symbionese Liberation Army decided to kidnap Patty Hearst, the millionaire heiress, brainwash her and rob the Hibernia Bank over on Noriega Street. Two bystanders were shot, and the left-wing-terrorist thugs got away with ten thousand dollars. Now, the entire force was on pins and needles from dawn to dawn, staking out store fronts, safe houses and communes, searching for the SLA.

Tony slowly drove his cruiser down Jones Street past St. Anthony's Dining Room. The Sunshine Bread truck was already at the cafeteria door, delivering the only bread that most of the visitors would eat that day. St. Anthony's was the backbone of San Francisco's Tenderloin District, feeding the meager spiritual and physical needs of the community. Tony grimaced as 'feeding the hungry' was one of the alleged goals of the SLA. Part of Patty Hearst's initial ransom was a two million dollar donation from her big-time papa to feed California's poor. The food distribution exploded into mass chaos as people fought for whole chickens and bags of carrots. Tony looked up at St. Anthony's steeple, thinking about all the good people who actually worked hard because they really cared about their fellow man, but around the corner or across the street was the other guy who had the devil hiding behind a deluded smile and glassy eyes.

The police radio chatter had died down, but Tony knew the city wasn't sleeping. He rolled down the car window to let in the chilly night air. Long, high-pitched whines drifted in from the fishing boats that were inching their way across the bay, laden with early catches of salmon. Ever since he was old enough to cast a line, the fog horns had a way of soothing Tony to sleep on the nights his father wobbled in late, all liquored-up and looking for a fight with his mother. Fiddling with the tail of his coonskin cap, he'd close his eyes and block out all sounds, except for the quiet songs that echoed from the bay.

Tony sucked in the salty bay air and stretched his shoulders back against the car seat to rouse awake for another few hours. As he turned left onto Turk Street, a sharp movement in the shadows of the bus stop shelter caught his eye. Slowing the cruiser, he leaned toward the passenger window and spotted a pair of pale yellow dog legs with thick, black paws folded under the bench.

"Catching a snooze, ol' boy?" Tony sighed. "Wish I could be doing the same." He settled back into the driver's seat and began to pull away, but something tugged at him. He stepped on the brakes and glanced in the rear view mirror. He rubbed his heavy eyes and stared back into the glass. A tangled mass of hair and large, round eyes had popped out from under the bench and was peering at the back of the cruiser.

"Goddamn," he grumbled. "There goes my hour of peace and quiet." He backed up the cruiser ten yards, stopped and slowly got out. Moving around the front end of the car with his hand held firmly on his gun, Tony could now see a small body wedged in the corner of the shelter.

He shined his flashlight in the shadows and feral green eyes glistened back. The urchin let out a sharp cry and covered her eyes with filthy fingers. The child looked like a night monkey with greyish skin and wide, dark eye masks. Tony shrugged, anticipating the pathetic story that was certain to follow. Tripping dad. Tripping mom. Mom's psycho boyfriend. Psycho mom. Abandoned. Hungry. The stories were different yet all the same. Tragic kids caught up in a cloud of dazed parents who couldn't escape their own youth. Tony shifted the bright light from the child's eyes and asked her to crawl out from the corner.

"Go away!" she screeched back at him and shrank deeper into her nest.

"Come on out," Tony commanded, shining the flashlight back into her eyes.

"Go away!" she screeched again, but this time she raised her moppy head and spat at him.

"Out, now!" Tony demanded. "And tell me what you're doing under there."

"I'm hidin'!" she hollered, still tucked tight into her corner. "Jack says hide from the cars."

"Who's Jack?" he asked, but the child didn't respond. Tony knelt down to get a closer look at the girl. "Where are your parents?" he asked again. This time she slowly pointed to a dimly lit window across the street, three stories up.

"Then, why are you down here in the middle of the night?"

"I'm waitin'," she snapped.

"Waiting for what?"

"Till Sue be done."

"Done with what?" he asked, eyeing her hollow, dirt-streaked face.

"A man."

Tony had had enough. He stretched out his hand and told her to come out. "Giant rats live under there," he warned.

"I ain't movin'," she said stubbornly. "Jack says I don't move I get a Snickers Bar."

"Are Jack and Sue your parents?" he asked.

She hesitated at first but then confirmed the question with a silent nod.

"Why did Jack put you out here at night?"

"'Cause of a man."

"What man?" Tony asked, shifting the weight on his knees.

"I told you! A man with Sue."

"Young lady, come on out from under of there. I've got a bag of Oreo cookies in the car. Are you hungry?"

She shook her head no and contracted deeper into the corner.

"Listen, your pops won't mind if you talk to a policeman. He just doesn't want you talking to bad guys. Right?"

The little girl just stared back at Tony. Still kneeling, he bent under the seat and said, "I'm Officer Tony. What's your name?"

"Star," she whispered.

"Star . . . that's a beautiful name. How old are you, Star?"

The little girl raised four fingers in the cool air. Tony shook his head. Her big attitude already defied her age. But the Tenderloin had a way of doing that to kids—ripping childhood right out from underneath their feet, leaving them with the gift of street smarts but stunted in most every other way.

"You want an Oreo, Star?" he offered again.

She nodded yes but coiled deeper into her nook.

"Then come on out with me." He stuck his hand under the bench again. This time she grabbed it and unravelled herself from the corner. Star stood just above Tony's knee and wore a mess of black curls that were matted around her face. Her thin arms and legs were lost in a baggy t-shirt that hung to her knees and was decorated with pictures of *Fat Albert and the Cosby Kids*. Her skin was grey, but Tony couldn't tell if the grimy hue was from poor health or from living in the four walls of a shithole for her entire life.

He led her to the door of the cruiser and told her to climb in, but she refused to budge. She just stood next to the door, looking up at him with thick lashes and heavy eyebrows that were hiding a lot of life for her young age.

"Have you ever been in a police car, Star?"

"Nope," she said with wide, frightened eyes.

"Well, jump in. It's nifty-neat and extra cool, and the cookies are in there, too!"

With another mention of food, she slowly climbed into the backseat and tucked her knees under her shirt. She waited quietly while Tony unlocked the trunk and pulled out a blanket. He wrapped the scratchy wool around her shivering shoulders and then called dispatch for backup and a family service counselor. She kept a close eye on him as he grabbed the cookies from the front seat and squatted down next to the cruiser door. He pulled an Oreo from the bag and peeled it apart.

"Look, they're Teddy bear eyes," he said gently.

Star gazed at the chocolate and cream without saying a word.

"How do you eat an Oreo? I pull mine apart and eat the inside first. Like this," Tony explained and then ran the creamy center across his teeth, leaving tracks in the hard chocolate cake.

"I never had a Oreo," she whispered.

"You've never had an Oreo!?" he asked in mock outrage.

"Nope!" she said, shaking her head earnestly.

"You've got to try one!" He pulled a cookie from the bag and gave it to her along with a tired smile. Star raised the cookie to her nose, took in a deep breath then clutched the disk in the palm of her hand.

"Aren't you going to eat it?"

"Nope," she whispered. "Gonna' let Jack and Sue have a bite."

Tony sighed, thinking that she was still young enough to love those assholes. In another few years, the illusion of parental love would be lost, and in a decade, Star would be perpetuating the same cycle of dashed dreams, neglect and waste when her own kid would surely be found roaming the streets at four in the morning.

Tony rubbed his eyes and shook his head. "Listen, go ahead and eat the cookie. I'll give you the whole bag if you promise not to eat them all at once."

"Promise," Star agreed and smiled for the first time.

Watching her relax, Tony pressed on with more questions. "Star, why's your mommy with the man? Is he your uncle . . . or grandpa?"

She shook her head no and took her first bite of cookie. A wide grin spread across her face as she crunched down on the chocolate.

"Why is the man at your house when it's bedtime?" he pressed again.

"To play," she mumbled with crumbs falling from her lips. "Fat Albert loves cookies," she giggled and pointed to the hefty black character in red on the front of her t-shirt. Star pushed her spindly knees to the front of the shirt to make her belly grow bigger and sang, "Hey, hey, hey! It's Fat Albert!"

Emerging from the over-sized t-shirt was the little girl's true four-year-old self, hidden behind the grit and grime of street life. Tony peered down at the girl's shirt and smiled. Fat Albert and his junkyard gang was the genius cartoon creation of Bill Cosby, a gutsy comedian from the tough streets of North

Philly. Cosby was pushing racial and cultural barriers with parents who were accustomed to pleasantville sit-coms like *The Andy Griffith Show* whose Sheriff Taylor spent his days keeping peace in the peace-loving white town of Mayberry R.F.D. *Fat Albert and the Cosby Kids*, on the other hand, tackled real issues that tormented black, inner-city streets across America. Andy Taylor's biggest threat was Otis, the town drunk, who let himself into jail on Saturday nights to sleep off his binge. Fat Albert faced real threats like the time when he mistakenly found himself entangled in a drug deal with Muggles, Franny's older brother. Whether Fat Albert and his gang were dealing with drugs, divorce, or bullying, they were always teaching a real lesson to real kids, which was part of Tony's mission in the Tenderloin. He looked down at Star and understood that she was one of the kids that Cosby was trying to save, but he also knew her chances of success in the District were slim or none.

"Do you like Fat Albert?" Tony asked.

"Yepparoo! Bucky and Dumb Donald are funny, but Fat Albert's the best," she said with certainty, reaching into the bag for another cookie.

"He's my favorite, too," Tony agreed. "Now, tell me about your mom. Why is she playing with the man in your apartment?"

"Sue and him plays naked. Sue says they wrestle."

"Does Sue wrestle at night a lot?"

Star nodded her head yes. "The man didn't want to play 'cause of me. That's why Jack says stay here."

So, this john had a conscience, Tony thought for a second. Nah, not down here in the District. A performance problem, most likely. Probably couldn't get it up with a kid in the next room. Eyeing the little girl behind her thick lashes, he was able to see the collateral damage brought down by needles and pipes and temporary joy rides. Just as he thought, she was one of hundreds of remnants from the psychedelic haze that blew over from Haight Ashbury, just one more kid who hid out in rancid apartment hallways while her old lady got some grandpa's rocks off, just so she could get her fix for the night.

Tony patted the little girl's thin knee and took in a heavy breath. She smiled with drooping eyes and rested her head against the seat. Tony tucked the blanket around her legs and stood up. He closed the door and leaned against the car, waiting for the social services counselor to arrive.

Despite its chronic depravity, Tony had been lured into the District over a decade before when he first heard Thelonious Monk at the Black Hawk. The jazz genius's radical harmonies and sharp melodies that took dramatic plunges into silence and then assaulted the audience with violent percussions echoed the cultural changes that were to come. Even before Bobby Kennedy and Dr. King were assassinated, friction had been sparking in the District. It started right in front of Compton's Cafeteria. The initial complaint was about rambunctious customers at the diner, but when the police answered the call, a few of the officers with attitudes roughed up the gender-bending patrons. The cultural clash quickly turned into days of violent protests between the transgender community and the force, but none of this ruffled Tony. The Tenderloin had become a part of him, for good or for bad. The dissonant energy of the streets was a strange intoxication that left the seedy smell of sin hanging on him long after he headed home to his wife, Julie. Even the motley children roaming the streets had become a part of his life.

Tony got to know many of these shell-shocked kids. He handed over a glazed donut or fifty cents when he found them scrounging around dumpsters for bits of food while their parents shot up in the alleyways. The Tenderloin had been his beat long enough, though, to watch the seedy Mandala spin. Many of the kids turned into broken-down users just like their parents. And most eventually became prostitutes or dealers in lieu of anything else, because there was nothing else offered to them in the Tenderloin.

He peered through the cruiser window at the sleeping child. She was already striking at the age of four with dark hair and thick brows. Her long lashes rested against her cheeks with her plump lips drawn into a ribbon across her face. He glanced up to Star's dingy apartment window and ran his fingers through his hair. With some luck, he hoped her destiny would take a sharp turn and torch a path somewhere beyond the broken lives of the District.

CHAPTER I

Peanut butter and white bread sandwiches . . .

Cincinnati, Ohio 1993

Cincinnati is a narrow town that sits snug along the Ohio River where the water runs muddy but the blood runs blue. Little more than a century before, Cincinnati was a gateway to freedom for slaves who lived just across the river in Kentucky. The town was settled by German Catholic immigrants who floated down the Ohio on flatboats packed with a hogs, barrels of malted barley and the family catechism. The town flourished for over one hundred fifty years when hog houses and breweries competed for space along the river and church steeples popped up on every other street corner. Even when American industry was flushed away to the other side of the world, Cincinnati survived—fortified by families like the Proctors and the Gambles and the Tafts. Through the hustle and bustle and change, the Germans' Ten Commandments survived, as well, clinging to the hills overlooking the city.

Staring out his office window high above the Ohio, Greer watched a barge creep down the river with a load of coal. The rectangular cargo vessel flashed back memories of the transport craft that dumped his unit on the beaches of Normandy a half century before. From his penthouse view, the black chunks of coal looked like the helmets of tightly packed soldiers who were headed for their Allied mission and, for many, their death. Greer reached down and rubbed his scarred thigh where a thick chunk of flesh had been spewed on the sands of Omaha when he took a mortar hit to his right leg. He was a lieutenant in the First Infantry Division, the *Fighting First,* who charged the initial D-Day assault at Omaha Beach during Operation Neptune. As his troops stormed up the beachhead, they came under attack, and Greer collapsed face down in the sand. Burning pain ruptured through his leg. He was certain that only a stump was left below his waist. He peeled open his eyes in the gritty sand and spied a severed leg three yards from where he lay. Later, Greer was happy to learn that the detached limb wasn't his, rather the leg of Patty O'Grady, an eighteen-year-old private in his unit who was blown in half that day. It was too bad for Patty, but there were always casualties in battle. That was one of the reasons why he never got too connected to his troops. He thought the entire fraternal, brotherhood notion in war made for weak leaders. The end-game was all that mattered to Greer.

Three months after the attack, Greer led his troops through the German city of Aachen, forcing the Nazi commander to surrender. As his men headed to the Ardennes forest and the Battle of the Bulge, Donald, his only child at the time, celebrated his second birthday. But before the German offensive was defeated, Greer took a second hit. His wife, Trista, sent news that Donald had died of rheumatic fever. Trista mourned her son's passing for many years, but for Greer, the loss was fleeting as he never connected with the boy who was born after his deployment to Europe.

Greer was snapped back to the present by a piercing voice that blared over the office intercom system. "Mr. Nox. Mr. Nox, your granddaughter's downstairs in the lobby. Should she come up?" the voice questioned.

He grabbed the phone receiver and dialed zero. "Tina, why in the hell are you paging me when I'm standing in my office?" he blasted. "You fucking forgot. Well, this is going to be the last time you'll forget. One more page like that and you're out of a job."

For a second, he actually contemplated firing the girl, but then her long legs and sumptuous breasts came to mind. "Tell Star that I'll be down in five minutes," he said instead.

Greer was accustomed to speaking and behaving however he wanted. For over seventy years, his formidable height and striking looks opened doors that would have been otherwise closed to him. And though he enjoyed Tina's cleavage, he wasn't in the mood for her airy antics today. Star was on his brain. In the eleven years that she had lived in Cincinnati, Star never once ventured downtown by herself. She spent the first twelve years of her life on city streets, picking through garbage cans for breakfast and scraping sidewalks for used needles for her parents. Downtown was the last place where she wanted to go, especially to lunch with him, for Star and he were never very close.

From her first arrival on their doorstep, Greer chose to ignore his granddaughter as he was waiting for that inevitable turn she was certain to take, following down the steps of Jack's polluted path. With not one but two parents as addicts, the kid couldn't avoid corruption. Her blood was contaminated with filth. Greer was irritable as he was now sure that Star had finally taken the plunge into Jack's underworld.

Greer stopped funding Jack and Sue's heroin addiction when Star turned one. The decision wasn't complicated; he decided the money was causing more harm than good. Presumably, the money Trista had been sending for baby food and diapers was shot up their arms. When Star was four, Trista got a call from a social worker, asking if the grandparents would consider temporary custody of Star. The four-year-old had been found by the cops wandering the streets of San Francisco's Tenderloin District at three or four in the morning. Jack had pimped a job for Sue, so Star was put out on the street for a few hours. Trista wanted the child, but Greer said no. If they took Star, the floodgates would open, and Greer was convinced that he'd be supporting Jack and Sue's heroin habit all over again. With no place to go, the little girl was placed in foster care, but within a few weeks, she was back with her parents and back wandering the streets of the Tenderloin.

Though he refused the child then, Greer was certain that at some point he'd be forced to take care of Jack's unsavory prodigy. Jack clung to life and to the needle longer than Greer anticipated. They didn't get another call from the cops for eight years. This time Jack was dead and Sue had no interest in the kid.

Though he'd never admit his feelings to Trista, Greer was relieved when Jack succumbed to his addictions. After Donald's death, Trista indulged and enabled their second son with misguided love. Greer resented the price he had to pay for her mistakes. Before the age of nineteen, Jack had been in and out of two military schools and arrested twice for dealing dope. After he was freed from incarceration, Jack bolted out of Cincinnati and cut off communication with his parents. Three years later Greer and Trista received a collect call from the San Francisco General Hospital maternity ward. Jack was calling to congratulate them—they were grandparents. Jack also needed cash. There was "cereal to buy along with diapers, baby powder, blankets and other shit," he explained.

For the first year, Greer permitted Trista to send money for the child, but after Jack called and asked for cash to bail Sue out of jail because of a mix up with "some prick," Greer stopped the money flow. Because the cash-cow dried up, Trista was never permitted to meet her granddaughter until after Jack's funeral. Their son had been dead for over a month before they were notified. Chet Wilson, a lawyer from San Francisco with baby-blue cheater glasses and an olive green leisure suit, contacted Greer at his office. His son, Jack, was dead, explained Chet, and Sue Nox was willing to give up full custody of Star for one hundred thousand dollars plus a thirty-three percent attorney's fee.

Greer's first inclination was to say fuck you and hang up the phone, but Trista threatened to leave if he denied her the child. This was one of the few times Trista really challenged her husband and the first to threaten their forty-two year marriage. In a different era, Trista may have found the gumption to divorce Greer's domination, but when role models like Mamie Eisenhower and Jackie Kennedy stayed, in spite of bad tempers and flagrant indiscretions, there didn't seem to be much of a choice. Trista may have also remained in the marriage because of a mandate she received from her father who was indulgent with his only daughter but was also a devout Catholic. "I'll permit you to marry this flimflammer," he said, folding to Trista's relentless pleas, "But once you marry him, you're married forever."

Unsurprisingly, shockwaves rippled through Cincinnati's social circle when Trista married Greer Nox. Trista was a highly sought-after beauty with porcelain skin, green eyes, and thick brown hair that folded into perfect bobbed waves. When she stepped onto the tennis court, country club members crowded onto the veranda to admire her grace, speed and agility. Greer was handsome, too, a debonair sort with jet-black, combed-back hair, a thin mustache and steely eyes, but the stuffy club mothers didn't trust their daughters with his dismissive edge and unproven blood. He gave some fuzzy claim that he was from Cleveland and that his family made a fortune in real estate investments along Lake Erie. But before Trista's father was able to confirm Greer's claims, Hitler was rolling through France and Greer was called to serve. Bending to his daughter's tears and pleas of marriage, a lavish wedding was expedited and Greer headed off to war.

Maybe Trista fell in love with Greer because he was the first man who presented a challenge to her, but when she fell, she fell fast and with her eyes slammed shut. Slowly but surely, his rough and domineering disposition battered her confidence and eroded her beauty. Left behind was a woman with a subservient and flaccid shell who found her only comfort in chocolate cake and prized rose gardens, rather than her husband's touch.

After the loss of two sons and years of loneliness, Trista viewed the opportunity to adopt her granddaughter as her last chance at happiness and fulfillment. So, for the first time in decades, she summoned her courage and will and fought for Star's adoption. Interestingly, Greer conciliated, and within a month, the girl had been purchased from her mother for one hundred thirty-three thousand dollars.

Life wasn't easy at the Nox's when Star first arrived. Trista envisioned a bright-eyed little girl who loved dresses, fingernail polish and hair ribbons. Instead, Star was a scrawny twelve-year-old with grey skin, dirt-caked fingernails and thick, matted hair, grimy as soot. During their first breakfast together, Star scratched her head like a hamster digging through cedar chips. She dug into her scalp, behind her ears and at the base of her neck. Trista gritted her teeth with disgust as flakes of skin fell onto the little girl's shoulders. Trista didn't want to offend her granddaughter at their first meal together, but soon goetta and eggs were rumbling back up her throat as she watched the thin fingers dig through the tangled mess.

Trista gripped the edge of the breakfast table and quietly asked Star if the scratching was a tick or nervous habit. The child shook her head no and continued to scratch.

Trista gave it two more minutes and then had had enough. She told Star that "young ladies do not, under any circumstance, scratch their bodies in public and that included at the dining table."

Star looked at her grandmother with a desire to please and shoved her hands underneath her bottom, but within a minute, the fingers crawled back to her scalp.

"Star, please stop," Trista said sharply.

"But Grandmother Trista, I can't!" she cried, turning bright red.

With that, Trista pushed her chair from the table and shimmied out of the seat to investigate Star's head. Glasses clanged as her thick hips and ample breasts bumped the table while she moved to Star. "Let me have a look," she said and pulled up the mass of waves from behind Star's ears. Tiny reddish-brown bugs were scurrying across her scalp. Strands of hair were covered with white eggs the size of a grains of salt. Star was completely infested with lice. Trista's stomach contracted. She dropped the hair and took hold of Star's chair to steady herself.

"My dear," she squeezed out. "You have lice!"

"She has what?" Greer yelled, jumping up from his seat. "She can't stay here with bugs crawling all over her scalp! We'll all be infested. Trista, she must go at once! Up young lady, up!" he commanded. "Up, up, up this instant!"

Star sprang up from her chair and ran out of the room without a sound.

"And where do you propose she go, Greer?" Trista demanded, still squeezing the frame of the chair.

"Who the hell cares?" he said, slamming his fist against the table. "This entire transaction has been an expensive nuisance, and I really don't want her sitting at my table with stringy hair hanging in her face for the next six years. This decision has been a major mistake. Jack failed us, and that ratty little thing is already walking in his footsteps."

"You don't know that. The poor girl hasn't said three words since she arrived."

"She doesn't need to speak to confirm that she's a failure. She was doomed before she saw the light of day with parents like hers. Find a foster family or an orphanage and send her off with a hefty donation. I'd rather pay somebody to take her off our hands than house her here," he concluded with his sharp chin raised in the air.

Greer still wore his pencil-thin mustache and combed-back hair, though both were now grey with age. Nonetheless, he bespoke elegance at sixty-two in his French-cuff shirt and custom suit. Towering over her, he was now a sharp contrast to Trista. Her hair was dyed into a flat, brown pageboy with little bounce. She squeezed into a floral poplin skirt and a white blouse with delicate buttons that were losing the battle with the weight of her heavy bosom. Her green eyes still reflected the beauty she once held, but her overall luster had been depleted years before.

In spite of his threatening stance, Trista scrambled for her newfound courage and challenged Greer once again. "She's our flesh and blood, and we adopted her," she began. "You can't keep casting off people just because they're a nuisance to you."

He lunged forward, grabbed Trista's arm and drew her within inches of his face. "What do you mean by that? When are you going to stop blaming me for Jack? That kid had everything handed to him on a silver platter by you. You're indulgence destroyed him. Not me. I tried to raise him to follow commands, but you defeated that!"

"Let go. You're hurting me," she said quietly, trying to yank her arm away. "She's not leaving, Greer," she said with trembling lips. "She is my granddaughter, and whether you like it or not, Star is staying."

He gripped her arm tighter and let go with a jerk and a shove, but Trista's girth held her steady. Greer grabbed the pastry plate from the table and threw it across the room.

"Here, have another five donuts, why don't you, while you're thinking about how to get rid of that kid! I don't want a thieving street scamp living in my house. I don't give a damn if she is a blood relative or not. We know nothing about her and have no emotional connection beyond the name. Find another place for her to live," he said and then stormed out of the room.

Trista stood before the table trembling. She watched as red jelly oozed onto the carpet from the donuts that were flung across the room. She fought back Greer's words, but through the years, his voice had become her reality. Greer had convinced Trista that she, alone, was the ruination of Jack. In some ways, he was right. She overindulged Jack, but she did so to make up for the distant relationship he had with his father. She carried regrets deep in her heart for loving her son too much, but she learned to live with this pain. She could not live with herself, however, if she would have loved Jack too little. Regardless of Greer, she was determined to avoid such mistakes with her granddaughter. She would fight for Star, even if it meant turning her back on her husband. But there was a part of her that knew Greer would never leave. With her newfound courage, Trista wished that she had summoned this knowledge of her husband years before.

Greer steered clear of the house for several days following Star's arrival. His absence allowed Trista to focus on Star's lice infestation and, all the while, learn about her granddaughter. Admittedly, she had never wiped scum from a sink basin in her entire life, let alone pick bugs from a child's head, but she did it. For five weeks, Trista painstakingly sifted through Star's hair, searching for louse eggs.

Star sat on a tall stool and held a cup of water while Trista searched through strand after strand of hair. When she spotted a bug, she snatched it between her finger nails and dropped the crawler in the water. The tiny eggs presented a greater challenge as they were cemented on with evolutionary super glue. Nonetheless, for one hour each morning and each night, Trista combed through thick waves, pulling out nit after nit and bug after bug.

Over the days of combing and picking, Trista learned that Star had never been on a bike nor baked a single cookie. She liked school because the nuns at St. Brigid gave her a hot lunch. Her favorite meal was fish sticks with tater tots and ketchup.

"Do you like lasagna? It's my specialty," Trista asked early one morning, satisfied because she had just captured three live bugs.

"Don't know lasagna," she said softly.

"Of course you know what lasagna is, Star. It is luscious layers of meat and cheese and pasta. Lasagna is simply divine, my dear. Jack loved las—" Trista began but then stopped.

Star bowed her head and shifted on the stool at the mention of her father. "I wouldn't know. Jack ate candy back home," she conceded. "He ate a bag of chocolate Kisses every day.

Never shared. Sue didn't eat much, either. Maybe a bag of Fritos. Chocolate and chips was all we had."

Trista stopped combing and put her hands on Star's shoulders. "He got the chocolate addiction from me," she said sadly. "His father always said that Jack was too much like me. Too indulgent."

Star rested the cup of water filled with bugs between her legs and sat up straight. "Don't listen to him," she said. "He's an asshole. Jack was right about him. I don't listen to assholes. They just get ya' into trouble."

"Star! Stop! You shouldn't say that about your grandfather. And please, never use that language in this house again," Trista demanded, withdrawing her hands from the girl's shoulders.

"I call an asshole, an asshole, when I see it, Grandma," Star said with complete confidence. "I called Billy Elrod an asshole when he walked by Blind Benny and kicked his collection can across the cement. Pennies went flying all over the sidewalk. I ran after him and shouted, 'Billy, you're nothing but a goddamn asshole!' He chased me and punched me in the gut, but I got him back . . . I kicked him the nuts—with all my might! He cried, 'wah, wah, wah,' just like a big baby," she continued intently.

"Star, please stop. That's enough!"

"Honestly, Grandma, if you can't spot the assholes where I come from, then you end up getting your brains beat out." She paused for a moment and added, "Oh . . . and by the way, Jack loved you. He said that Greer was the asshole, not you."

Star's vinegar and sass had leaked out during their many days of delousing, so Trista wasn't entirely surprised with her granddaughter's candor or gumption about Greer. The comment about Jack *loving her* left Trista breathless, though. She had stuffed away endless questions about Jack in fear of stirring up bad memories for Star, but now she could no longer suppress her desire to learn more about her son's life.

"Jack told you he loved me?" she asked cautiously.

"Basically. He didn't blame you for not helping," Star said, picking up the cup set between her legs. "Sue did, though. They fought about it. Jack said that Greer walked all over you. He was right," she added with unfettered honesty.

"Oh dear!" Trista said, grabbing her throat."

Star twisted around and looked up. "Grandma, I'm sorry. I'm just telling you what they said. If you don't want me to talk, I'll shut up."

"No. Don't be sorry," she whispered. "Jack was right. I should have been stronger. I'm learning that now," she said more to herself than to her granddaughter. "But it's too late."

"Nope. It's never too late to learn," Star said brightly and turned back around. "That's what Sr. Mary Gerome always said. I had her in the fourth grade at St. Brigid's. She taught me that lesson after I kicked Johnny Thompson in the nuts for stealing my ballpoint pen. She said it's never too late to learn to behave like a lady."

Trista breathed a heavy sigh of frustration. "Would you like me to make lasagna for dinner tonight?" she asked, changing the subject.

"Nah. How about peanut butter sandwiches?"

"Not for dinner."

"Why? I like peanut butter," Star told her. "St. Anthony's— just down from Turk Street, gives out a jar of peanut butter and two loaves of bread every week. That's mostly what I ate at home. I kept it in a tin box under my bed, so the rats couldn't eat it."

Trista cringed inside with talk about rats and peanut butter but showed no emotion to Star as she didn't want to embarrass the young teen. She knew that many pieces of her granddaughter's life were horrid. Debris from her dubious existence was in the adoption file, and Trista surmised the rest from the few conversations that she had had with Jack over the years. She knew that sharing stories at home about tin boxes and rats was one thing, but telling kids from St. Mary Magdalene Grade School would spell disaster for the girl's life in Cincinnati. As Trista resumed combing through a section of hair above the ears, she warned Star to never whisper a single word about her life in the Tenderloin beyond the walls of their home.

"I won't . . . but why?" she asked with an unfamiliar air of reserve.

"Because this town can be very unwelcoming to people cut from a different cloth, but more importantly, your privacy and reputation should be protected at all cost. People are going to talk. Giving them something to talk about is vulgar. So, pay attention—if you want to have friends around here, it is best that you not share your life with anyone beyond me. And that's a life lesson to follow forever," Trista said, slapping the comb in the palm of her hand.

Turning back to Star's head, she asked her if she liked Barbies. "I think you need a few normal toys to play with."

"Dolls? Nope. Don't like dolls. St. Anthony's gives them out every Christmas, but I always gave mine to Candy. She lived down the hall. I like books. But in the summer, I like to rock-cock the Nobbers who come down from the Hill. I was the best at it on Turk Street. Never got caught."

"What's rocking the Nobbers, Star?" Trista asked innocently as she gripped a tiny louse egg between her thumb and index finger and pulled it down the long strand of hair.

"It's rock-cocking the Nobbers," Star corrected. "Ya' hide between parked cars and sling rocks at the Caddies and Lincolns as they cruise down from Nob Hill looking for stuff. Dope. A girl. Maybe a guy. You know . . . stuff. "

"Star!" Trista snapped with her top lip curled under her front teeth. "That's one of those distasteful stories you should learn to keep to yourself. There is absolutely no reason to discuss those wretched things. From this point forward, I want you to forget that other life of yours. San Francisco is over and done with. We shall never discuss it again. Do you understand me?"

"Okay," Star agreed in a shameful whisper.

"Good. Now that that is clear, I think you need to play with Barbies," she said decisively. "We'll get you a few today."

"Nah. No thank you, I mean. I won't play with them," Star said, holding the cup of water filled with extracted varmints steady in her hand.

"What other things do you like to do for fun, then? Listen to music. What about Michael Jackson's new album? I think it's called "Scary" or "Thrilling" or something of the sort," Trista said, regaining her equilibrium by sifting through another section of hair.

"Music's okay. I don't have a record player or a radio, though. I just read—like I said, I like to read. I spent my days at the library."

"Well, Star, we already have something in common. I love to read, too. I learned all about boys with my very first *Harlequin Romance*, and I've been reading my romance novels ever since. Those *Harlequins* are clean enough, just a kiss or two. I'll have to buy you a few."

"No thanks. I'm not much into love stories," she said, resting the cup between her legs. "The only romance I ever liked was when Wilbur fell in love with Charlotte, and then she up and died at the end of the story and left him with all those baby spiders."

Trista laughed a sad laugh. "I really don't believe in love stories, either, dear, but I do like to dream."

"Not surprised," Star answered softly.

"Not surprised about what?"

"That you don't believe in love stories."

Trista bent down and kissed the top of her granddaughter's head. Later that day, she went out and bought *Where the Red Fern Grows* for Star to read aloud as she scoured her head. They both wept at the end of the story when Old Dan dies from the mountain lion wounds and Little Ann dies of grief a few days later while resting on his grave. As they both wiped away tears, Trista and Star agreed that Dan and Ann's love was the greatest love story of all.

During the hours her grandmother spent sifting through her hair, Star wanted to share the stories and poems she had written about life in the Tenderloin, but she quickly learned the lesson that sharing her life was a bad idea. Her grandmother was focused on eradicating any dirt and infestation that had built up through her years of living on the streets in the District. Rehashing one's life on paper for the world to read would be the worst possible idea for any Nox family member. So, from that point forward, Star learned to keep her mouth shut and her Tenderloin life hidden.

After Star's very first breakfast with Greer, she also knew to step lightly when her grandfather was around, and as time passed, they rarely crossed paths. Trista had enrolled Star in St. Mary Magdalene, the same school that Jack had attended and whose gymnasium was called Nox Hall. Teachers were kind to Star because she worked hard but also because her last name was Nox. She attended just one boy-girl party in junior high, came home early and refused to utter a single word about the night. From that point forward, Star refused birthday invitations and swimming parties at the country club. "I'm not going" was all she'd say.

Trista decided not to push Star into the St. Mary Magdalene circle. Her granddaughter would be better off if people knew less about her life, she thought. Star needed time and space to burn off the chaos left by Jack and Sue. The Nox family's old Tudor house and ambling gardens gave her the environment that she needed to repair her singed edges. On the weekends, she would crawl through the dirt and pull out dandelion roots from Trista's prized rose gardens, and in the evenings, she would escape into books.

Star endured high school at St. Angela Merici in much the same way. She kept her head down and thoughts close to her chest. The Tenderloin had taught her to survive with a big bark that wasn't afraid to bite, but Cincinnati quashed that side of her. Her new predators wore white skirts, carried tennis rackets and had engaging giggles. At least in the Tenderloin, she knew how to handle Slimy Jones or Billy Elrod when they tried to mess with her. Emmy Dribble and her posse were a completely different story. Star tucked her tail, lowered her gaze, and warily navigated her new terrain.

Other than scrutinizing her report cards, Greer stayed out of Star's business throughout high school. He was rarely home and had little interest in speaking with her at dinner when he was around. For the first year or so that Star lived with them, Trista tried to force conversation between Greer and his granddaughter. She only relented when he finally said, "As long as the girl performs well in school and isn't an addict, I don't really give a damn about a short story contest." He only became interested in Star's life when graduation rolled around and she had chosen Bosco, a Catholic university in the center of Cincinnati. In his mind, her bags were packed, and she would be out from under his skin forever.

"You need to move out and live on your own. Stop leaning on your grandmother. She's not going to be around forever, you know!" he argued.

Star had lived in survival mode for the first twelve years of her life and had spent the last six years tip-toeing around Greer, just to keep the peace. She finally found some stability and emotional connection with her grandmother and wasn't prepared to give up the security for college or for her grandfather. If she had to, Star was ready to call on her Tenderloin fury and fight to stay in Cincinnati, the strange, constricted place that she now considered home.

The battle with her grandfather never ignited as Trista didn't want her granddaughter to leave for selfish reasons but also because she was certain that Jack's brief stint at Clemson University had hastened his demise. And like Greer, she was also certain that the alcohol gene had contaminated Star's blood. If she could prolong her granddaughter's exposure to temptation for as long as possible, Trista was convinced that she could save Star from following in her parents' footsteps. Therefore, St. John Bosco University, located less than five miles from their home, was the *only* option.

The autumn of 1988 was lovely on Bosco University's campus with sharp blue skies and crisp, cool air. Star sat on a bench outside the student center to take in the sun before sitting in a stiff desk for two hours. She closed her eyes and caught snippets of a conversation about Tom Browning's perfect game pitched the night before.

"Yeah, I almost missed it. The game was delayed for three hours . . . Larkin got the only run . . . Reds' first perfect game . . . Twelfth in baseball history . . . Browning—he came to the Reds in '82."

Star opened her eyes and sat up. Tom Browning and she had arrived in the slow town in the same year. He found success, despite the pockets of small-minded people in Cincinnati. Star closed her eyes again, wondering if success was predestined. She imagined Browning's stars in the night sky, perfectly aligned in the form of a diamond with the pitcher at the center, controlling his own destiny. Star shook her head, stood up and headed off to class.

As the elevator slipped down thirty-three floors, Greer was already scripting Star's unavoidable descent to addiction. She had made it to her senior year at Bosco without mishap, but that was due to pure luck. He only hoped that she was now smart enough to seek help before spinning completely out of control. Either way, if she was into drugs or any other illegal activities, the free train ride was over. He would never bail her out.

The elevator doors pulled open and Greer spotted Star at the information desk chatting with Archie, the security guard. He hesitated and watched Star's head swing back with laughter as she listened to Archie, who was probably telling one of his obnoxious knock-knock jokes. *She must be okay if she can laugh with him*, Greer grimaced and headed toward her. As he approached, Star smiled and moved to hug him, but Greer stepped back and gave her only a brief nod.

"Apparently, Archie is quite the clown today," he said, without acknowledging the guard. "Let's go, though. We've got reservations at Orchids." Greer turned and headed toward the exit, with Star on his heels.

"Do you always treat him so gristly?" she dared, trying to catch up with his pace. "He's seems to be such a sweet, old soul."

"He's hourly and I'm not. Discussing a building guard has no relevance to me," he said with annoyance and pushed open the glass door for her. As Star passed him, Greer eyed her blue jeans and wrinkled shirt. "Why are you wearing jeans?" he complained. "I told you that we were eating at Orchids. It's in the Netherland Hilton, for God's sake."

"I've never been to Orchids, and this is what college students wear," she yelled through the wind that was now whipping her hair into a mass of knotted curls.

Greer just shook his head, opened up his stride, and charged down Walnut Street. Star struggled to keep up, but he didn't give a damn. The least she could do was comb her hair and put on a skirt for lunch. Orchids was Cincinnati's iconic French Art Deco restaurant built in 1931. Romanesque murals, Rookwood Pottery fountains and white tablecloths with crystal adorned the breathtaking space. Her wild hair and tousled clothes would be an embarrassment to the grandeur. *He should have known better!*

When they sat down at the table, Greer thought that Star looked pale and worn, as well as disheveled. Her wide, green eyes seemed pinched at the edges, and her black curls had settled into a mass of confusion around her face. As the waiter handed her a menu, Star's plump lips spread across her face, forming a magnetic smile. Greer watched as the young man paused and returned her smile with similar energy. Even if she looked tired, Greer had to acknowledge that his granddaughter was beautiful but in a raw and undomesticated manner that he found repulsive.

After the waiter took their order, she rattled nervously about school and complained that her academic advisor, Dr. Franklin, had given her fits about choosing the wrong thesis for her senior paper. Star wanted to compare how the spinster lives of Jane Austen and Emily Dickenson influenced their writing, but Franklin wanted her to invent a more radical thesis, something that had to do with phallic symbols and the gay reading of the two writers.

"I don't have a problem with the topic if the facts are there to support it," she said. "But to invent a thesis just to pander to a certain population is ridiculous. My friend Jimmy, who happens to be gay, agrees with me. He says that something so forced would be offensive to him."

As she was finishing her last sentenced, Greer stopped Star before she could continue.

"Do we have to discuss queers at lunch?" he demanded. "And don't tell me that you're hanging out with a bunch of faggots."

Star glanced up at the busboy pouring their waters and watched a frown shadow his face. "They prefer to be referred to as gay, and yes, some of my friends are gay," she said to her grandfather and then mouthed "sorry" to the busboy.

Greer ignored her comments and continued with his rant. "So, is your professor a lesbo or homo?"

"I'm uncertain about her sexual preference. She may be a lesbian, but that doesn't matter. Her professional opinion is what matters, and she believes that the only papers being selected for publication right now are those that reflect current cultural trends, which is what I call patronizing and pandering."

"Do what the lesbo wants you to do and move on," Greer insisted.

"I think that's stooping. If that's the case, I don't know if I really want a career in the world of academia. I'm beginning to second guess what I want to do with my life, anyway," Star answered sheepishly and then quickly glanced down at the table.

"It's already been decided. You're advancing on to Northwestern or the Iowa Writers' Workshop. That's it. Do what the lesbo tells you and move on," he said, tapping his knife on the table. "Your goal is to be published, not to be morally correct. It's time to grow up and start supporting yourself."

"Well, it's too late. I didn't heed her advice. The paper was submitted to the thesis committee a few months ago. I just got word that they approved it but with some reservation. They thought the thesis was *dated*. Straight from the horse's mouth. Maybe I'm not so concerned about getting published now, anyway."

"That's the second time you've mentioned changing course in the past sixty seconds, Star. Getting published is your goal. You're the one who chose that worthless English degree against my advice. Now, make something of it."

"Well, people change," she said, fiddling with her fork. "Circumstances change."

"What's wrong with you?" he demanded. "You're not acting yourself. Look at me."

Star looked directly into his eyes. "Nothing's wrong. I'm fine. No drugs, no nothing," she said defiantly.

"*Fine* is an ignorant word. Tell me the truth—why did you come downtown today, Star? Just cut to the chase. Did you get a rejection letter from one of the graduate programs?"

"Yes."

"So, who rejected you? Iowa?"

"No. Iowa and Northwestern," Star said, twisting the napkin in her lap.

Her grandfather sat back in his chair and shook his head. "Neither program? How can that be?" Visible disgust washed over his body. Greer picked up his knife again and began tapping the water glass.

"They didn't like my portfolio. They didn't like me. Guess I'm not polished enough for them, either," she snapped.

"What's that supposed to mean—the 'either'?" he seethed. "Don't start that. You sound like your grandmother. Always ready to raise Jack's ghost and blame me for his demise, aren't you?"

Star leaned forward with more backbone than her grandmother could ever muster. "Don't drag Grandma into this. Those rejection letters or your reaction to them have nothing to do with her nor Jack. I'm content with the letters now."

"Is that because you're content with failure? Daughter like father?" Greer said, slamming down the knife.

Star took a deep breath and slowly released the air. "Listen, it's been over ten years since Jack's death. Let's both allow his ghost to rest before someone says something they regret. I came to lunch to talk, not to argue."

"Agreed," Greer said sharply, seizing a roll from the bread basket and ripping it in half. Star watched as her grandfather grabbed a knife, stabbed a pat of butter and attacked the bread. They then sat in silence for several minutes until he again began pressing her about the future.

"Now that Northwestern and Iowa are out, what are your plans? It's time for you to cut the financial kite strings."

Star sat up straight, raised her head and gripped her thighs. "I do have a plan for my future. Ironically, the plan began to unfold last October in an English class when I read about Michael Henchard who sold his daughter for five guineas, an amount less than ten U.S. dollars."

"What are you talking about?" he asked with increasing irritation.

"It's a long story," Star said, stretching her shoulders back to relieve the tension in her neck.

"Well, I don't have a long time, so cut to the chase. Like I asked, what are you going to do with your life?"

CHAPTER 2

Ritz Crackers & cheddar cheese . . .

Autumn 1992

Star was mesmerized when Professor Perfidius read aloud in class. He had a way of standing that reminded her of Richard Gere, with his left hip and thigh thrusting forward. She discovered Gere's hip-thrust when he starred in *An Officer and A Gentleman*, the very first movie she ever saw in a theater. On the day that Trista declared her lice-free, the pair celebrated with a trip to the movies. She was delighted by the buttered popcorn and magnificent screen, but when Richard Gere paraded across the silver wall in his military whites, Star was besotted—love struck. Eight years later, Gere ensnared her heart again in *Pretty Woman*. This time she was much older and the story was much closer to home. There were many nights in the Tenderloin when she prayed that her prince would discover her, cherish her, and save her from the hellhole in which she lived, but he never came. Nonetheless, Star watched Julia Roberts being saved by her prince so many times that the VCR tape eventually snapped and knotted up inside the cartridge.

Over the weeks in class, Star entertained herself with other traits of Professor Perfidius that reminded her of Richard Gere. When he read, Perfidius titled his head to the side and looked up with a slight grin. He had thick, dark hair that swept back in waves, and as he became animated, a wavy lock would fall across his forehead, just like Gere's. Gazing toward the chalkboard, Star imagined herself to be Julia Roberts, pushing back the hair, softening his estranged heart.

Though the fantasies of *Pretty Woman* kept her occupied for many of the ninety minute classes, Star was caught off guard when her teacher read aloud the final lines of *The Mayor of Casterbridge*. Holding Thomas Hardy's classic high in his hand with his hip and thigh thrusting forward, Professor Perfidius read the final words as if he was revealing her own Tenderloin reality:

> "And being forced to class herself among the fortunate she did not cease to wonder at the persistence of the unforeseen, when the one to whom such unbroken tranquility had been accorded in the adult stage was she whose youth had seemed to teach that happiness was but the occasional episode in a general drama of pain."

Her cheeks burned as she discreetly wiped the trickle from her nose on her shirt sleeve. She glanced around the classroom to see if anyone had noticed. No one did, but why weren't they shedding tears, too? Didn't they hear Thomas Hardy's words? Happiness is fleeting. Nothing more. Don't hang your hat on it. Don't take it to the bank. Happiness is about as reliable as an addict. There's no Prince Charming handing out honest happiness, either. If you want that, read a book or watch a stupid movie. Don't depend on happiness and you'll be okay, she wanted to warn them.

After class, Star quickly shoved her spiral notebook into her backpack and stood to leave, but before she was out the door, Professor Perfidius called her back. After all the students had filed out, he asked if she was okay. "Just a long day and a head cold," she lied. How could Star possibly tell him the truth that she had learned a long time ago—that Happiness was and always would be an inconstant tease? Something you see on the silver screen or read about in books but nothing that ever exists in real life.

"Maybe I should be crying over the short story that's due next week," she tried to joke, dropping her backpack on the floor with a thud.

"Are you having problems with the draft?" he asked, leaning against the desk with his left hip thrusting forward.

Star shrugged her shoulders and turned away from his penetrating stare. Damn, his eyes are brown, too, just like Gere's, she thought.

"You've got a strong voice, Star. Be patient with your writing," he advised.

"I know, I know," Star said, grabbing her backpack and throwing it across her back.

"Stop by during my office hours, if you want help," he offered.

"Thanks. I usually come to class straight from work on Wednesdays, but if I'm really in a jam, Leo will let me leave early."

"Leo? Do you mean Leo's Coffee House over on Ambrose?"

"Yep. The one and only," she said with honest pride.

"Does he still have that amazing Italian chocolate roll?"

"Are you talking about the chocolate salami?"

"That's it, that's it!" her teacher said, shaking his head.

"We usually have chocolate salami once a week. Leo bakes everything himself in a tiny kitchen above the shop."

"I haven't been there in years," he conceded.

"I'm sure nothing has changed, including the pastries," she smiled proudly. "You should stop in some time and bring a friend. Leo needs the business."

"I'll do that," he said, folding his notes and tucking them into his briefcase. As he bent down, a lock of hair fell onto his forehead.

Star smiled to herself, turned and headed out the door. Crunching through leaves that were collecting along the sidewalk, she thought about *Pretty Woman*. The story was just another Pygmalion myth, much like Colette's *Gigi*. Pygmalion was famous for breathing life and love into a beautiful female statue that was captured in stone. Gaston Lachaille does the same for Gigi. Duped by her grandmother, the pitiful girl unknowingly is groomed to be a genteel Parisian courtesan, a prostitute. Oh, but alas, Gigi is saved from a life of vassalage by the wealthy Gaston who falls in love and marries her. Just like in *Pretty Woman, Cinderella, Sleeping Beauty* or scores of other stories, the gallant Pygmalion prince charges in, swoops up the girl, and saves her from a life of drudgery. But that was just it. All of the stories were flipping myths, fairytales, hogwash! Thomas Hardy was the one who had it right. There is no real happiness at the end of the story and no real prince! She kicked through the autumn leaves and forged on to the library for a night of homework.

As Star climbed the library steps to the second floor, she spotted Kory and Emmy at the study table where they typically camped out. Star whispered hello as she approached the table and quietly unpacked her bag. Kory raised his pencil in acknowledgment while Emmy continued to punch numbers into her calculator.

Star had known Emmy for longer than she liked to remember and had met Kory in an anthropology course the year before. He was what Bosco called an alternative student, a twenty-eight-year-old who had served in the military for eight years before going to college. When they first met, Star would have described him as unremarkable. Her prince was typically taller with wider shoulders and more hair. Kory was muscular but compact, not much over five feet nine inches tall. His brown hair was shaved into a crew cut, and his jeans were always neatly pressed with parallel crease marks.

She and Kory were serendipitously thrown together for a class project with which they were required to observe and track specified mating patterns of male homosapiens. Their test sample included college age men who hung out on the green, Bosco's student commons. Star and Kory designed a study that was to observe and record involuntary behaviors of men while attempting to attract the attention of young women. The three behaviors tracked included the number of times a male touched his crotch, touched his hair or touched his pecs while talking to a girl.

Because Kory was a commuter, arranging their schedules for observations was a challenge. With the due date looming, a frustrated Star finally gave him times and dates, hoping he would show up. On the day of their first observation, she rushed across the green, heading toward the old sycamore where they had planned to meet. Her black curls, tethered in a tight ponytail, bounced in the air trying to break free. She was wearing faded cut-off shorts and a clingy tank top that revealed a tight but shapely body. Though she was actually petite, her long legs and quick stride created an illusion of much greater height. Clutching a blanket and a bag of snacks close to her chest, she hurried along, searching for Kory in the distance. Star spotted him already seated under the tree and watched absently as he scanned the full length of her body. His approving look and her unmindful stare were no surprise. For her entire life, Star had been disconnected from her beauty and from the effect that she had on men. Behind thick black lashes and full brows, her untamed green eyes cast a sensual, earthy glow, drawing men toward her. Her body wasn't sexy and voluptuous. It was animalistic with taut arms and legs that moved in unison with the curve of her surroundings. Whether by choice or by oblivion, however, Star's aura never seemed to flow into her own consciousness.

"Am I late?" she asked breathlessly, drawing nearer to Kory.

"No. Right on time. I'm just chronically early," he said, standing up to help her.

"Good. We'll get along well," she said, handing him the grocery bag. "I'll spread out the blanket while you unload the bag. I need food. My blood sugar is ready to tank, and if it does, you'll want to jump ship," she explained, bending down to square off the corners of the blanket.

"Why would I do that?"

"Sharp fangs and evil spirits escape from me with no food," she said, standing up to face him.

Kory caught the glow from her eyes. "That sounds ferocious," he said, holding her gaze.

Star turned away and grabbed the bag back from him. "My problem is a recklessly high metabolism. I drive people crazy if they are around me for too long. At least that's what I've been told—that I can never just relax."

"Is that true?"

"Maybe. But what's wrong with that?" Star asked defensively.

"I wasn't the one who said it's a problem," he said, raising his eyebrows. Kory sat down in the center of the blanket while she plopped down next to him, pulling Ritz crackers, cheddar cheese and grapes from the bag.

"Looks great. All we need now is a bottle of wine and music, and it would be the perfect date," Kory joked.

"I don't drink alcohol," Star said without a smile.

"Maybe you should," Kory mumbled to himself and grabbed a few grapes. Pulling the record sheets from his backpack, he complained that projects like this irritated the hell out of him. This was busy work of the highest order, he told Star, but she disagreed.

"Don't you think that Professor Dingleman is trying to teach us how to formulate hypotheses and test models, but in a fun way?" she asked.

"I'm not seven years old. I don't need this kind of *fun*. Observing weak attempts at mating has nothing to do with real life. When an AK-47 is launching bullets at your head, you're not thinking about a goddamn hypothesis. You're thinking about covering your buddy's ass and saving your own."

33

"Maybe, but you've got to be practical. Most of us have never been shot at and most never will. We're in college, not on the battlefield."

"That's the problem with this country. All these guys," he said, looking toward the center of the green, "they've had cushy lives and pampered self-esteems. But in reality, they're nothing but a bunch of inflated pussies who've never heard the word no," he said, grabbing for the cracker box. "Can we open these?"

Star took the box from him and opened it. "You may want to soften the edges a bit lieutenant. This is just an anthropology project, not a paper for the Pentagon." As she handed him the crackers, Star wondered if Kory was some kind of mental case.

"I'm not uptight, Star. I just like to live in reality. Take the dude with the flipped collar over there," he said, pointing to a student in khaki shorts and a pink golf shirt. "Little Josh has been told that he's a superstar all of his life, even when he struck out and left three men on base. The harshest word his mommy ever muttered was "inappropriate." And if I hear the words "inappropriate behavior" one more time, I'm going to puke. Some squatty nine-year-old careened a grocery cart into a beer display at the store yesterday, and do you know what his mom said?"

"Should I really care?" Star asked, raising her eyebrows.

Kory ignored the comment and continued. "She said, 'Honey, that's inappropriate behavior.' My mother would have spanked my ass straight to Hades and back, right then and there. But, hell, now you get arrested for disciplining your kids. Tell me, do I want some little shit who's grown up into a big shit covering my back in real life? Hell no! Let the shits design their own clever hypotheses. They won't understand the value of the process anyway, because they don't take anything seriously, including life."

"Do you always get so bent out of shape over other people's behavior? You sound like my grandfather. Maybe the shits who don't take life so seriously are better off in the long run. They're probably a lot happier than the stiffs who always think that the sky is about to fall."

"Do you really think that?" he asked, narrowing his gaze.

"Yeah, I do. It's not a cop-out. Life is hard. It can be a relief to be around people who don't take it so seriously."

Looking at Star as if she'd never had a hard day in her life, Kory said, "That's why we have children. They're supposed to act like three-year-olds. It's a problem when a twenty-year-old can't get past the mental age of thirteen."

"Maybe," she said curtly to end the discussion. "But I'm not here to reform mankind today. I'm here to spot crotch-grabbers. *And*, whether you like it or not, I'm one of those people who is obsessive about A's. So, if I have to watch guys grab their balls for three days for an A, I'm going to do it."

"I get the point," he said, leaning back on his elbows. "Sorry. I get caught up in my own tangents sometimes."

"That's okay," said Star as she threw a grape, hitting him between the eyes.

"Nice shot."

"Learned it in the 'hood," she said.

"Yeah, right," Kory laughed.

"No, really, in the hood," she said, picking up the tally sheets.

By the end of the study, Star and Kory observed one hundred thirty-two men flirting with women. The majority of the men, sixty-seven, touched their pecs during the conversation while only forty-two grabbed their crotch, and the remaining played with their hair. Kory also observed, during the three days, the greenest eyes and the longest lashes that he had ever seen on a woman. Star's hair tangled in the black fringe when a brisk wind whipped through the trees, and several times during those three days, Kory was tempted to reach out and untangle the strands and peer into her eyes.

Star was resting on her stomach and erasing smudge marks on the tally sheets when she rolled over on the blanket and eyed Kory. "Well, Lieutenant Huber, was this assignment that painful after all?" Kory looked down at Star and ached to touch her cheek, to brush his lips across her lashes.

"Officer, I asked you a question. Was this study that painful?" she repeated.

"No, not at all," he answered. "But what does this information really tell us about men and their mating patterns?" he asked.

Star flipped over and sat up straight. "Oh, God! From a female's point of view? Everything!"

"Everything. Really?"

"Heck, yeah. A guy who plays with his hair—a pretty boy. Spends way too much time primping. He's high maintenance, worse than a girl. The crotch-grabber—insecure. If he has to double check to see if he's a man, who wants him? The pec-petter—masculine. In shape but full of himself."

"Do girls really think that way?" he asked.

"Of course! So, tell me, which one are you?"

"You tell me."

"I don't know. I haven't watched you hit on a girl yet."

Kory didn't diddle with his hair, pecs or crotch. He didn't need to. He was a Marine, one of The Few and The Proud hard bodies on campus, but Star would never know it unless she saw him buck naked. He was five feet, ten inches tall with one hundred seventy pounds of sculpted tissue underneath his jeans and t-shirt. Yet, in the year that followed their anthropology project, they became good friends and studied together most every day, but she never once gave his body the slightest nod.

Star was a contradiction to Kory. She seemed so intense and serious about life, yet when he caught a glimpse of her on the green or in the dining hall, she was hanging with some jock wearing parachute pants and Air Jordans. They were all pretty much the same, the type of guys who attended class only if required and bought stolen exam answers from shyster teaching assistants. They graduated late and their first job was selling used cars, and they still never took life too seriously.

Across the study table, Emmy and Kory huddled close to compare balance sheet numbers while Star settled down to work on her story for Professor Perfidius. She had known Emmy Dribble for years, and like a bad reputation, she never really went away. She followed Star from middle school to high school and then again to college. To Star's dismay, their paths converged again during Rush Week when she spotted Emmy at a party wearing her Cincinnati blueblood uniform: Topsiders, corduroy slacks, and a pink monogrammed sweater. The only conclusion that she could draw from the boxy fashion statement was that thick cords must look better rolled down around the ankles after the consumption of several Little Kings beers. Nevertheless, Rush week ended predictably for both. Emmy was invited to join the coveted Tri Delta sorority while Star landed a job at Leo's Coffee House.

Emmy was the type of girl who always wore a bright, stiff smile and who remembered birthdays and to send thank-you notes. She also remembered the details of her friends' lives that they, themselves, tried hard to forget. She could pinpoint in which bathroom stall at the Sigma Chi house Crystal Winters fell asleep after yakking on her date. She carefully noted who slept in the Tri Delta house on Saturday nights and who didn't, male or female. Emmy never wore gym shoes unless she was playing tennis, and her pink and green hair ribbons that held her ponytail never came untied. After Rush Week, Emmy remained acquaintances with Star, even though she "couldn't possibly understand how a run-down coffee shop could be more interesting than a sorority house."

As Emmy crunched numbers on her calculator, Kory dug his nose deeper into the pages of his accounting book. He raised his head only to snarl, "Star, the Hulk's walked around the library three times looking for you. He was shocked that there were 'like, so many books on the shelves,' but I educated him for you. I told him that if he bench pressed an entire stack of books then he would grow big and strong and that you love big and strong men."

"Very funny, Kory. Why are you so nasty tonight?" Star asked as she flipped through the pages of her notebook.

"I'm not nasty. I'm just wondering why you always fall for idiots?" Kory returned.

"Maybe there's a pearl in simplicity. Try it sometime. You might have a little fun," she snapped back. "Oh, I forgot. You're a serious man. No fun allowed."

"Would you two quiet down! I have an accounting exam in twelve hours and so do you, Kory," said Emmy.

"I'm ready for it. And I'm out of here," Kory said as he chucked his calculator into his backpack, stood up and walked away without saying a word.

"What's wrong with him?" Star asked.

"Forget about it. The Hulk will be back any minute," Emmy mumbled.

"What's that supposed to mean?" Star asked, tapping her pen on the table.

"Nothing. It's just midterms."

Kory went back to his apartment that night and tore off his t-shirt. He grabbed the pull-up bar that hung within a doorframe and began pounding out the tension that ripped through his body. He battled guerillas in Mogadishu and witnessed genocide in Bosnia. So, why couldn't he just blow her out of his mind? *Goddamn you*, he grunted as his body pulsated up and down. Why do intelligent, beautiful, witty women always go for the bums? It was one of the great mysteries of life, he thought. Star should be different, though, because she *was* different. She had a dimension to her that most people never developed. Kory knew that Star had a cache of experience that taught her about real life and real people, an awareness that didn't come just from reading Shakespeare or Hawthorne. She never told him about her childhood, but he read about her life between the lines of her short stories that she shared with him. Kory sensed an understanding in her similar to what he had learned when he uncovered his first mass grave in Bosnia. In a tangle of broken arms and legs, he spotted an intact body of a woman that was clinging to the body of a small child. That's not the kind of human understanding that comes from a book. That picture of pain and agony is drawn through experience, and Star could etch the curves, the valleys, the sharp peaks and dramatic descents of misery.

He wanted to know more about her, but she would never let him in. He wanted to know about the circular scars on her forearms that looked like cigarette burns. He had seen similar scarring in Bosnia where cigarettes where used as a handy tool of torture. He wanted to know what she ate for breakfast and what she wore to bed. He wanted to know what her last thoughts were before she fell asleep at night. He wanted to know about the crevice between her small breasts and the taut muscles curving her backside. He wanted to take his fingers and slowly learn about every part of her body. He wanted to take his lips and press them against her temples and absorb the thoughts that flowed from her mind.

He could do none of this, though, for she would never let him close to her. Kory squeezed the pull-up bar and yanked his body up and down until his arms gave way and he dropped to the floor. A bolt of pain flashed through his body. "I can beat this!" he swore. "I can beat this!"

CHAPTER 3

Bobbing Carrots . . .

L eo's was always dead at two in the afternoon. Star polished the coffee urns and reorganized the beans alphabetically. She wiped down the countertop and scrubbed the bar stools and café tables with lemon juice and ammonia. The shop was sparkling, and Star liked the fact that Leo would be pleased. She knew that he looked forward to Mondays, Wednesdays and Fridays because he could rest. Leo Bartatello was eighty-two and had lived above the store since returning from the war in 1945. His wife, Nella, died four years before from emphysema. She was the one who kept the place spotless, Leo told Star. The couple never had children, and Star never asked why. She guessed that it had something to do with Leo's twisted limp in his right leg. He had contracted polio from swimming in a city pool, just after returning from the war, but Nella married him anyway.

After Star's shift ended at five, she would go upstairs to eat dinner with Leo. They had the same routine each day. Star would crack open the door and yell, "Yoo-hoo, Leo, I'm hungry." He'd wobble out of the kitchen with a proud smile and say, breaded veal and polenta for you tonight. Three nights a week Star could count on an Italian masterpiece from Leo's old Roper gas stove with its trademark double oven.

There was just a single customer in the shop that day, a girl Star recognized from her biology class the year before. Her head was buried deep into charts and theorems, so Star dragged out her own notebooks to occupy her time. Once the shop was clean, Leo didn't mind if she sat at the bar and studied. The spiral notebook was filled with narrow, even script that told her stories, mostly about life and about suffering. Star turned to the last few pages and paused at the title of her working draft, "Paper Moon." She frowned and began to read the final lines of the story:

> Rich walked out of Belinda's apartment, trying to convince himself that this would be the last time. Her eyes glistened as Happiness walked out with him, the two, side by side. They were best friends, Happiness and Rich, mere reflections of each other. It was past eleven when Rich finally walked through his own front door. He clicked off the hallway light that his wife kept shining to help him find his way. Rich undressed for the second time that night and climbed into bed. He pulled Joy close, and she fell asleep with a smile on her face because, after all, Rich was wrapped around her for the night, and Happiness was there, as well.

Star read over the lines once more, worrying that the metaphor was too sophomoric. Happiness and Rich were both cheats. Happiness was nothing more than an unfaithful lover—promises the moon but dishes out jack shit. Maybe it needs to be more subtle. Kory usually read over her stories to provide a completely objective male perspective, but she hadn't seen him since he bolted from the library. She had called his apartment a few times but received only the mechanical ring droning in her ear.

Just as she began to splice her words, the sleigh bells nailed to Leo's door jingled, and Star looked up from her story to see Professor Perfidius walking toward her with his Richard Gere swagger. He wore grey flannel slacks that sat low on his hips, a black v-neck sweater and a crisp white shirt underneath. His deep olive skinned glowed from the windy chill outside.

Star was taken aback. She closed her notebook and slid off the stool to greet him. "Professor Perfidius. This is a surprise. Welcome to Leo's," she spewed.

"Hello, Star Nox," he said and sat down at the bar. "Does Leo have that chocolate salami today? I've been craving it since our last class."

"No," she said, pointing to the pastry dome. "Biscotti or Torta Di Meliga, which is cornmeal cake," she explained. "The cake is my favorite."

"You've sold me. A piece of cake and a cup of black coffee."

As she walked around to the backside of the counter, her teacher picked up the notebook, "Doing a bit of homework on the job?" he asked.

Star's hand shook with nerves as she lifted the glass dome and pulled out a slice of cake. "When business is slow, I do a little work. Leo doesn't mind," she said, setting the pastry on the plate and pushing it toward him. "I'm working on the story for your class, as a matter of fact."

"This shop could give you great fodder for a story," he said, looking around.

While his eyes roamed the room, Star noticed the copper specks in his brown iris's and the grey hair that was gathering around his temples. She wondered how old he was. Over forty, at least. She was still young enough when everything over thirty seemed old. Nonetheless, there was a strange tension balling in her throat that she tried to push down with a hard swallow. As his eyes returned to her, he asked about the story.

"Are you having problems with plot development or is it a technical issue," he asked.

"It's not finding the story that I have a problem with," she explained. "It's getting the words out in a way that will make people want to keep reading. That's my garden to grow, so my grandmother would say."

"Ah, be patient with yourself. It was Thomas Hardy who wrote, 'If a way to the Better there be, it exacts a full look at the Worst.' Looking at the worst in life or yourself can draw tears sometimes, but that's how we grow," Professor Perfidius said as he took a bite of cake.

Star cringed as she poured his coffee from the brass urn. She was certain that he saw the single tear trickle down her face during class. What a juvenile response she had given when he asked if she was okay. Why didn't she just say that she was moved by Hardy's description of pain? That was the truth. No, instead she rambled on about a stupid head cold. Very clever, Star Nox. Very clever.

With a deep breath, Star turned to Professor Perfidius and set down the coffee. "So, what brings you to this part of the campus?" she asked.

"I'm giving a lecture in an hour."

"Sounds fun." Star closed her eyes in embarrassment. *Sounds fun.* Just another brilliant comment for my esteemed English instructor, she thought. Trying to recover herself, she opened her eyes and asked, "Is the talk about writing fiction or nonfiction?"

"Neither. I'm discussing how the fusion of cult and philosophy fueled Christianity's success during the Middle Ages."

"You're talking about religion?" she asked, confused.

"I am. Theology is actually my area of expertise. I teach English courses for entertainment."

Star paused and thought before responding this time. "Interesting," she slowly noted. "So, are you calling Christianity a cult?"

"Of sorts. Both are a means to an end. Historically, cults have been a tool for people seeking an emotional and social connection that's often consummated through ritualistic behaviors. Does that sound familiar to you?"

Star shook her head no, so he explained. "Think about your own Catholic mass. You go to church on Sundays for communion with your god and with those who have similar needs. And, how is this connection accomplished? Through ritualized consecration on your part and the priest's part. You sit, you stand, you kneel, you chant, you share in ritualized bread and wine. By definition, Star, that's a cult."

Star shifted on her feet and cleared her throat. "Professor Perfidius, I have to tell you . . . I'm offended by the fact that you just called the Catholic faith a cult. The Church has guided me through some pretty bad storms in my life." Star took a rag and began cleaning the counter around his coffee cup.

"Star, I'm not trying to condemn the Catholic faith nor any other faith, for that matter. You take offence because the term 'cult' carries a negative connotation. Cult simply means a denomination. The freakish nature of the term has come about because not all cults have been driven by morality. That's where philosophy came into play for early Christians. Early on, when Christians were promoting their faith, philosophical schools were searching for the key to life's mysteries through rational reflection and a preoccupation with moral admonition. Combine cult behavior with philosophy and you had a perfect pathway for Christians to promote their cause. That's what my discussion is going to be about tonight."

Star stopped wiping the counter and asked, "Sorry if I seem stupid, Professor Perfidius, but are you telling me that God is just a tool or something, not our Creator?"

He took a sip of his coffee and set the cup down, "Star, I look at religion as a means to an end, which is a reduction of a lot of my thoughts."

"Okay," she said, not knowing what else to say.

"Let's talk about something far more exciting. Let's get back to your story. How is it coming along," he asked, finishing the last bite of cake.

"It's okay. I'm just worried that the audience will find the topic too common. The story is written as an extended metaphor for happiness. It's the metaphor that's risky," she said, leaning on the bar.

"Do you want me to take a look at your draft," he offered, glancing at her notebook that was decorated with flowers and peace sign doodles.

"Nah. I still have time to polish it." Star took the notebook and shoved it underneath the countertop.

"Well, the offer is still on the table. Stop by during my office hours if you have any problems."

"Thank you," she said and turned to two more customers who sat down at the counter.

Professor Perfidius drained his coffee cup, pulled a twenty dollar bill from his pocket and slipped it under his plate. When he said goodbye, Star moved to give him change, but he waved her away. "You're a starving college student. Keep it," he charged.

Star smiled and offered a quick wave, but as she went to grab his dirty dishes, a slight tremor rippled through her body. She was well aware that her instructor's imposing presence made her feel electric, but she wasn't certain if she liked the sensation that he stirred. For the most part, Star had been indifferent to boys and men, for that matter. She went out on dates once in a while, but what Kory didn't know was that the "hulks" bolted once a quick feel was met with a stony stare. This safe zone was easy for Star to maintain for no one had truly tested her own margins of physical desire. She rolled her shoulders to shake off the sensations, whatever they were, and looked around the shop for Kory, though she knew he wasn't there. She grabbed a soft cloth and began polishing the coffee urns for a second time that day.

Jimmy, the shop's only other employee, arrived at five to start his shift. He had silky blond hair with playful blue eyes and a narrow nose. His great sense of style and generous fashion advice made him the closest thing to a girlfriend that Star had on Bosco's campus. When he came into the shop, the two had a habit of welcoming each other with a kiss on both cheeks in a very European way.

After their cheeky greeting that day, Star untied her apron strings and made her way up the squeaky staircase to Leo's door. She cracked it open and yelled in, "Yoo-hoo, Leo, I'm hungry." He came wobbling out of the kitchen and said, "Risotto and Stracciatella for you tonight." Leo was a slight man with only a few wispy hairs left on his head. He walked with a limp and was hunched over from the heavy weight of life. Star had never seen him without a steady smile, though, or a crisp white apron secured around his waist and neck.

"It smells wonderful," she said, walking in and giving him a kiss on his forehead. Star followed Leo back into the kitchen and lifted the lid to the tallest pot. "What's Stracciatella?" she asked, peering into the sweltering soup.

"Egg soup," he said, handing her two bowls to fill.

As she ladled the soup into the bowls, Star complained about Kory's irritability and aloofness.

"Put the soup on the table," he directed and then added, "That young man has a lot on his mind. Be patient."

"Oh, Leo! He's always so serious. I have a lot on my mind, too, but I'm not glum," she said, picking up the bowls.

"Kory's not glum. You don't know the battle pack he may be lugging around from the service. Soldiers don't share with civilians," he explained, shuffling to the table with steaming plates of risotto. He sat down and told Star to do the same. "Eat. The risotto is getting cold."

She followed his direction and sat down but continued prodding. "Why don't soldiers talk? Maybe if Kory did, he'd have some friends. He's scares people off with his soldier attitude and military lingo. Everything's 'yes sir' and 'no sir.' People don't talk that way."

"The world would be a better place if people took the time to show a little respect like Kory," Leo argued.

"He's not normal," she said, taking a bite of risotto. She closed her eyes and swallowed. "Mmm! This stuff melts in your mouth, Leo. How do you do it?"

"Pazienza, Stella! Patience is in that rice. I slice my onion very thin, no chop-chop. When I sauté it in butter, the onion becomes clear and melts, giving up its flavor. A good cook takes the time to respect the process," he explained.

She looked up at him coyly, understanding that he was making a point about something other than food. "You know that patience isn't one of my virtues, Leo. I've always thought that patient people were secretly wrapped up real tight, like rubber bands inside a golf ball, ready to snap. Kind of like Kory."

"You surprise me . . . to hear you talk that way about him," Leo said with his voice dropping.

"He needs to learn to relax. That's all I'm saying. Live a little."

"Kory has lived a lot more than you think. That may be what keeps him wound up so tightly," Leo said, narrowing his eyes into a pointed gaze.

"Leo, please don't give me one of your looks. I'm right this time. Maybe Kory needs to talk a little. Get it out. That helps some people."

Leo put down his own fork and scooted his chair back from the table. "Mi Stella," he said firmly, "Sometimes soldiers can't just get it out. Unless you've crossed the battlefield, it's impossible for a civilian to understand the death and carnage that a soldier sees."

Star peered up at him. "But I do—" she started to explain but then stopped.

"Listen, Stella," he said, folding his arms across his chest. "What if I told you that I shot a kid who stood no taller than a broom stick when I was your age? You'd be shocked. You'd say, 'Leo! That is horrible!' You'd ask why. Why? Because he was gripping a grenade in one hand and had his finger on the pin with the other. By killing that kid, I saved nine soldiers, including myself, but for another fifty years, not a single day has passed by me without thinking about the boy's face as he crumbled to the ground. He was somebody's son, Stella. Did I do the right thing? To this day, I don't know. Maybe that's why God decided that Nella and I couldn't have kids."

Star swallowed hard and looked down at her plate. "I'm sorry," she whispered. "You never told me." She picked up her fork and began to toy with it.

"There's nothing for you to be sorry about. Maybe I shouldn't have lobbed the story in your lap. If Nella was here, she'd be kicking me under the table. After this meal, we'll never discuss it again, but I care about Kory and have a sense of duty to take his back. I started caring about that boy the first day he came into the shop all hot and bothered, looking for you.

Through all his steaminess, I saw it in his eyes. Soldiers know the look the first time they see it in a comrade's stare, and once they see it, they never forget it."

"Leo, what 'look' are you talking about?" she asked, shaking her head.

"Pazienza! Ascolta! Listen to me. Kory carries a lot of living behind those eyes, and it's not all good. I told you my story to make a point. Maybe there are things that Kory doesn't share for a reason, but they're still with him. Once you touch war, it never leaves you. It hangs in your nostrils during the day and rings in your ears at night. I'm just trying to help you understand Kory. He's a fine young man."

Star sat back for a moment without saying a word. She decided not to tell Leo that she understood the haunting scars of warzones. Battles weren't just fought gun to gun or bomb to bomb nor was there a clear definition of enemy territory. She understood all that and had buried her own battle srench and chaos a long time ago.

"Okay," she conceded. "But maybe it's not the military that's bugging him. Maybe it's something much more mundane, like girls."

"Could be," Leo said and scooted his chair back to the table.

"But who would know," she complained. "I've known him for a year, and he's never once mentioned a girl. Nothing."

"Do you talk to Kory about your fidanzati . . . your boys, Stella?"

"I don't need to. Kory comments to me about them. Calls them all *Jock Strap*. 'Saw you talking to *Jock Strap* today, Star . . . *Jock Strap* got lost in the library trying to find you, Star.'"

Leo grinned. "You see! Kory has a fine sense of humor."

"Yeah. At my expense."

"Ah, tease back. You don't have a shy bone in the body."

"I could never do that, Leo."

"Why?"

"I wouldn't want to hurt him. It's different with me. I don't take things so seriously. The topic of girls is off limits with him."

"Why?"

"Why? Leo, I don't know why. Why! Why do you think?" she said exasperated.

"What do I think? I think it's like a big pot of chicken stock with a single slice of carrot floating on the surface," he half explained with his hands. "Kory's standing over the pot with a wooden spoon, chasing that carrot, but every time the spoon gets too close, the carrot bobs and dives away."

Star looked up from her rice. "Leo, sometimes you are so infuriating!"

"Why, Carrot?"

"Very funny. And stop asking me why, for God's sake!" she said, dropping her fork a little too hard on Nella's plate.

"Star, don't break that boy's heart," he said, growing serious. "He's special."

Star pushed her chair from the table and stood up. "I know, I know, Leo. He's perfect and I'm not!" she said with unusual irritation directed at Leo. "You don't have to remind me that he's so special."

"Sit back down and listen to me," he said firmly.

Reluctantly, she did as she was told and Leo continued. "You need to figure out what's important in relationships. You've worked at the shop some three years. In all this time, not one of those *Jock Straps* has stopped in for a cup of coffee or a single cannoli."

Star's head snapped up, "Leo! You're as bad as Kory!"

"Stella, listen. Those boys don't come in the shop for one of two reasons, either you're not proud of them or you don't mean that much to them. When Nella worked at Andollina's Bakery, I bought crostata di mele three times a week. Gained five pounds in a month from that damn apple tart, but seeing her lovely smile behind the glass case was worth every ounce. If these boys don't think you're worth a walk across campus, then they're robaccia, trash."

"Leo, but those guys mean nothing to *me*. I don't want them hanging around. They're not like Nella and you," Star tried to explain.

"No. I don't buy that. You're a pretty girl. Robaccia! And when Kory comes in, you change. I watch things. He sits at the bar. You pour his coffee. Then you push him that little notebook of yours with all those stories scribbled in it. And he reads them. And you two talk. Now, that's what relationships are all about. The talking. I know. I talked with my best friend for over fifty years, and it all started with an apple tart." Leo paused for a moment and gazed out the window.

Star followed Leo's eyes, and with a slow, melancholy pace he started to sing, "Don't sit under the apple tree with anyone else but me, anyone else but me . . . anyone else but me . . . ." He finished the first verse, stopped and looked up at Star. "That was our song for almost fifty years. Glen Miller came out with that little number two months after Pearl Harbor took its hit. Been our song ever since. Nella and I planted the apple tree that sits right out there by the curb," he said, pointing toward the window. "Did it for good luck when we first bought this place. Nella still has an apple tree with her. Had one carved on her tombstone. That's what true love is about. It's about being rooted together. Kids, nowadays, think love is all about shooting stars. I'll tell you what . . ." he paused.

"Go on," she whispered, though she'd heard most of his stories a dozen times before.

"If a man makes you see stars, my advice is to turn and run the other way. Stars burn too hot and fizzle out. Find yourself a solid tree."

"Leo, I know what you're saying about romance, but I'm not talking about that kind of relationship with Kory. He is my best friend, not my boyfriend."

"Stella, best friend is where romance begins and ends," he said, opening his arms wide apart. "Beginning. End. Don't let anyone tell you otherwise. Kory is a good man. You listen to me. He's got the virtues, and don't you forget that."

"You lost me, Leo. He's no saint," she said with an edge.

"No, no. The cardinal virtues of an ideal citizen of Rome—prudence, justice, strength and temperance."

Star threw her head back and laughed. "Stop, Leo! Stop with the Roman-soldier-hero worship garbage!"

"No, no! You listen, young lady," he said wagging his finger. "Without the virtues, the man is robaccio. The world doesn't make men like Kory anymore. I watch these fellows who come into the shop. I wouldn't want any of them covering my back. Now, Kory—he's a real man."

CHAPTER 4

Baked cod, buon pesce . . .

Star held her spiral notebook close to her chest as she walked toward class that evening. Leo's advice rang in her ears. He had spent a lot of time with Kory and knew him well. Everything that Leo had said about him was true. No one needed to tell her that. As she crossed the green and headed toward Beekman Hall, Star spotted Kory sitting under the same tree where together they tracked Homo sapiens for their anthropology class. Emmy was with him, resting her back against the trunk of the sycamore. Star glanced at her watch. She had a few extra minutes before class, so she headed toward them. He couldn't avoid her now. Approaching the pair, Star watched as Kory leaned over and kissed Emmy on the lips. *On the lips!* A long, lingering kiss on the lips!

"What in God's name was that?!" She stopped and blurted out. A wave of confusion washed through her as she stood there, staring at the couple. When the interlude finally ended, Kory tilted up his head and looked out across the green. Star was shocked and embarrassed to find her eyes staring back into his. She turned and hurried away.

She rushed into Beekman Hall and up the steps to her class, cursing, "Happiness, I hate you. I hate your flimsy promises. You're a lying cheat. You're an asshole! An asshole!"

She yanked open the classroom door with more strength than intended and cringed as it swung back and hit the wall. The entire class, including Professor Perfidius, spun their heads to look at her.

"Sorry," she whispered and slunk into her seat. Star's stomach fell with dread as she slowly pulled her notebook from her backpack. She was in no mood for the "Read-Around" that her professor required for what he called "critical peer review." The room was sticky and the class was irritable. Mike Wilkens, whose ambition was to be a sports writer for *Sports Illustrated,* offered to read first. He was trounced on by most of the females in the class for writing a trite tale about a high school football coach who saved a kid from the ghetto. The theme was tired and worn out and teetered on plagiarism, his classmates complained. Knowing that her storyline and imagery weren't, at least, plagiarized, Star raised her hand to go next, and she began:

. . . Rich pulled Joy close, and she fell asleep with a smile because, after all, her husband was wrapped around her, and at least for the night, Happiness was there, as well. Clutching the paper moon that Rich left behind, Belinda never fell asleep that night as Happiness, the inconstant lover, walked out with Rich, shoulder to shoulder.

Hands shot in the air before Star finished her final line. Mike was first. "Talk about tired? That's just another story about a victimized woman," he explained. "Women like that are never happy and always have to blame the guy for their misery. Belinda's sleeping with a married man who's a cheat, and Joy is sleeping with a husband who's a cheat. Losers!" Mike made his index finger and thumb in the shape of an L to confirm his statement.

"'Paper Moon' is not about women, in the least bit," Star tried to explain, but Becca Peters, the class Tree of Knowledge, interrupted and told Star and Mike to face the facts. "When men are grappling for a topic, they revert to misogynistic sports stories. When women are under pressure, they fall prey to the whiny 'men are the ruination of society' themes. Both themes are flat and boring. The characters are stereotypical and uninteresting."

As the Tree of Knowledge rattled on, Star's face passed from scarlet to maroon. When the girl took a breath, Star informed Becca that "'Paper Moon' wasn't really about victimized women, just like Jonathon Swift's *A Modest Proposal* wasn't really about feasting on children. The story was a metaphor for happiness; it's like the inconstant lover of which you have no control."

Becca argued that the concept was still the tired pitiful-victim theme. "Happiness is something that you make happen. You can't rely on other people to make you happy or unhappy," she concluded.

Star stood strong and defended her story. "I agree with half of what you say, Becca. You can't rely on other people to make you happy, but you sure can't control whether they make you unhappy. You can't control other people's behavior, just like you can't control happiness. If Jake calls you on the phone tonight and dumps you, then that's going to make you unhappy, no matter how happy you try to be. So, like I said, Happiness is the inconstant lover."

After class, Star grabbed her backpack and nearly sprinted out of the room. She headed toward the library but then stopped dead in her tracks. She hadn't the time before class to process how she felt about seeing Kory's lips locked with Emmy's. She wasn't prepared to face either of them, but if they weren't at the study table, she wasn't prepared to face that either.

She turned around and decided to head home anyway, but the kiss between them was relentless. "Stop thinking about it!" she chastised herself. "He's not *your* boyfriend."

Star realized that she could have dated Kory at any given time in the past year, but she avoided it by dating other people. For a few months, she had an on-again, off-again thing with Cosmo, the captain of the lacrosse team, but he finally broke it off, telling her, "You're very cool, but I'm tired of dating a virgin. I'm in college, man, what do you expect?"

But if Star was really honest with herself, Cosmo or any other guy wasn't the real reason for not dating Kory, they were the excuse. Leo didn't know how close he was to the truth when he lectured her about Kory. The real reason that Star chose not to date him was because she was frightened of his intensity and of their palpable connection that she repressed. Star spent more than half of her life shepherding intensity, tragedy and chaos, and now she wanted a break from the three evil step-sisters. Kory, on the other hand, was just beginning to burn off the chaos and calamity that permeated his skin while he was in the military. Star understood that about him. She also understood that they could be soul mates if she would have allowed him to move any closer into her life, but she was emotionally exhausted and was willing to risk losing even Kory to maintain equilibrium.

Star worked very hard at creating a prophylactic world so the past couldn't re-penetrate her life. She never drank alcohol, never was late for work, never skipped a class nor forgot an assignment, never had sex, and, never lost control, and most importantly, never got too close, and because of these decisions, life was bearable. If she crawled out of her synthetic barrier, Star was afraid that she would lose her balance. In the end, staying away from any form of vulnerability sustained her sanity.

As she walked back past Beekman Hall, Professor Perfidius was coming down the wide, stone steps of the building. Star glanced up and quickly shifted her eyes back to the pavement. But it was too late.

"Star, wait a minute," he called and hurried down the steps.

She looked up and reluctantly stopped. "Sorry, Professor. You caught me trying to avoid you," she said with candor.

"Why is that?"

Star started to walk slowly and he followed. "I'm not in the mood for any more literary criticism tonight. I'm headed home to read a little Jane Austen where everything turns out happy."

"That's funny coming from someone who doesn't seem to believe in happiness."

"It's called escapism. I write realism, but I like to read escapism."

"What are you trying to escape from?" Professor Perfidius asked, looking down at Star. She only shrugged her shoulders and continued walking at a measured pace.

"I'm not going to critique you. I actually disagreed with Becca and Mike tonight, but that was student-guided peer editing. If I interrupt and give an opinion, it defeats the entire process."

"I'm not fishing for any compliments."

"You've experienced my grading for a semester now. I don't dish out compliments just to make people feel good. That won't make you a better writer."

"You're right."

"Star, let me give you some advice. If you are really serious about writing, and I think that you should be, you can't let every negative comment by someone pretending to be Starswati get you down. Ninety-nine percent of the great writers wouldn't be writers, if they had listened to the nay-sayers."

"Who's Starswati?" Star stopped and asked.

Professor Perfidius stopped and turned to face Star. "Star-swati is the Hindu Goddess of Wisdom. That's a good name for you, by the way. "Miss Star-swati." He grabbed her shoulders and said with reassurance, "You're wise beyond your age, young lady."

Star looked into his eyes and saw an intensity that made her heart pound. She felt warm, and her arm pits began to sweat. His olive skin was rich in the moonlight and his lips were swollen with color. Strands of grey glistened in his dark, wavy hair. Blood rushed through Star's body making her breathing heavy and labored. She pulled away.

"I've got to get going," she said, turned and rushed down the sidewalk. After twenty paces, though, she glanced back and saw that Professor Perfidius was gone.

Nine days had passed since Kory chucked his calculator and bolted from the library and five had passed since the kiss. Star missed him. Every time the sleigh bells jingled on Leo's door, she looked up to see if Kory had come in. She wanted him to read "Paper Moon" and to ask how he did on his accounting exam. What she really wanted was just to talk.

Later that evening, Leo watched Star as she pushed around baked cod on her plate until it broke into crumbled pieces. He finally asked, "Do you know the difference between a king and me?"

She looked up curiously and shook her head no.

"The king eats as much fish as he likes. I eat as much fish as I've got." He put down his fork and continued. "So, tell me, is there something wrong with my dinner tonight?"

"No, Leo. It's great as always. I'm not very hungry. I'm sorry," she said and looked down at her plate.

"Don't apologize, just eat. You're going to be hungry at some point, so you might as well eat what's in front of you." Star felt his eyes burning through her as she took a bite of fish.

"Did you patch things up with Kory?" he asked.

"There wasn't anything to patch up."

"No? Have you seen him, then?" Leo asked, taking a drink of milk.

"Why do you ask?" Star asked, lifting her head.

"Only asking. No harm in that."

"But you're asking a lot of questions about Kory. Have you seen him?"

"Sure, Stella. He's a regular at Leo's."

"Kory hasn't been in for almost two weeks."

"Sure, he has." Leo didn't lie to her.

"Just not on the days I work, right, Leo?"

He nodded yes and added, "He's got a nice friend. Blonde. Like that Marilyn Monroe."

Star burst out with a nasty laugh. "Emmy's no Marilyn, trust me. I've known her for ten years. *And*, I wouldn't call her nice, but either way, I haven't seen a hair on their lovely little heads in quite a while."

"He seems happy."

"I'm glad that he's happy, Leo. But in nine days, has the guy fallen in love with Emmy Dribble, who's a sorority girl, for God's sake, and, in the process, dumped his best friend? Tell me what *that's* all about! You're the one who thinks that he walks on water!" Star said with her cheeks turning red.

"Stella!" Leo said sharply, "I never said that Kory is perfect. He's a man who's looking for a good woman. And men are simple that way. When I was a young man with the same itch, my babbo always said that finding a good girl was like finding buon pesce at the fish market. You look for bright eyes and firm flesh, and you got yourself a good piece of fish. And that Emmy has bright eyes."

"Oh, please! Emmy's a knock-off, a fake, rotten fish. She's got bright eyes but none of those Italian virtues you talk about. The next time you see her, ask what she said about Leo's when I came to work here, instead of joining a stuck-up sorority. She called this place a 'run-down dump.'" Star watched as Leo's eyes darkened and instantly regretted her last words.

"I'm not Judas, Star," he said firmly.

"Leo, I'm sorry. This whole thing has nothing to do with you or the shop. It all has to do with me," she said breathlessly.

Silence and tension invaded the table, and Star struggled to catch her breath. "Just tell me what I did to make him hate me," she finally pleaded. "One day we're best friends, and then the next day he doesn't talk to me, and then the day after that, you're best buddies with Tuna Fish," she said with her cheeks burning. "Really, Leo, tell me why I should trust anybody in this world."

"Because if you don't, you'll never find devozione. You know that neither Kory nor I have betrayed you. We both love you. *That's* Kory's problem. It's not that he hates you."

Star was sick to her stomach as she walked to her English class that evening. Not only was she a tangle of nerves over Kory, she was confused about what transpired between Professor Perfidius and herself the week before. She struggled to understand if she was being a childish school girl with a wild imagination or if he really looked into her eyes with fever. Either way, she was determined to walk into the classroom and act as if nothing happened.

Star always sat in the bank of seats closest to the window. She was settled in and reading over her final draft of "Paper Moon" when Professor Perfidius walked into the room. Instinctively, she looked up and smiled. He smiled in return, but no other emotion flittered on his face. Star sighed with relief but also embarrassment for thinking something *deeper* may have transpired between them. A lump of disappointment was lodged in her throat, though, which was irritating, for she had always scoffed at the miniskirts who flirted with their professors. Inevitably, they sat in the back row wearing skinny tank tops in the dead of winter, and with derisive grins, they would cross and uncross their legs throughout class. Sometimes they'd choose not to cross their legs at all.

Star was never a miniskirt. So, she chastised herself as her eyes kept drifting from her notebook to Professor Perfidius' body. Most of her professors were either fat and florid or pencil-thin and pasty, but his body was different. She marveled at how his grey flannel slacks stretched across his thigh when he put his foot on the rung of the stool, hugging lean, hard muscles.

As she chronicled the outline of his quadriceps, somewhere in her mind Star heard Professor Perfidius say something about the importance of "showing vs. telling" in decent writing, but her eyes wandered back to his lithe legs. Her gaze was slowly travelling up to his chest when she realized that he was talking to her.

"Miss Nox. I will ask again. Please read a passage from your story where you are showing a character's thoughts as opposed to directly telling the reader about the thoughts."

"Yes, yes, of course," she stammered and fumbled through the pages of her story. Then she began to read:

Belinda finally mustered the courage to open the door of the pawn shop. She brought the sapphire ring to her lips, kissing it before handing over her heart to the cashier. A single tear welled in her eye as she took the $1,300 from the man. She then turned and headed out the door. The sun was shining.

Becca's arm was jumping in the air as soon as Star's last word was uttered. She refused to argue with the Tree of Knowledge or Mike, no less. She was shrouded in embarrassment. Not only did she have the audacity to think that her teacher may have been eyeing her last week, now Professor Perfidius caught her staring at his chest. The only thing that she wanted to do was run from the room and find Kory. She wanted to talk to her friend. Couldn't he understand how much his silence was tormenting her? The loneliness was making her behave like an imbecile.

After class, Star walked straight to the library and found Emmy and Kory at the study tables.

"Hey guys," she said drily. Kory glanced up and waved his pen at her while Emmy grinned like a sly lioness, protecting her dinner. Prickly heat crawled around Star's neck and scalp, but she dropped her backpack anyway and stood before them.

"It's been awhile. What have you two been up to?" she began.

"Homework," Kory grumbled and returned to his spreadsheet.

"Leo said you've both been in the shop. How do you like it, Emmy?" Star asked, twiddling her pen in the air.

"It's quaint and romantic," Emmy said with awkward pomp.

"Are Tuesdays and Thursdays the new 'happening' days at Leo's?" Star prodded, but no one answered her. "Kory, didn't you hear me? What happened to Monday-Wednesday-Friday coffee hour at Leo's?"

"Nothing's changed," he said, without looking up from his work. But Emmy chimed in.

"We have lunch there on Tuesdays and Thursdays. That's best for my schedule. Sorry we can't come when you're working, Star," she explained with her sweet, cortical smile.

Blah, blah, blah, Star wanted to shout in her face but instead said, "Whatever works best for your schedule. Any business is good business for Leo."

"Oh! He is a darling little man." Emmy said. "His stories about his wife, Nelly, are just delightful."

"Nella. It's Nella," Star said bluntly.

"What's Nella?" Emmy asked.

"Leo's wife's name. It's Nella, not Nelly." With that, Star sat down, pulled out a textbook and began to read. The words rolled by like a stream of hieroglyphics. Nothing was making sense to her except that fact that Emmy thought that she was Leo's new best friend and that Kory was sitting there like a mute main frame, punching in numbers on his calculator. Star quietly closed her book and packed up.

"You two have a good night," she said and turned to walk away. Ringing through the air, Star heard Emmy yell, "Leaving so soon?"

All six hundred forty muscles in her body were required to keep Star from turning around, stomping back and pouncing on Emmy. She represented every reason why Star had no close female friends. She didn't trust the petty, feline side of women.

They were opportunistic hunters who would tell a best friend that a pair of jeans looked terrific when they really made her butt look wider than a station wagon. Women were Machiavellian. When hard-pressed, they would sell out their best friend for a guy.

The crisp night sobered her mind as she headed back to her apartment. She kicked a rock sitting in the middle of the sidewalk that was bigger than it looked. She yelped in pain and cursed Kory. *Damn him. Damn me.* The leaves crackled under her feet as the wind shuffled through the trees, seeming to whisper her name. "Oh, gallant prince. Come and save Starlight Nox from her dreary, dreary night," she chided herself, but then she actually did hear her name being called.

"Star! Star!" the voice grew louder. She turned and saw Kory running toward her with his backpack flopping against his side.

She squeezed her eyes shut. When she opened them, he was upon her. "Star, please stop! I need to explain."

"Explain what? There's nothing to explain," she said, turned around and started to walk away.

"Come on. Stop for a minute," he said, following on her heels.

"What? What do you want?" she said, trying desperately to suppress her emotions—the stinking pile of garbage that she'd spent so many years working hard to keep hidden.

"I want to tell you why I haven't been around lately. It's only fair to you that I explain."

"Kory, you don't have to explain anything. I know you're busy. And now you have Emmy on your schedule, though there is something odd in that whole thing, but it's not my business to comment," she said, walking faster, with her eyes focused in the distance.

Kory's head dropped when Star mentioned Emmy. "This isn't about Emmy, Star. Now, stop, please!"

Star stopped dead in her tracks and swung around. "I wasn't suggesting that this is about Emmy, but I am curious about one thing. Have you gone to your first sorority formal? You know the dances where the girls get trashed by seven and laid by eleven?"

"Quit it and listen to me."

"You can tell me. I won't laugh. We're best friends, or we used to be." Star was fighting back tears. "Tell me, what is so intriguing about Emmy Dribble? Is it her ability to plan a terrific toga party or the way her polka-dot bows are always tied so perfectly around her ponytail?"

"Star, I asked you to stop," Kory said, dropping his backpack to the ground.

"No, you stop. You're the one who decided to stop being my friend, without telling me about it. Then I see you lip-locked under *the* sycamore with Emmy! Now tell me, who should *stop*?" Tears were welling in her eyes, but she forced them back with all her might.

"I had to stop the relationship for my own sanity."

"Why? How have I damaged your sanity?" Just as the words flew from her lips, Star knew that she had asked a dangerous question.

"Star, it's what you haven't done. And I think you know what I'm talking about. I can't take it anymore. I can't do it. I can't be friends with a girl I love. I want to touch you and feel you. I want to wake in the morning with your musky scent between my sheets. I watch these lacrosse sticks walk in and out of your life while you treat me like your big brother. It's driving me crazy, pure crazy. For my own sanity, I have to move on. I'm sorry."

"But you're my best friend, and you left me, just walked out of my life with no warning," Star said, blunting the tears that were begging to flow.

"Be honest with yourself. You know the reason. Everybody around us knows the reason. I can't play by your rules any longer. I quit," he said.

Star was winning her battle with the tears, but she wanted so much to tell him that she loved him, that she wanted to be his lover, but she couldn't. Because one day he would figure out that she wasn't who he thought she was—that her parents were drug addicts and that underneath the surface, she was just the daughter of drug addicts, losers. She was spent goods. Tainted. Wasted when she was just ten. Some john had offered Dirty-Syringe-Sue a *horse* ride to Never-Never-land in exchange for thirty minutes with her kid. Star knew that Kory was too smart and too decent for Tenderloin trash. Eventually, he would figure it all out, and then, yes, he would leave her.

"Do you love me?" he asked, raking his fingers through his bristly hair.

She stared into his searing blue eyes. They glistened back with volts of energy. "Kory, please!" she pleaded. "Why do we have to go there?"

"Because I *am there*, right smack in the middle of love with you. I'm not one of your guys who's just thinking about his next lay. I love you."

"For your information, I don't sleep with them," she said through clenched teeth.

"Then everything but. Though, that's not the point. The point is—do you love me?"

Star stood in silence. *Do I love him? Can I love him? How could he love me? He's pristine*, she thought. *I watched my mom go down on men for a nickel bag or an H pop. I've dug through garbage cans for half eaten corndogs. You can't possibly love me,* she wanted to scream. *I'm filth! When you find out, you will leave me. Can't we just be friends? Friends accept the dirt that lovers never would. I need you in my life too much to become your lover. Please be my friend. You'll never leave me that way,* she wanted to cry, but the words wouldn't come out. A long time ago she stuffed that voice deep down inside her, into a black hole where gravity blocks everything from escaping.

"No need to answer, Star. I get the picture. I got it a long time ago," Kory said sharply. He picked up his backpack and started to walk away but then stopped and turned. "Have a good life, Star. I've loved every minute of knowing you," he said and then walked on.

She watched as he walked down the path, unable to run after him or to walk away, but a smacking sound, growing louder and louder, forced her to turn around. Emmy Dribble was running toward her from the opposite direction, yelling, "Where is he, where's Kory?"

Star just shrugged her shoulders.

Catching her breath, Emmy demanded, "Why can't you just leave him alone, leave *us* alone? He's great when you're out of the picture!"

Star picked up her own backpack, turned and walked away.

CHAPTER 5

Salame Di Cioccolato, Chocolate Salami . . .

S tar kept her mind off Kory by writing and cleaning. She was scrubbing her way through every inch of Leo's shop, attempting to wash away the loneliness and loss that he had left behind. As she wiped down the baseboards and polished the brass, Star acknowledged that the loneliness was mostly her fault, but the fear of rejection was much greater than the fear of loneliness as she had more control over the solitude. Star had decided long ago that if she never got too close to the fire, she would never get burned. She applied this philosophy to girlfriends, as well, which left no one with whom she could share the pain. Alicia Salinger had been her only true girlfriend, and that was in the seventh grade, her first year at St. Mary Magdalene. Alicia didn't look like all the other girls at school who had tanned skin from summers at the country club and blonde ponytails. Alicia had orange freckles and red hair styled in a shaggy mullet. She was the only other girl in her class with an "alternative" family, as her grandmother liked to say. Her parents were divorced, which was the social death knell at St. Mary Magdalene. There were roller skating parties, slumber parties, tea parties, and "just because" parties organized by mothers who assumed that Alicia would not like to attend, so she was never invited. Star was included because of her last name, but the mothers were incorrect in assuming that she wanted to attend.

Star told Alicia how she felt "inside-out" all of the time, like everybody could see her tattered seams and read her tags. Alicia was confused at first, but then Star told her about Jack and Sue. "I'm made from trashy material, Alicia, trashy material. Like itchy polyester that sticks to your skin in the summertime, something nasty and cheap," she explained. "That's what these people 'round here think about me, that I'm nasty and cheap. They act all nice in front of the teachers, but I know what they're thinking."

Alicia understood. *Her* tags were already exposed: Divorced. That meant that somehow she was going to corrupt all the other girls at St. Mary Magdalene, even though she wasn't the one who got the divorce.

Star was on her knees, dragging a bucket of soapy water along with her as she cleaned Leo's baseboards. Squeezing out the thick sponge, Star thought about the last time she saw Alicia Salinger. On the final day of seventh grade, Alicia yanked her into a bathroom stall and told her that they would never see each other again. Her mom had decided to pull her out of St. Mary Magdalene because she was "sick and tired of all the hypocrites that filled the church pews every Sunday." They hugged each other and cried. They promised to write, but Alicia moved to Florida, and Star never heard from her again. Something inside her told her that she would never see Kory again, either. A teardrop tried to roll down her cheek, but she pushed it away with the grimy Playtex glove and moved the bucket along the baseboard.

Sleigh bells jingled on the door, interrupting her pity party. She pushed the hair from her face to see Professor Perfidius standing in the middle of the shop. "Down here," she called out from the corner of the room and pulled herself up from the floor.

"That's quite a job," he commented and casually shoved his hands in the front pockets of his slacks. His left hip and thigh were thrust forward.

Star peeled off the cleaning gloves and dropped them in the bucket. "I'm used to it. Leo likes the baseboards cleaned twice a month. Nella, his wife, did it right up until she passed." Star walked around the counter and washed her hands while Professor Perfidius seated himself at the bar.

"A cup of coffee?" she asked over her shoulder.

"Sure. Is that chocolate salami sitting in there?" he asked, spying into the pastry glass.

"Today is your lucky day. We've got a few pieces left."

"I'll take both pieces, then."

After scrubbing her nails, Star poured the coffee and dished up the chocolate roll. "Leo made it this morning," she said, placing the plate in front of him.

Professor Perfidius stuck his fork into the dense chocolate and took a bite. "Delectable. Just like I remembered," he mumbled through the crumbs. "I'll be back for this."

"Good, and bring your friends. I keep telling everyone that he needs the customers. A Subway shop opened up down the street, and it's hurting business."

"Sounds like you really care."

"Care? Leo is family. He's like a father and grandfather all wrapped up in one."

"Where is your father in the mix?" he asked and took a sip of coffee.

"Jack . . . the father, died at thirty-three."

"*The* father," he said inquisitively, narrowing his stare.

"Yeah, *the* father."

"I'm sorry. Why so young?"

"Don't be sorry. It's not your fault. He was a junkie and an—" Star stopped.

"And a what?" he prodded, taking another sip of coffee.

"Listen, I'm just rambling on and don't know why. It's not my policy to talk about Jack."

"Why? He was your father."

"No point," she said and grabbed a rag to wipe down the counter.

"You do an awful lot of cleaning, don't you?"

"It cleanses the mind."

"You seem to carry a lot of life with you for someone so young. How old are you, Star?" he asked, pushing his cup toward her for a refill.

"Twenty-two," she said and picked up the cup.

"How about your mom? Where's she?"

Star set down the cup. "Funny you ask, Professor Perfidius. Instead of the five guineas that Michael Henchard received for his wife and daughter, my mom sold me for over one hundred thousand dollars to Jack's father. Haven't seen her since, and that was ten years ago."

Professor Perfidius looked into her eyes. "So, that's the reason for the tears in class when I read from *The Mayor of Casterbridge*. Michael Henchard is a horrible, horrible character in that book who spends twenty years of his life seeking reformation."

Star bent down and leaned her elbows on the counter. She quietly yet firmly said, "Maybe, maybe not, but I'll tell you this much. There are some sins people commit in this world that cannot be forgiven, no matter how hard a person seeks redemption. But the sad fact is that most of the assholes who commit those sins never look in the mirror long enough to ask for forgiveness."

Professor Perfidius straightened himself on the stool and looked into her eyes. "Other than for myself, I try to be no one's judge and jury, but I've never carried a burden like yours. I am sorry for you."

Star stood up and stared back at her teacher. "That's just the problem. That's one reason why I don't tell people my story."

"What do you mean? How did I offend you?" her teacher asked in confusion.

"What are *you* sorry for? I don't want pity from you or anyone else," she snapped. "If I choose to talk about my life, I only talk to strangers who have no vested interest or pity in me."

Professor Perfidius stood up and came around the counter. He grabbed Star by the shoulders for a second time and said in a deep voice, "I'm sorry. I have no pity for you. I pity the weak who succumb to their burden."

Star pulled herself from his grip and, in doing so, knocked a coffee cup that shattered on the floor. "Damn it!" she yelled and quickly bent down to grab the broken pieces.

"I'm sorry! I'll get it," the professor offered, but just as he was bending over to pick up the glass, Leo wobbled into the shop from the backroom, brandishing a baseball bat.

"Stop! What are you doing behind my counter!" he roared.

Both Star and her teacher slowly stood up.

"I asked, 'What are you doing back there!' Get out before I club you," Leo demanded.

Star stepped from behind the counter. "Leo! Put the bat down. This is Professor Perfidius, my English teacher. He was helping me clean up the mess I made."

"English teacher or not, he's not going to upset you. I heard things. I might be old, but I'm not deaf," he said, moving closer to the man.

"He wasn't upsetting me. I was talking about Jack and got upset. He was trying to calm me."

Leo lowered the bat but kept his eye on the teacher. "Okay, okay. I just got to be careful," he said, seeming unconvinced.

Professor Perfidius stepped around the counter and extended his hand to Leo. "I'm sorry for the misunderstanding, sir. Janus Perfidius. It's a pleasure to meet you."

"Leo Bartatello," he said without a smile but shook the man's hand anyway.

Over the next few weeks, Professor Perfidius stopped by the shop three or four times for a pastry and a cup of coffee. Star became less skittish with each passing visit and finally accepted the warmth she felt when the sleigh bells jingled and he came through the door. She tried but couldn't deny that he helped fill the void that Kory had so abruptly left behind.

The loneliness and silence were still difficult, though. For the few first weeks following their final clash outside of the library, Star lurked about the study tables, hoping that Kory would show up. She found herself following men on campus resembling him. A student carrying the same type of army-green backpack that Kory carried stopped her on the green one evening and asked why she had been following him around for two weeks. She was mortified. Part of the problem was that she had no one with whom to share her turmoil. Leo, her typical beacon of rationality, was sympathetic to Kory. And without discussing the matter, both Leo and she refrained from mentioning his name. Her grandmother wasn't an option either as she was carrying her own heavy load that grew greater each day that she lived with Jack's father.

Star was still mystified by the fact that her grandmother remained married to the man. From the first day she moved into her grandparents' home, Star realized that Greer was a tyrant. She was also smart enough to realize that she was in way over her head. So, for the first six months, she worked hard to keep her mouth shut and her head low. Her Tenderloin rage unleashed itself within a year, however, when the man slammed her grandmother with one of his condescending comments one too many times in her presence.

Just as Star was finishing her last bite of pancakes, her grandmother tapped on the *Wall Street Journal* that her husband hid behind each morning. "Greer," she said hesitantly, "There's a new movie out called *E.T.* It's about a little monster from outer space. Let's take Star to see it tonight. What do you think, dear?"

Greer slowly lowered the newspaper and peered at her above his reading glasses. "Trista," he said slowly, "What makes you think that I would want to see a movie about a midget extra-terrestrial with you two? Besides, we already have to buy two theater seats to accommodate your fat ass," he smirked.

Star's head shot up and turned toward Greer. The straw had finally snapped. She jumped to her feet with both barrels loaded. "Listen, Asshole! Shut your fucking mouth!" she yelled. "You're the only fat ass in the room! And, I'm tired of you slamming Grandma. You don't care about anyone but yourself!"

Greer stood up and roared across the table, "Sit down, you ingrate! If you intend to live in my home for the next six years, learn to keep your mouth shut."

"Go to hell. You don't scare me. You wouldn't survive five minutes on the streets where I come from. You learn to keep your mouth shut and leave Grandma alone! You're nothing but a bully," Star blasted back, carving their battle zone in stone.

Greer reached across the table to grab her, but at that moment, Trista shimmied out of her chair as quickly as she could and stared down her husband. Something passed between the couple that Star didn't understand, but he pulled back.

After that day, most of the assaults were hidden from her, but Star was certain they weren't any less frequent. Though the confrontation forever severed any real relationship that she may have had with her grandfather, the fight solidified the bond Star established with her grandmother.

CHAPTER 6

Salsicccia Italiano—delizioso. Pig innards—disgustoso . . .

After a month or so, Star's dependency on her friendship with Kory began to dissipate. The sharp pain that he left in her gut changed to a manageable dull ache. Professor Perfidius continued to visit Leo's a few times a week, though the semester had ended after Thanksgiving. He stopped in the shop just before Christmas, carrying a package decorated with deep purple wrapping paper and a silver bow. He set the present on the countertop and smiled at Star.

"Merry Christmas," he said and pushed the gift toward her.

She looked at the package curiously but didn't touch it. Her heart began to race, but her mind slowed. *Whoa! Why a gift? He's an instructor with greying hair, for God's sake, not a friend.* The wrapping alone looked outrageously expensive. And as much as she tried to ignore them, forebodings of a bat-wielding Leo began rolling around in her head.

The professor lifted the package and handed it to her. "Aren't you going to open it?" he asked.

"I don't mean to sound ungrateful, but this seems a little weird. Why are you giving me a gift? You're my teacher," Star said, grabbing a cleaning rag to steady her thoughts.

"I'm no longer your teacher, Star. Grades were submitted last Friday. We're friends now, unless you don't want to be my friend."

"No. I mean, of course I want to be your friend, but even new friends don't exchange shiny, expensive gifts."

"How can you reject a present when you don't know what it is?" he said, resting the package on the counter. "Go ahead and open it—from friend to friend. Don't over think a gift."

Now she felt like an idiot for intimating that he meant something else by the gift, other than a kind gesture. "Okay, Professor Perfidius, if you insist," she said, pulling the present toward her. Opening the card first, she read the message twice. *For a woman who is as beautiful as she is wise. With deep affection, Janus.* She looked up with flushed cheeks.

"Janus? Professor Perfidius?" she questioned.

He stood up from his stool and reached across the counter for her hand. "Yes, Janus. Please call me Janus."

Star blushed to a deep garnet and pulled her hand from his grasp. She toyed with the ribbon while keeping her eyes fixed on the gift.

"Open it, please," he prodded and sat back down on the stool.

"This is awkward," she said, still staring at the gift.

"Only if you make it awkward. Don't make this mean more than a nice gift, Star. It is nothing outrageous."

Again, she was embarrassed for suggesting a deeper meaning behind the present. So, without haste, she began to unwrap the present. The paper felt thick and glossy as she slid her fingers under the flap. Her heart fluttered again and her knees trembled. When she lifted the lid to the box, a fresh set of Thomas Hardy's major works in leather binding was before her. She picked up *The Mayor of Casterbridge* and smiled sadly. "Strangely, this story gives me great strength. If Elizabeth Jane prevailed after being sold for five guineas, mark my words, 'I will prevail.'"

"You've already prevailed, Star," he said softly.

"I'm not so sure about that. I just received my grades in the mail. *And*, you gave me an A- of which I intended to dispute. How can I challenge you if I accept this gift?" she asked with a nervous laugh.

He shook his head with a puckish grin. "It was your grammar, Star. You still haven't learned how to use a semi-colon. I'll win the challenge."

"That is not true!"

"Oh, so true. Come on, accept the books and enjoy them. You'll hurt my feelings, otherwise."

She gently touched *Far From the Madding Crowd,* her favorite of Hardy's works. Gabriel Oak was a hardworking farmer whose life was molded by suffering. Happiness was *his* inconstant lover. Yet, he faced life with a steady sense of dignity and stoicism. He looked fate straight in the eye and was galvanized by it. In Star's mind, he wasn't the perfect hero, though. He opened himself up to love and was quickly punished for it.

"What are you thinking right this very second, Star?"

She shook her head to clear her thoughts. "Oh, just about Gabriel Oak."

"What about him?" he pressed.

"About his tragic flaw."

"Tragic flaw? He was Hardy's perfect hero."

"So untrue, my sage professor. He indulged himself in love."

"Why is that so tragic?"

"Because Bathsheba quickly kicked him to the grassy fields for years of suffering. Love was his hamartia."

"Star, how can you call love a weakness? If a person never experiences the power of falling in love, how can he or she become fully alive?"

"That's romantic hogwash. Look at me. I'm almost twenty-three, and I've never fallen in love and don't plan on it anytime soon," she said with both hands on her hips, "and I'm fully alive."

He laughed out loud.

Star became indignant. "Are you laughing at me, Professor Perfidius?"

"No, of course not, but you are just barely an adult. From a friend to a friend, though, I hope you take the chance on falling in love sometime. Yeah, love can be agony, but it can also be life's greatest ecstasy."

"Love wages war. Think of Helen of Troy. Paris started a war for that two-bit floozy!"

"That's mythology!"

"Anthony and Cleopatra, then. She seduced and distracted him from Rome, more than once, which ended in tragedy for both," she said smugly.

"Based on *your* examples, women should be feared in love, not men."

"This isn't a gender issue, Professor Perfidius. Love should be feared, not people. Any kind of relationship is a risk, friends included."

"Stop . . . the world would be pretty lonely without friends, Star."

"The world's a lonely place as it stands," she snipped.

"Why are you so down on humanity?" her teacher asked, gathering up the wrapping paper.

"Because friends can be brutal. My best friend dumped me—just like that!" she said snapping her fingers in the air.

"Ah, girls do that to each other ten times a day then kiss and makeup. Catfights are a perennial piece of sisterhood," he said, balling up the paper and tossing it on the counter.

"If you want to know the truth, my best friend was male, Mr. I-Know-Everything-About- Girls. And he dropped me like a load of warm turds. "

Professor Perfidius lifted his chin and smirked. "A load of warm turds? That's quite tactile, Star," he said, narrowing his gaze. "But your 'friend' is actually your boyfriend, isn't he?"

Star closed her eyes with embarrassment. Her coarse side of the Tenderloin seemed to slip out when he was around, which bothered her. She stood up straight and gathered her thoughts. "No. I told you. We were best friends . . . . It *is possible* for men and women to be best friends without being lovers, Professor."

"Never. That's impossible," he said with certainty.

Star crossed her arms in defiance and returned his narrow stare. "You're wrong. We were best friends."

"No. You are wrong, and I will tell you why after you pour me a cup of coffee," he said, pointing to the urn.

She poured his coffee and asked the question again. "So, why can't you understand that girls can be just friends with men?"

"Because that's impossible for a man," he said, raising his eyebrows with confirmation.

"That's myopic."

"No. It's naïve to believe otherwise. Men are incapable of being just friends with a woman. It's utterly impossible. Sexual tension always gets in the way. Always has and always will. End of story."

Star sighed and rolled her eyes. "I don't believe it. I just don't believe it."

"Star, it's a fact, not an opinion. You can't dispute facts. Ask any man. Take your friend who just dumped you. What's his name?"

"Kory," she said reluctantly.

"I bet your friend Kory dumped you because he was attracted to you, and the feelings weren't reciprocated." He caught a fleeting frown on her face and smiled. "Case in point. It's fact, Star. Being 'just friends' with a woman is impossible for a man."

A wide grin grew on Star's face. "Professor Perfidius," she said slowly, "you told me that you were my friend. Did you or did you not?"

He sat up straight and crossed his arms. Eyeing her, he finally spoke, "I stand by my position, Star. A man can never be just friends with a woman. To answer your question, I did call you my friend."

Star's neck burned with heat. *What was he saying? Stop. Do not read anything into what he is saying . . . but was this some kind of circular argument she didn't get?* Star was relieved when she spotted Jimmy at the door, arriving to start his shift.

Bundled in hiking boots and a scarf, Jimmy pushed through the front door, sending the sleigh bells flying.

"Hey, Jimmy," Star yelled a little too loudly as she quickly closed the lid on the box.

"Hey, sweet thing," he said, coming around the counter and tapping her on the bottom with his scarf.

"How's life?"

"All candy canes and sugar plum fairies," he said with a wink.

Star laughed and introduced Professor Perfidius to Jimmy. The two exchanged pleasantries, but then her instructor remained just a few minutes longer and left. Once the door closed, Jimmy said, "Sexy but a little old, though I might give it a shot. Is he available, Starlight?"

"Are you always hot on the prowl, Jimmy?" she asked with a wide grin.

He nuzzled his face in her neck and teased, "If I weren't gay, I'd be hot after you."

Star laughed and gathered up her gift. "Let me know if you need anything," she said and headed up the steps to Leo's apartment for dinner. She knocked a few times and cracked open the door. "Yoo-hoo, Leo, I'm hungry."

He came tottering out of the kitchen and said, "Gnocchi for you tonight."

Star walked in and gave him a kiss on the cheek. "What's wrong?" she asked reluctantly. "You only make gnocchi when you're angry or upset."

"Non è nulla . . . nothing is wrong," he said tersely and headed back to the boiling pot of gnocchi.

"Then why did you spend two hours pounding out potatoes, flour and eggs to make dumplings when you should have been resting?" she asked, following him.

Leo ignored the question and told Star to set the table. He was much quieter than usual at dinner, as well. He conceded that business was slow, but it always was around the holidays. He wasn't worried. And he didn't think that the new Subway store was going to hurt in the long run. He stopped in to see the competition. The joint attracted a different kind of customer. Besides, the people who worked there were odd. They wore long, matted sausage braids and had gigantic holes in their ears from tubular earrings. One guy even had an unlit cigarette inside one of the tubes!

But Star wasn't buying his Italian cacca about Subway. Something else was irritating him, and there was a part of her that didn't want to find out, especially if he was sick. Reluctantly, she finally summoned the nerve to ask.

"Leo, if business isn't bothering you, then what's the problem? Tell me the truth. Are you feeling okay?"

Leo jabbed the gnocchi with his fork and stuck one in his mouth. Star waited until he swallowed before she repeated the question.

"What's bothering you? Are you sick?"

"Nothing's bothering me. I'm as fit as a damn fiddle," he snapped.

"Come on, Leo. Be straight up with me. I know when something's eating at you."

"What's in that box you carried through the door, Stella?" he asked sternly.

"Books."

"Books from where?"

"Professor Perfidius."

Leo scrunched his brow and set down his fork. "What's he giving you gifts for? He's got no business doing that. He's your teacher."

"Not anymore. He's just a friend, now." The conversation about men and friends flashed through her mind.

"Men don't give gifts to friends, especially friends as pretty and young as you. I wasn't born yesterday."

Star's armpits began to grow moist. "Leo, why are you making such a big deal about a few books?"

"Mark my words. That man doesn't want to be just your friend. There's something about him I don't like."

"You're just upset because of Kory. You blame me for that mess. I didn't create it. He did," she said, dropping her fork on the table.

"This has nothing to do with Kory. I don't trust that teacher. He is un serpente! You are wrong about him. Mark my words, 'I frutti proibiti sono I piu dolci,'" he told her, pounding his fist on the table.

"What are you talking about, Leo? Speak to me in English. He is not a snake!"

"No, Stella, he is a snake. And to the snake, the forbidden fruit is the sweetest. To him, you are a peach ripe for picking."

"Honestly, Leo, he's just a friend," she said, with her face turning red. "Tell your soldier boy to show up every now and then so I have someone to talk to."

He looked up at Star with his eyes strained. "Don't you know?"

"Know what?" Star's heart missed a beat.

"He was called up."

"Called up to where?" she asked with dismay.

"Africa. It looks like there are some problems in Somalia. He was redeployed last week. Left on Saturday."

A deep flush washed over Star's face, but she forced back the tears cresting on her lashes. "He never called to say goodbye," she whispered.

Leo stood and dragged his chair around the side of the table and sat down next to her. He took her hand in his lap and squeezed it tight. "Mi bella, I'm sorry. It was Friday night when he came to say goodbye."

"That hurts worse. He knows my schedule." For the first time in many years, Star began to weep. She permitted the tears to flow. Leo pulled her close, rocking her for several minutes.

"Stella, he loves you so much," he finally said.

She pulled away from his arms. "No, he doesn't. He can't because he doesn't really know me. No one really knows my gig, including you—I mean everything about me. If you did, Leo, you wouldn't love me either," she cried, staring down at the floor.

Leo held her hands firm. "That's where you got it all wrong, Stella. Now, look at me," he demanded. When she eventually lifted her face, he went on. "You don't need to know all the ingredients of salsicccia Italiano to love it. Pig innards, alone, are disgustoso, but mixed together with fennel, anise, garlic, red pepper, and salt, innards become delicious Italian sausage."

"Leo, are you comparing me to pig guts?" she laughed through the tears. Star wiped her eyes and looked down at his hands wrapped around hers. She pulled one hand free and caressed the wrinkles and the dark age spots that decorated his skin like medals of honor. Finally, she said, "Leo, I know this is my battle to fight. I hope I can beat it someday, but who knows?"

Before leaving Leo's that night, Star tucked the box of books safely inside her backpack. The snowflakes soothed her tear-stained face as she walked home. She composed a letter to Kory later that evening, explaining how she hoped he didn't experience the desolation she felt when he left without saying goodbye. She hoped that when he unrolled his sleeping bag at night, he had a buddy with whom he could share his stories about home. She hoped that he found someone who would tolerate his AC/DC music, because, really, it sucked. Most of all, she hoped that he found a very best friend just like the one she so recently lost, a friend who would read her stories and honestly tell her what was good and what was bad. A friend who was kind and gentle and loved Leo as much as she. A friend who would listen. A friend who always smiled when he first saw her. A friend who was not a Prince Charming—a Pygmalion, breathing magical life into her through an electric kiss but, instead, a friend who was so important to her that she could not find the words to say *I need you*. A friend who was so immaculate that she could not find the words to say *I love you*.

When she woke the next morning, Star read through the letter once more. She held up her words, took a deep breath then tore them in half and then halved again and halved again until her thoughts were scattered on the floor. She bent down and swept the bits of paper into her hands and carried them to the bathroom. She dropped the bits into the toilet and watched as her words were sucked into the black hole.

"You're the one who lip-locked Emmy then left without saying goodbye," she whispered. "Not I. You left just like all the others."

During winter break, Star drifted in and out of Leo's and visited with Trista before her grandparents left for their annual hibernation in Florida. Her grandmother prodded Star to take a week off and visit them, but she refused as the tension between her grandparents seemed to grow worse when she was around. And, an irritable Greer was the last thing her grandmother needed.

To make matters worse, Professor Perfidius hadn't been in the shop since he gave her the gift. Wherever she turned, Star felt herself clinging to the damp, chilly walls of loneliness. She couldn't deny the fact, however, that she was the one who built the vacant space. She needed to learn how to cultivate friends, but first, she needed to learn how to cultivate trust.

On an early Saturday morning, Star went into Leo's to help him scrub down the coffee urns with vinegar and water. Leo insisted that his coffee was the best in town because of this process. As Star was finishing the final urn, the phone began to ring. She climbed down from the stool, but by the time she grabbed the receiver, no one was there. Once she was back on the stool, the phone shrilled again. This time she jumped down and grabbed the phone with vinegar dripping from her hands.

"Hello," she said irritably.

"Is this Star Nox?" the voice asked sharply.

"Yes."

"Star, this is your grandfather."

"Oh. This is a surprise. Why are you calling?" she asked confused. A sense of panic was rising inside her, though, as she asked the question. Greer never called her, especially at the shop where she had worked for three years.

"Are you alone, or is your boss with you?" he asked stiffly.

"Why?" she asked, but before the question was uttered, she knew something was terribly wrong. "What is it? Tell me!" she demanded.

"Star, it's your grandmother," he said and hesitated.

Star's hand began to tremble and her eyes searched the stairwell for Leo. "She's okay, isn't she? Grandma's not sick or anything?"

"She had trouble waking up this morning."

"What do you mean?" she shrieked. "Wake her, then!"

"I can't. The paramedics just left. She passed away in her sleep last night. They're certain it was her heart."

Star let out a wail and collapsed on the floor. Leo heard the commotion, and with his baseball bat in hand, he hurried down the apartment steps as quickly as his arthritic legs would allow.

"Stella, Stella!" he yelled. Leo spotted her behind the bar. She was moaning on the floor with the dead receiver still gripped in her hand. With the help of the counter, he knelt down next to her and gently coaxed, "What is it, mi bella? Tell me, what is it?"

Star lifted her head and drew herself up into a sitting position. "She's gone, Leo. My only family is gone. Grandma Trista has died," she cried.

Star's face was shrouded with a grim smile. She recognized most of the mourners from St. Mary Magdalene Church. There were a few people from the country club and, of course, a number of women from the horticultural society. She heard one grey-haired lady say to her humped-back friend, "This is my third visit to a funeral home in a week. I guess that's it for a while. You know they always say that death comes in threes."

"Who in the hell are 'they'? Once is enough for death!" Star wanted to shout back at the shriveled woman but didn't. Every few minutes she would peer at Trista resting in the coffin. The mortician did a decent job with her grandma, except for the hair. The woman never wore bangs a day in her life. Star wanted all of the people to leave so she could fix her hair and talk to her grandma by herself. Star wanted to tell her that she would take care of the rose gardens during the summer. She would make sure that Greer took Nana, Trista's prized French poodle, to the veterinarian to have her cataracts checked. Star wanted to assure her grandma that she always wore clean underwear without holes and put paper down on toilet seats. Star wanted her grandma to know how much she loved her for saving her life. She wanted her to know that she didn't really hate her for dying. She just hated the fact that her grandma, her only true family, had died.

Star swallowed hard and tried to smile. She spotted Leo in the greeting line and waved him forward. He wore a red and white checkered shirt with a green tie and gripped a brown wool cap in his hand. It was the first time she had seen him without his white apron tied around his collar and waist. Leo pulled Star into a tight hug, and she leaned into him for support. Finally, her face wrinkled up.

"It's so hard," she whispered into his ear.

"It's going to be hard for a long time," he whispered back. He released her and gave Greer Nox a powerful handshake. "You tell Stella to take a week off. I can keep the shop together for a few days without her."

"No such thing, Leo. I'll be in on Monday. It will do me good," Star interrupted.

Leo gave Star one last hug and moved on. She watched as he knelt in front of her grandmother's casket, making the Sign of the Cross. He pulled a hanky from his pocket and blew his nose. Star realized that those tears were not just for Trista. Nella was in the room that day, as well.

When Star turned back toward the greeting line, she saw Professor Perfidius standing a few people back. He looked suntanned and vital, a stark contrast to the occasion. Star smiled softly and held out her hand as he moved forward.

"Thank you for coming," she said.

"I am sorry for not seeing you sooner. I was out of town and just picked up a newspaper this morning. Your grandmother was a true philanthropist of Cincinnati. I never made the connection to you, Star. But sincerely, I am very sorry for not contacting you earlier."

"No need to apologize. I didn't think anything about it." Star was being honest, for she hadn't thought about her teacher since she received the call from Florida almost a week ago. She turned to Greer to introduce him, but he was too steeped in conversation with other guests to interrupt.

Professor Perfidius squeezed her hands tightly. "I'll stop in the coffee shop next week, Star. My prayers are with your grandfather and you," he said and then moved on with the flow of mourners.

After the funeral, Greer Nox was painfully quiet during the drive to her grandparents' home, a place she now rarely visited. When Star and he walked through the front door, Trista's poodle bolted out into the yard and ran from rose bush to rose bush, searching for her relentless adorer. Star stepped back outside and sat down on the front step while her grandfather closed the door behind her. She wrapped her arms around her knees and watched the dog's futile attempt to find Trista digging around her rose bushes.

Later, when Star gathered the energy to climb the stairs and crawl into bed amid the eerie stillness of the house, she stared at the spidery cracks in the ceiling, waiting to hear Trista's voice. Right before bed, she would always let the dog outside one last time. After Nana did her duty, both the dog and Trista would hurry up the steps to say goodnight to Star. Nana's paws would scratch at the door, and then Trista would open it with a warm smile. Now, Nana was too old to climb the stairs and Trista was gone.

Monday arrived and Star decided that the tile floor in Leo's needed cleaning because of the snow and salt the customers tracked in over the weekend. She used a toothbrush to scrub between the tiles around the front door. Trista and Kory swirled around her mind as she brushed the dirt from the grout. Losing them was so different from the times when she lost Jack and Sue. When Jack died, Star, who was just twelve years old, was the unfortunate one to find him. She arrived home from school, and like usual, Jack was asleep on the couch with a rerun of *Gilligan's Island* blaring from the television. She glanced at him and headed to the refrigerator, hoping to find remains of a take-out order or something. The racks were empty except for a six pack of beer and a bottle of vodka. She slammed the refrigerator shut and headed toward the door to go to the library for the night. She glanced at Jack, still glued to the couch, and said "See ya'" for no real reason. What caught her eye was the color of his lips. They looked blue against his brown-orange skin that had long been stained from an abused liver.

"Jack," she yelled, but he didn't rouse. Star went over to tug on him, but his body was rock hard. She calmly called 911 and told the operator that Jack Nox was dead. "He killed himself with the bottle," she said.

After the paramedics carried Jack out of the apartment in a black body bag, she never saw him again. The State of California cremated his body, and Sue dumped his ashes into the San Francisco Bay, because it was the cheapest thing to do. The day that Sue emptied the cardboard box of ashy remains into the rippling water was the same day that she sold Star to her grandparents. And that was that.

As Star scrubbed deeper into the grout, the door popped open and hit her on the backside. She looked up and saw Professor Perfidius staring down at her. He wore a creamy wool sweater and slim black slacks. Instead of an image of Richard Gere standing there, he reminded her of John Travolta when he starred in *Saturday Night Fever*. Star had discovered the movie hidden in a shoebox at the back of her grandmother's closet. She waited until 'garden club day' arrived when Trista would be out for a few hours and slid the movie into the VCR. Trista had a conniption when she came home and caught Star watching the scene where Double J and Joey rape the stoned chick in the back seat of the car. Trista didn't realize that the movie was Disney drama compared to Star's life in the Tenderloin.

She stood up and wiped her soapy hands on the back of her jeans. "Hey, Professor Perfidius," she said with less energy than usual. "No chocolate salami today, but there's something almost as good sitting under that pastry dome."

"Good, but I'm not here for the food today, Star. I came to check on you . . . . How are you?" he asked, reaching out to touch her elbow.

She looked down at his fingers and tugged away. "I'm hanging in there," she said and turned to wash her hands. Her instructor followed and took a seat at the bar.

He watched as she meticulously scrubbed her nails with a brush and finally asked, "Am I mistaken, or are you cleaning every time I come in here?"

"Cleaning is good for the soul," she said from the porcelain basin.

"Where's Leo?" he asked.

"Upstairs, resting. There's no reason for both of us to be on duty. It's always dead in here while school's on break. It'll pickup again."

"Well, let's give Leo a little business," he said, pushing his sleeves up to his elbows.

Star turned from the sink and her eyes fell on his deeply tanned arms and finely manicured hands. She looked up and saw him watching her.

"What's the pastry of the day, Star?" he asked with a slow smile.

"Polenta Dolce. It's good with coffee," she said, inhaling a slow, deep breath.

"Perfect."

Star felt his eyes on her as she poured the coffee. Her neck felt prickly. The cake dome shook as she lifted it from the plate. When she set down the order, coffee splashed across the counter. His eyes were still on her.

"You okay?" he asked.

"Fine." Star said as she cleaned up the spill. Looking up, she tried to relax and asked where he had gotten a golden tan in the dead of winter.

"Florida. Sarasota, to be exact. That's where I was last week."

"My grandparents have a home in Sarasota. It's ironic that you were there. That's where my grandma was when she had the heart attack."

Professor Perfidius raised his eyebrows. "That *is* coincidental, but Cincinnati is a very small world, too small sometimes. Lives collide."

"Yeah. In this town, everybody knows everything about you, but at the same time, they know nothing about you." She had moved from wiping the counter to polishing the brass hardware with a soft cloth. "The main thing is that people around here never seem to forget the bad stuff."

"Why do you say that?"

"It's human nature. You do a thousand good deeds in your life and do ten bad things, and people always remember that one percent of bad stuff. It's really crap, you know—think about it. People don't spread stories about all the good things you do. There's no fun in that, is there?"

"You have quite an edge about humanity for someone so young," he said, taking a bite of the polenta pastry.

Star stopped polishing the hardware and looked up. "It's life that gives you an edge, Professor Perfidius. I've had twenty-two years of living to sharpen my blade, and for the past few weeks, I've been cutting stone. So, yeah, maybe I do have an edge."

He reached across the countertop and grabbed her hand. "I know this is so hard for you."

She pulled away and resumed polishing the brass. "It's damn hard, if you want me to be honest. I've lost two of my best friends in the same number of months." Star closed her eyes and tilted her head back slightly, fighting back the pain. She took a deep breath and chastised herself. Why was she sharing her feelings with him again? *Dangerous! Damn dangerous!*

"I remember. Your friend, Kory . . . did he show up for your grandmother's funeral?"

"He's gone," Star said flatly. "He was called up by the reserves. He's in Somalia as we speak."

"That must have been a surprise."

"It was. He never said goodbye, but it only made me more certain about one thing."

"What's that?" he asked, taking a sip of his coffee.

"Getting too close to anyone is stupid, because somehow or some way, they will always leave you," she said, wiping the stem of the pastry plate.

"Do you really believe that, Star?"

"Yeah, I do believe it."

Professor Perfidius grabbed her hand again and pulled the cloth from her fingers. "Star, I think you need to have a little fun. Why don't you meet me for a drink tonight instead of dinner with Leo?"

"Professor Perfidius, I couldn't do that," she said adamantly. "I don't drink, and I always have dinner with Leo."

"I asked you to please call me Janus. And you don't have to drink, but I insist you get out a little. Some company will do you good. What time will your dinner with Leo be over?"

Star found herself agreeing to meet Professor Perfidius, or now Janus, at six-thirty, outside the coffee house. She toyed with her spaghetti at dinner and didn't hear Leo when he told her that some new place called a Starbucks was opening around the corner.

Janus pulled up in a Volvo, the quintessential "professor" car, but his was different. He drove a glistening black 940 sedan, not a rusted-out station wagon with a yellow "Baby on Board" sign suctioned to the rear window.

She waved at him through the window, opened the door and climbed in. "Hey, Janus," she said awkwardly and then looked down at her hands, letting her curls fall around her face to hide the anxiety.

Janus took her chin in his hand and turned her face toward him. "You look lovely in a soapy sweatshirt and gym shoes. It doesn't matter what you wear. You're stunning."

"Thank you," she said shyly and tucked her hair behind her ear.

"You need a little fun. I know a cozy blues club called *In the Pocket* just across the river in Kentucky. Are you up for it?"

"Am I dressed okay?"

"Honey, I told you. You're beautiful."

In the Pocket sat along the banks of the Ohio in an old row house. A massive mahogany bar and an old stone hearth, glowing with embers, offered warmth to the few early patrons who were scattered around the room. The bartender waved to Janus with familiarity as Star and he chose a table close to the fire.

"Do you come here often?" she asked.

"It's one of my favorite places. The music is great. I don't run into students here, and the gumbo jumps with spices and crawfish. You'll have to come here sometime on an empty stomach."

"I guess I will," Star said and pulled out her chair to sit down.

Janus moved around the table to push in her seat and touched the small of her back while doing so. Bending close to her ear, he asked what she wanted.

"Just a club soda, please," she said and then watched as he walked to the bar. His saunter was cool and smooth, sexy, she thought, but when Janus turned around and smiled, she berated herself. *Get control, Star. He's your teacher and probably old enough to be your father.*

Professor Perfidius, or now Janus, returned to the table carrying a tray of gumbo, popcorn and drinks. "Doesn't this place just kick ass!" he asked.

Star laughed. He seemed much younger with his giant smile and bowls of popcorn and gumbo. "Yeah, it kicks ass, all right."

Janus crumbled a packet of crackers into the soup and dug in. Between bites, he told her that Clemente, the owner, came from the Louisiana Bayou with his saxophone and ninety bucks. He played gigs around Cincinnati and Northern Kentucky. Made a name for himself and was able to get some financial backers to help him buy the place. He brought his mom and sister up from the marshes to do the cooking. As he finished with Clemente's history, Janus reached over and stuck a spoon full of gumbo before Star's lips.

"Here, at least taste this," he insisted. She hesitated but then opened her mouth, and he fed her a generous bite.

"It does kick ass," she agreed and took a few more bites from him but then pulled back. "That's enough. I'm feeling a little tipsy."

"It's not spiked. . . . Maybe you don't get out enough."

Maybe it's the fact that you're feeding me, she thought.

While Janus ate his soup, Star nibbled on popcorn and asked about his family. He was from Connecticut, which is where his parents still lived. His three sisters were scattered around the country. One was a doctor in Boston. Another was a patent lawyer in Chicago with two bitter divorces under her belt, and the third was a stay-at-home mom and the poorest but happiest of them all.

Just when Star asked him why he wasn't married, the piano player began to play "Georgia on My Mind." Janus stood up and took her hand in his. "Come on, let's dance. Hector's playing this for me. He knows that it's my favorite."

"No, I don't think so. That would be weird," she said, turning red.

"C'mon, Star. It's my favorite song."

She reluctantly stood, and he pulled her into a loose embrace. The bluesy rhythm and crackling fire were intoxicating. Star closed her eyes and, for a fleeting moment, thought about Kory. She had never been this close to him, close enough to feel an electrical charge between their two bodies, not like she felt right then, moving to the music with Janus. Her body tingled as she felt his hand press against her hip. When the song ended and she opened her eyes, Janus was staring down at her.

"That wasn't so bad, was it?" he whispered.

She shrugged her shoulders and shook her head no. The piano rekindled and Janus folded her back into his arms, this time pulling her closer. With her breasts pressed against his chest and her heart pounding in her throat, Star was certain he could feel her body reacting with a thunderous beat. She thought about wriggling away, but her body ignored her mind and remained in his arms.

Later on that evening when Star was alone in her apartment, tucked into bed, she stared at the Langston Hughes poster that was thumb-tacked to her wall. The picture was a sepia photograph of the poet that emanated beauty and strength. She closed her eyes and thought about his poem "50-50." She whispered into the darkness, "I'm all alone in this world, she said;

Ain't got nobody to share my bed; Ain't got nobody to hold my hand—The truth of the matter's, I ain't got no man."

Before that evening with Janus, Hughes' words irritated her. The voice sounded pathetic. No woman should ever scrape and grovel just for a man's attention. Strength comes from within. But Star had never felt the way she felt that night while in Janus' embrace. She longed for the touch of his hand, pressing against her back and pulling her close. As she was climbing out of his car that evening, Janus asked if she wanted to make it another date for the following Wednesday, and almost unwittingly, she agreed. She lay there now wondering if he really called it a date.

CHAPTER 7

Garum, a liquid squeezed from rotten fish used by
Ancient Roman cooks for flavoring . . .

The following week Star returned to school and was again balancing classes, homework and Leo's. Three weeks had passed since her grandmother's death, and the sadness was still a challenge to bear. Death was real to her but not this kind of loss. The pain would creep up her back and grip her chest for hours at a time. Through the years, when people asked her about Jack's death, she acted sad but immediately felt stupid for pretending. Now, she found herself pretending to be happy but immediately felt worse for acting. She even called Greer a few times to check in, but he seemed irritated, so she stopped calling.

When Professor Perfidius, or now Janus as he liked to be called, intruded on her thoughts, Star felt guilty about the twinges of pleasure that flashed through her. Despite the guilt, Star all but inhaled Leo's dinner when Wednesday finally rolled around again, and she was set to see her teacher in less than an hour.

"Slow down, Stella, what's the rush?" Leo asked. "You got a fire to put out?"

"Nah, Leo. Just a ton of homework. Heading to the library tonight," she said, glancing down at her plate to avoid his stare.

He eyed her closely and rested his fork on the table. "Ah, it's funny," he said and paused. "We have eggs on our plate, but I smell garum . . . do you know what garum is, Stella?" Without looking up, she shook her head no.

"Garum was a liquid squeezed from rotten fish. Ancient Roman cooks used it for flavoring. Awfully strong smell, I would say."

"Sounds disgusting," she said, still staring into her frittata.

"Not disgusting. Just fishy," he said and took a bite of eggs. The pair sat in unusual silence for a few minutes. Leo finally asked if she was wearing a new sweater. "You look awfully pretty in violet," he added.

"Thanks," she said sheepishly.

As the black sedan pulled up in front of the coffee house to greet her, Star didn't realize that Leo was peering out the window, one story above. She also didn't realize that he rubbed his eyes, turned away and slumped in his chair for the rest of the night.

In the Pocket was intoxicating that evening with the same warm fire and piano music. Janus ordered the gumbo and popcorn along with a club soda for her and wine for himself. He set down the food and drinks and pulled his chair close to her. He took a sip of his wine and then sat back and stared at her for a minute.

"Something's different about you tonight, Starlight," he finally said.

"I'm not sure what you mean." A few curls popped out from behind her ears and shielded her face.

"Do you do that on purpose?" he asked.

"What?"

"Use your curls as a diversion. Let them fall in your face to hide?"

"I don't know," she said coyly.

"You really are stunning, Star," he said in a deep whisper.

"Stunning?" she laughed. "I've been called a lot of things but never stunning. Must be the makeup and the sweater. You've never seen me in anything but ponytails and aprons."

"I did notice the makeup and the perfume. Are they for me?"

"I don't know. Should they be?" Star asked boldly and swallowed hard. She knew immediately that she was moving into untraveled territory and was completely uncertain if she should. Janus was a man. He wasn't some boy she met in a biology class or one who hung out on the green. He was legitimate with a nice job, a nice car, and nice clothes. And his age was an entirely different issue.

"I wouldn't mind that," he said, taking her hand and raising her fingers to his lips.

Star's breath caught in her throat and her body went rigid. She pulled her hand from his lips and tucked it in her lap. "That was different," she said and then fell silent. The fire snapped and crackled as the tension between them grew louder. "Why do you visit me at Leo's and invite me here?" she finally asked.

"Because I like spending time with you, Star. You're real. Everything about you shines differently. You're serious, yet you don't take life too seriously. You're beautiful, but you don't try to announce it to the world in flashy clothes. You're a perfectionist, but your sky doesn't come tumbling down when you fail. I've got a slow burn for you that won't go away. I thought that winter break would quell the blaze, but the distance made it worse for me."

Mingling with the sounds of the fire, Hector began the first few notes of "Georgia on My Mind." Janus stood up and reached out both hands to her. "Dance with me, please. Sitting here next to you is driving me crazy." She slowly rose and allowed him to lead her to the piano. He pulled her close, and they swayed to the music. The song flowed into Sinatra, and Janus pressed her into the curve of his chest, resting his chin against her head. When the music slowed, he tilted her head back, bent down and gently kissed her lips. Her body responded, and they shared a lingering kiss. When the music stopped, Janus led her back to the table but held tightly to her hand. They both sat in silence, staring into the blazing fire.

Star's mind and body reeled with passion and confusion. The man could be twice her age. My God, he probably remembers when Kennedy was president and Elvis was King. Who knows? He could have voted for Richard Nixon or could have protested against the Vietnam War. If he was an anti-war protester, she could just forget about ever bringing him around Leo.

"Janus," she said suddenly.

"Uhm?"

"Did you vote for Richard Nixon for president?"

He shook his head no and turned to look at her with knitted brows.

"What about the war? Did you protest at Kent State or somewhere else?"

"I didn't protest at Kent State, but I did my share of sign-waving. This is a strange line of questions, considering what just transpired between us," he said in a low voice. "What are you getting at?"

"Your age," she said and twisted in her chair. "I'm trying to figure out if I just kissed a man who is old enough to be my father."

"Oh, I see. The answer is yes but a very young father. I'll be forty-two next month."

"Mmm—you're over forty," she said, trying to suppress her shock.

"Yes, and I could have sired you. Does that freak you out?"

"Yeah. A little."

"That's understandable," he said and stretched out his legs toward the fire. "Star, I'm twenty years older than you. That is a little strange for me, too. I listened to Hendrix and the Beatles when you were in diapers. Now, I like U2 and Phil Collins. Same as you. I've done a lot of living in the past twenty years and never dreamed that I would have such a strong connection with someone who is barely old enough to drink alcohol. There are depths and dimensions of you that I see in your writing that I want to peel back and explore. Your mind and your soul are not twenty-two; they're an age so much older. Sure, I could fight the feelings, walk away and never see you again, but I don't want to. I'm electric when I'm around you. I haven't felt this way in a long time, if ever."

Star knew that some of what he said was true. Living in the Tenderloin District with Jack and Sue aged her well beyond her twenty-two years on earth. Her innocence was lost long before the first time Sue sold her for just another magical trip on her liquid horse. To cope, Star learned to take each day as it came, not looking back and not really looking forward. She tried to live in the moment as the past taught her that the future was just full of more pain. She learned that there was no point in dwelling on the agony before it arrived.

"I am who I am, and you've read about personal parts of me through the lines of my writing. I know that, and it scares the hell out of me. Rarely do I put myself in vulnerable positions, physically or emotionally, but when I wrote that stuff for the class, I never thought that I would be kissing you or feeling your fingers press against my back. I feel like I'm losing control. I hate the feeling, but I can't seem to control my body or my mind right now."

He sat up straight and turned toward her. "Star, why do you have to harness your feelings? Just enjoy the moment, the here and now. If next Wednesday comes and we're together, that will be wonderful, but if we aren't, then at least we have had today to hold onto. I never could have predicted what's happened between us, and I sure as hell can't predict the future. But for today, I can't stop thinking about you. I'm jealous of the other instructors who have you in class. I'm jealous of your dinners with Leo. I see students on campus and wonder if you've kissed them. . . . Listen, I'm not asking for your life, just an hour or two a week. Can you give me that much?"

"Janus, I don't know what that means. You told me, yourself, that men and women can never be just friends—that there's always sexual tension between them. Now, I know what you mean. When you touch me, my body responds in ways I've never experienced. So, what should I do with that?"

"Enjoy it, experiment with it." He slowly leaned forward to kiss her again but this time with a much deeper intensity. He wrapped his hand around her neck and pulled her closer. The touch of his kiss traveled down her body arousing every nerve ending from her lips to her toes. Star squeezed her thighs together to enjoy every bit of the tingling sensation.

Star's eyes scanned the campus for Janus as she walked to class the next day. They never ran into each other when he was still Professor Perfidius to her, so why should they see each other now? Either way, she wasn't prepared for the awkwardness of meeting him at school, trying to act like she was simply a student chatting with a professor. Lost in her reconnaissance, Star didn't realize someone was calling her name from across the green. She jumped when she received a tap on the shoulder.

"Hey, stranger. Long time, no see!" Emmy exclaimed.

Star hated how the girl towered over her. She looked up and said, "Hey, stranger. I'm seeing you now," with a southern drawl she never possessed.

"I've been looking for you all over campus."

"You know where to find me on Mondays, Wednesdays or Fridays. I'm still at Leo's."

"Oh, yeah, that place. Sweet man. Anyway, have you heard from Kory?" she asked, moving a little too close to Star. "I've sent him three letters in the past two weeks, and he hasn't responded. It's been the worst two weeks of my life. God! I'm worried a Russian Cossack may have captured him and sent him off to a Siberian labor camp."

"Ah, I believe he's in Somalia, which is in Africa, so Siberia is highly unlikely. Liberia, maybe. At least they're on the same continent."

"Siberia, Liberia, Star. You know what I mean. I am worried about him. Just tell me if you've heard from him."

"No, I have not," she hated to admit. "You could ask Leo. I'm sure they keep in touch, or don't you go in there anymore?"

"God, no! There's a new place called Starbucks. The Peppermint White Chocolate Mocha is to die for," she said, lifting the wrinkle from her brow.

Disgusted, Star simply said, "Can't help you, then. Might as well be moving on."

As Emmy turned around and walked back across the green, Star watched her for a minute. She was almost certain that Emmy's rear end was expanding into a station wagon, which satisfied Star momentarily.

A sinking emptiness overwhelmed her, though, when her eyes rested on the same sycamore tree where Kory and she had their first anthropology observation *and* where she spotted him kissing Emmy. As Star walked to class, she wondered what would have happened if they had kissed. Would she have seen the same stars that exploded in her head last night when Janus kissed her?

Wednesday evenings at *In the Pocket* became a standing date for Star and Janus. He picked her up at Leo's, they ate popcorn and danced and kissed before the fire. Each evening, she peeled back another layer of old skin that had grown callous over the years. She told him about meeting Officer Tony underneath a street bench at 4 a.m. in the heart of the District. The cop thought she was a stray dog taking a snooze, but the dog turned out to be a scrappy four-year-old with a mess of black curls.

From that point on, Tony became her guardian angel. When his graveyard shift ended at 8 a.m., he'd cruise down Turk Street to make sure he spotted her walking to school. St. Brigid's was just a mile and a half from Turk, but it was a dangerous mile. If he didn't spot her walking, Tony climbed out of the car and leaned on the buzzer to her apartment until she came running out the door. Most days he gave her a ride to school, and every September he replaced her grimy Keds sneakers with a pair of fresh white ones. If Star was going through a growing spurt and her toes poked through the front of the canvas, he'd buy her a second pair midyear.

When summer rolled around and hungry kids started to wander the streets from dawn to midnight, Tony would head home after his shift to catch a few hours of sleep. But by early afternoon, he was at St. Anthony's Dining Room, taming the unruly rabble-rousers who tried to push themselves to the head of the line for their only hot meal of the day.

Though he watched over her like a hawk, Star also found herself in the clutches of Officer Tony's angry grip whenever her mouth went wild and got her into trouble. Tony spotted her black curls flying one day in the middle of a raucous battle being waged on the cafeteria floor. He stuck his hand into the brawl, yanked Star out by the seat of her cut-off shorts, and held her up like a box turtle, kicking to be freed.

"Star, you hold still!" he shouted.

"Let me go, Officer Tony! I'm gonna' smash Billy's face, once and for all!" she shouted back.

"Stop moving or I won't put you down," he said, lifting her sixty-five pounds higher in the air with her curls tangling in her face. "Do you understand me?"

"No! I told you. I'm smashing that shithead's face."

"Starlight! You're really disappointing me now," Officer Tony said in a stern voice.

"I don't care. He's a shithead!"

Abruptly, Tony set her on the ground, grabbed her by the shoulders and demanded to know what was going on.

Pointing to the ginger-headed boy sitting on the floor with blood streaming out of his nose and two dinner rolls smashed inside his fists, Star roared, "Billy Elrod's a shithead. He just stole Sweet Sal's butter roll for the last time! If he steals her lunch again, I'll punch his lights out!" Looking down at the sniffling kid, she yelled, "Do ya' hear what I say, Billy? Do ya' hear me! I'll punch your eyes out!" With that warning, Billy's sniffling turned into a wail, and Star taunted him once more with, "Baby, baby suck your thumb, wash your face in bubble gum! Ha, ha, ha! You big baby!"

"Star, that's enough!" Officer Tony sounded.

Following the fight, Star was banned from St. Anthony's for three days, but Officer Tony made certain that she got a peanut butter and jelly sandwich for lunch on those afternoons. And Billy Elrod never again stole Sweet Sal's lunch.

As she finished the story, Janus was looking at Star with both admiration and amusement. He tugged on the arm of her chair to pull her closer and put his arm around her shoulders.

She sat in silence, wondering what he was thinking, hoping that he was neither disgusted by the story nor felt sorry for her. Sympathy would be the worst.

CHAPTER 8

Gnocchi, potato dumplings . . .

Ever since Starbucks moved in around the corner, business had slowed at Leo's. There was rarely the need for Star to scrub the floor tile with a brush and Borax because the grout wasn't dirty. She could wipe the entire floor with a rag and soapy water in a quarter of the time that it used to take her, and she wiped down the heart-shaped bistro chairs only twice a week now. To make matters worse, Star noticed that Leo was serving himself smaller portions at dinner. She wasn't sure if he wasn't feeling well, didn't have the money, or just wasn't hungry, but she was determined to find out.

"Why do have just a few gnocchi on your plate? Are you sick, Leo?" she pressed.

"Feeling just fine," is all he said.

"Why so quiet then?"

"Not quiet."

"Yes, you are."

"Nope."

"Why did you make gnocchi tonight? You never make it on Mondays. Are you upset about something?"

"Nope. Niente," he said sharply.

Star thought about leaving him alone but then remembered something she knew would ruffle him out of silence. "I forgot to ask you. Has that Emmy Dribble been in here lately? I saw her at school. She had the nerve to ask *me* if I've heard from Kory."

"Nope. Haven't seen her since the day he left."

"Figures." Star said flatly. "Told you she was a fraud."

"Watch yourself, young lady. There're a lot of frauds walking around here these days."

"What do you mean by that?" she asked hesitantly.

"I'm not blind. I know why you bolt out of here on Wednesday nights. It's that professor in his shiny black car." He dropped his fork and continued. "I know what he wants from you, and it isn't right. He's twice your age."

"Leo, nothing is going on between Janus . . . Professor Perfidius and me."

"Don't bother dancing the Tango with me. I know what's going on. Un vecchio gallo vuole una gallina giovane!"

"What are you talking about, Leo! Talk to me in English," she demanded.

"My nonna always said that an old cock wants a young hen. She was correcto!"

"Leo! I'm not sleeping with him," she cried.

"Not yet, but there's a reason why you haven't mentioned his name. I watch you skip into his car from that window," he said, pointing to the small window covered with a red and white checkered curtain. "Always parked right next to Nella's tree—Star, you listen to me. Any man who's cattin' around with a girl half his age is up to no good. You're an adult, but believe me, I'm not happy, and I know that your grandma wouldn't be happy if she was here."

Star looked down at her plate with her creamy skin turning to a deep burgundy. "I'm sorry for not telling you," she finally said. "You're right. Hiding things from you isn't right, but I really don't think there is anything wrong with us just talking. I'm lonely. What do you expect me to do?"

"Find a girlfriend. I never see you spending time with girls. Why is that?"

"I'm not a girl's girl, Leo. I don't trust them. I figured out a long time ago that girls are worried about two things, themselves and a man, and not always in that order. Maybe I would be different if I had a sister or, at least, a mom who cared. The only positive thing I can say about Sue is that she was consistent. A consistent pig. Once a pig always a pig."

Leo twisted in his chair to ease the pain in his arthritic legs. He shook his head sadly. "You've been through a lot, mi bella, things that I don't want to know. But I'll tell you what . . . Nella was a loyal woman. Find a friend like her. Forget about the professore. I told you . . . he's a serpente."

Star smiled softly into his eyes. "Leo, I don't understand why I have to have a bunch of friends when I have you," she said, reaching across the table and grabbing his hand. "But won't you trust my judgment about Professor Perfidius?"

He pulled his hand from her grasp. "Mai! Never! I will never trust that man."

On her frosty walk home that night, even though he reprimanded her about Janus, Star was certain that her teacher was not the only problem on Leo's mind. His health seemed to be stable, so she figured it was money. Nella and he had run the coffeehouse for fifty years with modest sales, but they were steady enough to pay the bills. Since Starbucks moved its savvy ass into the neighborhood, Leo was lucky enough to make fifty dollars on some days. She figured that the new-age shop was no better than the heroin dealers back in the Tenderloin. They were just pushing a different type of drug to hook a classier clientele. Either way, she had to stop the customer drain, or Leo would be out of business in a month. If she was wise enough to outsmart the drug dealers at eleven, she could outsmart a yuppie, here-today-gone-tomorrow coffee *bar* at twenty-two. Besides, she needed a distraction from her grandmother's death and from Kory . . . and Janus, for that matter.

After her morning classes on Tuesday, Star zipped up her puffy down coat, pulled on the bulky hood, donned black sun glasses and headed toward Starbucks. She spotted the bright green awning and grimaced. She took note of the warm, autumn colors greeting her as she opened the door. The stools and booths were upholstered with a gold and green plaid accented with a pumpkin stripe. "Aren't we cozy," she mumbled and headed to the counter. The menu was displayed in a bright white frame with green lettering. *My God, look at the selection*, she lamented. Caffè Americano, Caffè Latte, Caffè Mocha, Cappuccino, Caramel Macchiatos, Cinnamon Dolce

Latte, Espresso, Espresso Macchiatos, Iced Dolce Latte, Iced Peppermint Mocha, Iced Flavored Latte, Iced Flavored Mocha. She hadn't finished reading through the drink selections, let alone the food items, when she realized the peppy girl behind the counter was asking for her order.

Fumbling over her dismay, Star asked, "Do you sell basic coffee here?"

"Sure. One Caffè Americano! Would you like a warm scone or cheddar cheese croissant with your order?" the girl suggested.

Aren't we pushy, Star thought, narrowing her gaze, "Regular size coffee is all."

"That will be $1.50," the girl informed her.

"What? I didn't order a scone, too."

"The coffee is $1.50. That includes tax," she explained with a bright smile.

Star pulled two dollars from her pocket, paid the girl and went to find a seat. She chose a tall café table set close to the counter. She watched as the cashier greeted several other customers by name. All the employees wore white shirts, khaki pants and green aprons imprinted with the Starbucks logo, the same logo on the cup she was holding. Why in the hell was a sultry siren the central focus of their logo? That was easy, she decided. Starbucks really does sell sex *and* drugs, just like Diego did down on Turk Street back in the day.

Michael Bolton's crooning and Kenny G's clarinet cooing in the background barely soothed her anxiety as she took notes on the rest of the place. Service time was fast, just like it was at Leo's. Servers remembered repeat customers' orders, just like Leo's. The menu offered a wide variety of food and drinks, unlike Leo's biscotti and pastry of the day. The room was glowing with hustle and bustle and a happy hum of conversation, just like Leo's used to be.

Visions of Leo with only a few gnocchi on his plate galvanized her. Star was determined to turn business around. Leo's location was superior and offered parking. Leo's had authentic nostalgia and a sense of community. Leo's had Leo, an icon of the neighborhood. She had to admit, though, compared with Starbucks, Leo's had lost its sense of cool. Ambiance, music, variety—Leo's needed a makeover.

Star scanned the room and spotted faces she knew from Leo's. A few turned away or looked down into their cups of coffee when she made eye contact with them. *You should feel guilty*, Star wanted to sneer across the crowded room. Instead, she began scribbling down ideas for the reinvention of Leo's. She knew she could do it. Look at Cher. She was always reinventing her drooping body. Then, there was Elizabeth Taylor's recent marriage to the construction worker . . . maybe those weren't the *best* examples. She thought harder, and it finally came to her. Yes—Tina Turner. Penniless and divorced from madman Ike, she became sassy, sexy and strong again. That's it. Leo's was going to be sassy, sexy and strong.

Though she was enjoying her new sense of purpose, Star's enthusiasm dampened a little on Wednesday as she polished the coffee urn and sized up the few patrons scattered around the shop. Birkenstock sandals with chunky wool socks and flannel shirts was the trend at Leo's, quite unlike the pop-collared crowd at Starbucks who was willing to spend five bucks on a cup of coffee and a donut. How could she appeal to both groups? She looked around the room at the faded mint green walls and checkered curtains. The shop was cute for grandmas and granola grubbers but not for college students and yuppies. A duplication of comfy chair cushions and Michael Bolton music wouldn't work, either. Leo's had to offer something else. *Remember, something sassy and sexy*, she said to herself.

That evening, Star told Leo about her trip to Starbucks. She watched as the color drained from his face at the mention of the shop's name. He stretched his wrinkled hand across the table and patted her fingers. "Stella, I don't know how much longer I can hang on. I can't afford to pay Jimmy and you, and I'm too old to run the place alone."

"But I've got ideas, Leo. We can make it work. We can turn this place around!" she said, with glistening eyes.

Leo shook his head no. "I'm tired. I can't keep going like this, up and down those backstairs ten times a day. The place is paid off and has been for twenty-five years. I'll get some money out of it and move into one of those new retirement communities. It'll all work out."

Pain flashed through Star. She took his hand in hers and tried to smooth out the wrinkles and wipe away the age spots. "Leo, please don't do this," she pleaded. "You can't leave me, too. Just give me a chance. I know I can turn things around here. When I'm through, a line of customers will snake out around Nella's apple tree. I promise you. Don't pay me. I'll work for free. I'll paint the walls, make new curtains. I've got just a couple of easy classes this semester and then graduation. I've got all the time in the world."

"Then what? You graduate and go off to some big writing school. I know what your dreams are. I've got to be realistic. Nella would tell me so, herself. I'm no spring rooster anymore." With that, Leo pulled back his hand and pushed himself up from the table. He went to gather up his plate, but Star quickly rose to carry his glass and dish to the sink. He shooed her away. "If I'm not able enough to carry a dish to a sink, I'm not fit to own a coffee shop."

Star forced down the panic that was piercing through her. In two short months, her world had closed in on her. Her breath was hard to find. She was right all along. Happiness was just a selfish pimp with promises of a better life, but nothing ever changed. There was no use in trying to reinvent Leo's. She had been trying to reinvent her own life for ten years, but it was still the same. Loneliness was always lurking around her shoulder, breathing his hot, sticky breath down her neck.

Before leaving that evening, Star gave Leo a tight hug and a kiss on the cheek. She whispered in his ear to, at least, think about her ideas. Awkward tension separated them, though, as she headed out the door and down the steps. Janus was waiting for her when she stepped into the bitter, winter night. Before closing the door to the car, she looked up and saw Leo watching her. Star blew him a kiss, and he bowed his head in response but then turned away.

Her heart sank. Knowing that she was hurting him by climbing into Janus' car cooled her heels, but as soon as Janus took her hand in his, the excitement slowly rekindled. He pulled the car from the curb and told her that the past seven days had been "absolute hell" without her.

"Absolute hell without *me*? I've never heard that before," she said skeptically.

"Honestly. I searched for you on campus. You were nowhere to be found. Did you skip your classes?"

She raised her brow in surprise and tried to muster a smile. "No . . . I'm not on campus much anymore with just two classes."

"I waited outside Gonzaga Hall yesterday at 11:30, but you never came out."

"How did you know I was in Gonzaga?"

"I looked up your schedule. Professors have access to that information. Does that bother you?"

"I don't think so. It just surprises me. Actually, I'm not sure how I will react when I see you on campus. Do I say, 'Good day, Professor Perfidius' or 'I missed you, Janus?'"

He stopped the car behind *In the Pocket* and turned to her. "Either would be fine, but I prefer the latter." He raised his fingers just above her brow, brushing a few unruly curls from her face. He lifted her chin toward him. "Your eyes are intoxicating, like emerald ambrosia reserved only for the gods," he whispered. "I'm addicted to you, Star."

Janus twined his fingers through her thick curls and pulled her lips close to his. He kissed her deeply then lifted her full body toward him across the bucket seat and enveloped her in his arms. "God," he whispered, 'I've been dying to touch you for the past one hundred sixty-eight hours. I'm consumed with you."

Star closed her eyes and Leo's face slowly slipped from her mind. Janus' hands moved down her back, resting on her bottom. He drew her closer and kissed her more deeply. "I've got to see you and touch you—often," he said in a raspy voice.

"I'm here," was all she said.

Janus eventually pulled away from her body. "Shall we go in? I'm hungry, and I've got a little surprise for you."

Star untangled from his arms, crawled back across the seat and climbed out of the car. The familiar warm fire and soft piano music drew her in and clung tightly as she sat down at what had become their regular table. While Janus ordered drinks and food from the bar, she took in the full scope of his body that was perfectly carved for his jeans and light cashmere sweater. The trunk of his frame was erect and narrow while his broad shoulders and arms spanned out, dominating his surroundings. Star turned toward the fire blushing, remembering their first night out—the first time her body had ever spontaneously responded to a man.

Star was lost in her thoughts as Janus placed a tray of popcorn and drinks on the table before her. Sitting in the center of the tray was a pale, turquoise blue box wrapped in a white ribbon.

"Is that for me?" she asked shyly. Janus laughed. "Of course, it's for you." He grabbed the box and asked if she recognized the iconic color.

She shook her head no, but as he handed the present to her, Star saw *Tiffany & Co.* inscribed in elegant black letters.

"Tiffany? Are you serious?" she asked cautiously.

"Don't get too excited. It is something very small."

Star accepted the gift without the hesitancy she felt when he gave her the books, but she took her time untying the silky bow. When she removed the lid, a felt pouch of the same blue color was inside. She pulled out a silver necklace with a star pendant dangling from its links.

"Turn it over," Janus said with delight.

Engraved she read, *What you seek is seeking you.* *—Rumi*

"Oh, Janus, this is simply beautiful," she said breathlessly.

"I hope you like it, my Star Bright," he said, bringing his fingers to her face. "Do you read Rumi? He's a thirteenth century Persian poet."

"No. I've never read his work."

"He's a favorite of mine. Much of his later work was devoted to his close friend and master, Shams Tabrizi, who had left for another land after the two spent many years together. Shams is the Arabic word for Sun, the shining light of God. When they were apart, Rumi believed that Shams was shining God's love on him."

"That's beautiful, Janus."

"No, Star. You are beautiful. You are my shining light. I think about you day and night," he said, clasping his hands to hers.

"This is so unexpected," she said, swallowing hard. "We've known each other for such a short time—I mean in this way."

"I can't tie my feelings to a timeline. They are what they are. I'm not asking for anything from you but to think of me when we are apart. Will you wear it?"

"Yes," she said and secured the necklace around her neck. "It's lovely."

As they both slipped into the silence of their thoughts, Hector began to sing an old Sinatra song at the piano:

Before Lord God made the sea and land
He held all the stars in the palm of his hand
And they ran through his fingers like grains of sand
And one little star fell alone . . .

129

Star turned to him with a suspicious grin and asked if he had planned the song, as well. Janus smiled and pulled her up to dance. He held her closer than ever with his chest and hips pressed hard against her body. She knew that that night he would complete her as a woman.

As her head sunk into the pillow, Star wasn't quite sure why she felt a hard knot in her chest that was working its way into her throat. Janus was so gentle with her that night, taking his time, never moving faster than she wanted. He didn't jump out of bed or bolt out the door as soon as he was finished. Instead, he held her in his arms, and they drifted in and out of sleep together. Before leaving, he kissed the star pendant resting between her breasts and whispered, "Sweet dreams, Star Bright. Think of me."

Maybe the anxiety was born from unrealistic expectations. She expected the pleasure to be explosive. She wanted the feeling to be completely different from the times Sue had pimped her for a fix, but she had blocked out those memories for so many years that she now found it difficult to tell if making love to Janus was much different from the times she was prostituted. And, it scared the hell out her.

She ran her fingers across the bumpy scar on her lip, reminding her that there was at least one thing different from her last experience with sex. This time she didn't end up with a bloody lip and stitches above her brow. It was a rough night. Jack was out, God knows where, and Sue was in the living room watching *Johnny Carson* while some skanky john got a little too rough with Star in the bedroom. So, she bit him hard, bit his dick with her incisors, molars, everything. He screamed, knocked her in the mouth and threw her against the dresser. He laughed at the blood squirting from her face and then went out into the living room to share a needle and a bag of Fritos with Sue. Star couldn't stop the bleeding above her eye, so she waited until they were tripping, slipped on her Keds and crept out the door to find Officer Tony for help. She ran down the street and hid between two parked cars to wait for his cruiser to come along. A mass of curls popped up from between the cars whenever headlights turned down the street. Almost an hour had passed before she spotted the police cruiser coming toward her. She jumped up and ran into the middle of the street, waving her arms. Tony shined his bright lights on her and jolted to a stop when he saw the blood-stained shirt. Star looked like a cursed fairy with her curls bouncing in the wind and arms flailing about her.

He jumped out of the car and ran to her. "Star, what's happened to you?" he demanded.

"I was sleepwalking and fell down the hallway steps, Officer Tony, and no one's home to help. Jack and Sue are both working the night shift," she said, pressing the towel to her forehead.

Tony narrowed his eyes at her. "Let me take a look at that," he said, pulling her hand from the cut. "Something got you good. What about that fat lip? I didn't know that stairs could jump up and bloody a lip like that."

"Honest. I fell down the steps. It was like the stairs just jumped up and grabbed me."

"Do you always do your sleep walking with gym shoes on, Star?"

Star looked down at her feet. "Oh, yeah. Always. Sometimes I wake up in the morning with them on. Weird, ain't it?"

Tony knew that she was lying, but he also knew that he wasn't going to get a straight story, either. Star had been in and out of foster care over the years, and she wasn't going back. She would protect Jack and Sue with whatever lie that worked.

CHAPTER 9

Tortellini . . . arte del cuore, art of the heart . . .

Instead of scrubbing the floors on Friday, Star sat down to sketch out a remodeling plan for Leo's. The soft, earthy colors at Starbucks were soothing, but she needed something to wow the customers, knock their socks off. Starbucks had their sexy siren logo to stop traffic. What could do it for Leo's? She looked around the shop at the motley colors. Her eyes caught on a customer's scarf tangled around one of the chairs. Red. That was it. Hello! Stop signs, fire engines, women in red—they all stop traffic. She could paint the walls a deep, sexy-siren red and use buttery cream and black as accent colors. Red was it.

The mahogany bar and beveled mirror would look sleek with the garnet. On both sides of the bar she would hang big, creamy canvases painted with thick swipes of jeweled-tone colors. Jimmy was artsy. He could paint the pictures in an hour for less than thirty bucks. The window treatments would be easy, too. She would sew them using simple black valances hung midway up the long Victorian windows that lined the wall opposite the bar. Thank heaven Trista taught her how to sew. But the tables? How could she bring the wire and marble café tables into the twentieth century for cheap? Candles and flowers were listed somewhere in Trista's rules of entertainment. Flowers were too expensive, but candles would work. She could go to the Peddler's Market down in the East End and find holders for a dollar apiece. And they needed uniforms. Starbucks had those perky green aprons and khaki pants. Jimmy and she could wear all black with red aprons stenciled with *Leo's* in sassy, sexy black lettering.

Star jumped with excitement and headed up the back stairs to tell Leo about her ideas. She stopped, remembering that he was to be gone all afternoon, which was strange for him. Later, when she climbed the stairs for dinner, she found Leo asleep in the rocking chair. He always told her that it was Nella's favorite place to sit. The rocker was his spot, now, where he "did his thinking."

Star quietly pulled up Nella's embroidered step stool and sat down next to him. She looked at the wrinkled hands resting in his lap with a worn rosary laced through his fingers. Her heart sank with the heavy burdens she knew he was carrying. This was the first time that nothing was on the stove or in the oven when she walked through the door. She rested her head against his knee and prayed that he would listen to her.

Roused awake, Leo patted her head and said, "Oh, Stella, what am I going to do?"

"Leo, won't you listen to my plan," she said, lifting her head.

"I visited one of those fancy retirement communities today, a catholic one over on Lincoln. Nice people but old. I never heard so much talk about aching bones and cacare."

"What's cacare?" Star asked, sitting upright.

"Shitting. Eating prunes and shitting. Everybody's worried about the shitting. A man should shit in his own home. He don't shit somewhere else. Then, the ladies, they go to craft time to make a flower. And you know what, Stella?"

"I'm afraid to ask, but what?" she laughed.

"The men, they make the flowers, too. I don't make flowers from paper. Not Leo Bartatello. And, I've never been a joiner. Nella was the joiner. She was a member of the Italian Society down at the Sacred Heart Italian Church for forty-seven years. She ran their ravioli dinner. Now, that's who makes all the money. For eighty years, people line the street waiting for their ravioli. Nobody's waiting in line for Leo's, now, are they?" he asked despondently.

"Oh, Leo, just listen to me. We can change that. I've got ideas."

"No. No ideas. The man takes care of the child. The child don't take care of the man."

"I'm not a child," she said indignantly. "I've helped you run this place for three years. Are you saying that I've done nothing for you?"

"No! You know that's not it."

"Listen, Leo. You always say that an old pot still makes good broth. You can either believe what you say, or you can end up cutting out paper flowers instead of making cannoli and sweet polenta every day."

Leo leaned back in the rocker and closed his eyes for a moment. When he opened them, he put both hands on his knees and said, "I don't know about the shop, but I do know that I can't die talking about aches and pains and the shitting every day."

Star sat up straight and hugged his legs. "Now, you're talking. Just listen to me."

She saw a glint in his soft blue eyes. And by the end of the evening, she had convinced Leo to give the makeover a try. He liked the color red. Red was Nella's favorite color, the color of apples. He saw this as a sign from her. They planned to paint the shop right after midterms, which would give Star a few weeks to make the curtains and buy the candles.

Star was waiting in line for a cup of coffee at the student center when she was accosted. "Traitor!" a voice snapped in Star's ear from behind. She needn't turn around to know it was Emmy Dribble.

"Does that sweet little man know that his shining Star buys coffee elsewhere?" she asked with a toothy smile.

"Always sizing up competition, Emmy. So, how are you? Ever hear from Kory?"

"Finally! Three letters in a row. Silly me for worrying. I don't know how I'm going to last six more months without him, though" Emmy frowned, looking down at Star.

"I'm sure you'll find a way. Don't you have a sorority dance or something to plan?"

Emmy had stopped listening and was peering over Star's head and said, "Look at him! Wouldn't you just love to climb that ladder? A little old but think of the experience. Mmm! Mmm! Mmm! Mmm!"

Star turned to look and was surprised to see Janus standing at the entrance, eyeing the students. "Do you mean Professor Perfidius?"

"Who else? I'm taking one of his courses right now with other Tri Delts. All the girls are dripping with desire for him."

"Interesting . . . are you a dripper, too?" Star asked.

"Heavens no, I'm a committed . . . look, look! He's coming our way," Emmy said in mid-sentence. "I'm going to talk to him."

She waved to him with her lovely hand and toothy smiley. "Hey, Professor Perfidius! Emmy Dribble from your lit class," she said loudly to stop him, as if the waving wasn't distracting enough.

"Ah! Miss Dribble, how are you?" he asked, approaching them both with a broad grin.

"Keeping busy with William James and C. S. Lewis. I love how you integrate religion with literature," she exclaimed.

"Actually, theology is my area of expertise. I teach literature as a hobby, but I'm officially a theologian and an ordained minister."

"Now, that's a shocker. I wouldn't cast you as a religious one," Emmy said. "The Delts will be dreadfully disappointed," she said without embarrassment. "Well, toodles. I'm late for class," she said then turned and hurried away.

Once Emmy was out of earshot, Janus turned to Star and told her he had been scouring the campus for her. "I've got to see you, Star. Seven days away from you is torture."

Scanning the room for wily ears, Star's armpits stung with nervous perspiration. "Please don't say that here. Someone may hear you."

"No one can hear. We could be talking about Shakespeare or about your beautiful breasts, and no one would know the difference."

"Stop, please," she said in a deep whisper.

"I will if you promise to see me tonight. Can I stop by your apartment after my evening class?"

"You never told me that you're an ordained minister," she answered.

"I've been one for years. It never crossed my mind to tell you. We can talk about my religious responsibilities tonight, if you like," he said, moving closer, "while I kiss every inch of your delicious body."

Star took a step back and looked around the room nervously. "Please, Janus. Someone may hear you."

"Agree to see me, then," he breathed.

"Okay," she whispered.

"Perfect. . . . You know I want to touch your titillating breasts right now, don't you?"

Star was working on homework at the kitchen table when the bell rang. She opened the door, and Janus greeted her with a bouquet of roses and a bottle of wine. Star was stunned by the flowers, which were the color of amethyst irises.

"Janus, those are amazing," she said. "My Grandma Trista grew prized roses, but I've never seen anything like these."

"They're called Ebb Tide roses. I know a lovely woman who grows them in her greenhouse throughout the winter.

"Here, take the wine, as well," he said, handing her both.

"You know I don't drink."

"Yes, my darling, but I do," he said, kissing the top of her head.

Star turned and headed toward the kitchenette in search of a vase. She pulled one from under the sink, which was a remnant of her grandmother's funeral. A sad smile crossed her face as water from the faucet flowed into the container. Looking through her cabinets, Janus asked if she had wine glasses.

"No wine glasses and no wine opener. Sorry."

"Not a problem," he said, pulling a set of keys from his pocket. "I've got an opener on my keychain."

"That's a strange thing for a minister to have on his keychain," she said and turned to him, holding the flowers and vase. "They're unbelievably beautiful. Thank you, Reverend Perfidius. Now, please, tell me about your ministry. I'm quite curious."

Janus ignored her question about his religious service. Instead, he took the flowers, set them on the table and pulled Star into his arms. "God, I've wanted this," he said in a deep groan. "You don't know what you do to me." He ran his hands up the inside of her shirt to feel the warmth of her back and then lifted the top over her head. He picked her up, cradled her by the arms and legs and buried his face between her breasts, right where the star pendant was resting. "Mmm—jasmine. You smell delectable," he whispered."

"Reverend," she teased. "How did you know that was jasmine?"

Immersed in her body, Janus didn't answer. Instead, he carried her to the living room and set her on the couch. Slowly, he slipped off her jeans, took the sides of her pink panties and rolled them down her legs. Starting with her lips, he began to kiss her entire body. When his mouth was satisfied, he stood and undressed. He bent to his knees and pulled her onto the floor to join him.

Hours later Star woke up in her bed, screaming, "Stop! Stop! That hurts! Get off of me! Stop! Help me! Clawing at the bed and tearing at her pillows, she pleaded, "Help me! Stop him! Please, stop!" Trapped in her dream, she clutched the baseball bat hidden snug against the bedpost, and with all her might, she smashed it against the other side of the mattress, beating a lumpy mess. Wham! Wham! Wham! Eventually, the bed lay still, and she was able to break free from the tangled mess. She stumbled out of bed, searching for the light switch. She flipped the button and turned to her bed. Crumpled in the center of the mattress was a tattered feather pillow and a pile of blankets.

Exhausted, she slid to the floor and hung her head. She thought the memories had stopped taunting her. She hadn't had a nightmare like that in months. She cradled her arms around her legs and pulled tight. *Who was she fooling? Honestly, who was she fooling?* She would never escape her past. The pieces of hell would stalk her until she breathed her last breath. For over a decade, the terrifying images refused to rest. And some memories were more horrifying than others. She was alone at the kitchen table that night in Jack and Sue's dingy apartment, studying for her science test. She needed to know the three types of rocks and their characteristics. "Sedimentary rocks were formed from sand, shells and pebbles," she whispered. "Igneous rocks were formed when magma heated up and then cooled. Metamorphic rocks were formed under the—Ahhh!" she screamed, without finishing the definition. A horrendous pounding exploded against the steel apartment door that then flew wide open. Standing there was a stubby, bald man in a black leather jacket with a face like a mashed ball of hamburger.

"Where's Jack and Sue?" the man roared.

Chalk white, Star whispered, "I don't know."

He charged forward, grabbed her by the throat, and slammed her face up to his. "Are you lying to me?" he demanded.

"No," she trembled. "Haven't seen them in two days."

"They owe me a lotta' money, little girl! A lotta' money," he grunted.

"I told you. They're not here. Look for yourself."

He let go of Star's throat and eyed her up and down. She was wearing a Big Bird nightshirt that she got from the Salvation Army a few years back. He grabbed her by the front of the shirt, dragged her to the couch and threw her into the corner of the grimy cushions.

"Don't move," he commanded and began to interrogate her about Jack and Sue's whereabouts. Once he seemed convinced that she knew nothing, he moved closer to her. "Somebody's gotta' pay," he whispered. Star shook violently as he reached under the Sesame Street shirt and ripped off her underwear. When he was through, he told Star to tell Jack and Sue to get him the money, or he would be back. Unlike Jack and Sue, she knew he would keep his promise.

Star dragged herself up Leo's narrow steps for dinner the next evening. When she yelled yoo-hoo, her voice was barely audible. Leo wobbled out of the kitchen and was shocked to find Star looking a pasty grey under her normally radiant skin.

"I'm fine. Just a restless night," she assured him. "What's on the stove? That's more important for a tired and hungry girl."

"Splash water on your face and clean your hands, mi bella. We have pasta of the lovers for dinner tonight," he claimed.

"What?" she asked irritably. "There's no such thing."

"Ah, go on, go on," he said.

When Star returned from the bathroom, plates of delicate tortellini were sitting on the table, and Leo sat proudly with his napkin tucked into his collar and fork in hand. He drew his fingers to his lips and exclaimed "Delizioso!"

Star laughed and sat down. "You promised lovers and drama. I see tortellini," she charged.

"Isn't there any romance or imagination in your heart?" Leo stuck a fork into the ring-shaped pasta and held one before her. "This here is the navel of Lucretia de Borgia, the bewitching daughter of Pope Alexander VI. An innkeeper fell in love with her. Then, he pressed the pasta into the shape of her navel. Arte del cuore! Art of the heart," he pronounced.

"Oh, Leonardo, I didn't know you were such a romantic," she teased.

"I was the romanziere, not Nella. She won my heart with pastries. I won her heart with romance," he said with his voice rising proudly.

Star laughed and took a generous bite of the tortellini. She closed her eyes and opened them with pleasure. "Delizioso!" she exclaimed, pressing her fingers to her lips.

"Grazie, grazie. Tender veal, parmigiano, and nutmeg, perfecto," he agreed.

As Star unraveled from her sullen mood, they chatted about the renovation, and she told him about running into Emmy Dribble. Kory had already sent her three letters, and Emmy had no idea how she was going to survive the next six months without her soldier!

"Blah, Blah, Blah, Blah is what I wanted to tell her," Star said. "Emmy Dribble's never been six days without a man, let alone six months."

"What," Leo asked, not paying any attention. "What's that star hanging on your neck?" he asked instead, narrowing in on the necklace Janus had given her.

Star put her hand to her chest, forgetting that she was wearing the star pendant. Without thinking, she said, "Oh, it's new."

"What's that writing on there? Too small for me to read," Leo said, leaning forward.

Heat began to rise up the back of Star's neck and spread around the front of her chest, and her pasty face grew blotchy. "It's just a line of poetry. No big deal."

"I like poetry. Go ahead," he prompted.

Star recognized that there was no way of avoiding Rumi's quote or Leo's stare, so she quickly said, "What you seek is seeking you."

"Too fast for my wrinkled ears. Go ahead, ripetere."

This time she recited the line of poetry slowly.

Leo was quiet for a moment and then repeated the line. "'What you seek is seeking you.' Curioso, molto curioso, Stella." He sat back in his chair and eyed her. Clever, you think?"

She nodded yes.

"So, tell me. What is seeking you?"

"Oh, I don't know, Leo," she said, exasperated. "Nothing. It's just a stupid line from a poem." She took a sip of milk and then tried to divert him with talk about the shop. "Listen . . . I forgot to tell you. I found great material for the new curtains. I'm going to start making them tomorrow."

"Fantastico. But you haven't answered my question. What or *who* is looking for you?" He narrowed his eyes at her again and said, "It's the professore. No boy would give you such a gift."

"Maybe I bought it," she tried.

"Maybe, but you didn't. It's the serpente. He's the reason you look like potato dough tonight." Leo pushed his dish away and leaned on the table. "I'm going to tell you again, Stella. E 'un serpente pericoloso in acque profonde—he is a dangerous snake in deep waters.

She reached out and took his hand in hers. "Leo, trust me, please. I've had my run-ins with bad people. I can spot a snake a mile away. I promise to be careful, but Janus isn't one to worry about."

Leo yanked his hand away and pounded his fist on the table. "I don't trust the serpente. Il suo amore è veleno. His love is poison, Stella!"

Later that evening, she was relieved to have the night to herself. Star needed time to process her conversation with Leo and to let the smoke burn away from the Tenderloin memories that had resurfaced. When she got to her apartment, Star was too restless to study or to sleep, so she began cleaning. She ran the sweeper in the living room and then vacuumed every nook and cranny of the couch with the upholstery attachment. She changed her bed sheets and eventually made her way through the bathroom and the kitchen. Star couldn't fall asleep that night until her everything around her was spotless.

The next afternoon Star headed down to the building's storage bin in the basement. She carried up her grandmother's old Singer sewing machine that was given to her long before Trista died. She wiped away the dust from the throat plate, feed dog, and bobbin, inspected the hook and oiled the race. She spread out the fabric across the apartment floor, pinned on the simple pattern that she designed and began cutting. She pinned and cut eight separate curtains before she was ready to sew. As she pinned and cut, pinned and cut, Star wondered how many times she would have to make love to Janus before the Tenderloin memories would slip back into their underworld and lay dormant.

CHAPTER 10

Turkey sandwiches and macaroni salad . . .

Star was perched on a step ladder, organizing coffee beans behind the bar when the sleigh bells jingled. She turned from the shelves and was delighted to see Janus walk through the door. A week had passed since she last saw him, and the hours and days in between were becoming longer and longer.

"Wow! Finally!" she said spontaneously but then checked her enthusiasm as she peered around the shop. She scrambled down the steps with her heart pounding and went to the sink to scrub her hands. She poured a cup of coffee and set it before him with a wide smile.

"Would you like a piece of zuccotto or biscotti?" she asked loudly enough so the other customers could hear her but then whispered under her breath, "I can't wait for tonight."

"Star, that's why I'm here. I need to cancel."

She twisted the bar rag in her hand and a shadow crossed her brow. Memories of the Tenderloin had dissipated over the past few days lifting her mood and desire for him. She felt in control again and was anxious to make love to prove that she could beat the memories.

"Could we have lunch tomorrow, instead? After that, I will be leaving town over the school break," he explained.

"Sure, I understand," she said but really didn't. Wednesday was their night together.

"Great. I'll get you at one, and we'll spend the afternoon together. I don't teach until six."

He finished up his coffee and said goodbye, but before leaving, he raised his fingers to his lips for her, then turned and left. Star took his coffee cup from the counter and held it to her own lips to taste what was left of him. Without thinking, she then slipped the twenty dollar tip into her pocket.

Both Star and Leo were happy at dinner, rattling on about the renovation that was set to begin on Friday afternoon, just as the students exited Bosco for their holiday weekend. The curtains were complete, and Jimmy was finishing up the pictures that evening. She found an old leather loveseat at the flea market along with two comfortable chairs to place along the front window to create a lounging area. Once business got rolling again, she wanted to have the place wired for a sound system. College students wouldn't stick around very long without music, something Starbucks clearly understood.

Star hurried home from class the next day to prepare for her afternoon date with Janus. In between the flea market, sewing and school, Star managed to buy a new blouse and heels to wear with jeans, something more mature for Janus' taste, she thought. Mariah's "A Vision of Love" emanated from the clock radio as she buttoned up the silky blouse and slid into the black stilettos. Star turned toward the mirror and smiled. Her curls were as wild as ever, but she was satisfied with the rest of her reflection. The blouse revealed just enough of her small cleavage while the jeans and heels drew a long, sleek line.

She was still grooving to Mariah in front of the mirror when the doorbell rang. She ran her fingers through her untamed hair once more and hurried to open the door. Before her was Janus, holding a picnic basket in one hand and a bottle of wine in the other.

"I thought we'd have a romantic afternoon here, if that's okay with you," he said, handing the bottle to Star. "Who wants to track through slush and dirty snow on a cold day like this, anyway?"

Star looked down at her new shirt and shoes. "I thought we were going out on a date."

"You won't be disappointed with what I brought," he said, dismissing both her comment and clothes. "Bracke's, a charming delicatessen over on the east side, prepared this for me."

Star was familiar with Bracke's. The *charming* grocery was less than a mile from her grandparent's home. She walked there fifty times a summer for Nutty Butty Bars and Snickers.

He set the basket on the kitchen table and pulled off the plaid blanket to spread on the floor. Looking around, Janus finally noticed the loveseat and two bucket chairs crammed into the center of her tiny living room. Stacks of black and white material and boxes of dishes littered the couch, as well.

"What's all that junk?" he asked flatly. "And, how did you drag it in here?"

"The stuff is for Leo's makeover. Remember? I told you about the plans. The guys downstairs carried up the couch and chairs for a couple dozen cookies. I think it was a fair trade."

"Guess that mess blows the picnic idea . . . we can eat here at the table," he said irritably, unpacking the basket.

Star glanced down at her shoes once more and tried to push back the disappointment. "Leo says that a small kitchen makes a big home," she said, sitting down at the table. "What's your kitchen look like?"

Janus didn't answer and, instead, pulled out two turkey sandwiches and macaroni salad.

"Your kitchen—is it big?" she asked again, glancing at the basic lunch fare.

"Normal" was all he said and grabbed the wine bottle. He dug his keychain from his pocket and uncorked the bottle with the dangling wine opener. "So, when does the renovation commence?" he asked, pouring wine into a glass he had pulled from the basket.

"This weekend. I just finished sewing the new curtains."

Star continued to chatter on about her plans to revive Leo's while Janus ate his turkey sandwich and sipped on wine. The curtains turned out perfectly after she decided to go with a bold black and cream paisley instead of plain black material. The exaggerated lines that blurred together created a modern feel, she explained.

"They're over there," Star said, pointing to the material on the couch. "Do you like them?'

"Like what?' he asked.

"The curtains I made, Janus. Aren't you listening to me?"

"What curtains? I didn't realize people still sew, especially young girls."

With that, Star stood up, folded the wax paper around her half-eaten sandwich and tossed it in the refrigerator. She washed her hands and twisted the towel in her grip. *Don't get upset,* she told herself. Grandma always said that no man was perfect, including Jack's dad, but that was obvious.

She sat back down and asked about his trip. He was flying to Vail for the weekend with a group of old college buddies. The trip was something they did every year. As she sat and listened to stories about fast ski slopes and too much brandy, a wave of loneliness spread through her. Leo was right. She really had no close friends to ask to the movies, let alone a trip to Colorado.

When they finished lunch and Janus had consumed much of the wine, he took Star's hand and led her to the bedroom. He fumbled with the buttons on his shirt while she undressed. With too much alcohol flowing through his blood, he had trouble getting aroused, but she patiently coaxed him along. When he finally came, he quickly fell into a deep slumber without attempting to satisfy her. She glanced at the alarm clock and then at Janus. *It was only two o'clock in the afternoon, and he was passed out with a deflated dick and a full stomach*, she thought.

Star lay there, staring at the cracks in the corners of her ceiling while Janus snored. The growing frustration and discontent spreading through her body invited the Tenderloin into her bedroom that day with an ornery grin. As hard as she tried to push back the disconcerting memories, the District prevailed and gurgled to the surface. She was standing at the podium of St. Brigid's auditorium, searching through the crowd for a familiar face. Though Star was only in the fifth grade, she had won the English award for a story she had written about a homeless man and his dog. Walking home from school each day, she passed the pair along Pine Street. Rain or shine, the young man sat in a wheel chair, boasting one leg and an ugly stump. He had matted brown hair and orange, leathery skin calloused by life. His partner, who had similar matted hair, rested his furry head on the guy's only foot. A large sign made from brown cardboard was propped in front of them that read, "Homeless War Vet. Food for Prayers." On days that Star wasn't so hungry, she wrapped up her food from the school cafeteria and saved it for the two comrades. The guy never talked to her when she dropped the food in his lap. He only smiled and bowed his head in prayer. Star would pat the dog's head and move on. On a blustery day in January, she spotted only the dog shivering next to a phone booth. His buddy and the wheelchair were nowhere to be found. Though days and weeks passed without the man, Star kept feeding the dog, until he was nowhere to be found, as well. She wondered how many people ever noticed the missing friends.

Star sat in St. Brigid's auditorium waiting for her name to be called to the podium for the award. She was hoping that Officer Tony would show up, even though she knew he was on duty. When the principal finally announced her name and she got up to walk to the stage, Billy Elrod stuck his foot in the aisle and tripped her. He whispered "Shithead" under his breath as she crumbled to the floor. Star's first inclination was to jump up and pound the shit out of him, but she didn't.

Instead, she kept her mouth shut and headed to the stage. As she accepted the award, Star looked into crowded room of parents, except for hers.

When she got home that night, Jack was passed out on the couch with a girl who wasn't Sue and with a needle still hanging from his arm.

None of that mattered now, though, for she had a charmed life. She would never have to worry about going hungry again, and she really did have a best friend. As she listened to Janus' snoring, Star thought about Leo, hoping and praying that the coffee shop would make it.

She woke up early the next day to bake cookies and make cinnamon buns for her movers who lived one floor below. At 8 a.m., Star hurried down the steps with the food and knocked on Ricky and Kevin's door. After the sixth knock, Ricky opened the door and a draft of stale beer and cigarette smoke knocked her in the face.

"Nasty, Ricky," she said, waving her hand in front of her face. "What did you do last night?"

"Probably had a lot more fun than you, Star. Should have come down for a while," he said, rubbing his burning eyes.

"Maybe someday I'll take you up on that. But right now, we've got to get moving," she said and stuck a cookie in his mouth. "Where's Kevin?"

"Asleep. Calm down. We'll get the job done. Leave the door open, and we'll bring the furniture later. Nick is letting me use his truck all day."

"Nope. You promised. I've made you cookies everyday for the past week. Now, come on." Star headed to the closed bedroom door and knocked. "Kevin! It's Star. Cover up 'cause I'm coming in." She opened the door, walked in and found him sound asleep with his face planted in the pillow. Star grabbed his blanket and yanked it from the bed. Startled, Kevin jumped up from his bed, wearing only white sweat socks. He grabbed a pillow to cover himself and then blasted her.

"What in the hell are you doing?!"

She just laughed and said, "You're late. Get your naked butt moving."

Jimmy and Leo were sitting at the bar having a cup of coffee when Star arrived with a truck full of paint, curtains, candles, furniture and two semi-sober college boys. Leo's eyes sparkled when she walked through the door. Star ran over and gave him a giant hug. "This is it! This time tomorrow Leo's is going to be the saltiest joint in town." With that, Star directed Ricky and Kevin to carry the furniture into the back room while Jimmy and she brought in the paint and the rest of the boxes. Before the boys had unloaded the furniture, Star had already slapped on a few strokes of primer.

Kevin watched her for a minute and laughed. He walked over, took the paintbrush from her hand and said, "Twinkles, you know you can't do everything perfect." He pointed to the floor where she had already splattered paint and asked, "Where are your drop cloths and the caulking for the walls? You've got to fill the holes before you paint. Oh, yeah, and you'll need some turpentine to clean up this mess, as well." Kevin gave the truck keys to her along with a list of items to get at the hardware store. For another week of cookies, Ricky and he agreed to stay and paint the shop with Jimmy.

Aside from a few holes that needed to by filled, the primer was dry and the walls were ready for the first coat of paint by the time Star returned from the hardware store. The day of reckoning for Starbucks had finally arrived. Leo's would finally don its own sultry siren. Star carried over a can of the actual paint color and set it in front of Kevin. Jimmy, Ricky and Leo gathered around with anticipation. Kevin pulled out his car keys and shimmied the can open with the thickest key. When he peeled back the lid, a rich red glistened back. Star looked up at Leo, and they shared a wide smile.

By lunch time, the boys had finished the first coat of paint, and by three, the job was complete. Star directed Ricky and Kevin to move the couch and chairs to the front of the shop and asked Jimmy to arrange the tables with the candles from the flea market. Leo and she got busy hanging the café curtains with spring rods. As Star was twisting the rod to fit the width of the window, Leo nudged her.

"That Kevin. Egli è buono. He's a good guy, yes?"

"Sure," she agreed.

"What's he take at college?"

"Engineering. Nuclear, I think."

"Smart, then?"

"Yeah. Ricky's a techy, too. Computers, though. Both in cutting edge stuff, unlike the Miss Unemployable English Major."

"Ah, you missed your calling. You should've been a decorator, Stella." Leo looked around his coffee shop and smiled. "Così bella! So lovely. I wish Nella could see."

"Nella can see it. Trista and she are up there yakking about it right now."

Leo gave her a tight squeeze around the waist and whispered, "Now, what about this Kevin? I think he has his eye on you."

Star dropped the rod and burst out laughing. "That's the most hilarious thing I've heard all year." She turned to Kevin and yelled across the room, "Hey, Kev—Leo wants to know if you have your eye on me. Tell him that's a joke!"

"Twinkles, maybe it wouldn't be such a joke if you learned how to have fun. Want to try?" he yelled back.

Star turned as red as the walls and laughter filled the room.

"Seriously, we could start tonight!" teased Kevin.

She ignored him and turned to Jimmy. "Don't you think it's time to bring out the finishing touches?"

"Leo and you can go on upstairs while we hang the pictures," Jimmy told her.

"That's okay. Leo's tired," Star said. "He doesn't want to go up and down those steps."

"You follow me, Stella. If Jimmy wants us gone, we go," Leo said, shuffling toward the stairs. "We got to make these men some pasta, anyway." With that, Leo headed up the steps with Star in tow, talking about mostaccioli and garlic bread.

Ricky lit the candles and arranged the chairs while Kevin and Jimmy hung the paintings on either side of the bar. Dusk was setting in and a soft glow spread across the room. Kevin looked around and admired what was accomplished in a single day. "Twinkles did a damn good job for that old man, Jimmy. What's the connection?"

"Don't know, but they watch out for each other. Star's special that way." The room fell silent with exhaustion for a few minutes, but then Jimmy continued. "She's cool but odd sometimes. Only let's people so close."

"Odd? Yes. But hot as hell," Kevin admitted.

"Crazy hot, but different from other girls. She takes care of that old man. Both her parents are gone. Maybe it was fate. Maybe they both needed a friend. I don't know, but I sure as hell hope that this place takes off. Otherwise, Leo's going to end up eating prunes and pissing in a diaper with a bunch of old people," Jimmy conceded.

"That's tough for Leo. Tough for Star, too," Kevin said thoughtfully.

"Yeah, but either way, get your ass in here with your buddies. Otherwise, this place is going down the shitter. Starbucks is killing us."

"Ricky!" Kevin yelled across the room. "Did you hear that? We've got to help out old Leo. No more Starbucks for your ass." By then, Ricky was stretched out on the loveseat, but he lifted his head, waved, and fell back to sleep.

Jimmy moved into the center of the shop and looked around with satisfaction. "Well, it's time to call the 'dynamic duo' down here for inspection."

Star let Leo wobble down the staircase ahead of her. When he walked into the glowing room, he just kept shaking his head. "She did it, Nella. She did it. Il posto è bellissimo, just beautiful!" Together, they turned and looked at Jimmy's work. Both were stunned. He created paintings with bold flashes of colors as Star directed. But as a surprise to her, in one of the pictures, amid the jeweled-tones, were strokes of an old man sipping a cup of coffee at a café table. The other picture had the same sharp strokes and vivid colors, but in the midst of the kaleidoscope was a woman sitting at a similar table, reading a book. Resting on her table was an apple painted in chunky strokes of red. Jimmy came up from behind and wrapped his arms around them both.

"You remembered Nella," was all Leo could say.

Star was counting the cracks in her ceiling again to help her fall asleep when the phone rang. She scrambled for the receiver on the nightstand and heard her grandfather's voice as she drew the phone to her ear.

"Star, are you there? It's Greer," he kept repeating.

"What?" she grumbled.

"It's Greer, your grandfather. Star, we just talked a few weeks ago. What's wrong? Don't you remember?"

"I'm fine. No blackouts, no memory loss," she said highly annoyed. "It's me. I'm not Jack. Remember? You woke me from a dead sleep," she lied.

He ignored her words and went on to explain the purpose of his call. The Cincinnati Horticultural Society's annual Flower Show Gala was going to be honoring Trista posthumously and wanted Star and him to be their guests of honor.

"Do you have a nice dress to wear?"

"Not for something like that."

"Well, find something appropriate," he said then bid her goodbye.

Something appropriate lingered in her mind as she returned to the cracks in the ceiling. She remembered those same words coming out of her grandmother's mouth before she went to her first boy-girl party at St. Mary Magdalene's.

Before she left the Tenderloin to meet her grandparents, Star asked Officer Tony to take her shopping for a decent outfit. They went to Thom McAn, where she bought a pair of Earth shoes with brown rubber soles that tilted up in the front. All the cool kids in the District wore them. She also bought a short-sleeved, mock turtleneck and a pair of baby-blue Bobbie Brooks slacks that sat high on her waist. Her stomach tingled with butterflies when she saw her reflection in the mirror. This was her first outfit that wasn't from the Salvation Army.

Star fought with her grandmother on the night of the boy-girl party about what to wear. She wanted to wear her Earth Shoes and Bobbie Brooks while her grandmother demanded that she wear *something appropriate,* like the pink Lilly Pulitzer jumper she bought for Star that was embroidered with green whales. But Star was convinced that no twelve-year-old girl in her right mind would wear such a ridiculous dress.

"I look like a peppermint ice cream cone in that thing," she insisted. Star stood her ground. So, equipped with only her street smarts of the Tenderloin, she headed to the party in her Earth shoes and mock turtleneck. When Emmy Dribble opened the front door wearing her own Lilly dress and saw Star standing there in all her powder blue and brown glory, she burst out laughing.

"Ya! And where's your macramé purse and granola bar?" Emmy quipped with a tilted head and a cortical smile.

Star's first inclination was to punch her in the face like she did with Billy Elrod, but her grandmother's warnings rang in her ear. From that point forward, however, the battleground between Emmy and Star was established. Ten years later, she was still contending with the preppy thorn in her ass.

When the phone rang and roused her out of sleep for a second time that night, she was shocked to hear Janus on the other end of the receiver, for he never called her at home. "Star Bright," he whispered. "I miss you."

"I miss you, too, Janus. When will you be home?"

"Before Wednesday, of course. I'll see you then," he said and quickly hung up.

Her body kindled at the sound of his voice. Their last day together was awkward and tense, but she couldn't change that now. She was just glad that he still missed her.

Star went to Leo's on Monday expecting a twisting line of customers overflowing onto the sidewalk. When she walked in, Leo was behind the counter and only a handful of the regular customers were scattered about the shop. Her heart sank as she looked at the deep crevices above Leo's brow that were etched with worry.

She went around the back of the bar and rested her arm across his bony shoulders. "Not everyone's back from break, Leo. They'll be in," she assured him, but Star was worried, too. He needed the cash flow now. By Wednesday, the pressure inside her was surging and her anxiety was throbbing.

"Stella, you can't take on this responsibility. It's been my place for fifty years. Let me do the worrying."

"I'm not worried. It's going to work. I know it," she said unconvincingly.

"I don't know which crystal ball you're looking into, but I'm not so sure."

"We need to get the word out, do some advertising. No one knows that we painted the walls unless they come in and look. I'll talk to Jimmy about it."

"The money has run out. I don't have a nickel for paper and crayons."

"Just give me a little longer, Leo. Trust me." But, why was she telling him to trust her when she didn't trust herself?

The magnitude of the responsibility was stifling. With a spinning head and churning stomach, she slipped outside into the cold air to wait for Janus that night. His shiny black sedan never looked so inviting when she saw it turn the corner. As soon as he stopped, Star climbed in the car and crawled across the seat. She ran her hands up under Janus' coat, pulled him close and kissed him deeply.

"I've missed your body," he whispered, pressing his lips against her cheek.

"I've missed more than that," she murmured inaudibly.

As Janus put the car in drive, Star didn't notice Leo closing the red checkered curtains in the window, one story above.

While they were sitting before the fire at *In the Pocket* that evening, Janus apologized for being poor company the week before.

"I'm working on a major project outside of school that's consuming my time," he explained. "I was stressed and preoccupied."

"I'm glad to hear that. I thought it was me."

"No, Star. You're perfect in every way. Let's dance," he said, taking her hand. I need to touch you."

Swaying to Hector's music, Star could feel Janus' body responding to her. She rested her cheek against his chest and smiled. She knew that she was in love and couldn't be happier than she was at that very moment.

CHAPTER 11

Hothouse grapes . . .

Star twirled around in front of the mirror when she saw her reflection in the strapless, canary-yellow dress and deep purple heels that she had chosen for the Flower Show Gala. The heart-shaped neckline made her breasts look unusually voluptuous. She wished that Janus could see her. *In the Pocket* was fine, but the bar and her apartment were the only two places Janus wanted to go. When she suggested Chinese or Italian food, he said that his life was chaotic everywhere but with her. He didn't want any outside influences to taint their time together.

Star's heart fluttered when her grandfather knocked on her door. The vision she created was a shock for even him.

His eyes flew wide-open. "Smart selection, Star. Your grandmother would approve."

"I'm not so sure about that. Our fashion ideas never jived. Remember the Madonna-ripped-fishnet-stocking phase I went through? Grandma Trista really thought that Madonna was the Devil in drag," she laughed, but Greer did not.

On the way to the gala, Greer kept turning to look at Star. "There is something different about you, but I can't quite put my finger on it."

"It's the makeup."

"No. Something else," he said, stopping in front of the valet service.

"I'm just excited," she said, gazing out at the white tents and walkways lined with Romanesque vases, billowing with flowers. "This is amazing," she whispered.

The flower show was held at Ault Park, one of Cincinnati's crown jewels. The lush urban park with world-renowned gardens was home to an Italianate pavilion built during the days of Jean Harlow and Charlie Chaplin. Star felt like she meant something to people as she walked up the broad stone steps consummated with a cascading fountain. When she reached the top of the stairs and saw the sparkling lights and champagne glasses, her heart sank and a frown flashed across her face as she remembered why she was invited to the very adult event. A granite marker was being placed in The Garden of Old Roses in honor of her grandmother's dedication to the park's gardens over the past quarter century.

"Smile, please. There will be pictures," Greer insisted. For the next hour, Star met and shook hands with people from Cincinnati, around the country and even England as the event attracted local philanthropists as well as horticulturalists from around the world. Even though the flowers were brilliant and the people were dazzling, Star couldn't shrug off the weight of her grandmother's memory. She stepped away from her grandfather and the well-wishers as soon as possible, desperately trying to gather her thoughts. As she walked along the flower displays decorating the pavilion, she thought about how much Trista would have enjoyed the evening. There was a "Cottage Garden" with a cobblestone path and English roses set next to a "Woodland Wonderland" with its own trickling brook. The "Wine and Cheese Garden" was breathtaking with succulent burgundy grapes dripping from the vines.

"How do you get perfect grapes to grow for this event," she asked one of the horticulturists tending to the garden.

"They're hothouse grapes. We begin planning twelve months in advance for this event to make certain that all the plants are in full bloom or ripened on time. We're already planning next year's exhibit."

"It's lovely," she said and moved along. When she came upon the "Book Lover's Escape," her heart stopped. Janus was there, leaning over the display to see what book had been placed on the garden table.

"Janus! My gosh! What are you doing here?" she exclaimed, trying to contain her excitement.

"Oh, hello," he said and slowly stood upright. "How are you?" he asked perfunctorily.

Star narrowed her gaze and asked, "What do you mean 'how are you'? It's me, Star? You know *how* I am."

At that moment, a lovely blonde walked up to them and hooked her arm through Janus'. Her blonde hair was pulled into a tight chignon, emphasizing her long, elegant neck that matched a long, elegant body. Her lips were thin but highlighted in a lovely fuchsia lipstick, and her blue eyes matched the striking sapphire dress she wore. "Who is this lovely girl, Jan?" she asked, eyeing Star from head to toe.

"Hillary, this is Star Nox, Trista's granddaughter," he said, without a smile.

"Star Nox . . . Trista's granddaughter!" she repeated with delight. Releasing Janus' arm, the woman grabbed Star's hands and pulled her close. "My dear, Trista was my mentor—we served on the Horticultural Society's board together."

"Grandma Trista loved her roses," Star answered while trying to piece together where this woman fit into the picture.

"Oh! She taught me everything I know about begonias, roses, buddleia, rhododendron. Your grandmother could make rocks blossom. I was devastated when I couldn't attend her funeral. I was in the hospital with preeclampsia, so Jan went in my place."

"Preeclampsia . . . what is that?" Star asked with her mind still swirling in confusion.

"It's pregnancy-induced high blood pressure," Hillary explained.

"You have a child?"

"Yes. Our first," she said, freeing Star's hands and pulling on Janus' arm. "Her name is Katie Ann."

Unable to move her feet or to breathe, Star grabbed onto the white picket fence that surrounded the flower display. The past few months came tumbling over her in nauseating waves. She closed her eyes to steady the white tent that was spinning around and pelting her with sound bites of voices and music. She squeezed the fence with a death grip as the sounds and sensations grew dimmer and dimmer and her legs grew weaker and weaker.

"Star, listen to me," she heard from somewhere deep in her psyche. "Listen to me. I can explain," but there was no way for her to hold onto the words. She was falling, falling hard and then hit bottom. She opened her eyes, and Jack was there, kneeling over her, shaking her, shaking her. "Listen to me, Star. Listen to me. I didn't mean for this to happen. I just needed the money. We'll get rid of it. Listen, you'll be back to school in no time." Then, her world went black.

Star rested her head against the cool window as her grandfather drove her back to his home instead of her apartment. Both were silent until he pulled around the front drive. "Are you okay to walk?" he asked with irritation. She nodded her head yes, and he came around the car to open the door.

"I didn't mean to ruin your evening. I'm sorry. It's just exhaustion. And, I was caught off guard by Grandma's memories that kept flooding back to me. I am so sorry," she said, empty of all energy and emotion.

The next morning Greer fixed goetta and eggs for breakfast, but the mixture of sausage, oatmeal and eggs was nauseating to Star. She drew the fork around her plate instead of taking bites. Greer cleared his throat twice, indicating that it was time to eat and to stop playing with the food, but Star continued with the zigzag design in her eggs.

"Aren't you hungry?" he finally asked with irritation.

"No. Not at all. My stomach still feels queasy after last night."

"Did you have anything to drink?" he questioned.

"No, I didn't drink any alcohol, if that's what you mean," she said and put her fork down.

Greer set the newspaper down, as well, and said, "Star, I've got to talk to you about something, an issue of great importance."

She closed her eyes and tilted her head back against the chair. *My God, if he knows about Janus, I'll die,* she thought.

"What is it?" she asked with her eyes closed.

"Open your eyes and listen to me."

Listen to me, listen to me, listen to me, listen to me! Is that the only thing people can say to me anymore? Somebody listen to me. Anything I've ever cared about has shattered around me. Somebody please listen to me! I can't take the shots through my heart anymore. Fuck happiness, fuck everybody.

She opened her eyes with a vacant look and said, "Go ahead, tell me."

"Star, I didn't create this mess."

But maybe you did create part of the mess. Maybe you did do something wrong somewhere along the way in your desire to control everything around you. Maybe Jack just couldn't live up to this house's standards where everything has to look perfect on the outside, no matter how it feels on the inside. Grandma, too. She had a way of dressing up pain in flowers and pretty dresses and acting like it wasn't there, but it was. The pain never went away.

But, on the other hand, Star knew that was wrong, too. She knew that Grandma Trista tried as hard as she could to balance the perfection that Jack's father demanded. She tried too hard, probably. If perfection was the worst thing that Jack had to deal with, then he was a fucking coward. She wasn't going to be a fucking coward.

"I know you didn't create the mess. It's just life," she said, rubbing her temples. "Tell me what you wanted to say."

"Right before your grandmother died, we decided to sell the house. I'm going to go ahead with the plan and sell it. I've already had a few buyers approach me."

"I understand. Don't worry about me. It will be sad to see it go, but now is a good time. Maybe I'll be able to deal with Grandma's memories a little better once you sell the place."

"Well, I'm glad you understand," he said and went back to reading the newspaper.

Leo was horrified when he saw Star drag herself into the shop the following Monday. Her skin had turned to the same pasty grey that it had been a month earlier, and her eyes hung with dark circles. When she came back behind the bar to give him a kiss and grab an apron, he shuffled her right back around to a stool, sat her down, and then sat next to her.

"Tell me," he demanded, "Who gave you those black circles around your eyes?"

"I'm just tired."

"No. Not tired. You look like Rocky Graziano the day after Sugar Ray spanked him," he said.

She looked up at him with confusion. "Boxers? Are you talking about boxers right now?"

He nodded his head yes.

"Ah, Leo," she shook her head and laughed a tired laugh. "It's just plain wrong to tell a girl that she looks like a beat-up boxer." She put her arm around his frail shoulder and assured him that she was fine. "There were a lot of hard memories to deal with over the weekend. For the past few months, I've been sweeping Grandma's death under the carpet to avoid the pain, but the misery has finally caught up with me. On top of all that, I'm worried about you. I'm worried about the shop making it. Not many people listen to me, but you did. I feel a gigantic load of responsibility to make this place go."

"You don't worry. I told you, the man takes care of ten children. Ten children don't take care of the man. I'm fine."

"I'm not worried about you. It's the shop."

"It's fine. Sales were ten percent higher this week with that new chalk board sign out front. And Jimmy's friend, he's going to do a story on Leo's for *City Beat*. We're going to start carrying a rack of the papers at the front door. Mess or no mess, Jimmy said that kids read it."

"Leo, that's wonderful!" she said with the first bit of happiness she felt in seventy-two hours.

At dinner that night, Leo wanted to know why she wasn't wearing the poet's pendant necklace. Star put her hand to her throat and said that she had forgotten it.

"Onestamente? I haven't seen you without that chain since Signor Professore hung it on your neck. So, Stella . . . how is your old professor?"

"Fine" was all she said. *Fine*, that special word that females master to mean their world is about to crumble and fall.

On her way out that evening, she thanked Jimmy for arranging the *City Beat* story.

"No problem, Star," he said. "Remember that we're all in this together. It doesn't have to be a one-woman parade."

When she turned to leave, Jimmy yelled, "Oh, yeah, I forgot to tell you. That English prof—Perfect or something was in here asking about you a while ago."

What little color she had in her face drained away at the sound of his name. Jimmy gave her a curious look, but she ignored him, zipped up her coat and headed out the door. She wasn't thirty paces down the street when Janus' car pulled up next to her. The passenger window was rolled down, and he yelled to her.

"Can we talk?"

"Go away!" she shouted back.

"Star, please, just listen to me."

"Go away!" she shouted again.

"Damn you! Stop and listen to me!" he yelled.

With that, she turned toward the car and stuck her head in the window. "No, you listen to me, *asshole*! You let me fall in love with you, flat-on-my-face in love. You courted me, kissed me and made love to every part of my body. I shared parts of my life with you that I've never told anyone. Why? Because you let me fall in love with you. You had no right to do that. Now, here I am in love with a married man, and what am I supposed to do with it? Bundle it up and toss it in the shitter? Why? Because that's what you've done to me and to every part of my being that I have given to you. Just thrown it down the old shitter. That may be easy for a shithead like you but not for me. I've given myself rarely, cautiously and never to a *man* for this exact reason. I spent the first half of my life in the bottom of the shitter, getting crapped on and pissed on every day. When I moved to Cincinnati, I promised I'd never be at the bottom of that shitter again, because now I was in control of my life—Jack and Sue were gone. But look at me now, shining Starlight is right back where she was meant to be, at the bottom of the goddamn shitter. So, fuck you Janus Perfidius, take your fucking, married ass back to your wife and get the fuck out of my sight forever!"

Star then turned and headed down the street, fighting back tears. Her lips and cheeks began to quiver and her eyes pooled with tears. "Just walk, just keep walking," she said through gritted teeth.

From the corner of her eye, she could see Janus get out of his car and hurry toward her. She stopped and turned. "Leave me alone, shithead," she warned. "I've brought down bigger wanks than you back in the Tenderloin."

Janus ignored the warning from Star's five-feet-three-inch frame and kept moving toward her. When he got close enough, he grabbed her by the shoulders, turned her around, and pleaded, "Just listen to me!"

With that, Office Tony flashed through Star's mind. She cranked back her leg and jammed her knee, as hard as she could, into Janus' crotch, just like Tony had taught her. Janus doubled over in pain.

"Take that nasty nad-sac back to your pretty little wife, Wank!" As Star turned around to go, she said, "Remember— once Tenderloin, always Tenderloin. And damn proud of it!"

She had suppressed the Tenderloin for ten years, trying to make believe she was someone different, someone without that baggage. She put up with a lot of shit from a lot of people over the years to prove that she wasn't Tenderloin. When Emmy Dribble laughed at her Earth shoes, she should have done a Billy Elrod and punched her lights out. But no more trying to be someone else. *Salty Miss Tenderloin* was back. She cocked Janus, just like she cocked Kenny, that punked-out friend of Jack's, who pushed her into the closet and tried to stick his shank in her mouth. Yes, Salty Miss Tenderloin was back, but she was different. She was stronger. She was beginning to accept herself. *I am dirty. I am clean. I am powerful*, she thought.

CHAPTER 12

Rotten cabbage leaves . . .

Leo and Star huddled together at the bar, crunching numbers for the shop. Leo was right. Sales had increased by 10% in February but seemed to hit a plateau in March. The modest growth was good but not good enough to sustain Leo for much longer. She was tapping her pencil on the coffee counter to generate ideas when the sleigh bells jingled and in walked Emmy in all her pink and green raiment.

With the simple debonair he possessed, Leo scooted off the stool and greeted her. "Sweet Emmy," he began, "you're a bella rosa on a cloudy day."

"Ugh, Leo. I'm already nauseated. Do you have to make it worse?" Star moaned and closed the ledger.

Leo responded to Star's unusually rude candor with a sharp stare and then turned to Emmy and asked, "How's my soldier in Somalia?"

"I've gotten a box full of letters from him. He doesn't say too much about what he's doing over there, though. He just asks a lot about what's going on in Cincinnati. He always tells me to stop in and see you, so here I am!" Emmy said, twirling her ponytail around her finger.

"Well, what can I get you?" Leo asked, shuffling around to the back of the bar. "It's on me."

"Oh, God! I'd love a peppermint mocha latte, Leo," Emmy said, taking a seat.

Star burst out laughing. "Oh, God, I bet you would, Sweet Emmy, but you'll have to take your polka-dot ponytail down to Starbucks to get that."

"Stella, behave yourself!" Leo demanded.

"Leo, don't you worry your little head about her. I ignore Star. I've ignored her for ten years. I will take a coffee and whatever is under that lovely glass dome," she said sweetly, pointing to the pastry dish.

"Ah! Molto buona. Tortini di Riso. Little rice cakes," Leo explained.

Star turned to get the order, but before setting down the plate, she noted that the pastry was two dollars.

Ignoring the comment, Emmy sat at the counter and began to pick at the cake. She dug out all the raisins before taking her first bite. Star watched Leo as he watched Emmy desecrate his famous Tortini di Riso.

"Oh, Star," Emmy began then stopped with a dramatic pause. "Did you hear about Professor Perfidius?"

Emmy didn't notice the color that spread over Star's cheeks at the mention of his name. "No clue," was all she could manage.

"He announced to our class that he's taking a leave of absence from teaching to start up one of those megachurches, but not like the Jim and Tammy Faye Baker type. He said that his church was going to be legit. I might have to change religions just to watch him up on the pulpit—what do you think about that?" she laughed.

"Cool for him," was Star's only response. "Are you through with that?" Star asked, looking down at Emmy's plate of crumbs and raisins.

"Yeah. I've got to run back to campus to print off a paper. The shop doesn't have a computer I could use, does it? It would save me a ton of time."

"I'm not sure Leo knows what a computer is," Star said, pointing to the adding machine on the counter. "That's as technical as we get around here. Right, Leo?"

Leo ignored Star and walked Emmy to the door, asking her to send Kory his best. Later that evening, Leo did not walk out of the kitchen announcing "risotto or polenta for dinner tonight." Instead, he greeted Star with stone silence.

"Go ahead and say it, Leo. I know you're mad at me," Star said, half embarrassed and half proud.

"Sit down, Stella," he directed. He wobbled toward her and held onto the back of his chair. "Whether you like that young lady or not makes no difference to me. What you need to know is this. Whether I like her or not, makes no difference in the way I treat her. That's how it works at Leo's. That's how it should be in life. Many people have come through that door in fifty years that I wanted to turn around and send right back out, but I didn't. Why? Because disrespect don't teach respect."

"Leo, she's a snot, and you know it."

"Yes. But so was Gladys Goodworth, and I gave her respect."

"Leo, if this is one of your lesson-teaching moments, please stop. You go on and tell me these pitiful stories, and then they haunt me for weeks. Don't you understand? I can't live up to your standards. And sometimes, I just don't want to."

"Silenzio! Hear me out. You might learn something," he demanded. "Gladys Goodworth was a grand old lady. She lived in a big mansion over there in Avondale. She come in most days at noon, unless she had a hair appointment. Nella and she—they talked about Clark Gable or Rita Hayworth. Shared pie recipes. She loved Nella's ricotta pie. Gladys was a steady customer. Brought in her friends, the kind of customer you need. She come in one day, same time as usual. I believe it was the end of June, nice weather. The Korean War just started—"

"Enough details," Star interrupted. "Get on with *my* lesson of the day."

"Star, you listen," he said with warning eyes. "Gladys looked around the shop like she owned the place. Her head jerked to a stop when she spotted a negro woman sitting at the end of the bar. The negro lady was enjoying a cup of coffee. Her bus wasn't coming around for awhile. You know what that old Gladie did? She called me over. Tells me she won't frequent an establishment that serves *coloreds*. So, there I was, stuck between a rock and a mountain. I had my best customer telling me to throw a new customer to the street."

Star was interested by now. "What did you do, Leo? Throw Gladys out on her ass?"

"No. I took her arm and told her that her dress was real pretty and that the flower in her hat was just right for June. All the while, I was leading Gladys to a table next to the window. I sat her down and waved to Nella to bring on over her regular order."

"Did she stay?" Star asked.

"She looked up at me and said, 'Leo, I'm no fool. I know what you're up to. I'm not staying.' I looked down at her and said, 'Gladys, I know you're no fool. So, I know that you know disrespect don't teach respect.'"

"Go on, Leo, what happened?"

"She stayed put and ate her Crostata di Ricotta in silence."

"That's a good story!" Star said but then paused with tempered enthusiasm. She looked at Leo with narrow eyes and said, "But that doesn't apply to me. Emmy acts like Gladys, not me. I'm not a racist nor am I a snob."

"You're no fool, either, Star," he said and smiled.

"Yeah, but I've been played like a fool one too many times by Emmy Dribble and a lot of other people. If I can help it, I'll never be somebody's chump again," she said with a harsh edge.

Leo pulled out the chair and sat down. "What's wrong with you today?"

"Nothing."

"Niente is no good. The past couple of days you haven't been yourself."

"Maybe this is really who I am, Leo. Maybe I'm just white trash from the Tenderloin. Just like what they say about taking the country out of people, maybe you can't take the white trash out of me."

Leo shook his head. "That man's done something to you, Stella, hasn't he? You tell me what he's done."

"I can't, Leo. I can't tell you." Her lips began to tremble but she refused to cry. "You're going to hate me, just hate me."

"I'll never hate you. Now, tell me," he demanded.

"Leo, you're going to be so disappointed in me. Grandma and Grandpa were always disappointed in me, but you never were. Now, it's all changed."

"Unless you killed a man, nothing is that bad."

"No! I didn't kill anyone," she cried, dropping her head in her hands.

"Stop burying your face, Stella. Look at me," he directed. "Only the spoon that's stirring the pot knows what's cooking. So, you tell me."

As Star slowly raised her head, Leo announced, "The serpente is married. Isn't he?"

Her eyes shot wide-open. "How did you know that?"

"Of course the man is married! I tried to tell you, but you weren't ready to listen."

"Leo, how did you know, though?" she demanded.

"Facile, easy. All the signs were there. You just never saw them."

"Like what?" she asked incredulously.

"Like, the fact that he took you out only on Wednesdays. Never Saturday night dates. You go to the same place, week after week. Serves the same drunks, day after day. Once he trapped you, he stopped coming in here. Signor Professore was smart enough to know I had his number."

"Leo, I've worked so hard for the past ten years to prove that I was good enough—to prove that I wasn't Tenderloin. To this day, Jack's father is still holding his breath, waiting for the real *Jack's daughter* to stand up and fall right back down, flat on her face, drunk as a skunk. To this day, when he first sees me, Greer stares into my eyes a little too long to see if they're bloodshot or gets a little too close to smell my breath. He thinks he's discreet, but I know all the tricks of the trade. I did the same things to Jack and Sue for ten years. Now, I've proved *him* right. I'm nothing but trash."

"Your grandparents were good enough people."

"Leo, I know that. But I couldn't mess up with them. I felt a lot of pressure. Still do. Now look at me. I've gone and done everything they warned me against. I've committed one of the seven deadly sins," she cried.

"You mean the Ten Commandments, Stella. And no, you're not going to die and go to hell. He's the serpente, not you. Calm down," he said and reached for her hand. "Your biggest sin was ignoranza. And sometimes we don't know that we're acting ignorant when we really are."

"How could I be so stupid, though?"

"Stella, I called you ignorante, not stupido. The professore is stupido."

"They're the same thing. You're playing games with me," she said, pulling her hand away.

"No, I'm not. You're ignorante but not stupido. Ignoranza is no knowledge; stupido is slow to learn. You're ignorante and he's stupido. If you see the professore again, then you *are stupido*!" he said.

Star hated the word stupid as it was Sue's pet name for her, a word typically associated with "worthless cunt." Star first heard this string of words when she was forced to go down on one of Sue's wanks, and her teeth got in the way. Her mother was pissed. The Jolly Pop refused to give Sue her chiba, junk, smack, brown sugar, skag, white china, Dragon, dope, or whatever she called it that day. No matter the name, it was still heroin, something a lot more important to Sue than her stupid, worthless daughter, *Cunt.*

On the way up the steps to her apartment that night, Star stopped at the bank of mailboxes. She pulled out her key and opened the slot. Stuffed in the corner was what she had been silently expecting. The rejection letter from Iowa's Writer's Workshop had come months earlier. Northwestern's final notification deadline was April 1st, just a few days away. She ripped open the envelope and began to read, "Dear Miss Nox, we are sorry to . . . ." She closed her eyes and quietly said, "Not good enough for them, either."

That night, Star reluctantly climbed into bed, which had turned into a battleground for her. Through the night, sleep taunted and tormented her with visions of her grandmother, worries about Leo, guilt over Janus, and now Northwestern. How was she going to tell her grandfather that she had finally followed in Jack's footsteps?

Several nights passed and her mind continued to spin with chaos and dread, throwing her into nauseating turmoil every morning. Her routine of cornflakes, orange juice and the newspaper were interrupted as the cereal and juice began to work their way back up, and she'd find herself gripping the sides of the toilet, begging for mercy.

Her blankets were particularly bad-tempered one night, tangling around her as she rolled onto her stomach. The chafing against her breasts was almost painful. She remembered the discomfort the next morning when she went to put on her bra, which felt tighter than usual. Star slowly sat down on her bed and tried to remember the last time that she had had a period. There had been a few in the past year, but when, she could not remember. Star never kept track of her periods because she had so few, and it didn't matter, anyway. She had been told a long time ago that her chances of getting pregnant ever again were slim or none. She was only eleven then, but the memory was so palpable that she could reach out and touch it.

By the time she had gotten home from the Tenderloin library that evening, it was 9:30, and she was hungry as hell. Cautiously, she opened the apartment door, hoping there wasn't a john inside waiting for her with his dick half hard. Jack and Sue's habits were becoming insatiable, and she had become their only nickel left to chase the Magic Dragon. When she peeked through the door crack, she spotted both Jack and Sue sitting on the couch, watching *Three's Company*. She knew which show because of Chrissy's high-pitched voice that bounced off the door.

Star opened the door and walked past Jack and Sue without saying hello, but Sue called out, "Don't get too comfortable. We gotta' go somewhere."

Star turned sharply and looked at Sue. "Where? It's late and I've got school tomorrow."

"Don't worry about it. You're just going," Jack said, standing up. Sue grabbed a sweatshirt and headed out the door behind Jack. "Get your ass going," she yelled back to Star.

Star stumbled on broken glass as Sue dragged her along Turk Street and down past Jones, a street she never went down. Officer Tony had always warned her that the area between Mason and Jones was off limits, even for people who lived in the Tenderloin. Jack was ahead, waving them toward a dark alley. When they caught up, he grabbed Star's arm, hurried her down the alley, and knocked once on an old screen door. An Asian woman, without teeth or shoes, opened the door with her finger pressed over her lips. The three followed her into a back room, stepping over rotten cabbage leaves and cat shit. Jack squeezed Star's arm harder and harder with each step. The room they entered was dimly lit with a single bulb hanging from the ceiling. A twin bed was in the center of the room, set high on cinder blocks, like a Buick ready to have its transmission removed.

In the corner, Star spotted a giant pair of scissors or tongs of some sort. She had never seen anything like them before. The Asian lady with chopped grey hair and deep wrinkles with their own story to tell began barking orders at Star. Though she didn't understand the words, Star understood where she was meant to be, on the bed, high atop the cinder blocks.

Fear gripped her entire body and she turned to run, but Jack had her by the arms. In spite of her kicking and screaming, Jack and Sue managed to tie her arms and legs to the bed while the woman prepared to get to work. She barked out more orders, and a boy not much older than Star carried in a bucket of boiling water. A grimy, little girl, plagued with fear in her eyes, carried in a basket of rags and set them next to the bed. She gave Star a sad smile before she left.

Star had given up screaming because it was no use. The magnitude of what was happening to her was incomprehensible. She had no idea that a baby was growing inside her. It never crossed her mind. Why would it? She was just barely eleven. A missed period meant nothing to her, but Sue obviously noticed. Star closed her eyes and let the tears stream down into the pockets of her ears. She thought about what Charlotte said to Wilbur just after she spun her sac for her new baby spiders, "This is my egg sac, my magnum opus, my great work, the finest thing I have ever made. Inside are my eggs . . . . I guarantee it is strong. It's made out of the toughest material I have." That was the last thing Star remembered before everything went black.

She woke up the next morning in her own bed, and after feeling moisture between her legs, she was reminded of what had happened atop the cinder blocks. She reached down and found blood on her fingers. She closed her eyes and decided not to cry. Instead, she climbed out of bed, carefully, cleaned up and put on her school uniform. She had to steady herself several times while getting dressed but finally made it out the door and down the apartment steps. She sat down on the stoop for a few minutes to catch her breath and sighed when she spotted Officer Tony's car coming toward her.

He pulled along the curb, and she got up to catch a ride. "You feeling okay, Star?" he asked as she gingerly scooted in the car.

"Sure" was the only word she said in the four or five minute drive to school. During her language arts class, Star felt the moisture begin to spread between her legs again. She quickly excused herself and went to the bathroom. Minutes later, a first grader rushed into the stall next to hers, gripping a heart-shaped hallway pass. As the little girl was trying to hold up her skirt and balance herself on the toilet seat, she dropped the hallway pass which slid into Star's stall. When the little girl crouched down to pick it up, she saw Star crumpled around the toilet with blood pooling on the ground. When she woke, Star heard the emergency room doctor telling Sister Mary Gerard that he did his best but was worried that the young lady may not be able to have children in the future.

Eleven years later, here she was sitting on the edge of her bed, shocked and frightened of finding herself in the same position. She cupped her breasts and realized that they had grown much larger over the past month. She pulled on her jeans, tucked in a sweater and headed down to Walgreens. She spotted the unmistakable **e.p.t** box on the top shelf, sitting next to the K-Y Jelly. Hands shaking, she picked up the box and read, "So accurate, we call it the 'error proof test." She purchased the beacon of truth and headed home.

Star read the directions carefully and opted to pee in cup as opposed to relying on hitting the stick in the toilet. Her hands trembled as she held the dipstick in the cup for five seconds. She then carefully placed the stick flat, on top of the toilet tank. Her life rolled past her in the three minutes she had to wait for the results. She really didn't need that stick to tell her she was pregnant and that the father was a low-life, two-timing wank. When the minutes passed, she looked down at the stick and saw the distinctive pink double lines, confirming that she was pregnant. This wasn't Sue's fault. This wasn't Jack's fault or anyone else's. The responsibility was hers and hers, alone.

Star sat down on the toilet seat and was very still. Her heart was pounding fast and hard. A ringing in her ears mingled with the blood gushing through her arteries created a symphony that was timed by the beat of her heart. So, she was pregnant, indeed. So, what was she going to do?

She sat perched on the edge of the toilet seat for several minutes, counting the tiles in the bathtub. She finally concluded that the world was going to continue to turn. The sun would set that night and rise in the morning. The same would happen the next day and the day after that. And she would still be here, with child. And she would be okay, she would be okay, she decided.

Star stood up and wrapped the dipstick in toilet paper and put it in a plastic bag from the kitchen. She pulled a shoebox down from a shelf in her bedroom closet that held other trinkets and dropped it in with a hodge-podge of items. She looked through the memory keepers with a sad smile. Her first library card. Several bumble bee pins for winning spelling bees. A statue of Mary from her first communion. A plastic pearl necklace from Officer Tony that he gave her when she moved to Ohio. A stack of holy cards she got from St. Anthony's for helping serve lunches in the summer. All her baby teeth wrapped in felt that the tooth fairy forgot, or so she thought. A school picture of Alicia Salinger, the only best friend she ever had. A St. Rose medal from Grandma Trista for her confirmation.

She kissed the medal, closed the lid and put the box back in her closet. Star then placed a call to a gynecologist that she found in the Yellow Pages and scheduled an appointment.

She took her time walking to Leo's, for she knew the shock had numbed her. The world was going on with its daily life, but she couldn't see or feel anything. She wasn't sure if the temperature was hot or cold that day or if the sky was clear or cloudy. Somehow, the sun had completely disappeared, but she thought the sky was blue.

By the time she arrived at work, the spring air had sharpened her senses a little. Star smacked herself in the face several times, telling herself to pull it together. "You have to spend the next eight hours acting like the world is turning just like it was when you woke up this morning, because it is. The world's not going to stop just because you went and got your ass pregnant!" she mumbled but quickly looked behind her, hoping no one was near.

As she turned the corner to the shop, Star found Leo outside, pruning the lower branches of Nella's apple tree.

"What are you doing, young man?" she teased. "You pay me to do that kind of work," she said and tried to pull the shears from his hands, but he refused.

"You go on inside. Nella and I are talking out here," he snapped.

"Okay. I understand," she conceded, but before going in, she looked up at the sky, half expecting to see the Moon turned upside down. It wasn't and Leo didn't seem to notice anything different about her, either. So far, so good.

When she went in the shop, aside from the furniture and the tables with the flea-market candle holders, the place was empty. Not a single customer was there, and it was almost lunchtime. Star's stomach fell for the second time that morning. "No wonder he's out there talking to Nella in that tree. Tell her we need some divine intervention," she whispered.

With that, the sleigh bells jingled and in walked Kevin and Ricky. She welcomed them with a broad smile and waved them to sit down at the bar. "You saved Leo's day, guys," she told them with a deep sigh. "Not a single person has come in here all morning."

"We saw Leo outside talking to a tree. Is he losing it or something, Star?" Ricky asked, taking a seat at the counter.

She laughed and explained that it was his wife's apple tree that they planted together fifty years ago. "Leo prunes and talks to the tree, just as if Nella was standing right there, telling him which branch to cut. It's a beautiful connection, don't you think?" she asked wistfully.

"Yeah, I guess, Star, if that's what you think," Ricky reluctantly agreed, tugging on his baseball cap.

Star rolled her eyes and set out napkins and spoons on the counter. "So, what brings you two boys in here at this time of day?" she asked, relieved to have any diversion from the turmoil swirling around inside her.

"We're celebrating. General Electric offered me a job in their defense division," Kevin explained as he sat down next to Ricky.

"Congratulations! You're officially an adult with a job like that," Star said and grabbed two cups from the shelf. "Will you be building rockets and stuff that blow up people, though?"

"That's topic secret," Kevin teased. "I'd have to kill you, if I told you."

"Roger, Mr. Torpedo!" she laughed. "So, Ricky, why are you still hanging out with such a dangerous dude?"

"Hell, I'm celebrating. The dude can finally buy his own beer," he said, punching Kevin's arm.

"Why do guys do that . . . punch like that?" she asked, turning to fill their cups.

"We punch. Girls squeal and hug," Ricky explained.

"Not all girls," Star countered over her shoulder.

"We don't consider you a girl, do we, Rick?" Kevin said, pulling off his jacket.

Star turned around with a frown and placed the steaming coffee cups before them. "Be careful, Kevin. You could hurt a girl's feelings with a comment like that." Star stood up straight and patted down her curls. The inner chaos she was working hard to suppress seemed to be spiraling from the ends of her hair.

"It wasn't an insult, just a fact," he explained and took a sip of coffee.

"Ignore him and give me one of those things in there," Ricky said, pointing to the pastry plate.

Lifting the dome, Star pulled out a cannoli and thanked them again for coming in. "I really thought a facelift would change things around here, but look at this place. Dead, dead, dead—dead as doom! People walk right past here and go straight to Starbucks."

"Starbucks is cool right now. Comparing Leo's to Starbucks is like Tang versus Gatorade or Tab versus Diet Coke. It's a no-brainer," Ricky explained, before biting into his cannoli.

"I understand, but this place doesn't strive to be cool. *It's Ahead of Cool.* Leo's is authentic. It's original. Cool follows Leo!" Star told them, with her curls springing back into action.

"Yeah, but people aren't authentic. They're mainstream. People just want to jump on the bandwagon of cool," Ricky continued.

"If your angle is originality, then offer something original," added Kevin. "Offer something that Starbucks doesn't, something more than coffee," he said, raising his cup.

"That's what I thought I was doing with the makeover," she explained.

"The place looks great, Star, but that's just packaging," Kevin confessed. "Fulfill a need. What do your customers want that you don't have?"

"Alcohol, but that's not an option. Bacon and eggs, but that's not an option either because we don't have a full kitchen. People keep asking if Leo has a computer. They hate walking back to campus to print a paper, but we're not Kinko's," Star sighed.

"That's it, Star! You're a genius! Computers and a printer! Put three or four computers in here with a printer and magic will happen," Ricky said with excitement.

"Ricky, I'm talking about practical stuff. That's far-fetched," Star said, refilling his cup.

"No, it's not. In ten years, this world is going to be a different place. I just know it. There's a new thing in cyberspace called the world wide web. A nuclear dude in Geneva wrote a program that can potentially link all information on the internet by individual addresses. This shit's amazing. It's kind of like having your own personal post office, but instead of the mailman delivering your letters and crap, they travel in cyberspace and land in your computer. Do you get what I mean? That's the best way I can explain it without all the tech talk."

"I kind of get what you are saying, but what does that have to do with Leo's?" she asked.

"Techies say the applications are endless. Think about it, Star. You could just sit in Leo's and do research from the library through the internet with your cup of 'joe and biscotti. Write a short story and, boom, send it to ten people just like that, just sitting at Leo's. No postage, no paper, just cyberspace.

Mark my words. Someday we'll be able to share music, share pictures, watch movies, or even talk to friends, face to face, on our computers. I'm telling you, this shit is truly amazing."

"I get that, Ricky, but Leo's doesn't have ten years to wait," Star said, leaning on the bar.

"I understand, but get ready for the change now, 'stay ahead of cool.' Put a few computers in here with a printer, and this place will be a finely tuned money-making-machine, maestro!"

"Star, Ricky's right. People hate walking back down to campus just to print a document. This is good, real good," confirmed Kevin.

"But where am I going to get the money? Aren't computers thousands of dollars?"

"You forget so easily, Twinkles. Your buddy, here," Kevin said, nudging Ricky, "is a world-class computer geek. He'll build them for a fraction of the price. This time next week, you'll have two computers and a printer in that little lounge area you created."

"Kevin's right. We're always building and rebuilding systems in class. I'll talk to a few instructors to see if we can get a couple of the old dogs donated until this place starts popping."

"Instead of *Leo's Coffee Shop*, this place is going to be called *Leo's Coffee and Computer Bar*. Next thing you'll need is a beer tap sitting nicely between those shiny coffee urns," Kevin said, pointing across the bar.

Star looked at Kevin and just shook her head but then ran around the bar and hugged them together. "Maybe this is it. Maybe Nella really did answer Leo's prayers."

CHAPTER 13

Breakfast of the Champions . . .

Star tossed aside the *Family Circle* and *Parents* magazines and opted for *The National Geographic.* After flipping through several pages of birds and reptiles, she landed on a series of photographs chronicling an elephant giving birth. The mother looked like she had a giant pink and grey balloon coming out of her butt in the first picture. In the next, she was leaning forward on all fours, but two smallish hind legs were sticking out of her back end. Star drew the magazine closer to her eyes and realized that the hind legs were part of the calf coming out of the mother.

"My God! Is that what it's like?" she exclaimed and slammed the magazine shut. "I am not doing that!" Star said a little too loudly. Embarrassment flushed over her. She bent her head and peeked around the room to see if anyone had heard.

All eyes were on her. "Well, did you know that elephants come out feet first?" she said to the other women. "That scared the heck out of me."

No one said a word. A few women raised their eyebrows and went back to reading. Another woman in the corner who looked like an older version of Emmy Dribble grabbed her toddler and tried to pull him onto her pregnant lap, but he squirmed down and said, "I want to see the elephant, Mommy." The mother caught his arm just before he darted across the room to Star.

When the nurse came out and called for "Starlight Nox," the same mother looked up with disdain. Star stood and said loudly, "That's me. My momma said she saw stars when I came out, feet first!"

The lanky nurse with cropped brown hair and sharp eyes didn't smile. Instead, she directed Star into the first room on the right, gave her a gown and told her to pee in the cup that she handed to her. "The bathroom's across the hall. Write your name on the cup with the marker on the shelf, and I'll be in to get it," she said and snapped the door shut.

Star was surprised when the doctor came in the examining room. The woman looked like Audrey Hepburn with her dark hair pulled back in a tight bun and neat little bangs. She wore kitten heels and a pencil skirt. Star quickly pushed her Keds underneath the seat with her bare feet and said hello.

The woman stuck out her hand and said, "I'm Dr. Vance, Starlight. So, I hear you're pregnant."

"You can call me Star, and yes I'm pregnant, but I really don't know how far along. It could have happened anywhere from early January to a few weeks ago, at the end of March.

"I see," the doctor said and began reading through her chart. "It's noted here that you haven't had a gynecological exam in the past four years. Is that correct?"

"Yes. I got checked went I first went to college because I thought I might have sex, but I haven't until now."

"But you checked off the box for one pregnancy at twenty-one."

"Yes, I was pregnant, but I wrote down eleven, not twenty-one."

"Oh, I misread it." Dr. Vance paused for a moment and finally asked, "So, how did that go for you?"

Star's toes began to curl and beads of sweat were forming on her brow. "Excuse me. How did that *go* for me?" she repeated skeptically. "Not well, but do we have to discuss it?"

"I'm afraid so. I need your medical history."

"I don't think you want to hear it."

"But, I do," the woman said with impatience

"Okay, then. It was your quintessential back-alley abortion by a shriveled-up lady who didn't speak a lick of English. My parents held me down while she did the cutting. The next day I hemorrhaged, and the ER doc said I'd probably never have kids."

The young doctor turned red underneath her lovely alabaster makeup. "I didn't expect that. I am sorry."

"Don't be sorry. It wasn't your fault. It was *chiba's* fault," Star said.

"Chiba?"

"Yeah, chiba. Brown sugar. H-bomb. Skag. Tar Horse."

"What are you talking about?" the doctor asked with increasing irritation.

"Heroin. You wouldn't know that, though, would you?" Star asked defensively. Her life was none of this woman's business, but if she was going to press her, 'Miss Hepburn' was going to get the full throttle from Salty Miss Tenderloin. She *was* back.

"Are you a user?"

"Doesn't it say right there," Star said, pointing to the medical record, "that I don't smoke, drink or use drugs."

"Yes. But what does heroin have to do with your first pregnancy, if I may ask?"

"My parents prostituted me for their little pony trips. I was lucky, though. AIDS hadn't quite hit the heterosexual scene in San Francisco."

"I see," was all the woman could say. She continued looking through Star's chart and finally said, "Other than sporadic periods, your health appears to be good."

"That is correct."

"Then, let me examine you."

Star climbed up on the table and stuck her feet in the stirrups. The doctor examined her and guessed that she was about eight weeks pregnant. An ultrasound would confirm her due date, but Dr. Vance gave an approximate date of early October. After the exam, she took her bag of prenatal vitamins and headed back to work.

An unfamiliar chatter of voices greeted her when Star pushed open Leo's door. A small group of students had papers spread out on the coffee table while another one was feverishly typing at the computer. The chatter was about a group project for a marketing class that seemed to be due within hours. Empty plates and coffee cups littered the table, as well.

She turned and spotted Leo polishing the coffee urns with more energy than she had seen in months. The Moon had finally swung right side up for him. Star went around the backside of the bar and gave him a warm hug. "Grazie, my little Stella," he whispered, trying to hide a tear.

"Oh, come on, you silly old man!" she teased, rubbing his balding head. "No tears for you today. Go on upstairs and take a load off," she said. "I'm looking forward to breaded veal and polenta tonight. It better be ready by the time Jimmy gets here."

Star picked up where Leo left off with the cleaning and continued to polish the coffee urns. She saw her reflection in the copper and shook her head. *You've got his life worked out. What about your own goddamn mess? No graduate program, no job prospects, an affair with a two-timing cheat, a baby with a two-timing cheat. Forget Hawthorne. You've written your own Scarlet Alphabet.*

As she scrubbed the dirty cups in the sink, Star thought about how Janus would react to the baby. She realized that he would have to be told eventually, but for now she chose to push him far from her mind. Star was careful walking home that night as heavy clouds were crowding around the Moon, creating dark shadows along the sidewalk. This irritated her for the Moon had always been her friend and guide. On the nights when there was a john on top of her, pounding away, she would stare out her bedroom window and watch the Moon tiptoe across the sky. Her eyes wouldn't move from the bright ball until the man had rolled away and walked out the door. On nights when her beacon wasn't there but replaced with lonely fog horns echoing across the bay, Star struggled to find any hope in her small life in the Tenderloin.

As the shadows on the sidewalk darkened, Star looked up into the night sky, searching for both direction and glimmers of hope. The clouds grew thicker in response, though, but she trudged on. Turning the corner onto Bank Street, she spied a man up ahead in the moon shadows, leaning against a car. She knew immediately that it was Janus with his left hip and thigh thrusting forward. She cradled her stomach and chest with the length of her arms and walked toward him. For a mere split second, she imagined that he would jump with joy when she told him about the baby. Leave his wife. Marry her. And they would live happily-ever-after. But then Star quickly remembered that this was her life, not someone else's.

When Janus saw Star emerge from the shadows, he bolted forward and embraced her. He held her tight, resting his chin on her head. "I've missed you so much, my Star Bright," he whispered.

Star stood still, resisting every nerve and muscle that was begging to respond. She closed her eyes and breathed in his presence. She longed to wrap her arms around his body and bury her face in his woodsy scent and taut chest.

He pulled away, tilted her head up and kissed her deeply. Star could fight her body no longer and gave into the kiss.

As her body melted into his arms, Star's brain slapped her silly. Leo's words ripped through her body, and she tore away from Janus. "I was ignorant before, but now I'm stupid. Stupido! I never knew you were married when I made love to you.

That was ignorance. Now that I know, kissing you is sheer stupidity. There aren't separate pathways in marriage. As long as you're married to your wife, stay on that path. She's no crazy Bertha living up in the attic. There's no excuse for your low-life behavior."

"Star, you can't do this to me. Being away from you is unbearable," he pealed.

"Oh, really? So unbearable that you would be willing to leave your wife for me, Janus? Is it that unbearable?" she demanded.

"Star, I can't do that in my position. That's preposterous. I'm establishing my dream, my dream church right now. The temple is almost complete. It expands across three acres. What would people say?"

"They'd say that you're a fucking hypocrite, and they'd be correct," she seethed. "Listen, Janus, you need to know that I have a different dream that's growing inside me, and that dream doesn't include a family with a married man."

He looked at her, narrowing his brow. "What are you talking about, Star?" he asked, not anticipating what was to follow.

"I'm talking about a family, a baby, my baby, our baby," she said breathlessly.

"You're pregnant?" he thundered.

"You look terrified, Janus. To make it clear—yes, I am pregnant with your baby," she said, standing up straight and pulling her head high.

"How could you be so fucking stupid, Star?" he roared with his terror turning to abject anger. He grabbed her by the arms and shook her, yelling, "How could you be so fucking stupid! How could you!"

"Stop! You're hurting me!" she screamed, but he wouldn't let go and kept roaring in her face, "How could you, you goddamn slut?"

"Stop! Stop! You're hurting me!" she kept screaming back, but he wouldn't stop. So, instinctively, Star cocked her leg back and, with all her might, rammed her knee so hard into his balls that he dropped straight to the ground.

"You'll never learn, you motherfucker, will you? I come from the Tenderloin, not Hyde Park. If you ever touch me again like that, I'll make sure your balls pop off. Snap! Just like that," she said, raising her fingers and snapping them. "Your balls will be rolling on the ground right along with you. I've made meaner men with bigger balls fall a lot harder." With those final words, she turned and headed home. The clouds were clearing, and the Moon quickly guided her home.

When she climbed into bed that night, Star turned off the light and fell sound asleep. Sometime in the night she was startled by a loud thump when her bedroom door flew open. She lay still as stone but saw from the moonlight that it was the vicious man in the black leather coat who was looking for Jack and Sue a few weeks back. She didn't move a muscle, hoping he wouldn't see her.

"Little girl, you in here? I'm back. Just like I promised," he said, slurring his words. "I'm back."

Star watched as he kicked off his shoes and fumbled with the zipper of his pants. He almost fell over twice, scrabbling with one of the pant legs. The freak, however, kept on his black leather jacket. He stumbled in the dark, groping for the edge of the bed, but by then, Star had slipped her hand underneath the pillow and gripped a knife. He heard the movement and lunged forward, but Star was quicker. She jammed the blade into the smack-center of his crotch as he was falling toward her. Jolted by the pain, he flipped back and slammed his head against the wall. Star jumped from the bed, flew out the front door, and ran down the street, screaming bloody murder for Officer Tony.

The screaming and thrashing among her blankets woke Star from her nightmarish memories. She sat upright in bed with her nightgown dripping in sweat. Staring into the darkness, she whispered, "Please, leave me alone. It's been eleven years. I need peace." A cold shiver ran down her back and a single tear slid down her face.

Still derailed from the torturous nightmare, Star sat in her kitchenette the next morning toying with her Wheaties and wondering when the relentless memories would go back into hiding. The dreams were the least of her problems, though. Janus' dissembling image was almost unbearable, for that was the here-and-now. Her fleeting hope that he would embrace the baby and her was as fleeting as the happiness in her life.

She stirred her cereal and thought about graduation. She received word that her senior thesis comparing the writings of Jane Austen and Emily Dickenson was going to be passed by the thesis committee allowing her to graduate on time, but she had no desire to participate in commencement ceremonies. Her grandfather may be provoked but not like he was going to be when he learned of her other nefarious news. Between the graduate program dings and the baby, his world was going to shake. Finally, she had lived up to her grandfather's expectations by following in Jack and Sue's footsteps. The gilded stool that Trista placed her on in hopes of some kind of eternal salvation had collapsed.

Later that day, Star was taking down the coffee bean jars from the back-bar shelf to dust when Emmy Dribble came bursting through the front door, waving a letter in the air.

"Star," she demanded, "Where's Leo? I've got great news," she said with a proud smile.

Star climbed down from the step ladder and came around the bar. "Leo's upstairs, taking his afternoon siesta, Emmy. Do you want me to give him a message?"

"No thanks. Kory sent the letter to me, not to you," Emmy said, shifting her eyes up and down Star's body.

"What are you looking at?"

Emmy stepped back for a wider look. "Something looks different about you, Star. Can't quite put my finger on it," she said, shaking her head slightly but then continued, "I know. It's your face. Your cheeks and neck look fuller," she confirmed. "You've put on a few pounds since I last saw you, haven't you?"

"No, not at all," Star lied.

"Now, Star, are we telling the truth? The extra pounds look good. I'd watch it, though. My mother always said that short people can look pudgy with just a few extra pounds. Thank heaven my parents are both tall."

"So, which would you prefer, Emmy, brains or height in your family?" Star asked with her neck burning.

"Oh, that's easy. Height."

"I thought so," Star said with a tilt of her head. "Well, I've got to get back to work. Do you want to tell me the news or come back later?"

"Oh, whatever," Emmy said, exacerbated. "Kory will be home by graduation. He wants Leo to join him at the ceremony as his guest."

"How will he graduate? He's been in Somalia."

"His professors worked with him to finish his last few courses."

"That's fortunate."

"Well, are you going to tell him or not?"

"Sure."

"Then, I'll write to Kory and let him know. Toodles," she said and turned to leave.

After she left, Star climbed back on the stool and whispered, "Toodles, bitch. 'Short people look pudgy!' At least I'm not a stupid bitch." The telephone rang and startled Star out of her private rant. She climbed back down the steps again and answered the phone.

"Hello. Is Starlight Nox available?" a woman's voice asked.

"Speaking. May I help you?"

"Can you hold for Mr. Wallace?"

"What? Can I hold for whom?" she asked.

"Mr. Wallace, attorney Mr. Wallace," the sultry voice repeated.

Star agreed, but she didn't understand why the man didn't call her directly and why she had to listen to Debbie Boone sing "You Light Up My Life" into the phone while she waited. Shifting her feet with impatience, she rolled her eyes and said, "What now, dear God?"

"Excuse me?" a male's voice said at the other end of the line.

"Oh, I wasn't talking to you. This is Star. Can I help you?"

"Yes, Miss Nox, you may. I represent Janus Perfidius with regard to his personal legal matters. I would like to schedule a meeting with you."

"What for?"

"To discuss the very private matter between the minister and you."

"This is between Janus and me. Stay out of it," Star demanded.

"I can't do that, Miss Nox. Reverend Perfidius hired me to represent him regarding the matter."

"Stop calling it a matter," Star said, throwing a rag into the sink.

"Okay, his paternity issue, then. Is that more palatable?" the man asked.

The Tenderloin was creeping into her psyche, but she wanted to remain composed and in control.

"Get to the point, Mr. Wallace. I've got to get back to work," Star said, wiping out the sink basin.

"Fine, then. Are you free tomorrow at nine a.m.?" he asked.

"No. I've got class. I'm free at one."

"Perfect." He gave her the address and hung up.

Star's hand was shaking as she clutched the receiver. Paternity Issue? What does Janus want? To take a paternity test? That's ludicrous. He knows the baby is his.

Walking back to her apartment that night, Star remembered the last time she spoke with an attorney, the man with the baby-blue cheater glasses from San Francisco. He was Sue's attorney who negotiated her purchase price.

She contemplated what to wear to the meeting the next morning. Trista would have demanded a dress, but Star opted for jeans, though they were tight around the waist. She slipped into her lucky Keds, the last pair Officer Tony had given her, and stood up. The shoes were tight, but without socks, they would be fine.

Right after class, she took the bus to Erie Avenue and got off in front of a three-story red brick building with white pillars and a black front door. The interior was decorated in navy blue and gold brocade. Austere men from the past century stared at her from their frames that lined the walls.

She took a seat closest to the door and waited. The men in the frames continued to glare down at her. Finally, with her back straightened, she blurted out to the nastiest of all, "What are you looking at?"

The receptionist looked up and asked, "I beg your pardon?"

"Don't these grumpy, old geezers get on your nerves?" Star asked, looking around at the pictures.

"Grumpy men like that pay my salary, so I guess not," she said and returned to her work.

Within a few minutes, the sultry voice from the day before appeared in the doorway, asking Star to follow her. She tagged behind the woman down a long hall and peered into each room as she passed. A quiet murmur swarmed through the place. The woman led her into a conference room with a long table, and sitting at the other end was Janus and a crusty, old man with tarnished white hair and a stiff, pin-striped suit.

For some reason, Star was shocked to see Janus there, but of course he had to be there to defend the fact that he *wasn't* the baby's father. Janus bowed his head in acknowledgement while Mr. Wallace stood up and paused. He looked at Star's gym shoes and turned to Janus with disdain and only then did he ask her to be seated. She chose the seat farthest from them and sat down.

"Miss Nox, we may have difficulty hearing you if you seat yourself so far away."

"Then, get up and move," Star told the man.

"Excuse me," said the lawyer.

"I said, Mr. Crusty, if you can't hear me then move. Who's the guest? You or me? Show some manners."

Mr. Wallace looked at Janus who rose to move, and they both gathered their papers to sit closer to Star.

Once he seated himself, Mr. Wallace began, "Miss Nox, we have a highly sensitive matter at hand with regard to your alleged claim that you are impregnated with Reverend Perfidius' child."

"Stop right there, Mr. Crusty," she demanded, glaring right back. "This is not an alleged claim. Janus' baby is a fact, and I have the dipstick to prove it," she said. With that, she reached down into an open zipper of her backpack and pulled out the pregnancy test that had been wrapped in toilet paper and tucked into her memory box. "Do you know what this little purple and white stick is? The 'Error Proof Test,' every woman's best or worst friend. Here, I'll show you how it works."

"Please, stop. You do not—" he began to say but quickly saw that his plea was fruitless.

Star took the dipstick from the baggy, unwrapped the toilet paper and held up the stick. "See these two windows," she said, pointing to a square and a circular window on the stick. The square box with the line is the control, but if you're pregnant, a line appears in the circular window, too. How many lines do you count, Mr. Crusty?" Star asked.

Mr. Wallace answered her question with only a menacing glare.

"What's wrong? The cat's got your tongue?" she taunted.

"Star, enough. I acknowledge the baby is mine," Janus finally said. "Let's move on."

"Enough? Let's move on? I'm not your child, this is," she said, pointing to her belly. "What in the hell am I doing here, anyway?"

She grabbed the stick and rose to leave, but both men quickly chimed, "Sit down! Please sit down."

"Get to the point. I've got to get to Leo's," she said and sat down. Without looking up, Star wrapped up the dipstick and tucked it back into her backpack and waited.

"Okay, Miss Nox, I will get straight to the point. Reverend Perfidius is willing to pay you a very generous sum of money in exchange for your silence and confidentiality regarding the baby's paternity. This sum of money will include an eighteen-year annuity for the care and welfare of the child along with a stipend for you."

Star sat very still as he finished his disquisition. Blood raged through her body, torching a vivid path through her heart and soul. She kept her eyes focused on her clenched hands knotted in her lap and tried to control her breathing. *Hold on, hold on*, she kept repeating to herself. *Hold on. You'll get through this.* She closed her eyes and focused on her breathing, much like she did when a john was fucking her brains out when she was little. *It will be over soon. Breathe. Breathe. You are in control. He is not. Breathe. Breathe.*

Star wasn't sure how many minutes had passed when she finally heard Mr. Wallace say, "This is a very sweet deal for you, Miss Nox. Five hundred thousand dollars. What do you have to say?"

Star slowly looked up and stared straight at Janus and said, "Five guineas. You can sell your child for five guineas." She watched as a grey hue spread across his face.

"What? What are you talking about young lady? Five guineas? That's not much more than fifty dollars."

"Just about ten dollars, Mr. Crusty," Star confirmed.

"He's offering you five hundred thousand dollars," exclaimed Mr. Wallace.

"Janus," she said with a sad smile, "Take it or leave it. That is my only offer. Pass over the papers, and I will sign them, here and now."

"With all due respect, Miss Nox, I think that you should take the time to think about what you're doing—for your child."

When Mr. Wallace finished his words, Star slowly rose to her feet, leaned forward, grabbed his tie, and whispered through gritted teeth, "Don't you ever tell me what is best for my child. Five guineas or nothing. Give me the papers to sign now, or I am leaving." She let go of his tie, sat down and waited for the papers.

Mr. Wallace handed her three copies of the confidentiality and custody agreements. Star read through the original document. When she arrived at the sum of money, she crossed out "five hundred thousand dollars," wrote in "five British guineas" and initialed the change.

A sharp pain pierced her heart as she signed, *Starlight Nox.* Did Jack and Sue really know what they were doing when they gave her such an ill-fated name? When she was through, Star stood once more and looked Janus in the eye and said, "I wish you good luck. You will need it as you have just unleashed your own ill-fated destiny."

With that, Star bowed to the men and gathered her backpack. She walked out of the office and crossed the street to the bus stop. She sat down in the bus shelter and hugged her backpack to her chest, resting her chin on top of the bag. The daffodils and tulips were in their full glory that day, craning their slender necks in the breeze to watch the tears stream down her face.

Star pulled her wallet from a side pocket in the backpack and took out the ten-dollar bill Janus had handed over. Slowly, she tore the bill in half and then halved again. She kept tearing the money into smaller pieces until only bits rested in her palm. When a strong gust of wind came by, she blew the bits of money into the wind. Her child was not for sale, not like she was, not for ten dollars, not for ten million dollars.

The coffee shop was swamped with customers when Star walked through the door later that day. Leo was behind the bar, beaming with a broad grin as he set a coffee and a cannoli before a stylish woman. Star looked around the room and spotted tables still littered with dirty cups and plates. She hurried behind the counter, kissed Leo on the head and grabbed a bin and a rag to begin clearing the tables.

Cleaning up other people's messes slowed the chaos roaring through her momentarily, but she was under attack and was quickly losing the battle. Janus' stony face bombarded her with bruising reminders of a bitter past but also with foreboding images of a volatile future. She dropped a dirty plate into the bin then reached up to feel her cheek. *Was the pain visible? Could people see the sins washing over her face?* Star squeezed her eyes shut and rubbed her fingers from her cheeks to her forehead, desperately trying to erase the anguish. But the crime was too big to wipe away. And who was the criminal? The man signed away the rights to his child without a grimace or a tear. The fact that she knew so little about his covert life and about his personality after six months of knowing him frightened her. Such artless, unquestioning acceptance was an atrocity. She was from the Tenderloin. She should have known better. His dick was no different from the johns in the District. They all wanted the same thing. And Tenderloin johns seemed to be far more dangerous than Janus—maybe not as smart but much more vicious. She should have known better. Leather Jacket taught her that much.

Leather Jacket's greasy face hung inches from her face the night he yanked her from the kitchen table and wasted her on the couch. The gross relief that spread across his face still made Star's stomach churn. A regret that remained with her was the fact that she couldn't see the whites of his eyes when she plunged the knife into his crotch, leaving a testicle hanging by a string of skin. The expression that she wished to wipe away most, though, was the one she saw in the courtroom the day the judge handed down his sentence.

Star was sitting behind the San Francisco County prosecutor with Officer Tony at her side when the jury reached their decision. Silence shrouded the room when the seven men and five women filed into the jury box and sat grimly in their chairs. Officer Tony took Star's hand and squeezed tightly. She closed her eyes and tried to think about a happy place. There was only one happy place for her—the library, the only place where she had control over what *she* wanted. She had no choice anywhere else in her life. She couldn't choose to have food on the table or sheets on her bed. She didn't choose to have Jack and Sue shoot up in the bathroom or to have one of their johns stick his cock down her throat. She couldn't choose to have this jury make the right decision and have Leather Jacket trapped behind bars for the rest of his life. The only thing that she could choose was which library book she was going to read that day.

Her thoughts were interrupted by the judge's sober address to the jury. She opened her eyes and took a deep breath.

With all eyes in the direction of the jury box, the judge asked the foreman, "Have you arrived at the verdict?"

The foreman slowly stood, looked at the judge and announced, "Yes, we have, your honor."

"Please pass the verdict to the bailiff," the judge directed.

The bailiff took the decision from the foreman and handed it to the judge who turned to Leather Jacket and asked him to stand.

"Are you prepared for me to read the verdict?" the judge asked, looking directly at Leather Jacket.

"Yes, your Honor."

With that the judge began, "We the jury find Mr. Ira Black guilty on one count of attempted murder and guilty on one count of attempted rape."

Star grabbed Officer Tony's arm and buried her head into his chest. He held her head in the palm of his hand.

Leather Jacket slumped down into his chair and refused to stand when the judge asked him to rise again. "Mr. Black, I am going to continue with the sentencing, so please remain standing for the duration." Leather Jacket dropped his head deeper into his chest and ignored the judge's directions. "For the last time, please stand or the deputies will assist you," the judge confirmed. The deputies then gripped his arms and lifted him to his feet.

"Mr. Black, I will now proceed. In accordance with the jury's findings of guilt for attempted murder and for attempted rape, I hereby sentence you in accordance with California penal code to a minimum of five years to a maximum of fifteen years for the attempted rape and to a sentence of a minimum of seven years to a maximum of twenty-five years for the attempted murder of Starlight Nox. The sentences will run consecutively. This means that you will be up for parole in twelve years."

With the judge's final words, Leather Jacket ripped his arms from the deputies' grip, turned to Star and shouted, "Remember my words, little girl. I'll be back. I promise."

Star buried her head back into Officer Tony's chest and shook wildly, for she knew he kept his promises.

A customer with frizzy red hair pulled Star from her thoughts when she tapped her on the arm, asking for another biscotti and a chocolate cannoli. Star struggled to smile then picked up the bin and carried the dirty dishes around the counter to get the order. When Jimmy arrived for his shift, Star dragged herself up the back steps at 5:30 to have baked cod with Leo. His sheer glee over the shop's success grated on her nerves that evening. She felt badly, but the number of pastries he sold seemed to have no relevance to her life at that moment.

After dinner that night, Leo jumped up from the table before Star could clear the dishes. When she moved to help, he said, "No, no, Stella. Stay put. I've got a surprise for you."

He grabbed her plate and tottered off to the kitchen. Star rested her head in her hands and listened to the tinkering of bowls and saucers, trying unsuccessfully to push Janus far from her mind. Buttery cream and vanilla began to filter through the air, which slowed her breathing, but Janus' steely image was relentless.

As the clattering quieted, Leo yelled from the kitchen, "Here I come, Stella. We're celebrating tonight!" He wobbled back to the table carrying two saucers and small bowls filled with sweet rice and raisens. He set down the dessert, and clasping his hands, he exclaimed, "Surprise! Just for my little Stella! Budino di riso dolce."

Star lifted her head with what little energy was left and breathed in the delicious aroma. "Oh, Leo, this is sunshine in a bowl. Thank you so much," she said quietly, but instead of eating the dessert, she dragged her spoon through the rice and around the raisens.

Leo eyed Star and sat back in his chair and finally said, "What's this? You don't like Leo's rice pudding, a delicacy that was once your favorite?"

"Yes, yes, I do like your pudding. I'm just full tonight," she said, rubbing her belly.

"You eat my pudding on a full stomach plenty of times before. Everything okay with you today?"

"Leo, I'm fine. Just a little tired."

"Stella, seems like you've been tired a lot lately, and you've been having swollen eyes, too. And I know about those swollen eyes. . . . They are cryin' eyes."

She looked down and shook her head. "No. You're wrong. They're tired eyes. Just a lot on my mind. Look what I've been through the past few months—Grandma—Kory and now everything with that idiot professor. On top of all that, I've been worried about you and the shop. Life is catching up with me. That's all, Leo. Honestly."

Leo's eyes followed the teardrops that were plopping into her lap. He asked Star to look up. She wouldn't. He asked her again, but she refused. "Listen," he finally said, "I am the boss, and today you begin vacanza. I don't want you back in here for at least one week. You hear me?"

"Oh, Leo, stop. This is my world. Of course I'll be back tomorrow and the next day and the next. The shop is not my problem."

"Stella," he said with deep concern, "What is going on? Is it that professore again?"

"No. It has nothing to do with him," she lied through the tears.

"Tell me what's wrong," he demanded. "You look different, and you're acting different. Go on, tell me."

"What do you mean I look different?" she asked, crying harder.

"I don't know. Nella could explain it better than me. You're like . . . ." Leo paused, raised his hands into the shape of a ball, and said. "Different, that's all I can say."

Star swallowed hard and raised her own hands and drew a shape of a ball in the air. "Do you mean I look rounder?"

Leo nodded his head yes, and Star pressed her hands against her forehead and wept. "Oh, Leo, you're going to be so disappointed in me!" she cried.

"No. Never. What is it, mi bella?" he asked gently.

"Leo," Star cried. "I'm pregnant. Four months."

"Oh, Madre Maria, come è potuto succedere?" he cried, rubbing his bald head.

"Leo, stop. I don't understand you!"

"Oh, Mother Mary, how could this happen? I just knew it! I just knew something like this was to happen."

"Oh, Leo, please calm down," she pleaded.

"It's that professore, that bastardo! I should have killed him with the bat the first day he walked in the shop."

"It's not him. I swear. I don't know whose it is. It happened right after Kory left. There were other guys," she lied. "I never did that with Professor Perfidius." Lying to Leo was killing her, but she had no choice.

"Star, you are a smart girl. Of course you know the father," Leo charged.

"I don't, and I'm not going to hunt guys down to take a paternity test. I have to deal with this. I'm the mother."

"But there is a father."

"No, Leo. No. There is no father here."

"Oh! Gesù! Che cosa posso fare? What can I do?"

Star knew this was devastating Leo, and she hated herself for it. Telling him was far more difficult than it would be to tell her grandfather. Greer would be disappointed for himself and for the way it made him look to other people. Leo was agonizing over the pain the situation brought to her.

"Please, listen to me, Leo," she said. "A baby can be a good problem. Bad things happened to me in the Tenderloin, so bad that I wasn't supposed to be able to have kids. And I know one thing. If I survived growing up in the Tenderloin, I can certainly handle a baby. I know that I've disappointed you, but I need you. I've never needed someone more in my entire life," she cried.

"Oh, Stella! This is no curse, no bambino is a curse. A bambino was Nella's dream. But a bambino at twenty-two and without a father?" he said, shaking his head, "That's a problema."

"You were leading your troops into battle against Hitler at my age. I think we can handle a little baby," she said, leaning forward and grabbing his hands that were knotted on the table. He tried to smile and nodded his head yes with his frail frame moving in tandem.

"I just have to ask you to promise me one thing," she said, squeezing his hands tighter. "This is the most important thing I have ever asked of you."

He narrowed his stare at her but didn't say a word.

"Please, never again ask me about the father or never speak to anyone else about the baby's father."

Leo pulled his hands away and placed them in his lap. He sat back and closed his eyes. Star watched him for several seconds before he spoke. He tilted his head forward and grabbed his chin. Eventually, he opened his eyes and said, "Star, this is grave and importante, but I respect what you ask. However, if that bastardo, that serpente ever steps into my shop again, I *will* beat the shit out of him with my bat!"

"I understand, Leo. Thank you," she said quietly.

CHAPTER 14

Puffed pastries . . . cream-filled donuts!

S tar stood at the bus stop, holding a piece of newspaper over her head. The weather was capricious that day with sprinkles of rain mingled with rays of sunshine teasing her hair into a massive ball of curls. Her stomach had contracted into an equally tight mess as she thought about her grandfather. He was going to be outraged over the rejection letters from Iowa and Northwestern, but she had no clue how his reaction would be to the news about the baby. He had anticipated her demise for the past ten years, but a baby just wasn't the bombshell he had predicted.

She climbed on the bus and seated herself next to a window for the short trip downtown to have lunch with Greer. Resting her head against the bus window, Star's vacant stare fell on a woman sitting in the front bank of seats who was fumbling with a pack of Winston's. When the woman finally managed to pull a cigarette from the pack, she tore apart the thin white casing and began to lick the tobacco from the paper. Brown bits flaked around her lips and fell into her lap. In that moment, Star promised herself that she would rise up against the Tenderloin. She would not slip back into the filthy chaos whose corruption seeps into your psyche, destroying every part of your ability to reason. She would succeed for herself and now for her baby. Turning her eyes from the woman with tobacco gathering on her chin, Star looked out the window and focused on the buildings rolling by.

Dilapidated businesses and tenement houses lined the streets as the bus approached Over-the-Rhine, a neighborhood that sat along the northern fringes of downtown and didn't look that different from the Tenderloin District. Both areas were born from the Victorian period with Italianate architecture and long-gone dignity. The buildings that once stood proud with ornate balconies and bay windows were now adorned with broken glass, crumbling stone and lost dreams crammed into doorways. Star befriended as well as fought with many of the same drug addicts, dealers, pimps and grafters when she was in the Tenderloin. The same lives just wore different faces. She closed her eyes and prayed for strength as the driver pulled into Government Square.

She climbed off the bus and hurried off to her grandfather's office building, in the same way she used to sprint to St. Brigid's. Within a few minutes, she stood breathless at the security desk, asking for her grandfather to be notified that she had arrived. Archie, the building's security guard, remembered Star, though she had visited the building only a few times in ten years. He entertained her with knock-knock jokes while they waited for her grandfather. Instead of being annoyed with Archie's inane jokes, she appreciated the distraction as her breathing steadied and her hands stopped shaking.

When her grandfather stepped off the elevator, Star's laugh grew stronger with nerves. She waved him over and said a little too loudly, "Where have you been? I'm starving! I finally come downtown for lunch and you leave me waiting for fifteen minutes."

"It's only been five minutes," he said with reserve. "And it looks like Archie was keeping you entertained. Let's go," he said, turning toward the door. "We've got reservations at Orchids."

Star gave a quick wave to Archie and followed Greer into the harsh wind that was blowing off the river. As they hurried up the street toward the Netherland Hilton, she rehearsed her speech. She planned to tell him about the writing program rejections first and then follow with news of the baby.

Greer was agitated and short when they sat down at the table. In spite of his ominous mood, Star decided to dive straight into the stormy waters and explain the problem with her senior thesis. She then followed with the disappointing rejections from both Iowa and Northwestern's graduate programs, but before she could finish, her heart began racing as she watched visible rage seethe through her grandfather's body. He sat upright with his chest puffed forward and grabbed the knife resting on the table.

Tapping sharply on his water class, he questioned, "Neither graduate program, Star? How can that be?"

His scorn was far worse than she had anticipated. She took in a deep breath and closed her eyes to calm her nerves.

"Open your eyes and answer me," he said through gritted teeth.

She opened her eyes and looked directly into his. "They didn't like my portfolio; they didn't like me. Guess I'm not polished enough for them, either," she said flatly.

"What's that supposed to mean—the 'either'?" he growled with a piercing stare. "Don't you dare get me going! Your grandmother and I never compared you with Jack."

With that, the onslaught began, and Star knew what was to follow. She sat back in her chair, closed her eyes and prepared herself for the diatribe about Jack that she had endured so many times before. She worked hard every day to manage the destruction Jack and Sue left behind, so she understood what Jack's father was trying to prove with *his* version of history. This understanding didn't make the besiegement any easier for her, though.

When her grandfather was through and she gave the waiter her order, Star tried to calm the waters with an apology in effort to brace him for the additional shame that was to follow. "The rejections from both schools were hard on me, but I realized that they would be much harder on you. I am so sorry for that. I'm sorry for disappointing you," she said.

He set down his knife and glared at her. "There are other schools. Those are the best, but there are others."

"Yes, I realize that there are other writing programs, but my plans have changed."

"So, *your plans have changed*," he said sarcastically. Now that graduate school is out of the equation, what is your *plan* for the future? It's time for you to cut the kite strings, Star. You've been hanging on to our financial resources for long enough. Now, tell me, what is your *plan?*"

She swallowed hard, picked up her spoon and drew circles on the table cloth while she contemplated what to say next.

"My plan . . . is a long story," she finally said.

"A long story? Are you in some kind of trouble?" he asked, sharpening his gaze at her.

"No, not really."

"Tell me what 'not really' means," he demanded.

Without answering, she continued to toy with her spoon.

"I'm waiting," he said with mounting disgust.

Star set down the utensil, took a deep breath and began, "It's not really a long story. Actually, it was only a one-night-stand. With whom? I'm not sure. But the fact is—I'm pregnant."

Greer shot forward in his chair and grabbed the sides of the table, "You're what?" he asked in a low voice.

"I'm pregnant. I'm due in October," she said, glancing around to see if other people noticed his reaction.

"Who's the father?" he demanded.

"I don't know. There were pretty many guys in January. I was upset about a lot of things and made some bad decisions."

"Are you telling me that you don't know who the fucking father is?" he said, frothing with anger.

Star looked around the room again and saw that patrons were beginning to stare. Her plan to tell him in public was backfiring. She had never seen her grandfather lose his cool around other people, only behind closed doors, but now he was on the verge of losing all sense of command.

"What do you expect to do now?" he asked enraged. "You're pregnant without a husband and no fucking future! Have the past ten years of my time and your grandmother's time been a waste of energy! You were supposed to be different, but as anticipated, you're just like Jack!"

"I'm pregnant. It's not like I robbed a bank or committed murder. My God, I am sorry," she said, determined to hold back the tears that were pooling in her eyes.

"Sorry doesn't take care of babies. It doesn't feed them, and clothe them and send them to school. Jack had you at your age and look what happened."

"I'm not Jack. Stop putting me in the same pile of crap that he sat in for his entire life. I'm a survivor. I'll make it with this baby. Whether or not you decide to be on my side is entirely up to you."

"Your grandmother enabled Jack, and that never helped him. I'm not going to enable your recklessness."

"Like I said, it's your choice. I'll survive, either way. But just so I'm clear, does this mean that you no longer want a relationship with me?"

"Not in this reckless state. Grow up and take some responsibility. Then, we can talk."

"Glad I asked," she said. With that, Star pushed herself from the table, stood up and, without looking back, walked out of the restaurant.

Instead of catching the bus at Government Square, she walked up Vine Street toward Over-the-Rhine. There was something about the panhandlers, the broken beer bottles and the storefront windows sheathed in metal bars that made her feel at home. She took in a deep breath and smelled the familiar stench of poverty that she avoided for over a decade. She was certain about one thing, though. The Tenderloin never made her feel so ashamed and disgusted with herself—like her grandfather just made her feel.

When she arrived at the shop later that day, Star ignored Leo, who was working behind the bar, and headed straight back to the storage closet. She yanked out a brush, plastic gloves, a bucket and a box of Borax. She dumped a cupful of powder into the bucket, filled it with steaming water and returned to the front of the shop. Taking no notice of customers, she got down on her hands and knees and began scrubbing the tile around the coffee table. Working her way around the table, Star bumped up against a pair of long legs and a tie-dye shirt, and without looking up, she asked," Do you mind lifting your feet?"

"No problem," the girl said, raising her legs in mid air.

As Star crawled under the girl's legs and cleaned at the other end of the coffee table, she turned around and asked, "You know what?"

"What?" the girl said, resting her feet back on the ground.

"Guys can really suck. It doesn't matter if they are seventeen or seventy. They can really suck."

"Yeah, you're right about that. They suck most of the time, but then they reel us in with that one time when they change our tire in the rain while we sit in the car listening to music," she said, leaning forward, looking down at Star. "Is that why you're scrubbing the floor?"

"Yeah, basically."

"I knit when I'm pissed. I made an afghan for my bed the last time my boyfriend and I had a fight."

"Must have been a big fight."

"It was, but at least I was productive."

"True. At least I've got a big floor to clean," Star said and pushed the bucket onward.

Leo left her alone while she worked her way around the couch and the computers, but when she moved in front of the door, he came over to halt her catharsis.

"Stella, you got to stop cleaning. The place is too busy. Someone's going to trip over you."

"They can go around me, Leo. They all have eyeballs in their heads," she said, pushing the bucket around his legs. "Move, please!"

"Stella, stop!" he demanded. "Put the bucket away and help me at the counter."

"I'm not stopping, Leo. People can go around me!" she snapped, and in that second, the front door flew open and banged her on the backside.

As the sleigh bells quieted, a voice from above asked, "Still scrubbing that floor?"

Star need not look up to know who was standing before her. She sat back on her haunches and hung her head. She dropped the brush in the bucket and peeled off her gloves. Leo wobbled forward in delight and pulled Kory into a tight hug.

"Kory, my son! Benvenuto, benvenuto!" Leo said, patting his back.

Kory pulled away and smiled. "Leo, it's good to be home. There's no place between Cincinnati and Somalia that serves up coffee like yours."

"True! True! But what do you think about the old girl, now?" Leo said, opening his arms wide toward the garnet walls. "She got herself a facelift."

"She looks like something swanky out of New York City."

"It's all Stella's doing," Leo said excitedly. "Starbucks killed business. So, we got ourselves a 'new angle.' We're a computer bar now, too. We can't serve customers fast enough," Leo said proudly.

"The place looks great, Leo. It's good to be home," Kory said, putting his arm around Leo's slight shoulder.

With that, Star slowly stood and said hello.

"Star, how are you?" he asked with a little too much enthusiasm.

"I'm jolly, soldier-boy! And how about you?" she quipped. Star took a deep breath and held it for a few seconds.

"Not bad."

Kory looked tan and healthy. His black t-shirt and jeans were molded around him, showing the taut body of a soldier. There were a few grey hairs and new lines drawn at the edge of his eyes, but he wore the battle scars well. Standing there before him, almost five months pregnant, with dirty water splattered on her shirt and sweat dripping from her curls, was the last place Star wanted to be. She bent down to grab the bucket and brush when the door struck her on the bottom for a second time.

"My God! I couldn't find a spot to park. Is this place really that busy?" Emmy rattled as she walked in, wearing a bright orange sun dress decorated with neon pink dahlia's. Her matching pink lips spread wide, and she squealed, "Oh, Leo. You lucky little fellow! Look at all these customers." She then turned to Star, eyed her up and down, and said, "You look different every time I see you, Star. Do you have a new hair cut?"

"Attitude, Emmy. It's pure attitude." Star balled her fists in a tight knot, but before she could say another word, Leo grabbed her arm and pulled her back behind the counter. "Behave," he whispered and let go of her arm.

Emmy and Kory followed, taking a seat at the bar. While Star scrubbed her hands, Leo poured Kory's coffee and clamored on about the shop.

"There's only one problema with all the business," he said, leaning on the counter for support. Leo's frail frame suddenly seemed lost in the oversized butcher's apron.

"What's that, Leo?" Kory asked.

"My old bones can't take the standing and the stairs. It's wearing me out."

Star quickly turned away from the sink with concern in her eyes. "That's the first I've heard of this, Leo. Why didn't you tell me that the shop is too much for you?"

"Quietare, calm down," he said, patting her hand. "I'm fine for now."

"Take a load off, anyway. Go on around and sit next to your soldier boy. You both have catching up to do," Star said and nudged him away.

While Leo was working his way around the counter, Emmy asked Star for a white chocolate cappuccino.

"Sorry to disappoint you, Emmy, but Leo's is still a coffee shop, not a candy store."

"That's fine. I didn't want anything, anyway. Kory was the one who wanted to stop in," Emmy said, fingering her ponytail. As she spoke, Emmy's eyes narrowed in on Star's chest and held their stare. Suddenly, she burst out, "My God. I figured out what's different. You've got boobs!"

Leo and Kory turned to Star who had grabbed a rag and was holding it in front of her chest. "I don't know what you're talking about, Emmy," she said, mortified.

"Oh, yes you do. Star Nox has always been as flat as a pancake. Now you've got yourself a pair of puffed pastries," she laughed. "Cream-filled donuts!"

Star's eyes darted to Leo for help, but he was too slow to respond. She watched as Kory's eyes turned to her chest and his brows gathered in question. She threw the rag in the sink, ran around the counter and headed up the back stairs. *Do not cry! Do not cry,* she repeated to herself, but Emmy's shrill voice won the battle, and tears streamed down her face as she reached the top of the steps. She threw herself into Nella's chair and wept, not only because of Emmy but because of Jack's father, her grandmother, Janus and everything else in her life that was making her so emotional. She hated being so emotional.

Shadows were crawling across the living room when Leo finally headed up the stairs. He found Star sound asleep, cradling Nella's needlepoint pillow. He sat down in his chair, leaned over and shook her by the knee.

"How's mi Stella?" he whispered.

She opened her eyes but didn't smile at him. "I've seen better days," she said, rubbing her temples. "If I had dated Kory a year ago when he wanted to date me, my life wouldn't be in the shithole that it's in, Leo," she said, hanging her head.

"Stella, look at me," he said, lifting her chin. "First, dwelling on the past don't make flat bread rise. . . . Second, you're only in a shithole if you smell cacca. There's no cacca here. We dig ourselves into holes for all different reason. Sometimes for bad reasons, sometimes for good reasons."

"Leo, there's never a good reason to be in a hole, shit or no shit, trust me."

"No, you trust me. On the battlefield, a fox hole is good. It's what you do with the shovel and the pile of dirt that makes the difference. Your world is turning for a reason. I've got some ideas why, but that don't matter. What matters is this. You can build a good life with the shovel and dirt, or you can just dump on yourself. You got arditezza, coragio. You got guts right here," he said, pounding his chest with his fist. "I'm surprised my Stella didn't slap the rag across her face."

Star grabbed Leo's hand and smiled. "She had it coming to her, but you would have killed me. And today just wasn't the day. It started out bad and just got worse."

"What else is stirring in that pot of yours? Nothing wrong with mi bambino, is there?" he asked with deepening concern.

"The baby's fine. It's my grandfather. I met with him today and told him about the baby," she said, caressing her belly. "It was terrible. He essentially reduced me to Jack and said that he wouldn't enable such deplorable behavior. So, here I am, pregnant, without a husband, and graduating next week, without a profession. Then, Miss Butterflies-and-Bows twits in here and makes comments about my boobs! She's lucky I didn't do a 'Billy Elrod' on her. She deserved it ten years ago and still deserves it today."

"What's a Billy Elrod?"

"It's a good, old Tenderloin ass-kicking . . . seriously, Leo, one day I am going to punch her lights out."

Leo smiled and closed his eyes. Star sat back in the chair and rocked for a few minutes. Finally, she asked him, "What in God's name am I going to do?"

He opened his eyes and looked at her. "Stella, it's time to talk," he said gravely.

She sat up straight and said, "We are talking. Stop right now if you're going to tell me something bad."

"No, no. It's not like that."

"Are you sick?" she demanded.

"No. I'm not sick, I'm vecchio, old. I can't keep going up and down those steps and standing all day long. My arthritis and the gout, they got me. I need somebody to take over Leo's, run the place. I don't want to ask you before—you had plans, but they've changed. You could manage the shop, take care of the baby, right here, at least until you land on your feet or until my feet are pushing up the daisies."

"Leo, stop talking like you've got one foot in the grave. . . . I'll do it. I'm here night and day, as it is. You might as well start paying me for it," she teased. Star reached into his lap and took his bony hand into hers. She brought his fingers to her lips and gently kissed the top of his hand.

"It would be my honor to manage Leo's."

Star had planned to wash all the windows and wipe down the tables and chairs on Sunday to keep her mind occupied while Leo was gone. He was joining Kory at graduation. She had no desire to sit in a hot auditorium for three hours and listen to everyone else's accomplishments. She had always promised herself that she would achieve greatness. She would be one of those success stories who would go on *Oprah* and tell how she went from child prostitute to Pulitzer Prize writer. From Tenderloin trash to television star. Her name would be her great destiny. She was meant to be different. She turned out different, all right. She was so different that she was shut down by both the Iowa and Northwestern writing programs. She was so different that she fell in love with the first smooth-tongued-hungry-dick she met. She was so different that she got knocked up by Mr. Married Pants, himself. *Yeah, right. I'm meant for greatness*, Star thought as she bent under one of the café tables to scrape off dried gum with a spatula.

Star was startled out of her greatness when the sleigh bells jingled and she popped up, banging her head on the marble tabletop. Kory had walked through the door and was looking around for Leo. She stood up with spatula in hand and greeted him.

"Hey," he said.

"I'll get Leo for you. Have a seat," she offered and turned toward the stairs.

"Is that it? Have a seat?" he asked.

Star slowly turned around and asked, "What do you mean 'Is that it'? What more do you want?" she asked, pulling down her tight top over her belly.

"More than your cold shoulder, Star."

"Okay. How about this? Have a seat, asshole?'"

"Why are you so angry at me?" he asked, moving closer to her. "I haven't been around in six months."

"Oh, don't you dare act so obtuse," she spat, raising the plastic paddle.

"Put down your weapon and tell me what I did."

"I should beat the shit out of you, Kory."

"For what?"

"You never said goodbye. You left and never said goodbye to me," she said, lowering the spatula.

"You're right, Star. But sometimes you can't say goodbye, so you just leave."

"I don't understand. Best friends don't do that. Do you know how much that hurt?"

Kory closed his eyes for a brief second and said, "In a different way, Star, I do know how much that hurt. I have . . ." he was about to say when the bells sounded again and Emmy came through the door.

"Oh, look. It's your infrared heat seeker," she said, turned around and walked up the stairs to find Leo.

CHAPTER 15

Candy and . . .

Star's twenty-third birthday came around with as much fanfare as her graduation. She couldn't hide the baby bump much longer as she was tipping over from looking fat to looking pregnant. Tension seemed to be softening with her grandfather, though, for he sent her a card asking to see her when he returned from a trip to Florida. She was relieved for that, but she also missed her grandmother more than ever. As different as she was from Trista, her grandmother was still the only female whom she had ever trusted. More than anything, she wanted Trista back to talk about the baby. Leo was a joy, but he didn't quite understand her excitement when she felt the baby flutter in her stomach. And he had no clue if the tingling in her hands and fingers or the itching on the soles of her feet was normal.

Star was rubbing her feet on a rung of the bar stool and arranging flower vases when the phone rang. She felt the weight of the baby as she padded around the bar to answer the phone.

"Hello, Leo's Coffee and Computer Bar," she said breathlessly.

"Hi, I'm looking for Star Nox. Is this the right place?" asked a deep voice at the other end of the receiver.

"Sure is. This is Star speaking."

"Well, hello, Star. This is Officer Tony."

"Officer Tony! This *is* Star! How are you?"

"I'm glad I found you," he chuckled into the phone. "I'm great. I just became a grandpa."

"Oh, that's wonderful," she said with genuine happiness. "Can we add distant uncle to that list, too?" Tony was one person with whom she was never embarrassed to speak the truth.

"What do you mean? Are you pregnant? You didn't mention a baby in your last card," he said dubiously.

"I'm pregnant like a rabbit. Due in October, but don't bother asking the sordid details. I've joined the ranks of unwed mothers. Other than that, I'm doing great," Star said, massaging her back with her free hand.

"Well, Star," he began with sincere interest, "I do want to know the *sordid details*, and I do hope that you are *doing great*. However, I have to talk to you about something else right now," he said with his voice falling flat.

Her mind quickly processed the date with the change in his tone. The date had been following her around for the past several months. How could she forget? June 16, 1993. She gripped the phone and leaned against the back-bar for support.

"He is up for parole, isn't he?" she asked, with her voice quivering.

"Star, the hearing is scheduled for the first of July. His record is spotless since he's been in. He's done all the right things. I have to tell you—he's got a good shot at parole. I'm buddies with the prosecutor, and he's written a decent Victim Impact Statement to keep the guy in, but I just don't know. I was wondering if you want to come out to San Francisco to appear before the parole board."

Star's heart was pounding in her throat. "Tony, I never want to see that man again. I couldn't appear."

"I understand. Anyway, you'll be receiving documents from the prosecutor's office in the mail. Is Leo's a good address for you?"

"Yeah, I guess, but," she paused, "could he ever find me here?"

"Not through the department or the prosecutor's office. That information is protected like Fort Knox."

After Tony reassured her that she was safe, they chatted a few more minutes about his family, her pending delivery and then hung up the phone. Star kept it straight while she was talking to him, but as soon as she set the receiver down, her legs started to buckle. She slid to the floor and rested her head against bent knees. *Breathe, keeping breathing*, she said to herself. As long as she could keep breathing, steady, just like that, she knew she would be okay. The mantra always worked when johns were pumping the hell out of her or when punks were chasing her for lunch money that she didn't have.

As her heart rate steadied, she remembered the sudden relief she felt when Leather Jacket was finally put behind bars.

She received unexpected relief from Jack and Sue, as well. Scared silly by the courtroom scene and police presence, they slowed down on pimping her out for a fix. Only one steady customer remained, and he wasn't so bad. He didn't hurt her, and he didn't smell. He wore nice cologne and was handsome. He reminded her of Prince Charming, but she was supposed to call him Pygmalion. He brought her gifts like candy and books. While he was undressing, he always tested her on the books he had left the week before. When he was on top of her and ready to come, he would whisper, "Elissa, my sculpted goddess" and then explode as if he were a Greek god, himself. She hadn't thought about Pygmalion in many years.

Star was pulled back to Leo's when a customer bent over the counter to ask if she was okay. Pulling herself up, she lied and said that she was reorganizing the coffee cups. She didn't care if he believed her or not. Star was just happy that closing time was fast approaching so she could go home and process Tony's phone call by herself. But as soon as she pulled the keys from the cash register drawer to lock up, the sleigh bells jingled and in walked Kory through the door.

"You looking for Leo?" she asked from across the shop.

"No. I am actually looking for you." He walked toward her, seeming taller than usual, and sat down at the bar.

"Where's your heat seeker?" she said and grabbed a rag for no real reason.

"Lay off Emmy, Star. I want to talk to you."

"Okey-dokey," she said stiffly. "Let me lock up. It's closing time."

As Star walked to the door, Kory's eyes followed, zoning in on her stomach. The shirt she was wearing was blousy, but when she walked, the material hugged her stomach, revealing a defined ball underneath.

"Star," he said, looking at her stomach incredulously. "Are you what I think you are?"

"Do you mean pregnant?" she asked nonchalantly and turned from the locked door.

Kory's head was cocked back and his eyes were wide. "Yeah . . . are you?"

"Yep. Over five months. Amazing, ain't it?" she said, rubbing her belly.

"But with whom? How?" he asked in utter shock.

"The whom I don't know. The how is obvious," she offered and walked back behind the bar to empty the coffee urns.

"Are you saying that you don't know who the father is?" he demanded.

"That's right. Things happen. Remember all those Jock Straps? Guess one got me good." Star twisted and faced the back of the bar as she spoke. Turning around and seeing the disappointment on Kory's face would be torture.

"My God, Star. How could you let this happen? You're so smart," he asked with palpable disgust.

"It just did, Kory. Grandma Trista had just passed away and you . . ." she started to say but then stopped.

"You what?" he said, banging his fist on the bar.

"Nothing."

"Star turn around and talk to me," he demanded.

"I am talking to you. I'm tired and want to get these things emptied so I can go home," she said, tugging on one of the coffee urns. "My bus is coming in twenty minutes."

"I'll drive you home."

"No, that's okay. I like the ride and the walk. It clears my head."

"What's going on with you, Star?" Kory asked, rising from his seat.

Finally, she turned around and looked him in the eye. "Kory, since you couldn't give me the dignity of a goodbye before you left for Somalia, I'm not sure you have a right to ask that question."

"That's not fair. You know why I couldn't."

"You're a Marine, Kory. Do you really want to talk about this in terms of fair? *You're* much smarter than that. I never talk about life in the realm of fairness. What's the point?"

"You've changed, Star. There's an edge about you that I don't get."

"Maybe it's your perspective that's changed. I'm not about pink bows and polo shirts. Never have been and never will be, but that's what you like now, isn't it?" she asked, moving closer to the bar.

"Why do you hate her so much? . . . Is it jealousy?"

"Jealousy of shellac, veneer? Ah, let me think real hard," she paused. "No. The answer is no."

"Well, I'm marrying her," he blurted out. "That's what I came here to tell you."

Star put the palms of her hands flat on the cold marble counter top and asked, "You're what?"

"I'm marrying Emmy," he said, shoving his hands into his pockets.

"I don't believe you, Kory. You'd never marry Emmy Dribble. Screw her, yes. Marry her, never! That's not you. We both know that. That's the life you used to mock and snarl at," she said incredulously.

Kory hung his head but then looked up and said, "She gives me what I need, Star."

"What's that?" she asked, furrowing her brow. Without waiting for an answer, she continued. "Whether you care or not, you were one of the only true friends that I've ever had. Those feelings haven't gone away. So, as a good friend, I must say that I think you're making a huge mistake. Maybe what she gives you is good sex, but that can't sustain a marriage."

"If you want to know the truth, Emmy does give good sex, and she makes me feel like a king while she's doing it," he spat back. "Whether she wears pink bows or not, she makes me feel like her hero, something you never did."

Star closed her eyes and took a deep breath and slowly released the air. "You're right," she finally said and opened her eyes. "I never treated you like my hero. Maybe I should have, but I know I treated you like my best and dearest friend. That wasn't enough, though, and now I understand why. Life is a shame sometimes . . . isn't it?" she asked herself more than Kory. Silence hung in the air for several minutes, but eventually Star walked around the bar, reached out her arms and asked, "Can we still be friends?"

"That's why I'm here," he said and moved closer to hug her, but as soon as Star embraced him, Kory quickly recoiled when her baby bump pressed into him.

"But you're different now. You're not the person I thought you were. The Star I knew would've never let this happen," he said, looking down at the bulge under her shirt.

"How could you not know the identity of your child's father? That's incomprehensible moral degradation! I know you had a rough life somewhere along the way, but that's no excuse." He reached for his car keys that were on the bar.

Star looked down at her stomach and then looked up at him. "You've changed much more than I have, Kory. Did Emmy help you climb up on this newfound, moral high-horse, decked out in shining white armor?"

Kory walked to the door but before leaving, he turned and said, "Listen, Star, I know that I can speak for Emmy. We're both sorry for your circumstance, but I hope you make the best of it for your child's sake. No child deserves a life of not knowing his or her father."

"That's not always true," she whispered, but Kory didn't hear her as he was already out the door. Star sat down on a stool and rested her head against the bar as the last bus for the night rumbled past the door. Kory had managed to climb up on the same self-righteous horse as her grandfather, grasp the same reigns of moral perpetuity and trample her sense of dignity. All the while, Janus was cradling his little Katie Ann and constructing his irreproachable megachurch, prepared to welcome both saints and sinners.

Star learned about Janus' progress serendipitously when a customer asked for the movie section of the newspaper, which was always kept on the coffee table. Leo sheepishly pulled the newspaper from the garbage and handed it to Star. Highlighted on the front page of the social section was a picture of Janus and his family, standing in front of a bankrupt Kmart that had been purchased for their new church. The building was in an area that was enjoying an influx of young people who were single or had new families, all ready to hear the word of God while drinking their cappuccinos and listening to good music.

Instead of going home that night, Star dragged herself up the steps to Leo's apartment and asked if she could sleep on his couch, which was really only a loveseat. He pulled a quilt from the hall closet that smelled of moth balls and gave her a satin sponge pillow from his room that was laced with rose water. Star snuggled into the curves of the couch and breathed in the old memories that were woven through the pillow and blanket. She closed her eyes and slept soundly until the gurgling hiccups from the coffee percolator woke her the next morning.

She pulled the quilt around her shoulders and headed to the kitchen table where Leo had set out warm rolls, jam and orange juice. "Morning, Leo," she said softly.

"Good morning, mi bella. How's my girl today?" he asked, wobbling over with a glass of milk."

"Better, believe it or not. I slept like a dog," she said as he placed the milk before her. Star took a roll from the pastry plate and looked up. "Leo, be straight with me. Did you know that Kory is going to marry that twit?"

Leo shifted his eyes to the floor then pulled up a chair that was as rickety as he. He sat in the seat but was quiet for a moment. "I did, Stella," he finally said. "Kory told me in confidence at graduation."

"Aren't you going to do something to stop him?" she asked, breaking up the bread and sticking a piece in her mouth.

"Of course not! You can't tell a man he is marrying the wrong woman. People have to figure that out on their own."

"See! You do think that Emmy Dribble is the wrong woman for him," she said emphatically.

"Now, don't go putting words in my mouth. I don't judge their relationship, and you shouldn't either," he said, taking a sip of coffee.

"Well, there's a lot of judging going on that's directed at me, Leo. Nobody seems to care about that, now do they?" she asked, pushing back her heavy curls.

"Stella, no, no! We're both made from flesh and blood. So, until either of us becomes one with the Spirito Santo . . . nobody around here should be judging."

"Well, you need to tell soldier-boy that exact point the next time he sticks his pointed nose into my business," she complained.

Leo tilted his head with confusion. To clear his hazy look, Star explained every detail of Kory's visit the night before. "I think his exact words were . . . 'How could you not know the identity of your child's father? That's incomprehensible moral degradation.' Leo . . . incomprehensible moral degradation! Where does he get off talking to me like that?" she yelled and banged her fist on the table. "Especially since he's marrying someone who's slept with every Phi Delt in this year's graduating class, including quite a few while he was in Africa."

Leo sat back in his chair and shook his head. "Stella, I'm very sorry. I'm surprised. Kory knows better than to throw live grenades like that. He's served in war zones. He knows the bombs. They come flying right back when you throw them carelessly." Leo leaned forward and took another sip of coffee. He sat for a moment longer but finally added, "I don't think he meant what he said. Kory cares too much for you to truly want to hurt you. I'm sure it was just the shock of the baby."

Star didn't respond for a few minutes. Instead, she sat there listening to Leo's heavy breathing. When she eventually looked up, sadness was crinkling around his eyes.

"What is it, Leo?" she whispered.

"I hate to see mi Stella in so much pain."

"Don't worry about me. This is a cakewalk compared to the Tenderloin," she lied. "Walking to school every day was like walking the gauntlet. You and me, we're both survivors."

"Sì, but I don't want you to go through life just trying to survive. I want more for you," he said with a gentle smile.

"Leo, let me ask you something," she began. "You've been around for a long time . . . you've beaten battlefields and bread lines. You've crossed a lot of paths and met a lot of different people . . . from what you've seen, do you think that people can honestly escape their lives and rewrite their own destiny, or do you think fate is already out there, dictating where lives will ultimately end up?"

"Are you asking that question because of Kory?"

"Maybe. I don't get why he's marrying Emmy or why he now thinks he's replaced St. Peter. But what I'm more concerned about is my own fate. Do you think my destiny is to be Tenderloin trash forever?"

"Stella! No! I'm no fatalista. Too many people have surprised me, for the good and for the bad. Life is a moving target. When you slow down or take your eye off the bull's eye, that's when you find yourself in trouble."

CHAPTER 16

Tomato soup and saltine crackers . . .

Though the sun had barely reached high noon in the sky, Star was already dripping wet. Morning fog hovering over the Ohio River had turned into a blanket of humidity hugging the city and was now clinging to her curls and cotton dress. Sticky silence drifted through the bus as it swung down Vine Street, heading into Over-the-Rhine. She spotted a few young girls hanging out of windows and chatting it up across an alleyway. Probably jazzing about Luther or R. Kelly or Janet or just about the humidity and their fuzzy curls, Star imagined, running her fingers through her own frizzy mess. Even though their apartments must have been blazing hot, the girls were laughing and cutting up as they sat upon their perches, high above the sidewalk. A sharp pang of anger and jealousy shot through her. Even though her grandmother was constantly telling her to stand up straight or to hold her stomach in, she missed their friendship. She wanted a girl-friend. She wanted what those girls had.

Star climbed off the bus and headed across Fountain Square to Hathaway's, a diner that had been around since the Eisenhower days. She spotted her grandfather at the entrance dressed in his quintessential pin-striped suit and neat mustache. He didn't bother to hide his displeasure when he saw her stomach outlined by a sundress that was glued to her clammy skin. She pulled the dress away from her belly, but the damp material fell back limply around her bulge.

"My, my, Star. You certainly look different," he said flatly.

"I'll take that as a compliment," Star said and opened the door to the restaurant. She felt sweat run down her back as she walked into the diner.

Greer ignored her words and headed into the restaurant. Star turned and watched his eyes scan the customers' faces as he requested a booth against the back wall. He then fell back several steps behind Star as they followed a server to the back of the room. Instead of going straight to the booth, though, she took a detour to the bathroom. While washing her hands at the sink, Star turned and spotted a full-length mirror hanging on the back of the door. The image before her explained her grandfather's overt disdain. Yellow smiley faces were laughing at her from the granny-style underwear that she chose to put on underneath the thin white dress that fit the summer before but was all of a sudden moist and skintight. Mortified, she picked up the hem of the dress and waved it in the air to dry out the sweat. But, before she made any progress, some woman began knocking on the bathroom door, forcing her to step out with the smiley faces still laughing.

She spotted her grandfather and quickly scooted into the booth. "You look very tan and healthy, Grandfather," she said politely.

Instead of a thank you, he asked, "Did you recognize anyone on your way to the bathroom, Star?"

"No. Why?"

"Don't you remember meeting Hillary Heisman and her husband, Janus, the night of the Horticulture Society dedication? You walked right past them just now."

Star's eyes shot around the room in terror and fell on a lovely blonde seated a few booths away. "My God," she whispered. His thick, dark hair and broad shoulders confirmed that the man seated across from the woman was Janus.

"My God what?" asked her grandfather.

"Nothing," was all she could say. Star squeezed her eyes shut and began her mantra. *Breathe, just breathe. You're in control.* As she was breathing, a delicate hand tapped her on the arm.

Star looked up and saw Hillary Heisman standing before her, dressed in an elegant tweed suit with a slim skirt and a collarless jacket that was trimmed in a cream braid and gold buttons.

"Do you remember me? Hillary Heisman from the Horticulture Society," the lovely blonde asked as she scooted into the booth, next to Greer. "Poor girl. That evening was so overwhelming for you, honey, wasn't it?"

All Star could do was stare across the table at the gold buttons on Hillary's jacket that were decorated with Chanel's iconic double C logo. Greer interrupted her gaping silence and asked, "Of course, you remember Hillary and Janus, don't you Star?"

Star nodded her head and looked up at Janus who was standing before the table without a smile. His right cheek was twitching from the corner of his mouth to his ear. *I could blow up your life, right here and now*, she said with her eyes.

He shifted his gaze to Greer who was speaking quietly with Hillary.

"Janus and Hillary are establishing a large community church on the east side of town," her grandfather eventually turned to her and explained. "It will be open to all Christian denominations. They're talking about naming the auditorium the Trista R. Nox Center . . . of course, the name would follow a significant contribution," he laughed.

"But you're Catholic," Star said, finally finding her voice.

"God doesn't give a damn about the name of the religion hanging on the front door, now does he?" Greer charged with a sardonic chuckle.

Star stared incredulously at the man whom she thought lived at the foot of the Roman Catholic cross. "Is this something Grandma would want?" she bluntly asked.

"Of course," said Hillary, reaching her finely manicured hand across the table toward Star. "I spoke to Trista about the idea right before she passed away. Trista thought this would be a wonderful opportunity for the family trust. We're building a contemporary stage with great acoustics to accommodate a top-quality band. We'll use music, drama, art—all magical forms of language to spread God's word. And there is *not* a better charismatic minister than my husband," she said, looking up at Janus. "He'll offer something special for everyone—choir, outreach ministries, bible study, support groups, all under one roof. One-stop-worshipping is what I like to call it," she said with a grand smile.

"It sounds like a shopping mall," Star said. "Will you have a food court, as well?" asked Star.

"Oh, you're so silly," Hillary laughed. "No food court, but we will have Christ's Coffee Kiosks throughout the complex."

"So, even God will have to compete with Starbucks," Star said, gaining back her equilibrium. "Will you serve Cajun gumbo and chardonnay in the evening accompanied with a little piano music?" she asked, looking up at Janus. "You've got to be a full-service church, don't you, Reverend?"

"Janus will be a full-service minister, but he isn't a good cook," Hillary laughed. "His message will be directed at the 'anti-church' Christian seekers. He doesn't want to spread God's word only on Sundays. He wants to be part of the anti-church-goers' everyday lives. Don't you, honey?" she said, reaching for his hand. "Passages Community Church will be an extension of people's homes, not just a Sunday obligation," she almost shouted. "In just a couple of years, Janus' home will be ten-thousand members strong."

"You'll be a busy man, Reverend, with your flock of children all over Cincinnati. How will you keep them all straight?" Star asked, looking directly at Janus.

"As a professor, Jan is used to a large flock," his wife answered. "But as a minister, the relationships will be much deeper and more moving for him. He's always complained about the fleeting relationships he's had with students. Haven't you?" Hillary said, taking a breath and looking up at her husband in admiration.

"So, you've longed for deeper and more moving relationships with your students, Reverend?" Star asked, again looking directly at Janus. She noticed a line of sweat forming around his hair line.

He returned her question with a piercing glare.

"Most professors don't want intimate relationships with their students. Conflict of interest, ethical issues seem to scare them away. Your desire for intimacy is unusual. Has it ever caused you any problems, Reverend?" she prodded.

"What do you mean by that?" interrupted her grandfather.

"You never know how young girls might interpret friendships. And Reverend Perfidius is such an engaging man . . . I just thought—"

"Star, that's enough," her grandfather said, cutting her off mid-sentence.

"Well, we've imposed on your lunch for long enough," Hillary said, wrinkling her brow. She scooted back out of the booth and stood up next to her husband who had yet to utter a single word.

After they walked away, Greer reprimanded Star for her inhospitable behavior. "That woman was your grandmother's friend, Star. Why were you so rude?"

Star didn't hear her grandfather's words as she was lost in the spectacle that had just unfolded before her eyes. When he questioned her a second time, she still did not respond.

"What is wrong with you? Did your brain die when you got pregnant?" he said, grabbing the table knife and smacking it against the steel napkin holder.

Star's head popped up at the sharp sound. "Sorry. I wasn't listening," she barely whispered.

"I asked you . . . why were you so rude to them?"

"I wasn't rude . . . I don't know. It was just that . . . Hillary Heisman was acting like she was Grandma's best friend, and it bothered me," she said breathlessly.

With growing agitation, her grandfather slammed down the knife. "Let's move on. They're not the reason why we're here today, anyway. I've got more important things to talk to you about, other than a goddamn church. This is the deal, Star. Megan Albers, Ralph and Judy's daughter, wants to buy the house. She has a baby due in seven weeks, so she wants to close before then. I've been dragging my feet on the estate because I've been in Florida, but now I've got to move on it."

"That's too bad. I'm sorry for all your problems," Star said with weak conciliation.

"It's the unfortunate part of death. Nonetheless, you're going to have to move your things out of the house sometime in the next week or so. Your grandmother wanted you to have a few pieces of jewelry and her gardening tools, if I remember correctly," he said and waived over the waitress. After the woman took their orders, her grandfather explained that his plan was to move to Florida permanently in the next month.

"I understand," she said, taking a sip of water.

"I also want to talk to you about another issue," he said and paused but then continued. "I've been supporting you for several years. Now that you've graduated from college and have gotten yourself into this unfortunate mess, you need to stand on your own two feet. Like I said in our last conversation, I can't support this behavior of yours, and your manners today were deplorable. This rude display of yours today serves to confirm that my decision is correct. I have already notified your landlord, informing him that I am no longer responsible for the rent. June 30th is your final day."

Star lifted her chin and tilted her head and said, "That's what I expected. I don't want a free ride from anyone." She grabbed her purse, fished out a five dollar bill, and set it on the table. "That should take care of my tomato soup. I've suddenly lost my appetite. Was there anything else you wanted to tell me, Grandfather?" she asked calmly.

"Don't be ridiculous. I invited you to lunch," he said, pushing the money toward her.

She scooted out of the booth, stood up and offered, "If you don't want the money, donate it to that new megachurch, you're so interested in." She then turned and walked away.

The dense sunlight and humidity accosted her as she walked back across Fountain Square to catch the bus. Droplets of sweat slipped down her breast and were soaked up by the yellow smiley faces covering her belly. She tried to pull her dress away from the moist underwear, but the two layers of fabric peeled back as one. She climbed on the bus frowning.

More than her grandfather's audacity, the bus' diesel fumes mixed with Janus' shrewd silence nauseated her during the ride back to Leo's. Because of her Tenderloin education, Star always thought she had the power to see through people, to see their real character. Janus had duped her, though, and she was pissed at herself and at him. Now, more than ever, she hated how his world was so perfectly aligned with adoration and wealth while hers was careening out of control and poised to crash.

Star recognized that with a few simple words she could have easily thrown Janus' entire world out of orbit, contract or no contract. The only silver-lining that existed in the whole mess was her balance of power. As it stood, she wielded the control. If she exposed him, the balance of power may change. Either way, if she was going to spiral out of control, she'd rather do it alone. She pressed her face against the bus window hoping for some relief from the heat and humidity. Scrubbing the floors was out of the question with the weather, so she planned to attack the coffee urns when she got back to Leo's. She closed her eyes and kept her head resting against the window for most of the ride home, desperately trying to stop her world from spinning. But when she pushed open the door to the shop, anything-but-soothing was sitting at the bar giggling with Leo.

As the sleigh bells jingled, Emmy jumped up from her stool and gasped at Star's belly, which was still grinning with sweat. "It's true! You *are* pregnant! I told Kory that I'd have to see you with my own eyes before I'd believe it," she squealed. "I'm not so sure about that dress you're wearing," she said, wagging her index finger back and forth, "but I'm sure you're pregnant, Star Nox. You're as pregnant as a dog in heat."

"You never make sense," Star mumbled and walked up to Emmy, grabbed her left hand, and said, "I'm pregnant, you're engaged, la-de-da. Now it's all old news. Let's talk about something else." She then headed behind the bar, pulled out a box of baking soda and a bottle of white vinegar, combined the two ingredients and began slathering the mixture onto the urns. As she wiped away the tarnish, she looked at herself in the copper reflection. *Breathe, just breathe*, she kept thinking.

Later that night, when Leo began to admonish Star for her abject rudeness toward Emmy, she stopped him. "Leo, I don't want to hear it ever again. Emmy Dribble came into this shop today with only one goal, and it wasn't to offer me best wishes or baby booties. I invaded her playground eleven years ago, and she's been throwing sand in my face ever since. Now, she's on my turf, and I'm going to start throwing back the sand."

"I understand, but you acted badly in front of other customers. Nella never did that," he said, sitting down in his wife's rocker.

"I'm not Nella, and you don't get it!" she said, plopping down on the loveseat and grabbing a pillow.

"Yes, I do 'get it', but you need to listen to me Star Nox. Acting out of revenge is malaccorto, unwise. Karma takes care of that. That will be true with Emmy."

"How's that?" Star asked, raising a skeptical brow.

"I've witnessed Emmy's attacks on you with my own eyes," he said, pointing to his face. "She has a mean streak that runs straight through her head and straight through to your heart."

"Leo, that's my exact point."

"Sì, but karma's already got her. Don't you see that? Poor Emmy got her man, but I'm not so sure she got his heart. Let that be your revenge, but keep it here and here," he said pointing to his head and to his heart. No need to throw sand in her face. That pain will be more than enough."

"Oh, Leo!' Star moaned, burying her face in the pillow. "Why'd you have to go and say all that?"

"What do you mean? You need to hear it," he said, rocking way back in Nella's rocker.

"Now, you've got me feeling sorry for that damn twit!" she moaned even louder.

Leo grinned at her but wasn't ready to let up. "Now that Emmy's settled, tell me why you were polishing those urns today," he said.

"They were tarnished," she said.

"Nope. Scorrectto. Wrong answer," he said sharply. "I polished them three days ago. You were fit to be tied when you came through that door today."

She was silent for a moment but finally said, "It's not worth lying. You're going to find out anyway. In six days, I'm going to be homeless."

He landed the rocker firmly on the ground, leaned forward and demanded an explanation. Star told him about the megachurch encounter as well as the loss of all future funding from the great Greer Nox.

"Stella, no! Forget the serpente. He means nothing. But Greer . . . he cast you off, just like that?"

She nodded her head yes and said, "For now . . . financially. He doesn't want to enable my deviancy," she said, cradling her stomach.

"Questo è pazzo! Crazy, plain crazy!"

"Kind of," she said, knotting her hands together. "But Leo, maybe this is how I'm so suppose to be . . . I was never comfortable being 'the rich kid.' I've always had a premonition that someday the money would disappear as quickly as it appeared in my life. That's why I never lived like I was rich. Why do you think I ride the bus?"

"Yes, yes. Stella, you were wise. But Greer is your nonno, you're flesh and blood. Is the money that importante to him?"

"To Greer, money is key. He's lived by the Golden Rule all of his life."

"Which Golden Rule?" Leo asked.

"He who has the gold—rules. And if you don't follow his rules, you're basically screwed," she explained. "Jack was a complete train wreck, but I often wonder if he would have been different if Greer was different."

"You'll never know. No use dwelling on it."

"I don't, but I do know one thing. Even in the Tenderloin, I always had a roof over my head," she said, holding her belly with both hands.

"Stella, you listen," he demanded. "A home is the least of your worries. As long as Leo is alive, you have a roof over your head. Nella always dreamed about making the attic a room for a bambino. Her dream will come true."

Star smiled, got up from the loveseat and pulled Nella's foot stool next to Leo. She sat down and rested her head on his knee. "Lines of fate mystify me, Leo, but thank heaven they drew us together," she told him. The baby kicked under her right rib, and Star stretched out her legs. "You know if this baby's a boy, his name is going to be Leonardo Nox."

"He will be coraggioso e intelligente!" he said proudly. "But what happens if it is a bambina?"

"She will be courageous and smart, too, but her name will be Rosa Leonardo Nox."

CHAPTER 17

Southern Comfort and smack . . . Vietnamese beef barbecue

That night Star packed up a few boxes and planned to ask Kevin and Ricky for help with the move, though she knew it would be awkward. Ever since she had become visibly pregnant, they seemed uncomfortable around her. But frantic desperation trumped pride. She woke early the next morning, made banana nut muffins and headed down the steps to make her case. Their door opened within the first few knocks, and before her stood Ricky with his girlfriend close behind.

She held out the muffins and smiled. Ricky laughed and asked what she needed.

"I'm moving into Leo's to save money, and I need help this weekend."

He grabbed a muffin from the plate but apologized. "Sorry, Star. I wish I could help out, but Beth and I are leaving on a trip to Colorado in a few hours," he explained, pointing to his backpack and gear.

"That's too bad," she said, still holding the muffins. "What about Kevin?"

"He's gone on a GE training trip for ten days."

"Oh, well," she said, lowering the plate. "There's always Movers and Shakers to call. You can still have the muffins, though," she offered.

"No thanks. They'd go to waste. We're leaving."

"Okay, then. Have a safe trip," she said and turned to go back up the stairs. Ricky closed the door, but when she was midway up the steps, he reopened it, holding a bundle of mail in his hands.

"Star," he yelled. "I've got some of your mail that landed in our box." He skipped up the steps and dropped the letters on top of the muffins.

She thanked him and continued up the stairs. When she walked into her apartment, Star dumped the muffins in the garbage and tossed the letters into an open box. She pulled out the Yellow Pages and called Movers and Shakers, knowing that their moving fee would decimate her savings.

With the confusion of the move, the first of July almost snuck by Star without notice, but when she signed for the coffee bean delivery, her stomach dropped. July 1, 1993, Leather Jacket's parole hearing. She stood up straight and took a deep breath. "Shake it off, shake it off," she repeated to herself, but each time the phone rang that day, her stomach heaved, and by early afternoon, she was a nest of nerves. When the phone rang at 3 o'clock sharp, Star somehow knew that the call was Officer Tony. She hurried around to the back of the bar and answered the phone with a terse greeting.

"Star, is that you?" the caller asked.

"It is, Officer Tony. Tell me. How did it go?" she asked, gripping the phone.

"I've got some news, honey," he said in a low voice.

She bent over and leaned her elbows on the counter for support. "Go ahead. I can take it," she whispered.

"He got paroled, Star. The prosecutor did everything he could, but it's the overcrowding. The prisons out here are at 115% capacity."

"What does that mean for me?"

"Your life won't be any different. He has no connections to you. Personal information of victims, especially minors, is sealed. Plus, your father is deceased and your mother hasn't been seen in the Tenderloin in over a decade. There are no ties to you, Star. Cincinnati, Ohio, is a world away from a guy like this."

"Okay" was all she could say. The baby kicked hard under her right rib.

"Star, listen to me. You're safe. He's on probation for the next five years, if he has no violations. After that, we continue to keep tabs on bastards like Black. Don't live your life in fear of him. If you do, then he wins."

"I know. I know. I'll be fine . . . I just feel like I'm standing out in a storm with a lightening rod strapped to my back.

Once the shock wears off, I'll be fine." Star had been mentally preparing for the news of Black's release, but when she actually heard Tony's words, a sharp tremor ripped through her body. The baby again reacted to her nerves but this time with a stiffer kick to the ribs that took Star's breath away.

"Calm down, Star. I realize this is a shock. But I've got your back. I always have and I always will," Tony reassured her.

After Star hung up the phone, she headed to the back closet and pulled a pasty mixture of beeswax and olive oil from the shelf along with dusting rags. She began polishing the front bar, desperately trying to rub out the scars and scrapes in the old cherry wood. By the time she worked her way to the back bar, Leather Jacket's face and the sounds of his promise were a little less clear in her mind. The tremors in her hands had calmed, and the baby had fallen back into a peaceful lull.

Later that day and for the first time in all the years that Star had worked at Leo's, Greer Nox walked into the coffee shop, carrying a large cardboard box. He set it on the floor and greeted his granddaughter. Star smiled. His dark suit and silk tie looked awkward in Leo's.

"I called your apartment, but the line was disconnected. I wanted to drop off these things before I left for Florida," he explained, glancing around the shop. "Nice place," he said. "Nicer than I thought."

"Thanks," she said, walking out from behind the counter. "I moved in with Leo last week. I'm renting his third floor."

"That's convenient. Do you like it?" he asked, caressing his pencil-thin mustache.

"We're still adjusting, but it's good." She bent down and grabbed a photograph from the box and stood up. "Is this

Jack when he was a baby?" she asked. "I've never seen the photograph."

"It is."

"Interesting."

"Yes . . . well, I've got to run. I'm catching a flight for Florida in a couple of hours."

"You sold the house already?"

"The closing was yesterday. The deal had been in the works for a while, actually. Well, I'm in a hurry," he said, turning to leave.

"See you, Grandfather. I'll miss you," she added as he walked out the door. She had no idea why the last few words stumbled out. What she wanted to say was, "I wish I could miss you. I wish that we were so connected to each others' lives that the pain of separation seemed intolerable," but that would never happen. His relationships were with silk ties and diamond-studded watches, not with people. And the severe distance that existed between Star and her grandfather had only widened since Trista's death. The schism had become so great that she almost felt sorry for Jack and his life with the man. A marriage with Greer must have been insufferable for her grandmother, too, Star thought.

Following their first few battles after Star moved in with her grandparents, she rarely observed Greer and Trista interact as husband and wife. The dinner hour typically included only Star and Trista, a time she cherished, for the pair actually shared conversations. Dinner hour in the Tenderloin was digging through a garbage can on the way home from the library or making a peanut butter sandwich from the tin hidden under her bed. Once in a while there might be a bag of Fritos or a box of crackers in a cabinet, but the fight for the food with Jack and Sue or the cock roaches was rarely worth the effort. She ate meals at home only when Pygmalion came for a visit. One too many times her rumbling stomach had deflated his efforts, so he got in the habit of bringing her beef barbecue from the Golden House, a Vietnamese spot a few streets over from Turk Street. As his visits and her waist line increased concurrently, the ten-year-old Star never dreamed that she was pregnant. She thought the extra weight around her belly was from the beef barbecue, not from Pygmalion's visits. She never connected that a full stomach would lead to a back-alley abortion.

As she matured, Star realized that the sporadic conversations her grandparents shared were only at breakfast, and they weren't really conversations but rather condescending lectures filled with Greer's overinflated and under informed opinions. His monologues were insightful to Star, though, as they had a way of exposing Greer's true self, like when a chemical plant in India leaked lethal gas killing thousands of people. Her grandfather called it an irrelevant and ineffective government conspiracy targeted at expendables, inconsequential laborers. When Trista suggested that he was being heartless, he called her a moron. He called her a moron again when she wanted to donate a sizeable sum to the Red Cross for the ten million Ethiopians facing starvation due to political unrest. "Let them kill each other," he said. "Why should my hard-earned money go to some savages who haven't gotten along for ten thousand years?"

Instead of sending money to Ethiopia or to India that year, Greer spearheaded a lavish fundraiser to have the men's locker room renovated at the Cincinnati Golf and Racquet Club. His campaign was a huge success, which was celebrated with a Memorial Day dance at the club.

Trista never had the courage to remind her husband that the trust money she wanted to donate was from *her* father's sweat and blood, not his. Instead, she slowly suffocated under the immense weight of his vile condescension. Like his mother, Jack never had the courage to stand up against the man, either. Instead of escaping Greer through the comfort of lasagna and chocolate cake like his mother, Jack escaped his father through a lethal cocktail of Southern Comfort and smack.

Star sat down at the counter and wiped away the dust from Jack's picture with a bar rag. The baby in the photograph resembled a galago bush baby with eyes too large for its head and ears that stuck straight out and came to a point at the top. When Jack was high, which was most every day, he had the bush baby's dark rings around his eyes, as well. Twelve years had passed since she had seen Jack or even a picture of him. Star recognized her own large eyes in the photograph, but that was all she saw of herself in him. Her thick, curly hair and petite nose and ears came from Sue.

Resting her hands on her belly, Star thought about her own baby. She was certain that Little Leo would have a backbone of steel bolstered by her own life in the Tenderloin. The child would need the strength if heredity mattered. The twisted gene of addiction seized both Jack and Sue and never let go. Star was determined to end the lethal legacy, freeing herself and her child from the grips of the disease.

She rummaged through the rest of the box in between taking care of customers. There was her Madonna cassette along with Tears for Fears and Whitney Houston tapes. A half empty bottle of *Heaven Scent* perfume had leaked onto few spelling bee ribbons and report cards from St. Brigid's. Her *Dirty Dancing* sound track and transistor radio were buried under Judy Blume books and a Cabbage Patch doll, which she hated. Its big eyes set too close together reminded her of a bush baby, like her father, but without the ears. That was about it, the culmination of her twenty-three years of life. The most interesting thing about the entire box, though, was the fact that her grandfather bothered making the trip to bring it to her.

Over her life, there were very few memories that Star had collected that she actually wanted to keep, and none of them were in that cardboard box. So, she bent down, lifted the carton, and resting it on her stomach, headed out the back door to the dumpster. She pulled open the steel door and tossed that part of her world into the trash. Slamming the door shut, she wished that the memories of Leather Jacket were as easily tossed away.

When she walked back into the shop, Star was confounded for a third time that day but this time by Kory and Emmy, who were standing at the bar, chatting with Leo. Emmy was leaning against Kory with her hand resting on his thigh. Star took a deep breath, walked behind the bar and wrapped her arm around Leo's shoulder. Though she was not much over five feet, Leo fit neatly into the crook of Star's arm. She gave him a tight squeeze and smiled warmly at the couple.

". . . Daddy wants a gigantic reception at the club, but Mom is in a panic because of the short notice," Emmy was explaining to Leo.

"Wedding plans already?" Star asked, interrupting the rapid flow of words.

"Yes!" Emmy said, turning her attention to Star. "Kory just got word that he may be returning to Somalia by October. We want time together as husband and wife before he leaves. Save August 2nd on your calendar. That's the magical date!"

"That's just a few weeks away," Star said, wrinkling her brow.

"I know! Isn't this so exciting?" Emmy gushed, gazing up at Kory.

He stood straighter than usual with his rock-hard chest thrust forward. "Exciting, Emmy. Damn exciting."

Star was uncertain if he was sincere or sarcastic, but the entire exchange seemed surreal.

"Leo and you are invited, of course," Emmy said with falling enthusiasm. "Kory asked Leo to be his best man."

"It will be my honor to stand next to him on your wedding day," Leo said with pride, not noticing or ignoring her change in tone.

Star squeezed Leo's bony shoulder then finally addressed Kory directly. "Selecting this comrade is a wise decision. With a fifty-year marriage under his belt, there is no better person to represent commitment at the altar."

"You're right," Kory said, putting his arm firmly around Emmy's waist.

Star tilted her chin up and said, "I wish you both the very best."

CHAPTER 18

Stiff rolls and ranch salad dressing . . .

The heat and humidity of August arrived two months earlier that summer, and the stifling guest hung around throughout July. By the end of each day, Star's feet were swollen and the baby was uncomfortable. The third floor was unbearably hot, so she slept on Nella's loveseat most nights. The highlight of her day was watching *The Tonight Show* after the eleven o'clock news. She missed Johnny Carson, but Jay Leno was funny enough. She really watched the show to hear Branford Marsalis break out into a saxophone solo. His long, deep notes pulled the heartbreak right through her.

"He's a powerful sax man, isn't he, Leo?" she asked one evening, stretched out on the love seat, with her feet propped up on the armrest.

"Marsalis doesn't do much for me. Doc Severinsen was *the* horn man and funny, too. Nella always had a crush on him. I told her that if I had a tromba like his, she'd have a crush on me."

Star laughed and reminded him that Nella's crush on him lasted over fifty years. "How long do you think Emmy and Kory's marriage will last?" she ventured.

Leo shook his head. "No, no. I'm not walking that mine field, Stella. Let's just hope for the best." Leo was sitting in Nella's rocker, still fully dressed with his shirt buttoned to the neck.

"Are you worried about Kory? Your bedroom light has been burning awfully late."

"No. No. They're grown adults. That's no problem of mine."

"Then, what is it?" she asked, sitting upright.

Leo sat for a minute with his hands pressed against his knotty knees, thinking, just thinking.

"Leo, go on. Tell me what's going on with you . . . I'm not blind. I see when you start dishing out just a potato or two on your plate. It's money, isn't it?"

The wrinkles in his forehead drew together in a tight web. "Stella," he said quietly with his soft blues eyes shifting toward the window, "I feel terrible, pessimo, about letting Jimmy go from the shop. He has no job, and I'm worried about you and that baby coming around in two months. Business is slow again."

Star hadn't heard such efficient pessimism from Leo in a long time, but she was worried, too. Business was steady, but she didn't know if it was strong enough to support the three of them, let alone, Jimmy.

"It's the summertime. No worries. As soon as students return to campus, Leo's will be back to its hustle and bustle," Star said cheerfully, but neither was convinced.

Star had no intention of buying a new dress for Emmy's wedding with just eight weeks left of her pregnancy, but her sundresses from the year before were now so tight that her belly button poked through like a headlight in the night. Her single pair of pregnancy jeans and shirts from Leo's closet wouldn't work either.

At breakfast on the morning of the wedding, Star bravely declared that she wasn't attending the "Event of the Century."

"Leo, you'll have to go alone. I look like a house. I feel like a house, and I'm not spending a dime on a damn housedress for this stupid wedding," she said artlessly. "You go alone. That way we won't have to close the shop."

"Assolutamente no! Che sarà presente. You're going to that wedding," he said, slamming down his fork. "Even if I have to go buy a dress this minute."

"You're not going to do that, and I have nothing to wear to the country club. Remember, I used to belong there. I know how those ladies dress. And this is going to be the wedding of the year. I'm fat. I'm pregnant, and I'm not married. So, I'm not going. You go and stand side-by-side with soldier-boy, have a delicious dinner and then come home. The End. Period."

"No, Stella," he said with a decisive edge. "Not 'The End. Period.' You're going. I don't intervene in your life, but today,

I do," he said, sitting back in the chair and folding his arms across his chest. "For your own dignity, you will go."

"Why, Leo? Give me one good reason," she argued.

"Because, if you don't go, then she wins."

"Oh, Leo, she won a long time ago. Don't you get it? Without Trista or Greer Nox within earshot, to these people, I was Jack Nox's pathetic daughter from California, and now I am Jack Nox's poor, pathetic, pregnant and unwed daughter from California. Emmy's smart, pretty, very blonde and soon to be married to the perfect man," she said, tapping her spoon on the table.

Leo reached out and yanked the spoon from her. "Enough with your pitiful pity parties, Stella!" he blasted her with shattered patience. "When the pie crust crumbles, you make apple cobbler. Leo don't want to hear you complaining no more. You got food. You got a roof. You got someone who loves you."

"But, Leo!" she interrupted.

"No, no! You listen. Emmy is very pretty and smart, but I'm not sure what else she's got. Depth? Coraggioso? Strength? I don't know. She's marrying a Marine. He's got a lot of years in the reserves. If the going gets tough for her, I don't know what happens."

"Stop patronizing me. You like that damn twit. You're just trying to make me feel better, so I'll go to the damn wedding."

"Liking someone is not the same as respecting someone. Nothing solid in that girl. I respect you. I like her."

"Whatever! I'm not going. I've got nothing to wear."

Leo was visibly agitated, but he sat quietly for a moment, fiddling with the spoon he had taken from her. Suddenly, he looked up with beaming smile. "I've got it, mi bella! I've got it!" he exclaimed as if he had just discovered electricity. "Nella's dresses! She was a little plump at it times. Surely, one of her dresses will fit you," he said, standing up and pushing back his chair.

"Leo, wait a minute! I'm not trying to hurt your feelings, but Nella was a bit older than me, by sixty years!"

"Ah, go on. My Nella had style . . . style eccellente, sopraffino. Follow me," he said, shuffling toward his bedroom. Before Star could say another word, Leo was pulling old dresses from the back of his closet. Most of the dresses were cinched at the waist with full skirts, but then he pulled one out that was bright yellow with big daises. The dress was sleeveless and floated down from a roll collar that fit high around the neck, something Twiggy would have worn on the cover of *Vogue*.

Leo looked at Star and smiled. "Nella wore this number with a pair of white patent boots to the Beverly Hills Country Club. We saw Dean Martin and Sammy Davis, Jr. that night," he said thoughtfully.

Star fingered the lemony dress. "You're right, Leo. Nella did have style. That's still pretty today . . . maybe with a pair of sandals."

"Here, go put it on," he said, handing over the dress.

Star took the chiffon flowers and headed up to her room. She pulled off her pajamas and stepped into the dress. The zipper was hard to reach, but she zipped it high enough to realize that, despite her pregnant breasts, the top section of the dress was too big. She gathered the material together under the armpits and looked down with approval.

"If I draw it in an inch, this may work," she whispered. She stepped out of the dress, put on a robe and began hunting in unpacked boxes for her sewing basket. Star made her way through four cartons before she spotted her sewing materials. When she lifted the basket, a bundle of letters tumbled out along with it. She picked up the mail and remembered the stack Ricky had given to her.

"Hope I'm not late on a bill," she said, picking up the letters from the floor. "It doesn't matter anyway. If you don't have the money, you can't pay the bill, can you, Lil' Leo?" she asked, patting her belly. Star threw the letters on the bed and grabbed her sewing basket. She pinned the dress under the armpits and tried it on again. The alterations seemed to work, so she quickly mended the dress.

Short on time, Star showered and pulled her curls into a high ponytail and tied it with a yellow ribbon from her sewing basket. She propped up a hand mirror on her desk to see if the dress looked okay, but only a bulge of chiffon daisies reflected back.

"Oh, well. This is as good as it's going to get," she said to the squatty mirror and headed down the steps, ready for Emmy's all-day event.

Star glowed when she saw the delight in Leo's eyes as she stepped from the stairwell. He came hobbling toward her and grasped her hands. "Nella dreamed of having a daughter like you, Stella," he said with tears cresting on his lashes. She pulled his hands to her lips and kissed them. "And I dreamed of having a mother like her, Leo."

His blue eyes twinkled back in a gentle smile. "Shall we?" he asked, reaching out his arm to escort her.

Star had not been in St. Mary Magdalene's Church since her grandmother's funeral. A wave of queasiness rushed through her as an usher stepped up to escort her down the aisle. She took his arm for support but did not realize that her fingers were set in a death grip until he tried to seat her. The pimply-faced teen, who was one of Emmy's brothers, peeled back her fingers, one-by-one, from his arm and left her shaking at the pew. She stood there, wishing that Leo was by her side for support. *Breathe, just breathe*, Star said to herself. *You can do this.*

When the wedding party was ushered in and Star spotted Emmy's mother, her heart shuddered once again. She remembered that Mrs. Dribble was on the board of the Horticulture Society. Certain they were invited, there was no need to look, but Star couldn't control herself. She slowly turned around, scanned the church, and found Hillary Heisman sitting alone, wearing an emerald dress with a matching bolero jacket. Her hair was pulled into a perfect bun resting at the nape of her neck. Star swallowed hard and turned her head toward the altar.

Emmy's dazzling gown set against her deep tan was anticipated, so seeing her walk down the aisle was bearable for Star. She felt her composure slip away when Leo stepped from the sacristy in his pale grey morning suit to escort the groom to the altar. Kory was dressed in his formal Marine uniform with a fully decorated white coat, white trousers and white gloves. As Emmy approached, Kory shook her father's hand and took the arm of his bride. Together, the couple cut a magnificent image.

Thank heaven her body reacted mechanically to the standing, kneeling and sitting required by a Catholic mass because her mind had grown numb. She watched carefully, though, when Leo fumbled in his pocket for the rings and, with trembling fingers, handed them to the priest. She waited impatiently for someone to stand up and object to the union, but before she knew it, Kory and Emmy were pronounced husband and wife, and she was working her way through the receiving line to greet the newlyweds. As she approached him, the laughter and chatter of the other guests became a muted din, for Kory seemed to be the only person in her world at that moment.

"You look like Prince Charming, Kory," she said honestly, taking his hand in hers.

"Wish me the best, Star," he said, standing tall and proud.

"I will always—," she started to say, but Emmy grabbed her arm and laughed.

"My, my! What do we have here? It's Jan from *The Brady Bunch*!" Emmy teased. "Star, where did you find that dress? Kory, isn't it a hoot?" she asked, releasing Star and grabbing her new husband's arm.

Even at your own wedding, you can never leave me alone, can you? Star wanted to say.

"Groovy," he conceded with a slow smile. "I'm only kidding, Star. I think you look great, seriously," he said, trying to straighten his face.

You're turning into her, she wanted to say, but instead, Star smiled seductively at Emmy. "You might want to make sure you husband doesn't try to eat the daisies," she advised.

At the reception, the first person to beeline to her was Hillary Heisman. Before uttering a single word, the woman started with Star's sandals and carefully took in the full floral ensemble. Star stood there wondering if Hillary's suppressed smile was from the giant daisies that now decorated her belly or from memories of the smiley-faced underwear that peered through her sundress at Hathaway's. Star's toes began to twitch and curl with anxiety, and in response, the baby kicked and poked around in her belly.

Hillary smiled a tight smile and explained that she had been trying to contact her grandfather about the endowment for Passages. "Janus has been working so hard with church renovations. He's there right now, as a matter of fact. The auditorium is almost complete, and we would love to have Trista R. Nox emblazoned above the stage."

"Grandfather moved to Sarasota last month. Didn't you know that?" Star asked when Hillary paused to take a breath.

A dark shadow crossed over the woman's face. "I didn't realize that he was leaving Cincinnati so soon. Will he be managing the trust from Florida?"

"I haven't a clue," Star said as she massaged a foot that was poking her rib.

"Well, then," Hillary said sharply. "When you speak with your grandfather, please ask him to return my calls."

"Of course," Star said and turned to find Leo.

She saw him seated at the table looking tired and frail. Guilt washed over her as she thought about the heavy burden she placed on him by moving in. Even if he wanted to close the shop and move into a retirement community, he never would with her living there. The steps were getting tough with his arthritic knees, and she thought she heard him stumble down the stairs a few times. In a little over a month, she was adding a baby to his sense of duty. She loved him dearly, but her love wasn't going to pay for coffee beans *or* diapers *or* relieve the burden.

She came up behind him, rested her hands on his shoulders, and bent down to kiss the top of his head. He patted her hand and asked her to sit with him. Star looked down at the stiff roll and ranch salad that Leo was picking through. Basic wedding-reception-fare. Nothing really that special for the very special Emmy Dribble, she mused. They were seated at a table with a few elderly ladies who seemed to be vying for Leo's attention. One with bluish, permed hair yelled across the table, asking if Star was his granddaughter. Her friend tapped her ear, reminding the woman to turn up her hearing aid.

"I can hear just fine, Ruth. Stop acting as if I'm deaf. I'm not deaf," she yelled across the table to Leo.

"Where's your husband, honey? Lucky man, I should say," the friend Ruth asked Star.

"I'm not married," Star answered with a smile, nudging Leo under the table.

"Oh, you're one of those new age girls," the woman said.

"Do you mean trailer trash?" Star asked with a wider smile.

Ruth raised her eyebrows and pursed her lips. "Of course, not," she said, and with that, both ladies turned their conversation away from Leo.

"Behave, Stella, behave. I told you . . . I don't want to hear no more pity-party talk from you." He leaned his head toward her and sharpened his soft blue eyes. "And look . . . now you gone and ruined my chances for a double date!"

"I'm looking out for you, Leo. They had "gold digger" written all over their foreheads," Star teased.

CHAPTER 19

Dirty dishes . . .

B
y the time they returned home that night, Leo was so exhausted that Star had to push him up the narrow staircase. She sat him in Nella's rocker and slipped off his shoes, but before she had time to boil water for tea, he was sound asleep in the chair. She wrestled him awake and sent him off to bed. Pushing the wedding to the back of her mind, Star climbed her own set of stairs to the third floor and was relieved to find cool air drifting through the open windows.

She changed into her nightshirt and sat down on the bed, thinking about the heartache she was causing Leo, as well as Jimmy, who no longer had a job. How could she conscionably rely on an eighty-three-year-old man for the support of herself and her baby? Her grandfather was right. Her reckless behavior was hurting many others beyond herself. If only she had listened to Leo when he first tried to warn her about Janus, then they all wouldn't be in this mess. Did she really think that she was so clever and engaging that a dashing, established man would want her for anything other than sex? And to never question if the man was married? Didn't the Tenderloin teach her better than that? He never took her anywhere beyond that dump across the river where afternoon alcoholics hung out. She met the same people stumbling down the sidewalk when she was a District street rat. Her grandfather had every right to disown her, just like he disowned Jack.

Star sat back on her bed pillows and rested her head against the wall. She needed more than a shovel to dig herself out of this hole. A backhoe crossed her mind as she felt something sharp poking her back. She reached behind her and pulled out the letters that had fallen from the box earlier that morning. Flipping through them, Star noticed that they were dated from last spring and winter.

"Really, Ricky," she mumbled. "Why couldn't you walk up a few steps to drop them at my door, junk mail or not?" Most of it was junk mail, but the last two letters were not. Both had the same return address of Robert M. Garrison, L.P.A. Star tore open the first envelope and pulled out the letter. Slowly she read:

Miss Starlight Nox,   January 15, 1993
5018 Marlon Avenue
Cincinnati, Ohio 45207

Dear Miss Nox,

We were saddened to hear the news regarding the death of your grandmother, Trista Rose Nox. We realize this is a difficult time for you and your family, and it is our wish to help expedite the legal process. As sole beneficiary of the Trista Rose Nox Trust, we would like to meet with you at your earliest convenience to discuss legal and tax responsibilities of the trust. If you have personal representation of your own, please feel free to have him or her contact our office on your behalf.

Again, please accept our sincere condolences regarding the loss of your grandmother. Your time and consideration are much appreciated.

Sincerely,
Robert M. Garrison, L.P.A.

Star read through the letter a few times trying to comprehend its meaning. How could she be the sole beneficiary of her grandmother's trust when her grandfather was still living? The only stuff she had received after her death was that box of rubbish containing the Cabbage Patch doll and old cassettes. This still seemed odd since her grandmother had always promised her the diamond engagement ring and a few other pieces of jewelry that had been in the family for three generations, but considering the position that she had put herself in, Star had no room to question her grandfather.

She dropped the letter and tore open the second envelope that was dated three months later. The letter contained essentially the same information but this time asked for her immediate response. Star folded the letter and tucked it back into the envelope. She was certain that this was some type of legal scam from a seedy lawyer. Instead of an ambulance chaser, he was probably a weird casket chaser, she thought. Star was tired of being fleeced. She would make a single call to this Garrison character, but that was it. Her salty edge was back, and she wasn't going to be taken for a ride again.

Early Monday morning, without any expectations, Star telephoned Robert M. Garrison, and by that afternoon, she was reluctantly following his secretary into a dark office that smelled of cigar smoke and scotch. When Star walked into the room, Mr. Garrison jumped up from his desk and tried to tuck in his dress shirt over a belly that far exceeded hers in size. He barreled around the desk, grabbed her hand and shook her arm up and down.

"Miss Nox, where have you been hiding, honey?" he said with a smile.

"I've been working, sir," she said, pulling her hand from his grip. *What have you gotten yourself into, now, Bright One?*

"Call me Bob and have a seat," he said, heading back around the desk to his chair-on-wheels. "I've been trying to find you since last January."

"I'm sorry, sir. I've moved since then."

"No problem. Situations like this happen with beneficiaries all the time. You've got to be patient in my business, but when money's involved, people eventually turn up."

Star sat down on the edge of a tattered leather chair. The office was as disheveled as the man who sat before her. He couldn't be her grandmother's lawyer. The woman was unable to control her appetite, but everything else in Trista Nox's world was in meticulous order.

"Excuse me, Bob, but how did you know my grandma?" Star asked with reservation.

He almost flew up out of his chair for a second time to answer the question. "Trista and I dated in high school. I would have married her if Greer hadn't beaten me to the punch. He had the looks, and I had the brains, and when you're a twenty-year-old girl, looks are more important than brains," he said, leaning forward on his chair. "But the problem with the good-looking ones like Greer Nox is that they don't develop other parts of their character. No need to be kind or loyal when you're that good-looking, now is there?"

Star looked at the man incredulously. "Who are you to say such things to me about my family?" she demanded.

"I was a friend of your grandma's for a good, long time. That's who I am," he said in all seriousness. "A part of me never stopped loving her. Watching Greer Nox make a fool of her has rustled me for years. She may have been the last to know, but when she finally accepted the truth, Trista was prepared to make him pay. And that is why you are now one very wealthy, young lady, Miss Nox."

"What do you mean?" Star asked, scooting to the edge of her chair.

"The affair—when Trista finally accepted Greer's philandering affair."

"What affair?" Star asked in disbelief.

"The relationship Greer had with Laney Walker, your grandma's friend. Didn't you know?" he asked, eyeing Star closely.

"No! Of course not! He cheated on Grandma?"

"For a long time. Laney wasn't the only one, but I understand they just tied the knot a few weeks ago down in Sarasota."

"What! Grandfather is married?"

"Young lady, are you telling me that you don't know any of this?"

"No, sir, I do not. Grandfather disowned me a while back. I got knocked . . . pregnant and disgraced the Nox name," she explained, looking down at her stomach. "He said that he wasn't going to support reckless behavior like Jack's," Star added quietly with her gaze stuck on her stomach.

Bob let out a deep laugh. "That sounds like Greer Nox. Always blaming the other guy. You know . . ." he began but stopped.

"You might as well finish what you started," Star said.

"Okay, then. Some say Laney's third child looks an awful lot like your grandpa, speaking of kids."

"No!" Star said, gripping his desk. "This all can't be true."

"The child gossip I can't confirm, but everything else is certain, including the fact that you are one rich, little lady."

"Starting when?" she asked in complete and utter shock.

"Starting today. There are some papers we have to file, but you're rich. Your grandpa's name was on the house, so he got that, and they had few other investments together that will set him for life, but the mother lode goes to you."

Star sat back in the chair and began panting. Her mind was spinning, and the baby was clamoring under her ribs. She grabbed the arms of the chair and pulled herself forward.

"Sir, can I ask you a question?"

"You just did, and the answer's yes as long as you call me Bob," he said, pulling a cigar from the top drawer of his desk. "I won't smoke this baby. I just chew on it," he added, sticking the cigar between his teeth.

"Why didn't you try harder to get in touch with me?"

"We did a little snooping, but you left no forwarding address. And Greer was no help after he discovered that Trista designated you as sole beneficiary. He said that you had fallen off the deep end, just like Jack. I was waiting to see which way the chips were going to fall. It's taken me a few years to contact beneficiaries. Six months or so is nothing."

"Well, I've got a baby due soon, and I'm flat broke. A little money is going to go a long way," Star said, leaning back in the chair with her heart throbbing in her chest.

"I can get you a distribution by the end of this week. What do you need? Will one hundred do?" he asked, biting at the cigar.

"Could we make it five hundred? I want to give my boss some cash. I've been living with him rent-free for a few months."

"What's this guy's name? Is he on the up and up, or is he trying to take advantage of you?"

"Bob, his name is Leo Bartatello, and he is eighty-three years old. When Greer cut me off, he took me in, even though he was broke, too. The man is a saint."

"Then, why does he need five hundred thousand dollars?" Bob asked, narrowing his gaze at Star.

"What! Are you insane? Five hundred thousand dollars? This entire conversation has been nuts. I think this whole meeting has been a sham." Star jumped up and grabbed her purse. "*Bob*," she said emphatically. "I'm reporting you to somebody. I don't know to whom, but somebody important. You can't yank people around like this."

"Settle down, Miss Nox. This isn't a sham. I'm the trustee, and it's my responsibility to protect the assets of the trust. So, if you're asking for a half a million dollars for your boss, I need to know why?"

"I was asking for five hundred dollars, *Bob*," she said angrily.

With that, Bob burst into another roaring laugh. He leaned to one side and pulled out a wallet from his back pocket, which was thick with cash. He counted out five crisp one hundred dollar bills and said, "Here, take this. It will hold you over until Friday. We'll transfer fifty thousand to your account instead of one hundred."

Star looked at the cash in front of her like it was toxic. "What do you want from me if I take that?" she whispered.

"You really don't get this, do you, Star? May I call you Star?" he asked.

She didn't respond.

"I'm on the up and up. I just wish Trista had some of your backbone, honey." With that, he rolled his chair close to the desk, opened the center drawer and pulled out a document that read *Last Will and Testament of Trista R. Nox*. He set the will in front of him and flipped through several pages, stopping at one that was paper clipped. He ran his finger down the page and read, "'The Trista Rose Nox Trust will be left in its entirety to Starlight Nox. No provisions will be made from the said Trust for Greer M. Nox, surviving spouse.' There's plenty more legal lingo that verifies your inheritance, but that pretty much sums it up, honey. Last month's financial statement for the trust balance was close to six million dollars. You're a rich, young lady," he said with honest affirmation.

Star dropped her purse and grabbed the arms of the chair, focusing on the sound of the blood pumping through her ears. Beads of sweat gathered on her upper lip, and the room shifted into a wild spin. She closed her eyes tightly trying to stop the whirling, but she couldn't pull herself from the devious carnival ride. 'Six million dollars' taunted her lips as the room spun. *Breathe, just breathe*, she repeated over and over again, but the only thought that swirled through her mind was . . . *Something wicked this way comes . . . Something wicked this way comes.*

"Are you okay, young lady?" Mr. Garrison asked, rolling his chair close to the edge of the desk.

Star looked up and shook her head. She stared at him for a minute longer and then asked a final time if what he said was really true.

"True as my love for Trista," he assured her. "This is a legitimate legal transaction, and you have the right to your own lawyer who can also help explain the trust. But for now, take the cash. You can pay me back on Friday," he said, pushing the bills toward her.

"Thank you Mr. Bob. I'm banking on the fact that you are the real deal."

"It doesn't get any realer than Bob Garrison," he said, sitting back in his chair. "I just wish Trista would have seen that fifty-some years ago."

When Star walked out of Garrison's office, the autumn air was crisp and the sun was glistening in the deep blue sky. Star felt her knees wobble as she made her way to the bus top. She sat down on the bench and gripped her purse close to her chest. She closed her eyes and listened to her heart pounding through her body. The thunderous beat reverberated from the top of her spine to her fingers and toes. Hairs on the back of her neck were standing on end and goose bumps spread across her arms and legs. Her entire body responded to the excitement and confusion with a fierce jerk and then relented. Star wondered if big-time gamblers felt this way when they unfolded a royal flush before them. She wondered if lottery players shook like this when they scraped off the black gum from their ticket, revealing a winning jackpot. Did bounty hunters tremble when they found their fugitive or did treasure hunters when they spotted gold coins buried in sand?

She was rich. Six million dollars rich. She silently thanked her grandma for saving her life for a second time, though this time it was at the expense of her grandfather. She smiled a sardonic smile. She was the rich one now. She *was* part of the fortunate few. But why was there that horrible, gnawing ache at the pit of her stomach? *The Mayor of Casterbridge's* Elizabeth Jane crept back into her mind. Star recognized that now she really was like Hardy's heroine who ". . . forced to classify herself among the fortunate . . . did not cease to wonder at the persistence of the unforeseen." Relentlessly, both she and Elizabeth Jane stood with their heads turned up to the sky, waiting for the thunder to crack and the clouds to burst open, washing away any glimmer of happiness.

For many years, Star had clung to Elizabeth Jane's melancholy belief that "happiness was but the occasional episode in a general drama of pain." Leo was right, though. The time had come to cast off this melancholy shroud that she hid behind. The opportunity for happiness had fallen into her lap quite literally, and the time had come to embrace life, rather than run from it with inexorable fear and cynicism. Nothing was wicked about the inheritance nor was the money the ultimate key to her happiness. However, the bequest gave her economic freedom and a chance at providing a comfortable life for herself and her child. She wrapped her arms around her belly and smiled with genuine relief.

Leo was perched behind the bar, reading the newspaper when Star returned to the shop. He peered over his glasses and smiled. She looked around and spotted a few dirty tables.

"Look at this place. It's a mess," she teased, heading around the counter to give him a hug.

"Ah, go on now. You sound like Nella. A few dirty cups make the place look busy."

Star tied an apron around her back and neck and picked up a dish bin. Before moving to clear the tables, she stopped and propped the bin on her stomach. "Leo," she began, "I think this place could use a sound system. A little light jazz in the background would really set the mood. Don't you agree?"

"Sure. A stereo would be wonderful. While you're at it, put in an escalator to carry my old war injuries up and down those back steps," he said and went back to reading.

After Star cleaned the tables and refilled a few cups, she sat down at that bar to rest while Leo worked his way through the sports section.

"Looks like the Pirates are going to face the Braves in the pennant race this year," he said, turning a page of the newspaper. "Atlanta's got that Barry Bonds. I don't think the Pirates can handle him. Reds ended up eight games behind the Braves this season," he grumbled.

"Maybe we'll get season tickets next year," Star said offhandedly.

"I want my seat right behind home plate. Hire a limousine while you're at it to drop my old bones at the front gate of Riverfront Stadium," he chuckled. "We'll buy peanuts and hotdogs for our entire row . . . damn, maybe Lou Piniella will ask me to throw out the Opening Day pitch." Leo closed the paper and looked up at Star. "You can still dream at eighty-three, Stella. Never forget that," he said wistfully.

Star reached across the counter and grabbed Leo's hand, pulling it toward her. "No need to dream anymore. I'm going to give you a pair of season tickets right behind the Reds' home plate for Christmas. I promise."

Leo rubbed his chin with his free hand and cocked his head. "Are you okay, bella?"

"I've never been better. And by the way, I'm calling an electrician to have this place wired for music speakers. I'm buying a stereo tomorrow. We need to boost the vibe in here if we're really going to compete with Starbucks."

Leo pulled his hand away and stared at Star over his reading glasses. "I'm not trying to rain on your happy parade, Stella, but I'm barely paying for the coffee beans. Where do you think I'm going to get the money for a stereo system?"

"I'm buying it . . . my gift to the shop for all you do," she said.

"I won't have it," he insisted, standing up as straight as his crooked back would allow. "If you can't afford a dress to a wedding, you can't afford music. And this nonsense about baseball tickets. What's got into you?" he demanded.

"Leo, come around here and have a seat," she whispered, patting the stool next to her. "I've got something to tell you."

He eyed her oddly but slowly shuffled around and sat next to her. "What is it?" he asked gruffly. "You're not talking with that professore again, are you? Don't tell me he's giving you money to make up for all his evil."

"Leo! Of course not! I can't believe you would say something so hurtful," Star cried, turning bright red.

"Ah, go on and calm down. Bread is bread, wine is wine. With you, a serpente is a serpente, Stella. If the professore raises his ugly head, trouble will follow!"

"Leo, he has nothing to do with this!" she insisted.

"Then, go on and tell me why you want to dump money you don't have down the toilet when you've got a baby coming in a few weeks. Talk some common sense."

Star was irritated with Leo, but even his mention of Janus couldn't bring down her mood that day. She leaned close to him and smiled. "Because I'm rich, Leo. I'm like . . . I'm like a millionaire," she whispered.

He leaned closer to her and whispered back, "Yeah, and I'm like . . . I'm like Howard Hughes. Congratulations."

"You don't believe me, do you?"

Leo just closed his eyes and shook his head no. His frail chest moved with his head. "Mama Mia! Do you think that baby is coming sooner than you thought? Maybe something took hold of your brain," he gently said.

"This is for real, Leo! My grandma left me her money. Greer was two-timing her, and she found out before she died. She left me her trust. I'm rich. We're rich!"

"You don't say?" was all Leo could answer.

"It's all true. Now, I know why Grandpa left town so fast. Leo, do you know what this means? I'm going to buy a nice house for you and me and Lil' Leo. The place will have a first floor bedroom just for you!" she said with excitement.

"Nah, Star. You won't be taking care of an old bag-a-bones, like me. I wouldn't have it."

"Leo," she said, looking into his eyes, "You're all I got."

CHAPTER 20

Warm milk, 98 degrees . . .

Accepting that she was now a millionaire was a challenge for Star. She had lived more than half her life in poverty, so living without was far more familiar to her than living with excess. With so many decisions tumbling toward, she planned to use the money to make life comfortable for Leo and the baby, but she wasn't intent on turning her world upside down with too many changes. A small house and car would be a good beginning, she decided.

Set out on a mission to buy a home before the baby arrived, Star quickly found a delightful bungalow in Hyde Park with a wide front porch and a first floor bedroom for Leo. Dark wood trim offset multi-paned doors and stained glass windows. The fireplace was decorated with Rookwood ceramic tiles and the rooms were expansive and bright. The second floor had two bedrooms and a bath that would be perfect for the baby and her. Most importantly, the home was on a bus line for Leo that went right past the coffee shop.

Leo resisted moving out of the shop at first, but once she decorated his room with soft greens and browns and hung a picture of an apple tree above his bed, he conceded. Star and he rode the bus together for the first few days, but then Leo got used to the comforts of her shiny red Audi. Within a few weeks, Leo had made new friends in the neighborhood and began spending less time at the shop. Jimmy was hired back full time and was given the title of manager to replace Star when the baby came.

Business picked up with school back in session, though Star was certain that part of the change was due to the new sound system she had installed. One morning in early October, while she was waddling around to Mariah Carey's *Dreamlover*, the sleigh bells chimed and in walked Kory. His eyes bulged at the sight of her.

She laughed and yelled across the empty shop, "What are you looking at? Haven't you seen a beached whale before?"

"My God, Star, you look like that baby's going to drop to the floor right here and now," he said, taking a seat at the bar.

"Well, it could drop right here and now. I'm due anytime," she said and walked around the bar, massaging her back with both hands. "What can I get you?"

"I'll have coffee and a piece of chocolate salami. It'll be my last one for a while. I'll be shipping out for Somalia tomorrow. I came to say goodbye to Leo and to you," he said with a soft smile.

Star smiled back and thanked him for coming in. "I'm glad to see you, Kory, and I'm glad you came to say goodbye this time," she said, lifting the cake dome for his pastry. "A lot has changed since you were last deployed. We both have changed. I'm pregnant and you're married," she laughed. Star held the glass dome close to her chest and continued, "I want you to know that I'm happy for you, as long as you are happy."

"Star, I am happy . . . Emmy shows me how to have a little fun. She doesn't take life nearly as serious as some of us," he confessed.

She dished out a piece of chocolate salami and pushed the plate before him. "I'm glad, and I mean that sincerely," Star conceded. She poured his coffee and set it down. "Thank you for coming to say goodbye this time. We'll miss you. I missed you a lot the-ah-ah-ah the last time," she said, almost panting.

"What was that?" Kory asked, eyeing her curiously.

"It's nothing. Just the normal aches and pains of pregnancy," she said through breaths. "Everything seems to hurt at one point or another. You'll understand when Emmy goes through this," she said, still breathing heavy.

"Yeah, but babies will have to wait. She can't get pregnant if they keep sending me to Africa or Afghanistan."

"Do you think she's prepared to be alone f—f—for so long?" she asked through another wave of pain.

"Why don't you sit down for a minute, Star? You look pretty uncomfortable," Kory advised.

"No, I'm okay. I've just been getting these sharp pains in my back since last night. I didn't get a wink of sleep. The baby must be kicking hard to get out. They weren't so bad before, but in the past few hours . . . man . . . man!" she breathed.

"Is Leo upstairs?" he asked.

"No. He's lawn bowling today with some ladies he met from the neighborhood. Now that he's settled in, he's really been living the life in our new digs. I wish you-u-u had . . . time . . . to see our house," she said as she breathed through another sharp pain. She looked up at him and tried to smile.

Hesitantly, he smiled back. "You look weird, Star."

"Thanks, buddy. So, how's that pretty wife of yours? She really was a gorgeous bride, but I knew she would . . . man, this hurts!" she grunted.

"Star, I don't think you're okay. You look awfully pale."

"No, I'm fine. Really," she said as another sharp pain gripped her body. She grabbed her back again and massaged her sides. "Honestly. It's just back spasms. The doctor says it's from carrying all the weight in the front."

But just as she was finishing her sentence, a horrible spasm ripped across her back and warm fluid rushed down her legs.

"Star! What's wrong?!" Kory cried.

"Kory, my, my water just . . . broke . . . oh my, God!" she yelled as another sharp pain ruptured through her. "Help me . . . I feel so much pressure all of a sudden," she said, grabbing the counter.

"My God! Are you having the baby?" he shouted. "Someone's got to help. Help!" he yelled to the empty shop.

"No! I'm not having the baby!" she yelled. "It's not supposed to come this fast. Oh God! Help me, please!" she pleaded as another spasm gripped her back. "Call 911! Oh, God!" she yelled, "I think I need to push," she screamed, squatting down. "Babies don't come like this. Something's wrong," she panted.

He ran around the bar, grabbed the receiver and slowly dialed nine-one-one on the rotary phone. "My God, Leo! A rotary phone!" Kory shouted.

When the operator finally came on the line, he shouted, "She's having a baby! We need an ambulance at Leo's Coffee Shop on Ambrose Avenue. You've got to hurry!"

"Sir, calm down, sir. Can you hear me?" the dispatcher asked slowly.

"Yes, I hear you, operator. She's pushing. Don't push, Star!" he yelled frantically. "You've got to stop, or that baby's going to come out."

"Sir, don't' try to stop anything," the operator calmly advised. "Have your wife lie down. Check to see if the baby is crowning."

"Star, you've got to lie down on the floor! Does the baby have a crown? The lady wants to know."

Crawling out from behind the bar, Star laid down on the floor. "You've got to look. Oh, God! I've got to push."

"Is she crowning, sir?" the woman asked again.

By now, Star hiked up her dress, tore off her underwear and was feeling for the head. "My God! It's crowning! The head is crowning! Help me!" she yelled.

"She's crowning. She's crowning!" Kory yelled into the phone.

"Sir, find a clean towel to catch the baby. Place clean towels under your wife."

"Star, where are the towels?" he asked frantically.

Star propped herself up on one elbow while cupping the crown with the other hand. Her head was flung back as another contraction rippled through her. "The middle drawer," she groaned. "Hurry! You've got to help me!"

"Don't hang up. I'm getting towels," he said, placing the receiver on the floor. He pulled out the center drawer, reached for a bundle of towels, grabbed the phone again and stretched the cord to Star.

"Kory! The head! The head!" Star yelled.

"Ma'am, the head is coming out. What do I do?"

"Sir, support the head with the towels and let the body come out. Do not try to stop anything."

Kory got down on his knees, looked between her legs and saw the head. "Oh, God! The baby is coming!" He dropped the phone, took the towels and cradled the head as it began to emerge. "Push, Star, push! It's coming!"

"Oh, God, what if I can't get it out?" Star cried.

"Star, just push. Just push. I'm right here for you," Kory reassured her. "I've got the head in the towel. Just get the shoulders out!" he yelled. "Now push, push the shoulders out!"

"I can't!" Star cried.

Holding the head with one hand, Kory grabbed the receiver, "It won't come out, the shoulders won't come out!" he yelled to the woman.

"Wait for the next contraction. Then gently push the baby's head toward Mom's back. The shoulder and body will then slip out," the operator calmly advised.

He dropped the phone and grabbed another towel with his free hand and gently pushed on the side of the baby's head. "With your next contraction, just push, Star, push," he urged her.

As the next contraction ripped through her body, she pressed her palms hard against the floor and pushed with all her might.

"Come on, Star, give it one final push. You can do it!" he directed, carefully manipulating the head.

With all her remaining strength, Star pushed one last time, and with a few twists and turns, the shoulders popped out and the feet followed. The afterbirth gushed out with the baby, splattering Kory's pants with blood and fluid. Quickly following was a thick piece of bloody meat that flopped on the ground close to Kory's knees. He looked down at the baby cradled in the towel and then at the placenta and the heavy bleeding flowing from Star. He turned back to the baby who had a dusty, blue hue and grabbed the phone with his free hand.

"Operator, are you still there?" he asked breathlessly.

"Yes, sir," the calm voice answered. "Is the baby breathing?"

"I don't know. She looks blue," he said, trying to remain calm.

"What! Blue! Is it okay? Is it breathing?" Star yelled.

"She's going to be okay! Quiet down so I can hear the operator," Kory demanded.

"Sir, clear the nostrils and mouth with a towel," the operator directed Kory.

He dropped the phone and wiped the baby's mouth and nose with a towel. She started gurgling, which was followed by a strong cry. He grabbed the phone again. "She's breathing, she's breathing," he said, and with that he heard the fire sirens. "Thank God, they're here," he said to the operator.

"Good luck, sir."

"Thank you, ma'am," he said and let go of the phone and turned to Star.

"You have a baby girl, Starlight. She's beautiful."

"Oh, let me see her!" she cried.

Kory tried to lift the slippery baby up between Star's legs, but the umbilical cord was still attached, and Star was bleeding heavily.

At that moment, the paramedics came through the door. They could hear from the baby's cries that she seemed healthy and strong.

The first paramedic set down his equipment next to Star while two firefighters wheeled in a gurney. "How are you doing, ma'am?" the paramedic asked as he took the baby from Kory to perform a quick Apgar test.

"Okay, but how's my baby?" Star whispered.

"Skin color is coming around, solid heart rate, reflexes okay. You can tell from her crying that her activity and breathing are solid. I'd say she's looks pretty good. How about you?" he asked again as the other paramedic began to take Star's vitals.

Kory answered for her. "She's bleeding a lot down there," he said, still reeling with shock.

"That's pretty normal. Mom looks like she's in good shape," the second paramedic noted. "Let's clamp and cut the umbilical cord so she can hold her baby."

While the paramedics were working on the cord and running through another Apgar test, Kory took a wet towel and wiped down Star's face.

"You scared the hell out of me!" he told her with his hands still shaking. "I came in here for a cup of coffee and came out with a baby. She's beautiful, Star . . . you did a magnificent job."

"Thank you, Kory," she whispered, looking into his eyes, but he quickly turned away and stood up.

"Mom, are you ready to hold her?" the paramedic asked.

Star reached out her arms for the bundle and pulled the baby close to her breast. She peeled back the blanket and saw a mass of curly black hair. "She is beautiful, isn't she, Kory?"

"Of course. She's yours. What are you going to name her?" he asked softly.

"Rosa. Rosa Leonardo Nox."

"You're wonderful. Leo will be so proud," he said, still avoiding her eyes.

"Your wife is about ready to go to the hospital," the paramedic said, standing up. "Dad, you can follow behind the ambulance."

Kory bent down and kissed Star on the forehead. "Take care of both of you, Star. I'll get Leo and bring him to the hospital," he whispered. He followed the stretcher out the door and watched as they were loaded into the back of the ambulance. Once the sirens were turned on and the vehicle pulled away, he walked back into Leo's and sat down at the bar to get a hold of himself. He dropped his hands in his head and tried desperately to push back the waves of emotion that were washing through him. "Don't think about her," he whispered. "Don't think another thought. You have no right." As the words fell away, he began to weep. This was the first time he had cried since his tour of duty in Bosnia when he found the mother still cradling her child in the tangled bones of the mass grave.

When the tears stopped flowing, Kory was able to push back thoughts of Star to the dark corners of his mind where he kept his feelings locked up and safely guarded. His decision to move on with his life had been made. Nothing more was to be considered. He blew his nose, stood up and headed out the door to find Leo as he had promised.

Star drew her fingers through Rosa's black curls, counted her toes twice, caressed her delicate lips and cheeks, and welcomed her child with the most certain and deepest love that she would ever receive. Star was confident that the attachment born with her daughter in those early hours was so profound that nothing, including death, would ever break their connection. And for the first time in her life, Star was truly and completely happy.

Enveloped in her glee, Star almost missed the familiar sound of Leo's shuffle, echoing down the hall. Her eyes flew toward the door, though, just as Kory walked in with Leo by his side.

"Oh! Nonno Leo! Come and meet your little girl!" she exclaimed.

Tears were already trickling down Leo's face as he approached the bed. He grabbed the guard rails to steady his legs then reached out to touch the baby's dark ringlets. "Look at all the curls . . . She looks just like Nella," he whispered. "Il primo amore non si scorda mai."

Star looked up at him quizzically.

"You never forget your first love, Stella," he said, patting the baby's back.

"Meet my first love, Leo. Rosa Leonardo Nox," she said proudly. "You can call her Rosie."

Kory stepped up, put his hand on Leo's shoulder, and with his best effort, smiled broadly. "Welcome to this beautiful, unpredictable world, Rosie," he said.

CHAPTER 21

Succulent red apples . . .

October 1998

S tar laughed at the mass of curls bouncing in Rosie's face as she scrambled down the long steps of St. Mary Magda-lene School. She bent down and held out her arms, ready to catch Rosie as she approached the last few steps.

"Hey, Rosebud! Jump!"

With three steps to go, Rosie jumped into her mother's arms, they hugged and then the little girl squirmed to get down.

"Mommy, let go. I have to show you something."

As soon as Star set her on the ground, Rosie pulled off her Barney backpack and tugged open the zipper. From the bottom, she pulled out a carefully designed collage of autumn leaves, orange construction paper and paste.

"I made it for you," she said, handing the picture to Star.

"Oh, my gosh! Where did you find such beautiful leaves?"

"Miss Jenny took us on a walk. Tommy couldn't go because he wiped a booger on Sarah."

"That's too bad."

"Yeah. He cried. I gave him some of my leaves."

"I meant that it was too bad for Sarah."

"Nope! She stole his red marker."

"How do you know that?"

"He got new markers for his birthday. Sarah's red doesn't work."

"Are you sure about that?

"Yes, Mommy! I used her marker when we made apples yesterday."

"Well, stealing seems to be worse than booger-wiping, don't you think?" asked Star.

"Yeah," Rosie agreed as she skipped off to the car.

When Rosie and Star arrived at Leo's that day, the carpenter was working on the finishing touches of a cherry wine rack that was being installed between the bar and the front window. Over the past few years, the college neighborhood had transformed into a cool, urban quarter dressed in renovated Victorian row houses and flashy BMW's that lined the streets. In addition to Starbucks, a high-end pastry shop had moved in two doors down from Leo's while a trendy new sushi bar sat directly across the street. Though the coffee shop still possessed its old-world charm, the new clientele was looking for sleek and sophisticated. To beat the competition, Star decided to give them what they wanted. Leo's Coffee shop was becoming Leo's Wine and Piano Bar. All the marble-top café tables and wire heart chairs had been replaced with tall, cherry-stained tables and tasteful stools. Low tables were to be placed in front of the wine rack to form a crescent around a piano that would be in full view from the street. She had already booked several local jazz groups through the winter and paid a ridiculous sum to have *R. U. Sinful* play opening night.

Rosie darted over to the carpenter as soon she ran through the door. "Hi, Charlie," she shouted over his scratchy wood sanding. "Can I help?"

"Certainly," the carpenter said, putting down the sanding block. "But first, tell me how school was today."

"Tommy got a time-out for wiping a booger on Sarah, but Mommy said Tommy was right because Sarah stoled his marker."

"Your mom's probably right," Charlie said as he grabbed a piece of scrap wood and set it on his tool box. "Are you ready to get to work?"

"Yeparoo!" she said, jumping up and down.

"Take this block and sand, just like I am," he said and then lightly stroked the wood. She took the block in her hand, bit her lip, and slowly, but surely began to sand down the wood.

While Rosie was busy with Charlie, Jimmy came in with a large portfolio containing the layouts for the new signage and logo designs for Leo's. He wore a camel-hair sport coat with a pale pink shirt and soft, glen-plaid trousers. His light brown hair was neatly trimmed, and his brown loafers gleamed with polish. He had joined Apex Graphic Design a few years back and was doing quite well.

He bent down to Star, giving her the familiar double-kiss on her cheeks. "How's my favorite girl?" he asked.

"Frazzled! The opening is in sixteen days, Jimmy, and we still have no logo or signage."

Opening the portfolio across the bar, he assured her, "Approve the copy, and you can hang your hat on the sign next week. You're going to love it. We developed a crisp, classic look. With the renovations and income growth in the neighborhood, you don't want to scream "college bar." You want to announce, 'Edgy, young, professional wine bar, the cool place to hang if you are *a somebody*.'"

As they paged through sample logos, Star was drawn to the design that had a tall black tree set to the left of the copy. Its branches reached to the right, creating a canopy over the lettering. Dangling from a single branch was a succulent red apple, and just below the fruit was "Leo's Piano & Wine Bar" in sophisticated black print.

"What do you think?" Jimmy asked, pointing to the apple. "Sin hanging within your reach . . . ready to be plucked and tasted."

Star slowly smiled. "Jimmy, this was worth the wait. I do love it. Leo is going to go nuts over the apple."

Star selected a form-fitting, red sheath dress with a deep neckline and a slit up the leg for the grand opening of Leo's. Her dark curls were tamed in a loose bun with errant ring-lets falling around her shoulders. She looked in the mirror and smiled with satisfaction. She had earned this night. She deserved it.

"Mommy, you look like a princess," Rosie whispered as she watched her mother brush on finishing touches of blush and mascara.

"Thank you, Rosebud. You look like a princess, too. Do you like your new dress?"

"I love it!" she exclaimed, twirling around in black patent Mary Jane's and folds of red velvet. At the age of five, Rosie was a brighter version of the little girl that Officer Tony had discovered under a Tenderloin bench twenty-four years before. She wore a massive head of black curls much like her mother but had chocolate-brown eyes instead of Star's evergreen hue. She was salty like her mother, but her manner was carefree. Rosie had none of the burdens that Star carried by the age of four.

"Run downstairs to see if Grandpa Leo is ready. There might be a surprise outside waiting for you," Star whispered with penned-up excitement.

Rosie spun around and bolted out the bedroom door, yelling for Leo. Star smiled with great joy. Her little family still lived in the comfortable bungalow she had purchased five years before. As her trust fund continued to grow, she could have easily purchased a statement house, a trophy that said she was finally *a somebody*, but she chose to stay in the quiet security of their small home. She sat down on the bed that evening to calm her nerves and to gather her thoughts before the night began. She closed her eyes and took in a deep breath, but unexpectedly, life on Turk Street came rushing in, blindsiding her. She shook her head, trying to clear her mind, but the memories fought back. The Tenderloin seemed so far away on most days, but at times like this, the District snuck back, taunting her, warning her not to enjoy life too much. The sins and demons of those times were dormant for now, but they could easily awaken at anytime. For the most part, she was able to ignore the threatening voices. In the past five years, she had seized happiness and held tight . . . and was almost certain that she had won the battle.

Star shook her head again and quickly stood up to repossess herself. When she walked down the steps and into the living room, Leo, Rosie and Meg, the babysitter, were all kneeling on the couch and peering out the window. Rosie heard her mother and squealed, "Mommy, there's a giant car outside! Come look!" Star hurried over and looked out the window with the rest of them.

"Our magic pumpkin is here! Let's go!" she beamed, almost as excited as her daughter. Star grabbed Leo's cane, and as he was unfolding himself from the couch, she asked if he liked the limousine.

"A little out of character for you, Stella. But for me, a stretch limo is perfecto," he said, straightening his tie.

"Jimmy said you either go big or go home," Star insisted. "We're going big! Wait until you see the guest list Ted and he compiled. It's the 'who's who' of Cincinnati."

"How does Jimmy know anybody?" Leo asked.

"It's Ted's doing. Remember, he's an entertainment lawyer."

"Let's go! Let's go!" Rosie interrupted, growing impatient. "Grandpa, hold my hand. I'm sitting next to you."

When the limousine arrived at Leo's, Ted and Jimmy were at the door greeting guests. Ted was Jimmy's partner who was also Star's business lawyer. He was in his mid-forties, tall and slender with dark, short-cropped hair. He wore only hand-tailored suits and Italian shirts. More notable, however, was the fact that he knew *everyone* who was important to know in Cincinnati. Ted hurried down the steps to help Leo out of the car while Rosie crawled out behind him, dragging his cane along with her. Jimmy walked down and reached for Star's hand as she stepped out of the door in her siren-red dress. As she took his hand, the long slit of her gown fell open, exposing thirty-two inches of leg. "You look sinfully delicious, my dear. Almost tempting enough to make me leave Ted and marry you."

"I'm not the marrying kind, Jimmy. Stick with Ted, but don't leave my side tonight. I'm a nervous wreck," she whispered.

As Star and Leo entered the bar, the crowd hushed and then began clapping with generous approval. Overwhelmed, Star quickly scanned the room, looking for familiar faces. She first spotted Bob Garrison standing at the bar. He raised a glass of scotch to her as their eyes met. She smiled with some relief. Ricky and Kevin were at a four top, chatting with their pretty wives. They waived when she caught their attention. She scanned the room once more but was disappointed when she couldn't find Kory. Leo and she hadn't seen much of him in the past year or so as he was buried under managing Emmy and her father's medical supply company. If he didn't show up tonight, Star knew that both Leo and Rosie would be greatly disappointed. She tugged on Jimmy's ear to ask if he had arrived.

"No, but look who *is* here. That's Mark Hanson, the quarterback for the Bengals," he said, pointing to a divine man in a double-breasted suit. "Standing next to him is Mad Mikey-Mike, the DJ from Q103.3. And, the mayor's in the back with her own entourage. Star, what more could you want?" he asked, pulling her toward the crowd.

"Where did you find him, Jimmy? Ted's flipping amazing," Star said appreciatively. "He knows everybody."

"Ted *is* delicious, but look over there!" he directed, turning toward the piano. "There's Reverend Jan, the megachurch star. Ted just signed him with a major Sunday morning cable show. It's national. Didn't you take a class or two with him back in the day?"

Suddenly, Star grew ice cold. "Where's Rosie, Jimmy? Where's Rosie?" she demanded instinctively.

"Calm down. She's already at the bar with Ted and Leo, talking to the manager of the Reds, for God's sake."

Star turned to the bar and saw Leo's hand firmly set behind Rosie's back as she sipped on a Shirley Temple. Leaning forward with his good ear, he was hanging onto every word the man was saying about the Reds. The hand gesticulations told her that it was some epic story about a World Series or something of that nature. *Breathe, just breathe. You can handle this*, she said to herself.

"Oh, look again, Star," Jimmy said. "Sir Gawain, the gallant knight, and Lady Bertilak have just arrived. When is he going to stop wearing that damned uniform? He makes all the other men in the room look like pussies," Jimmy insisted. "Ted thinks he's hotter than hell."

"I think you just answered your own question," Star said, still trying to recover from the initial shock of seeing Janus in the same room as Rosie.

"He *does* look good," Jimmy conceded. "Why he married Miss Bells-and-Whistles, I'll never know. I really thought you two had a thing."

Jimmy's chatter was irritating Star, for she was having difficulty regaining her equilibrium and devising a plan to handle Janus without making a scene. Why wasn't she told that he was invited? She approved the final guest list, and his name was nowhere on it.

"Hello! Are you listening to anything I'm saying, Star?" Jimmy prodded.

"Of course, I am," she said, refocusing.

"Well, listen up. Here comes the Reverend J, himself, and his dynamite wife."

"Star Nox!" she heard from behind her. "Look at this place. Trista would be so proud of you right now." Star cringed as Hillary Heisman's words rang through the air. She slowly turned around and greeted the perfectly coiffed couple. Janus wore a black double-breasted suit while Hillary wore a strapless, black velvet cocktail dress that looked exquisite against her blonde hair.

"Hillary. Reverend Perfidius. Welcome to Leo's," she said, glaring into Janus' eyes. "This is quite an honor to have the Most Reverend Janus Perfidius at Leo's."

He nodded, but his wife was not so coy. "I told you five years ago that he was going to be glorious. Fifteen thousand followers in Cincinnati, alone! No one is permitted to know, but he just signed a national deal with a cable company. On television! Can you believe that, Star?"

Star pressed her fingers to her lips and said, "I promise not to tell a soul. How is your daughter, Katie Ann," she asked with firm lips.

"Little thing's been sick lately. Must be the flu," Hillary explained while her husband stood silent.

"I'm sorry to hear that."

"That's grade school for you. Germs everywhere. Don't you have a little one?" Hillary asked.

"Yes. Her name is Rosie, which was Trista's middle name. She's at the bar with Ted," Star said, not taking her eyes off of Janus as he turned to look at his daughter. The man was devoid of all emotion.

"What do you think about my daughter, Reverend Perfidius?" Star pressed.

"Lovely" was all he offered.

Star thanked them for coming and excused herself to greet other guests. Throughout the night, however, she kept one eye on Janus and the other on Rosie, making certain their paths would not cross.

She spotted Kory and Emmy working their way through the crowd and headed toward them. The years had softened Star's edge with Emmy, but dissatisfaction with her own life seemed to harden Emmy's attitude toward Star. Leo had been right. When the going got tough with the military, Emmy resented Kory's time away. Tension had been heating up in the Middle East, and Kory was spending a lot of time between the States and Afghanistan.

Six months had passed since Star had last seen him, but Jimmy's assessment of Kory was correct. His deep tan set against the Marine Blues looked devastatingly sexy.

"Kory! Emmy!" Star proudly hailed as the two approached. "What do you think about Leo's now? It's come a long way in the past fifty years!" She leaned forward, kissed Emmy's cheek and quickly hugged Kory.

He gazed around the room with approval. "Star, you've transformed her again. The place *is* unbelievable."

"Thank you, Kory. We're so glad to have you back," she said with all sincerity. "And you're killing Jimmy in that uniform. He thinks you're damn hot!"

Kory laughed, but Star noticed Emmy raise her eyebrow in disapproval. *The woman never stops judging.* "Don't worry, Emmy," she quipped. "Jimmy's taken by the most eligible bachelor in Cincinnati, Ted Richards. Your mother certainly knows who he is."

"Yes, I know Ted, as well. I'm not worried about Jimmy. I was simply thinking that Kory needs to buy a new suit and stop playing soldier. That's all."

Star was stunned by her words. "Stop playing soldier, Emmy? That's his job, part of his profession!"

"Don't worry, Star. She doesn't mean anything by it," Kory said, pulling Emmy close to him. "The years in and out of the States have been hard on her. My duty is coming to an end, though. Final discharge is in December."

"We'll all be glad to have you back to stay, especially Rosie," Star added, but not without noticing how Emmy edged away when Kory touched her.

Star was relieved when Jimmy summoned her to greet other guests, for she wanted no part of the sticky heat that was simmering between the couple. This was her night for once, not Emmy Dribble's.

Star smiled broadly and her green eyes glistened as Jimmy guided her around the bar to meet and greet. She was struck with a certain pang of jealousy when he introduced her to a couple of writers. Maybe someday she would sit down and tell *her* own story, but somehow she knew that there were many more chapters ahead of her before the time was right to put her life on paper.

Her private reverie was interrupted by a gentle tug at the knee of her dress. "Mommy, I have to go potty," Rosie whispered up to her. Star looked down and saw Rosie holding herself. She grabbed her daughter's hand and hurried back to the restroom, but Rosie had waited too long to tell her. As Star pushed through the bathroom door, little trickles ran down Rosie's leg. Star lifted her in mid-air, kicked open a stall and sat her on the toilet. As she listened to her daughter tinkle, Star glanced down at her own dress that was wet, as well. Rosie saw the mess and tears began to stream down her face.

"Mommy," she cried. "I ruined your princess dress."

"Don't be silly, honey. My dress will dry," she said, helping Rosie off the toilet. "Come out of the stall, though. We're going to have to take off your stockings. They're all wet."

Rosie stood in silent dismay while Star got down on her knees, unbuckled the black patent shoes and rolled down the damp stockings. "You're not going to have any stockings or underwear on, honey. Are you going to be okay?" she quietly asked. Rosie shrugged her shoulders and nodded her head yes. Just as Star finished up, she heard distinctive whispering outside the bathroom door.

"When can you break away?" the man asked in a low, raspy voice.

"I can't tonight. We drove together," the woman whispered back.

"Tell him you're sick and you want to leave now. He can catch a ride with someone else. Ask Hillary or Star to drive him home. No one will question it. Meet me at the church in an hour. I'm leaving here in thirty minutes."

"Maybe. I don't know. It's too risky tonight."

"Then, tomorrow?"

"Yes, that would be better," the woman confirmed.

Star hung her head and pulled Rosie's belly close to her for support. "Mommy, what's wrong? Are you mad at me?"

Before Star could answer, the door pushed open and in walked Emmy. Without missing a beat, she looked down and exclaimed, "My, my! What's happened here? Made a little mess, Rosie?"

Star stood up, and for the first time, Rosie heard her mother tell a lie. "No, Emmy. Some sloppy drunk spilled a drink on her. Almost ruined my dress and Rosie's." She then took her daughter's hand and headed out the door.

Star found Leo still sitting on the same bar stool, absorbing all the attention but drooping with exhaustion. She rounded up Meg and sent the three home in the limousine while she stayed until the final guests chose to leave.

CHAPTER 22

Broken eggs . . .

The grand opening of Leo's was a bold success, which was only the beginning of its popularity. *Cincinnati Magazine* dubbed it as the Midwestern "SoHo," a cool bistro that would be a likely rage in New York City. *The Business Courier* believed the verve was copied from a Chicago club in Lincoln Park. Then there was the human interest angle, "With Sixty Years Between Them, Unlikely Investors Create a Winning Cocktail." Star believed that Ted was the driving force behind the press, but with lines out the door on weekends and busy weekday nights, she welcomed his help.

Most evenings Star worked no later than eight o'clock. She hired two experienced restaurant managers and paid them well, so she could feel comfortable leaving early enough to put Rosie to bed. On a Tuesday night in early December, The Dave

Mandingo Trio was playing and the place was slammed, so she stayed a little late to clear tables and help some of the servers. As the rush slowed down, Kory surprised Star as he came through the door, without Emmy.

"What are you doing out this late on a Tuesday night. Aren't Marines in bed by nine?" she asked as he took a seat at the bar. She noticed dark circles under his eyes, and his clothes seemed unusually disheveled for Kory.

"I've been kind of restless lately. I needed to get out of the house," he explained.

Star put a cocktail napkin in front of him and poured him a glass of cabernet. "When do you officially hang up your uniform? I thought the date was in December."

"That's been done, for the most part," he said, dropping his head.

"Do you miss it already?" she asked, pouring herself a club soda.

"I don't know. Being a Marine gives you a true sense of purpose, something different from working at Dribble Medical Supply. Don't get me wrong, the company is thriving and the clients are terrific, but running a medical supply company isn't what I saw for myself ten years ago."

"Kory, do you think I ever dreamed of owning a bar? Both my parents were addicts, but life evolves. Embrace what you have," Star said with honest satisfaction.

"Yeah, but you control your own destiny. I don't think I do. What would happen if Emmy woke up and walked out on me one day? I'd be out of a job and a wife." He looked away, raised his glass and took a gulp of wine.

Her heart sank for him. Star tried to forget what she heard behind the bathroom door opening night, but maybe the core of the conversation was rearing its ugly head. "Are Emmy and you going through a rough patch, Kory?" she asked, treading lightly.

"Oh no, it's nothing like that," he reassured her. "It's the military. I feel like I'm losing a good friend, someone I could depend on."

"I know the feeling," Star said quietly, leaning against the bar.

"You do?"

"Yeah, I do, Kory." He was either being obtuse or had forgotten that she lost her best friend in him. Either way, she refused to push him on the issue. Many years had passed and none of that mattered anymore. "You have a wife now, Kory, and she should be your best friend, not the Marines," she told him.

"Emmy *is* my best friend," he said, running his fingers through his short, thick hair. "The service was hard on her, though."

"I understand that, but now you have time to really get to know each other." Star walked around the bar and sat next to him.

"You're right," he said dejectedly.

"Kory, where is Emmy tonight," Star finally asked.

"She's at Passages Community Church working on a social outreach project. The place has been a godsend for her while I've been gone. I think she's made a few good friends."

I bet she has, lamented Star. "How many nights a week does she spend volunteering there?" she asked, taking a sip of soda.

"Maybe three. Sometimes five," he said, toying with the wine glass.

"That's lonely for you. Why don't you go with Emmy? Join some of the programs," she pushed.

"We've talked about it. I don't think she wants me to. I'd be invading her space."

"She must really like the venerable Reverend Jan?" Star asked, inching the questions closer to her target.

"'Awe-inspiring'! She says he's fucking 'awe-inspiring,'" Kory said, taking another big gulp of wine.

"Sounds like I touched a nerve." Star reached out and grabbed his arm. "Tell me what's going on, Kory. I've never seen you this way."

He slowly shook his head in confusion. "I fell in love with Emmy because I was her hero. I need to be somebody's hero, Star. I don't think I'm her hero anymore."

"Are you saying that the Reverend is her hero?"

"No-yes. Not in a sexual way. She's mesmerized by the whole church, including him. I feel like we're in two different worlds."

"Well, that's probably how she felt while you were in the Middle East and Africa."

Kory didn't respond. He sat staring at the wine spinning in circles as he twirled the stem. "You're right," he finally said. "All of this is my fault."

"Kory, that's not what I'm saying. There is no fault here. I'm only trying to figure out what's going on between you two. I'm trying to help."

"Star, I know. I'm sorry," he said and patted her hand.

"There's nothing to be sorry for, but Kory . . . I feel like there is something more, something that's not being said here.

I've just got to ask you—do you think that there is something more than spiritual between Emmy and the Reverend?"

"My God, Star! How could you accuse Emmy of such a thing?" he demanded, jumping to his feet. "I know you two never got along, but to call her a cheat is outrageous."

Star stood her ground. "Calm down. I didn't call her a cheat. I simply asked if their relationship was more than spiritual. The conversation was winding down that road. I'm sorry. Honestly."

Kory sat back down and took another sip of wine. "With your wife gone five nights a week, you might think that she's cheating on you . . . so I asked her that same goddamn question last night, and now I feel like a shit. I was the one who was gone for six months at a shot. Not her."

"Don't beat yourself up over this, Kory. I think it's a fair question. I asked it."

"The question blew up in my face like a land mine. Then, she throws that thing in my lap about Perfidius' sick child. What a selfish piece of shit I am."

"What are you talking about? Is his daughter ill?" Star asked, straightening her back.

"Don't you know? She's got leukemia. They're looking for a bone marrow donor."

"My God, I didn't know . . . I'm shocked," Star said, setting her glass on the bar.

"Yeah. People at the church are volunteering to be tested to see if they're a match. Emmy was tested. You'd think that with fifteen thousand members in the congregation, they'd find somebody."

"Wow, unbelievable. Unbelievable," Star said, shaking her head. "I had no clue. Has she been sick for long?"

"Months. Apparently, it is pretty aggressive. If a donor isn't found soon, it looks like she's not going to make it." Kory rubbed his eyes and sighed. "I really feel like a self-centered shit. The little girl is gravely ill."

"What a horrible shame," Star said sincerely, "But with all those supporters, you would think a match could be easily found."

Meg put Rosie to bed long before Star arrived home that evening. She peeked into her daughter's bedroom and saw black curls sprung across her pillow. Tip-toeing close to the bed, she knelt down to listen to her daughter's breathing. Hillary's pain must be unfathomable, Star thought. Rosie was her world, and she figured that Katie Ann was Hillary's world, as well.

As much as she disliked Emmy at that moment for hurting Kory, her willingness to be tested for a bone marrow match was admirable. She rested her head against Rosie's bed and contemplated being tested. Why not? If Rosie was in that position, she would want every healthy family member, friend and acquaintance to be tested to save her child.

In that moment, Star suddenly sat back on her heels and grabbed her chest. *Oh my dear God,* she thought. Rosie . . . Rosie was Katie Ann's half sister. The room was swirling around her. Why hadn't Janus contacted her? Rosie could be a match. Rosie could save Katie Ann! Why hadn't he contacted her? Why hadn't he contacted her? The question was relentless. Should she contact him? Was he concerned about their confidentiality contract? No, for he certainly wouldn't let that hold him back from saving his daughter. Did she, herself, have a duty to remain silent? But, could she conscionably stay silent knowing that Rosie could be the match? Rosie could be the key to that little girl's life. Her mind was spinning.

Star slowly stood and kissed the pile of curls that slept so peacefully. Rosie looked a little like her father. Their eyes were the same shape and color. She wondered if Katie Ann was light like Hillary or dark like Janus. Either way, Star knew that she could not stand by and allow a child to die, knowing that she could have done something. But on the other hand, images of Rosie in a hospital bed, connected to IVs and monitors, scared her to death. Her heart pounded at the thought of putting her own daughter in any type of danger to save a child she did not know. With her mind racing throughout the night, Star didn't fall asleep until 5 a.m. and was awakened only a few hours later when Rosie snuck into her bedroom and crawled under the covers.

"Mommy," she whispered, "St. Nicholas left M&M's and candy canes in my slippers last night! Did you hear him?"

Star sat up and silently thanked Leo for remembering St. Nicholas's Day. Jack and Sue never celebrated Christmas, let alone a saint's holiday, which made it difficult for her to remember the date.

"No! I didn't hear St. Nick last night. I don't believe it!" Star teased.

"Honestly, Mommy! Look," Rosie said, opening her hand that was filled with chocolate candy.

"Rosebud, it's too early for candy. Hand that over," Star said, reaching out for the M&M's.

"Nope," she giggled and rolled away from her mother.

At that moment, visions of IVs and hospital monitors flashed through Star's mind. She swallowed hard and allowed Rosie the candy.

"Okay. You win but only because I got home late last night and missed putting you to bed. Uncle Kory came to visit. He was sad, so I couldn't leave," Star said, pulling Rosie close to her.

"Why's he sad, Mommy?" Rosie asked.

"Because he's not going to be a soldier anymore, and that's a big change."

"He should be my daddy, then," she concluded.

Star dropped her arm from Rosie's shoulder and peered down at her. "What do you mean, honey?"

"In circle time, Lucy said her daddy helps mommies have babies. Uncle Kory helped you have me."

"Do you think because Uncle Kory helped deliver you, then he should be your daddy?"

"Yeah, that's what Lucy said."

"It doesn't quite work that way, babe. Lucy's dad is a doctor. He helps deliver the babies, but he doesn't make them. And that doesn't make Lucy's dad the father to all those kids. Kory was kind of like a doctor. He was at Leo's when you wanted to come out of my belly. So, he helped me, but that doesn't make him a daddy."

"Oh. Then, why don't I have a daddy?"

"Honey, remember. I've told you. Your daddy was sick and had to go away a long time ago."

"Did he go to heaven?"

"I'm not certain where he went. God has those answers."

Star pushed the blankets away and tapped Rosie on the head. "Hey! First one downstairs gets to wake Leo!"

Rosie scrambled out of bed and ran down the steps to Leo's room. While chatter about St. Nicholas and candy ricocheted up the steps, Star reached for the phone and called information, asking for Passages Community Church. After speaking with the receptionist, she was surprised to be connected directly to his office.

"Janus?" she asked hesitantly.

"Yes. And this is?"

"Star—Star Nox. I'm calling to talk about something terribly important," she said as her hand began to tremble violently.

"We have nothing to talk about."

"I'm not calling about us. I'm calling about Katie Ann. I understand that she needs a bone marrow transplant," Star said as she stood up from the bed.

"Star, stay out of my business," he said sharply. This has nothing to do with you."

"Are you forgetting that we have a child together?" she whispered.

"Stay out of this. I'm warning you."

"Janus, maybe Rosie is a match for your daughter. She could save Katie Ann's life. Don't you understand?" she asked incredulously.

"The person who doesn't understand is you, Star. This is my private life, something that you have absolutely nothing to do with. Do not intrude," he demanded.

"But we may be able to help," she pleaded.

"I'm warning you to stay out of my life," he said and slammed down the receiver.

Star sat back down on the bed in shock. What was he saying to her? How could he not understand that she was trying to help Katie Ann? She dialed the number again and asked to be reconnected, but this time she was denied access to him. My God, she thought, how could she reach him to explain that she wanted nothing to do with his life—that she only wanted to help Katie Ann?

For several minutes Star thought about Rosie and about Katie Ann. She thought about Hillary, too. Would Hillary try to help Rosie if the tables were turned? Of course she would. Hillary was a mother, just like herself. Star jumped up from the bed with determination. She had to help save this little girl if she had the means to do so. She would go to Janus immediately and explain that the confidentiality agreement would be upheld. If Rosie was a match, she would remain anonymous. She needed to tell Janus this face to face.

Star quickly showered and threw on clothes. When she ran into the kitchen, Rosie was standing on her step stool, next to Leo, breaking eggs into a large bowl.

"Mommy, we're making pancakes!"

"Oh, honey. Will you save one for me? I've got to run out for an hour or so," Star explained. "Meg should be here any minute. Will you two be okay?" she asked, turning to Leo who was eye level with Rosie when she was standing on the stool.

Leo tilted his head forward and narrowed his gaze with an omniscient stare. "Stella," he said decisively, "What's the big hurry?"

Star knew that if she stayed a second longer, he would drag answers from her. So, without a pause, she dashed for the door, yelling, "I'll explain when I get back."

Passages Community Church was an imposing place with several ancillary structures adjacent to the central building. Star parked her car in the lot where she spotted a cluster of other vehicles, including a late model black Volvo sedan. "Bingo," she whispered. As she hurried into the main entrance, Star felt as if she was walking into a cool, urban movie theater with the auditorium directly in front of her. Two coffee kiosks were positioned on both the north and south sides of the wide foyer. Small pockets of loveseats and matching chairs were set strategically around the expansive space. Star glanced at the entrance to the auditorium and above the doors hung a large brass plaque emblazoned with "The Dribble Family Auditorium."

"No fucking kidding," she whispered. Her astonishment was interrupted by a woman's voice from behind.

"May I help you?" the woman asked in a nasal, high-pitched voice.

Star turned and saw an attractive blonde in a smart blue suit and brown heels. "Yes. I'm here to see Reverend Perfidius," she said, tucking her purse under her arm.

"Do you have an appointment?" the woman questioned.

"Yes. At nine-thirty," she said, looking down at her watch. "In five minutes."

"Follow me, please."

Star followed the woman down the south hallway past small meeting rooms and well appointed offices. Above each door was a wooden cross surrounded by a circle with curious wavy lines.

"That's an interesting cross," Star said to the lady as she followed her.

"Yes. That's Reverend Jan's vision of the many paths we must cross to reach our savior."

"Well, he's got that right," Star said.

The woman stopped and with an echo of condescension said, "Here we are. His receptionist is through that door."

Star walked into the office and approached a lovely girl seated behind the reception desk. She was wearing a bright pink sweater and a wavy, blonde bob pinned back at her temples with flowered barrettes. *Yet another blonde, Star mused. Wonder how I squeezed into his picture?*

When the Kewpie doll looked up to greet her, Star explained that she was there to see Reverend Perfidius, but the girl immediately turned her away.

"I'm sorry, ma'am. There is nothing on his calendar. Would you like to make an appointment for next Thursday? That is Reverend Jan's first available time slot. He is a very busy man," she said protectively.

"No. There must be some confusion. Reverend Jan asked me to be here at nine-thirty. Maybe he forgot to tell you," Star said, smiling sweetly. "If he is in, please tell him that Star Nox has arrived, right on time as he directed."

The young receptionist looked at her sharply but stood up, knocked gently on the office door and stepped in, closing the door behind her. When she reopened the door, she looked at Star with awkward disapproval and said, "Reverend Jan is ready to see you now."

"You all are friendly bunch, aren't you?" Star commented and walked into the office and closed the door.

Janus didn't bother getting up from his desk to greet her. Instead, he asked, "What do you want, Star, to save your own soul by saving Katie Ann? She's my sacrifice to bear, not yours."

"You've been thinking about this, haven't you, Janus?" she asked, narrowing her stare. "That's not a normal response from a father who may have a chance to save his dying daughter."

"I asked, are you here to repent? If that's the case, I absolve you from all your sins," he offered, leaning forward in his chair.

"What are you talking about? I'm not here to repent. You're not my God! I'm here to help save a child. My relationship with God has nothing to do with you or the reason why I am here," she said, taking a few steps closer to his desk.

"I told you on the phone, stay out of my business, or you will pay."

"Go to hell! Though you probably have one foot stuck in the river already. But, on your way, know that my own conscience won't allow me to stand by and do nothing. If I thought I had the direct power to save a child's life, even your child, I would and will do it."

"Leave me alone. Leave my family alone," he demanded. "I have sinned, and if I have to sacrifice my daughter for my sins, then that is God's plan."

"God doesn't punish like that, Janus. He doesn't punish our children for our sins. He'll punish both of us for eternity if we stand by and let Katie Ann die, knowing we could have saved her."

"You're wrong, Star. This is my judgment to bear in silence. I am a revered minister. Thousands of people receive their spiritual revelations and rebirth through me every week. I cannot destroy their faith because of my own sins," he explained, sitting back in his chair with the palms of his hands pressed together as if in prayer.

"We are talking about a child's life, *your* child's life, not about a congregation of people. Those people are responsible for their own relationship with God. God is where they gain their true strength in faith. They answer to God, not to you. You are only a man, Janus. You are not their God. You are a mortal father who has the chance to save your child's life."

He gripped the arms of his chair and sprang forward. "Stop, Star! Stop what you are doing. This will destroy me. If my followers know that I have fathered a child in sin, they will abandon me. Passages is a movement much bigger than Cincinnati. Passages is a movement across the country, across the globe. Soon, millions of people will follow my word."

"You are disgusting. This is about your ego and your power and your television show and your donations. You are willing to let your child die to retain your own glory."

"You're wrong. Katie Ann is my sacrifice for my sins," he charged, in a throaty growl.

"Yet, you continue to sin, Janus. You're a fraud. I know about your affair with Emmy Dribble. You're nothing but a fraud. You're worse than the slime on the streets who prostitute their kids for drugs. At least they're honest about what they're doing. You are the lowest of the low," she said, now standing just a few feet away from him.

"Star, I'm warning you," he seethed. "Stop what you're doing."

"Fuck you," she said calmly. "You forget—I grew up in the Tenderloin. Your pussy-ass means nothing to me. As soon as I walk out of here, I'm calling Hillary. She either hears it from me, or she hears it from you. That's the only choice you've got, *Reverend*!"

Star turned around and walked out, but before leaving, she stopped at the receptionist's desk for Hillary's number. "Reverend Jan has asked that you give me Hillary's contact information," she said sweetly. "He had to take an emergency call."

Once the girl handed over Hillary's information, Star rushed out the door and headed to her car. She turned on the engine to activate her mobile phone, but before dialing the number, she thought about what she was about to do. This one phone call could annihilate Hillary's marriage as her daughter lay dying in the hospital. And there was the very real possibility that Rosie couldn't help. How would she feel if the woman's marriage was destroyed, but Rosie wasn't a bone marrow match? On the other hand, how would she feel if the child died, and she never made the effort to find out if Rosie could help? Which was more precious to Hillary, her child or her marriage? Janus and Emmy's whispering voices swirled around in her mind. She took a deep breath, reached for the phone and dialed the number written on the pink telephone slip. Star recognized Hillary's voice as soon as she came on the line, though her words were entirely drained of any life.

"Hillary," she began hesitantly. "This is Star Nox."

"Hello," she said softly.

"I understand you're facing a tough challenge right now."

"I am," she said barely above a whisper.

"I would like to talk to you as soon as possible," Star said and took a deep breath. "Rosie and I may be able to help Katie Ann . . . do you have a little time to talk this morning?"

"Thank you for your concern, but this is a bad time. I am walking out the door this minute, headed to Children's Hospital."

"May I meet you there, Hillary? I promise this is important."

"Star, please. I don't mean to be rude, but I need my privacy right now," Hillary said, with her voice cracking.

"Hillary, from one mother to another, please let me see you. I'm pleading with you."

"Okay, then," she said weakly. "I'll wait for you in the hospital lobby, near the gift shop in an hour."

Star found Hillary sitting in the main lobby looking exhausted and pale. The bright colors and tropical zoo animals decorating the walls seemed to give little relief to the anxiety that stretched across her face. Star quietly greeted her and sat down. Before Star had a chance to say a word, however, Hillary explained that Janus had called just before she left the house.

"What did he tell you, Hillary?"

Tears began streaming down her face. She dotted the corners of her eyes with a used tissue. "He said that you two had a brief encounter many years ago when you were his student . . . it meant nothing to him . . . but you ended up pregnant," she murmured, then the tears flowed faster.

Star could not imagine what Hillary was going through at that moment, but she thought that honesty would be the best way to handle the situation. "That is correct, Hillary. I hope he also told you that, at the time, I had no idea he was married," Star said, squeezing her purse.

"He didn't mention that. He only said that there was flirting on your part and that he faltered."

Taking a deep breath to gather her composure, Star chose not to respond to Janus' lie but, instead, explained that she was shocked to discover that he was married, which she learned the night of the Horticultural Society dinner.

"I was overwhelmed, if you remember. After that night, we met with his lawyer. I released him of all parental obligations and agreed to complete confidentiality regarding the paternity. Beyond his lawyer, you are the only other person who knows that Janus is Rosie's father. I would like to keep it that way."

"What do you want, Star? Why are you doing this?" she implored.

"I want to help save a child's life. I have no other motives. I want nothing to do with Janus' life or yours, beyond helping Katie Ann."

"Janus tells me you are seeking salvation through our daughter. He says that you are a sinner and that you want to use Katie Ann as your penance."

Star shifted in her chair and looked directly at the woman. "Listen," she said indignantly, "We're all sinners, and sins are relative. My relationship with God has nothing to do with your family and, especially, with your venerable husband. If you are interested, I will have Rosie tested to determine if she is a bone marrow match. Otherwise, you will never hear from me again. I came to you as one mother to another mother, nothing more. Your marriage is your cross or crown to carry. I never intended to be a part of your marriage six years ago, nor do I now." Star stood up and added, "I greatly apologize for interfering. If you are interested, the offer still stands."

As Star turned and walked away, Hillary jumped up and shouted, "Don't go! Please help my daughter! We can talk with the transplant team right now."

Star turned back around, and within a quarter of an hour, they were meeting with an expert from the bone marrow transplant team where they both learned much more about tissue typing, which was more formally called human leukocyte antigen (HLA) typing. Dr. Sherman explained that since Rosie and Katie Ann had the same father, four of their eight antigens could match. However, with two different mothers, there was a one in a million chance that the other four antigens would be a perfect match, as well.

"Ms. Heisman, with the same biological parents, the chance of a sibling match is twenty-five percent, but in Katie Ann's case, the chance of a perfect match is similar to a grandparent match, which is extremely rare."

"But do matches ever occur, doctor?" asked Star.

"I've seen a grandparent match twice in my career," he confirmed. "Similar ethnic and racial backgrounds play a significant role in HLA gene matches, as well."

"Oh," Star said grimly. "I'm Irish and German, Hillary. I know you've got some German blood in you, but how about Irish. You've got to be Irish."

Hillary looked up sadly, but confirmed that her mother was an O'Sullivan. Star took Hillary's hand in hers and squeezed hard. The only thing that she could think about was that she just destroyed this woman's marriage for a one-in-a-million chance at saving Katie Ann's life. Was Janus right? Was she trying to be the hero for her own damn sake? No, she thought.

There was a force driving this that was much bigger than her ego or her desire for redemption.

"If the stars line up perfectly straight, who is to say that Rosie can't be the perfect match, or close to a perfect match?" added Dr. Sherman. "Seven of the eight antigens could match, which would work for us. It's only one blood test away from knowing the answer. You can have Rosie's test drawn tonight or tomorrow."

"Doctor," Star began. "Something tells me that my daughter is a perfect match. I don't know if it's a mother's intuition, hope, fate, or divine intervention, but I believe that Rosie can help Katie Ann."

"Let's hope so," he said with little optimism. "But, Ms. Nox, if she is a match, I want you to know the risks to the donor. Though the risks are very slight, you should think long and hard about the process. There are two types of treatment, bone marrow extraction and peripheral blood stem cell transplant. The marrow extraction is done under a general anesthetic, so Rosie wouldn't feel anything, but later, she may suffer from lower back pain, fatigue and stiffness. In about one percent of all cases, there is damage to the muscle, nerve or bone at the extraction site, which is the hip."

"What's the blood transplant option?" asked Star.

"It's a process that is similar to donating blood. In order to collect a sufficient quantity of stem cells, injections are given to mobilize stem cells to travel from the bone marrow into the circulating blood. The stem cells are collected through a procedure where a cell separating machine filters out the stem cells. The good thing with this process is that no anesthesia is required. The amount of blood we take is less than one quart, and it won't weaken Rosie's immune system. I will give you plenty of literature on both processes."

"Okay. That would be helpful, but I do have another question."

"Yes, Ms. Nox?" he said, leaning forward in his chair.

"Due to the delicate circumstances, I want to make certain that we can maintain strict confidentiality about the donor's identity. For my daughter's sake and the Perfidius' privacy, I do not want Rosie's identity revealed."

"That is standard procedure. I can assure the strictest privacy," and for the first time, the doctor offered her a gentle smile.

"Well, then, I will bring Rosie here tomorrow for the blood test. Does that work for you, Hillary?"

She looked up with a dismal smile and said, "Please. It can't hurt."

When the two women walked out of the doctor's office and into the hall, an awkward silence separated them.

"Thank you, Star," Hillary finally said.

"None of this is comfortable, Hillary. But as one mother to another, I am on your side."

Later that night after Star put Rosie to bed, she went back downstairs to talk with Leo. She hated to interrupt him while he was watching *Home Improvement*, but she couldn't hold it in any longer. "Leo, do you think I can tear you away from the show for a few minutes? I've got something I need to talk with you about," she said, sitting down on the couch.

He grabbed the remote and turned down the volume. "Surely, Stella," he said. "But if it is something bad, I'm going back to Tim Allen," he teased.

Star didn't smile and said, "I wish it was something good."

Leo came forward in Nella's rocker, landing with both feet firmly on the floor. "Is something wrong with you?"

"No, Leo, it's not me," she said, slipping her hands between her knees. "Nor is it Rosie. It's another little girl."

He sat back in the rocker and let out his breath. "You had my heart racing for a second, not that I want to hear about any sick child. Is this one of Rosie's classmates?"

"No. Her name is Katie Ann, Hillary Heisman's daughter."

He looked at her with a blank look, so she went on to explain that he had met Hillary at Leo's grand opening with her husband, Reverend Perfidius.

"Oh," he said shortly. "I'm sorry to hear that. I'll keep the little one in my prayers to the Santa Madre," he said and pointed the remote at the TV.

"Wait, Leo. That's not all. They are looking for a bone marrow donor. Katie Ann has leukemia."

"Like I said, I'll prayer for her," he said, raising the volume.

"But Leo, what if Rosie could help Katie Ann?"

"She'll pray, too" was all he said and turned backed to the show.

"Leo, what if there is more we can do—like what if Rosie's bone marrow is a match for the little girl? She could save her life." Star grabbed a pillow and squeezed it hard.

"There's no reason why she would be a match, so let's stop talking about it," he snapped.

"Leo! Leo, listen to me! What if Rosie is Katie Ann's half sister?"

"Stella," he slowly began. "Six years ago we agreed to remain silent about the serpente. Remain silenzioso! Zitto! Say no more. There is no point in digging up dried shit now."

"Leo, whether we like it or not, sometimes you have to stir up shit to help other people."

"Listen here, Star! That serpente did niente, nothing to help you. It broke my heart. You are a proud woman, and I respect that, but I respect nothing about that man. You're not risking Rosie's life to help a man who abandoned his own daughter."

"Leo, it's just a blood test, and if Rosie is a match, she will most likely donate blood rather than bone marrow. The risk to Rosie is very small. She may be tired for a few days but not much more. In only twenty percent of the cases do doctors extract actual bone marrow, and the risk is still slight."

"Sorry, Starlight. Any risk is too much risk in my book, especially for a man who abandoned Rosie. I'll say this once and only once. You cannot make Rosie pay for the sins of her parents. That is wrong."

This was the first time in years that Leo had used her given name. His disdain was painful. Tears welled up in Star's eyes and spilled over, running down her cheeks. "Leo," she whispered. "That is the cruelest thing that you have ever said to me."

"Star, you know I love you more than I love my own life, but I won't let you risk Rosie's life. Never!" he yelled.

Star struggled to maintain her composure. She took a deep breath and continued. "I don't look at the situation in the same way. My belief is that, in spite of my sins, I could never let this little girl die if Rosie could save her."

Leo crossed his arms and shook his head. "You will regret this decision for the rest of your life. Si pentirai!"

"Leo, listen," she cried. "There are scores of terrible decisions that I have made in my life that I fall asleep thinking about and wake in the morning still contemplating. Letting a little girl die, knowing that I may have had the power to help, would be the worst decision of my life."

"Seems to me you made up your mind. There's nothing else to talk about," he said, pointing the remote at the television and raising the volume even higher.

Leo stayed in his room the next morning while Star talked to Rosie about going to the hospital. She used a baby doll to explain how she might be able to help another little girl become healthy, just by getting poked with a needle. Rosie didn't quite understand what Star was talking about. The only words that she hung onto were those that promised ice skating after the hospital visit.

CHAPTER 23

Bottom of a wine glass . . .

Star was busy at the bar making flower arrangements with holly and red roses while the servers prepped their stations for the night. With *Soul Sista* playing that evening, the place would be slammed from Happy Hour until closing, so she wanted everything well-oiled before four o'clock. As she hurried through the flowers, Star checked off her mental Christmas list that still included a Tickle Me Elmo doll for Rosie and something clever for Jimmy and Ted. Her holiday angst was distracted by the jingle of Leo's sleigh bells that still hung on the door after fifty years. She looked up and was surprised to see Kory walk through the door, especially so early in the evening. His pin-striped suit seemed to constrict his stride as he approached her. A body like his was made for jeans or military gear, Star thought, not Emmy's hand-selected uniform.

He sat down at the bar with a thud. "Is it too early for a drink?" he asked without a greeting.

Star shook her head no and asked the bartender, who was busy slicing lemons, to pour a cabernet. "The cheapest we've got," she half teased.

"I wouldn't know the difference," he said, looking at the vases. "Need some help?"

"Why? Is the medical supply business slow today?"

Kory undid the top button of his shirt and loosened his tie. "No. We're busy. I'm just tired of going home to an empty house."

Star stopped arranging the vases and peered up at him. "Kory, is Emmy still consumed with Passages five days a week?"

"At least five days," he said and then gave a thankful nod to the bartender for the drink. He took a sip of wine and added, "It seems like she's there day and night."

"Maybe you should join her every once and a while or drop by some night. Get involved," she said, returning to the flowers.

"She doesn't want me there. She's made that loud and clear. I had my space in the military. Now, she has hers at Passages."

"Has she been at the church during the last week or two, while Katie Ann's been so sick?"

"Sure. I asked her about that, but she says that Reverend Jan visits his daughter during the day. His wife sleeps most nights at the hospital."

"I see" was all Star said, returning to the last vase that needed flowers. She finished with the arrangement, stood up from her stool and handed two vases to Kory. "Do you want to help set these on the tables?"

Kory slowly rose to his feet and began distributing the flowers around the room. Star kept him at a distance to avoid any further discussion about the daily routine of his marriage, but knowing that he was being taken for a fool still tore her apart. His blind acceptance of Emmy's chicanery was disturbing. She thought Kory was a stronger man, a man who wouldn't choose to deceive himself like this. She already took the chance and led him down the path with questions about Emmy's faithfulness, but he exploded with an attack directed at her, instead of his wife. Star was half-entangled in the mess, as it was. Kory would have to handle Emmy on his own, she decided.

When he returned to his seat at the bar, though, Kory started up the conversation once again. "Star, you're a woman and you know Emmy. So, tell me something. What does she get from that church that she can't get with me?" he asked, picking up his glass, emptying the wine in just a few gulps.

"That was an expensive cabernet," she said. You're supposed to sip it," she said flatly.

"I'll sip the next one," he said, waving to the bartender.

"Kory, slow down. It's not like you to throw down drinks."

"Well, maybe if I had a wife who came home at night, I wouldn't have to drown my loneliness in booze."

"That's tired and trite," she said, moving closer, glaring down on him. "If Emmy's not coming home at night for some reason or another, go home and figure it out, because you're not going to find any answers in the bottom of that wine glass."

"That's a real sympathetic ear," he sneered.

"No. It's called honesty, Kory, honesty. I care about you too much to see you crash and burn. This is how I see it. You feel guilty about your time in the service, so now you're willing to accept any sound bites that she feeds you, just to keep her happy. That's not like you. Be a man, because, as a woman, I'm certain that she wants a man."

"What 'sound bites' are you talking about?" he said, leaning across the bar.

"That's between Emmy and you. I have no idea. But if my husband wasn't coming home at night because he liked church better than me, I'd march straight to that church and figure out why."

Kory stood up, pulled his wallet from his back pocket and took out a ten-dollar bill. "I don't want your free advice tonight," he said then turned around and walked out the door, with the sleigh bells jingling behind him.

A few days had passed since their visit to the hospital for the blood draw. Star woke early with Rosie to make French toast for Leo as a peace offering. Standing on her step stool, Rosie carefully dipped bread slices into an egg wash while Star buttered the pan and began to fry the bread. Rosie sprinkled powdered sugar and cinnamon on each piece as Star removed them from the skillet. Once she was satisfied with the presentation, Rosie jumped from her stool and went howling for Leo. The phone started to ring at the same time. Star answered it with a perky "Good morning! Happy Holidays," but at the other end, she received a stern greeting asking to speak with 'Ms. Nox.'

"Yes, this is Star Nox. May I help you?"

"Ms. Nox, this is Dr. Sherman from the Children's Hospital Medical Center."

"Yes, doctor. I've been hoping that you would call soon. I've been waiting on pins and needles." Star leaned against the refrigerator while she listened to what the doctor had to say.

"Well, Ms. Nox, your mother's intuition paid off. Rosie is the one-in-a-million. There is an eight of eight antigen match which means that there is a match at A, B, C, and DRB1 markers. This is truly a miracle for Katie Ann. We would like to proceed with a bone marrow extraction instead of the peripheral blood stem cell process, which is still somewhat investigative."

"My God," she whispered, with her full weight pressed against the refrigerator. Her heart was pounding in her chest while her body began to shake violently with the same beat.

"Are you still prepared to give your consent, Ms. Nox?"

"Yes," she answered, squeezing the phone receiver. "I'm overwhelmed, doctor . . . I'm overwhelmed . . . this is unbelievable . . . but I'm . . . I'm worried for Rosie."

"That is understandable," he said perfunctorily. "But let me tell you what will transpire with Rosie."

"Go ahead," Star said, still shaking.

Dr. Sherman explained that Rosie would first receive an overall physical to determine her state of good health. She would then be scheduled to arrive at the hospital early in the morning for an overnight stay and receive general anesthesia to block the pain. During the donation, she would be lying on her stomach while the doctors made one to four very small incisions over the area of her pelvic bone. A syringe would be attached to a needle to draw out the marrow. She would be closely monitored as she awakened from the procedure and then closely followed for several weeks to detect any side effects, which typically were minor.

By the time the doctor wrapped up the explanation, Star's breathing had calmed.

"Doctor," she quietly said, "I have a question."

"Yes?"

"Am I risking my child's life? Am I making a decision that I will regret forever?"

"Ms. Nox, other than temporary fatigue and achiness, the side effects are minimal. I can't say that there are zero risks as anesthesia is involved. However, I would make the same decision if I were in your shoes."

"Okay, then. We'll move forward."

Leo was outraged at Star's decision, but on the day of the procedure, the only place where he wanted to be was by her side. The doctors had given Rosie a book and two dolls to help her understand the procedure. However, five-year-old oblivion and thoughts of Santa Claus seemed to ease her fears more than anything.

The waiting room was filled with beleaguered couples hoping to hear that their child would be back to making snowmen in the front yard by Christmas Day. Star noticed a lot of hand-holding and hugs shared among the husbands and wives. One woman dressed in a peach velveteen sweat suit was resting against her husband while another kept patting her husband's leg seemingly to convince them both that everything was going to be okay. Pangs of jealousy struck her as she watched the couples share their struggles together. But when she looked at the soft wrinkles etched on Leo's face, she was comforted. Fate had pulled them together, and for that she was thankful.

While Star was studying the hands on the clock and Leo was dozing, Hillary Heisman walked in the waiting room, carrying Starbucks's coffee and rolls. On a different day, Star would have taken anything from Starbucks and dumped it in the garbage, but not on this day. Quietly, she looked up and greeted Hillary, who sat down next to her. Hillary handed her a cup of coffee and a donut, and then the two women sat in silence.

Eventually, Hillary tried to express her gratitude, but Star interrupted her. "Please don't. There is no need to thank me. I understand. Words aren't needed right now."

"Star, but you *don't* understand. Katie Ann was my last hope. We tried fertility treatments for years with no success, and then, unexpectedly, she fell from heaven. I'm almost forty-five. Katie Ann is my life. You saved two lives today."

"No. Rosie did."

"Yes. Rosie, your brave little girl," Hillary said, falling back into silence. She toyed with her purse straps and turned the rings on her fingers for a few moments, but finally, she looked up at Star and asked if she would like to meet Katie Ann.

Star shook her head no. "This isn't the best time. I need to figure out how I plan to handle the situation as Rosie grows up. Today's procedure will eventually dim in her memory, but neither of us can deny that they are half-sisters, living in the same city. Someday you and I will have to come to terms with that fact, but now is not the time."

"You're probably right but, but . . . Star . . . Janus is now convinced that your encounter with him was divine intervention. He told me that God sent you to him as a sacrificial lamb to save our daughter."

Star bolted upright in her seat in utter disbelief, ready to unload, but then she stopped. *Breathe, just breath, she kept repeating to herself. Don't unleash on this woman; she has to accept her husband's lies for her own survival. Think of Katie Ann, not Janus. Calm down. Just breathe.*

With her back still stiff, Star eventually regained her composure and explained, "I crossed paths with your husband for some reason or another, but my plan was never to cross paths with him again. I made that decision six years ago when I relinquished Janus from all parental obligations. Revealing the connection beyond the transplant is not something I want, especially now, nor would the revelation be good for your husband's career." Star added the last few words with exaggerated concern that was lost on the woman.

Hillary thanked her one last time and then excused herself to return to Katie Ann. When she was out of earshot, Leo opened his eyes and sat up straight. "Asino! She's a donkey's ass!" he charged. "You—a sacrificial lamb! That's insane!"

Star gently slapped his leg. "Calm down and ignore her. Someone may hear you. Hillary needs to believe her husband right now. Ignorance by choice is a coping mechanism. Unfortunately, it seems to be a popular trend right now," she said with her voice falling away.

When the doctor finally walked into the waiting room, he was smiling. "The extraction was a great success," he explained. "The entire procedure went off perfectly, except for one hitch."

The color washed from Star's face, and Leo grabbed her hand. "What?" she demanded.

"I promised Rosie that Santa was going to bring her a Tickle Me Elmo for being so brave. My daughter wants one for Christmas, too, but my wife said they're impossible to find."

"If I have to call *Sesame Street*, I'll find one for her," Star said with a wide smile.

"That's a good idea, and you've got an excellent reason. Rosie's beginning to rouse in recovery and will be taken to her room. Plan on meeting us there in less than an hour," he said and turned to go back to the recovery room.

Star and Leo grabbed a bite to eat in the cafeteria and then headed to Rosie's room. As they were walking down the main hall to catch the elevators, she spotted his broad shoulders and wavy dark hair. "Jesus, Mary and Joseph! Do we have to deal with him today, too?" she growled.

"Who?" Leo asked, looking around.

"The venerable Reverend Jan, Leo. That's who! Look! He's straight ahead, walking toward the elevators."

Leo stopped his slow shuffle to let Janus step into the elevator. "Don't worry. You won't have to deal with the snake today," Leo said protectively. "I should have beaten him with my bat when I had the chance."

"Okay, Mr. Tough Guy, can I feel your muscles?" she teased.

"Don't test me! My knees may be weak, but I still have my swing."

"Oh, I believe you. I've watched you do pushups, but let's go. He's gone," Star said and moved toward the elevators. She pressed the 6th floor, and when the doors opened, Janus was standing directly in front of them at the nurses' station.

"My God! What's he doing here?" she demanded. "This isn't the oncology floor."

As they stepped off the elevator, Janus turned and walked toward them. "Star," he said, extending his hand, "I came here to personally thank you for your generosity. The doctors tell me the procedure was a great success. You truly are one of God's golden lambs."

"Put your hand down, Janus. I'm not interested in shaking it, and cut the crap about the sacrificial lamb. We both know what I really am. I'm your scapegoat."

"I came here offering thanks and peace," he said with his face turning red.

"Don't bother. You can't play your holier-than-thou crap with me. I've learned to see right through your bogus act. I only wish I was so smart six years ago when Leo tried to warn me about you," she said, wrapping her arm around Leo's shoulder. "And please, stay away from my daughter. Rosie is here to save a life, not to have you in *her* life. That decision was made long ago, if you recall."

"But, Star, things are different now."

"Do you really take me for a fool? If a kid from the Tenderloin is fooled more than once, she ends up dead. I'm no fool, golden-boy, so listen up. If you don't stay away from Rosie and me, I will do everything in my power to destroy your holy kingdom. And you can take that to the altar!"

Leo smiled proudly. "That's my girl! Bravo, bravo!" he said with sheer pleasure. "You can run along now, Reverend J, or whatever they call you. But remember one thing while you're up there on the pulpit—you're no Billy Graham. Arthur Dimmesdale is more like it. The sins you hide under that preacher's collar will be exposed," Leo said, pointing to Janus' neck.

"Leo! Arthur Dimmesdale! You've read the *Scarlet Letter*! Foretell, foretell," Star said with great amusement.

"Maybe the good Reverend J could learn a lesson or two from the story. What do you think, Stella?" Leo asked, taking Star's hand and leading her away.

When Star and he walked into Rosie's hospital room, Leo let out a delightful laugh. The room was decked in a winter wonderland with snowflakes and candy canes hanging from the ceiling. A miniature stuffed Santa and Mrs. Claus were sitting atop a sled in the corner with eight tiny reindeer. Garland and red bows decorated the windows and a red velvet blanket trimmed in white fur was set at the foot of the bed. "Ah, Star! She won't feel a thing once she's in here! How did you arrange this?"

"I've got a treasure chest of money. I might as well use it to make Rosie more comfortable, especially today. In twenty years, I want her to remember the winter wonderland, not the needles and the pain."

Leo wobbled over to a chair and sat down. He looked up at Star and said, "I need to say something."

"Go ahead," she said, sitting on the edge of the bed. "I'm listening."

"The past two weeks have been terrible, cattivo. I didn't like what was stirring in your pot. I thought this idea was self-serving, a shot at redemption. Now, I feel like the *serpente* for questioning you. Putting Rosie through this was really about saving a little's girl life, nothing more."

"Nothing more, Leo."

"You're a good woman, Stella. I'm so sorry for not trusting you. Nella would be ashamed of me," he said, wiping a tear from his eye.

"Don't worry about it. There's nothing to forgive. I realized that you were angry because you love Rosie. I can't ask for much more than that." When she stood up to give him a hug, the door opened and Rosie was being pushed into the room. Seeing her little body on the bed hooked up to IVs and a monitor was overwhelming. Suddenly, the winter wonderland lost its glow and reality set in. Star rushed to the bed and took Rosie's hand. Tears billowed from her eyes and doubt flooded her mind. *Breathe, just breathe*, she repeated to herself.

Star took a deep breath, bent down and whispered in Rosie's ear, "Mommy's here, Rosebud. I've got a surprise for you." Rosie opened her eyes and smiled a sweet, soft smile, but then her eyes quickly closed.

The nurse asked Star to step aside so Rosie could be settled in. "When she fully wakes, her bottom may be tender, and she'll be a frightened by the IV, but other than that, I think she'll be fine. And with a room like this, Rosie will feel great in no time," the woman said reassuringly.

Once the nurses left the room, Star sat down next to Rosie's bed and hummed Christmas carols to help her wake. Wrestling with her own self-doubt was tough for Star as she watched the confusion spread in Rosie's eyes as she roused awake. Her gut was confident with the decision, but her heart was washing away the euphoria she felt when Dr. Sherman confirmed that the donation was a success. Star's racing thoughts slowed only when Rosie's little fingers tugged on her hand.

"Mommy," she whispered. "Are we at the North Pole?"

"No, honey," Star smiled. "You're in the hospital, remember?"

"Why?" Rosie asked groggily.

"You just gave a little girl the best Christmas gift she'll ever receive."

"A Elmo doll?"

"Oh, Rosie! Something much better! Remember, you gave her your "Super Hero–Super Marrow!"

"Did she like it?"

"Golly, yes! It's the best Super Hero–Super Marrow in the whole wide world."

"Really?" Rosie asked with her eyes growing wide. "What color was it?"

"Pink. Your favorite color!"

"That's good," Rosie said with her eyes floating around the room. They came to rest on the reindeer, and she grinned. "Mommy, can I hold Rudolph?"

"Of course you can. I'll have to tip-toe. Grandpa's asleep in the chair. Can you see him over the bed?"

Rosie strained to raise her head but couldn't. "Let's wake him up!" she giggled, becoming more herself. "Grandpa Leo, Grandpa Leo!" she tried to yell.

Leo jumped in the chair with a start, knocking over his cane.

"What! What's going on?"

"You were snoring," Rosie teased.

"You better not scare me like that, little girl, or I'm going to tickle you," he said as he pushed himself up and out of the chair. He shuffled around the side of the bed and saluted Rosie. "Hello, my brave comrade. Colonel Grandpa is very proud of you!" he said, and Rosie giggled again.

"Grandpa, I gave a pink super hero to a girl. She liked it."

Leo bent down and kissed her forehead. "You gave her much more than that, Rosebud."

Within a day, Rosie was able to bundle up Mr. and Mrs. Claus and the reindeer and head home. Leo built a tent over the couch, and Rosie and he sipped hot chocolate and watched *Arthur* and *Dora the Explorer* while Star played waitress. Rosie stayed on the couch for most of the first week and grumbled about body aches. Leo whittled a matching cane out of a broom stick, and Rosie and he would waddle around the house until she got bored and ran for a toy. By Christmas Eve, she was back to her five-year-old self, bouncing off the walls from sugar and excitement.

Star and she made chocolate chip cookies for Santa and set them out with a tall glass of milk. Leo and she carefully counted out eight carrots for the reindeer and put them in the front yard with a mixing bowl of water. When Rosie went to bed that night, she cared about only one thing, a Tickle Me Elmo doll. When she scrambled down the steps the next morning, Elmo was sitting next to the fireplace in all his red glory.

CHAPTER 24

Liquor bottles . . .

Afew days after Christmas, Leo informed Star that the time had come for her to return to work. If not, she was going to turn Rosie into a hypochondriac by measuring and monitoring every cough, sneeze and whine from the child. He assured her that Meg and he could do a fine job of playing house and watching *Barney* while she was at Leo's.

Leo was right about returning to work. Star was counting wine and liquor bottles for December's inventory when she realized that the ball of panic that was stuck in the base of her throat for the past month was no longer there. She was looking forward to *R. U. Sinful* playing on New Year's Eve and wanted something sassy to wear. Her plan was to finish up the inventory, call in the holiday order, and leave to go shopping just as soon as the crew began to arrive. However, when the sleigh bells chimed and in walked Emmy Dribble, Star was shocked but also certain that her shopping plans had changed.

Star turned from the wine rack and headed behind the bar as Emmy strolled up to the counter and threw down her heavy purse. She smiled sweetly and said, "What's up, Starlight? How the hell are you? Oh, wait, don't answer, because I really don't give a fucking rat's ass how you are. What I want to know is why *your* white, trashy ass is trying to destroy my life."

Star set down the inventory record and stood up straight. "Lay it on the line, Emmy, because I really don't have time for your pissing and moaning. What have I done wrong now in your polished little eyes? Used the wrong fork at dinner or forgot to send a thank-you note? Which important matter is destroying your life? Oh, I know. I wore white after Labor Day. So sorry. I promise never to break one of your Ten Commandments again. You can go home now," she said, looking at her nails casually.

Emmy stretched over the bar top and through gritted teeth said, "Don't play games with me. Why did you tell Kory that I was cheating on him?"

"Tell your husband to be a man. He shouldn't blame me for his suspicions," she said. Star turned around and picked up the phone. "Let's call Kory right now and ask him if I accused you of cheating, okay, Emmy? As far as I'm concerned, I could care less about what you two do. So, please, keep me out of your screwed-up marriage."

"Don't you dare call my marriage *screwed-up*!"

"Don't you dare come into my place of business and chastise me for something I never said. If your husband has suspicions about you, then discuss it with him, not me. I'm not part of your love triangle."

"There is no love triangle," Emmy said, banging her fist on the counter.

"You don't need to convince me of that. I don't give a shit. Tell Kory that. Call him and tell him that you're *really not* dropping your drawers for somebody else five nights a week."

"How dare you question my life! You're the one with the love child who has set out to save the world."

Star stopped dead in tracks and looked Emmy directly in the eye. "Explain what you mean by saving the world, Emmy," she asked calmly.

Emmy smiled a sharp smile, knowing that she finally hit a nerve with Star. "I know all about Rosie donating bone marrow to save Katie Ann."

"I have no idea what you're talking about," Star said with the utmost control.

"Look who's lying now," Emmy said, leaning back on her heels with a smirk. "It slipped out. He told me. Janus told me about the two of you, including details about your bastard child together. My, my, my, Star," she said with a contrived southern accent. "You can certainly take the girl out of the trash, but you can't take the trash out of the girl. Once white trash, always white trash, is what my momma always told me about you."

Star moved closer to the counter, reached out and grabbed Emmy by the shirt. She pulled her across the bar and growled, "Shut the fuck up!"

"Let go!" Emmy shrieked. "Let me go!" Squirming in Star's grip, Emmy raised her arms to break free.

But Star was too quick and too strong. With her free arm, she hauled back, and with all her might, smacked Emmy right across the face. "I've been waiting sixteen years to do that," she snarled, tugging Emmy's face closer to hers. "And I'm warning you—leave my little girl out of your mess, or the ass-kicking will be much worse, 'cause your momma was right. My white, trashy ass will beat the motherfucking shit out of you, if you draw Rosie into your stinking pile of lies."

Emmy yanked herself out of Star's grip and touched her stinging cheek. "You will pay for this! You've destroyed my marriage *and* my spiritual journey with Reverend Jan."

Star laughed out loud. "Oh, Emmy, Emmy," Star laughed again. "We both know that I'm not the dick destroying your marriage, nor am I the dick you're riding during your spiritual journey. Now, am I?" she asked, still grinning.

"You're a whore, Star, a low-life whore with a bastard child whom you prostitute to get what *you* want. But it didn't work with Kory, and it won't work with Janus. You didn't win Kory back by having him deliver your kid, right there on *that* floor," Emmy said, pointing to the area where Rosie was delivered.

"And you won't get Janus back by risking your own kid's life to save Katie Ann. You're nothing but a whore, and you turned your child into a little whore as she was coming out of the womb," she added with a tilt of her head. "Somebody's going to pay here, and it won't be me." She picked up her purse and headed for the door, but before leaving, she turned and said, "You'll pay, Star Nox. Your straw house is going to go up in flames quite soon, so you better prepare yourself."

Star was stunned as she watched her walk out the door. Emmy had no clue how close she was to the truth yet so far from reality. Nonetheless, a battle with Emmy was not one that she sought, nor one that she would deny any longer. The woman had been waging war against her for over a decade and winning, but in the past, the territory was not worth the fight. However, Star would fight this battle and defeat the woman, once and for all, as Rosie would never again be a casualty of Emmy's envious wrath.

The parking lot was crowded when Star pulled into Passages, so the calm of the foyer surprised her as she walked into the main entrance. Standing below the Dribble Family Auditorium copper plate was Janus being interviewed by a woman Star thought she recognized. Immediately, a man dressed entirely in black stopped her and said that the public was not permitted in the building as filming was in progress.

Star smiled graciously and whispered, "I am so sorry, but Reverend Jan is expecting me."

"Where is your pass and identification needed for entry?"

"Oh goodness, I ran out of my office in a ruffle and left it on my desk," she told him. "Just let Reverend Jan know that Star Nox has arrived. I'm legitimate."

The film cop eyed her from head to toe and then waved over an assistant to relay the message. When there was a break in filming, Janus was told of her arrival. Star watched a sharp scowl flash across his face as he glanced in her direction. Eventually, though, Star was escorted to the conclave huddled around the cameras and learned that the woman who was interviewing Janus was Joan Simon of *20/20*, a national news show.

Star stood silent until there was another break in filming and then asked to speak with Janus. He stared her down but then requested five minutes from the director. Janus followed Star into the Dribble Auditorium for privacy. Not until she was certain that they were out of earshot of the entire crew did she begin to unleash her fear and anger.

"First, I won't even ask why you told Emmy about Rosie's donation because, at this point, it does not matter, Janus. What matters is that you get your scorned lover under control as she has threatened to destroy my life, my daughter's life, and it seems," she said, glancing toward the door, "your life, as well!"

"Star, I'm sure you are overreacting," he said irritably. "When did you talk to Emmy?"

"She stormed into Leo's an hour ago," Star said, moving closer to him. "Listen, Janus. Take her back. Screw her until she turns blue, but do whatever you have to do to silence her rage. Rosie and I saved your daughter's life—now save ours."

"There's no need to be so crude. We're in the house of God," he admonished her.

"Look, Janus. I'm not so sure we're in God's house right now. The Big Guy shies away from camera crews and extra-marital affairs. This is about *you* fucking a loose cannon that waged war on me years ago. Somehow, you need to muzzle her, or both our lives will be obliterated."

"Calm down. You're being irrational. What can she do to hurt me? She has no evidence. No one will corroborate whatever she has to say," he said, standing tall.

"You're a reckless man, Janus. Don't be so arrogant. Hillary swallowed your relationship with me because of Katie Ann. That copper sign hanging over the auditorium door may not be big enough for Hillary to stomach your infidelities, once again. When those stories begin blowing in your face, there is no pulling back. Bits and pieces of you will be scattered all over this world. Instead of *20/20* doing a story on the dramatic

ascension of your megachurch, Joan Simon will be document-
ing your grand fall from grace."

"By destroying my reputation, she destroys her own," Janus
told her. "Emmy cares too much about her status in society
to do such a thing. And furthermore, I truly believe that she
wouldn't want to hurt me. I'm her spiritual adviser," he added
with certainty.

Star shook her head and laughed a dark laugh. "You're
crazier than cat shit if you truly believe what you are saying.
Pop that twisted ethereal bubble you are living in, because it's
going to burst anyway. Don't you think the outcome will be
better if you control when, where and how it pops? Whatever it
takes, though, make sure that my family stays out of the path
of Emmy Dribble's rage," Star demanded in a deep growl.

"After the filming, I promise to take care of it."

"I don't want your promises. I've dealt with your paper
pledges before. I want action, and I want it now. If you do
nothing to tether that beast, I'm going to Hillary."

Janus glared down at her. "Star, I said I'd take care of it.
Filming is over tomorrow. I'll talk to Emmy then."

"I hope that's not too late, Janus. I've been stung by her
wrath for a very long time. She's a dangerous woman who
gets what she wants," Star warned. "Call me at Leo's tomorrow. I'll be there at least until midnight. Remember, it's
New Year's Eve," with that, Star turned around and headed
up the aisle.

On her way home, she was tempted to call Kory for help,
but she was certain that he possessed little influence over
Emmy at this point. His purpose in his wife's life ended five
years ago, a time long before his service in the reserves ended.

When Star walked into the back door that night, Rosie and Leo were at the kitchen table eating spaghetti and meatballs. He was teaching her how to twirl noodles around her fork, but the mess on Rosie's face and on the front of her shirt proved the technique to be a challenge. Star kissed them both on the head and sat down next to Rosie.

"Can you twirl a bite for me?" Star asked. "I'm starving."

"Sure, Mommy," Rosie agreed, and all eyes focused in on the twirling process. While she was maneuvering the fork, Leo told Star that Kory had been by the house earlier that day.

"He thought you'd be home. Don't know why he'd leave work in the middle of the day, looking for you," he said, raising his wise eyes. "Any idea why?"

"It's ready, Mommy," Rosie interrupted excitedly and lifted the fork to her mother's face. Star bent down and opened her mouth, conveniently preventing a response. She chewed and chewed and chewed and then asked for more spaghetti, but Leo stopped her and asked for an explanation.

"Stella, tell me what's going on. Kory è rosso di rabbia. The man is red with anger!" Leo said, dropping his fork on the plate. "Why didn't you tell me about Emmy and the serpente?"

"I didn't tell you because it wasn't my business to share. And to be quite honest, I can't worry about Kory's feelings right now. I raised red flags about Emmy weeks ago, but he simply wouldn't listen and accused me of lambasting her. He has to work through his own issues with Emmy. My sole concern right now is my family's privacy. She has no right to expose our connections with Janus. And if she does, the media will grab hold of her tales and scatter them like parade confetti. The bits and pieces of stories will swirl around until they land in piles of confusion along streets and alleyways from Cincinnati to San Francisco. This cannot happen, Leo, for more reasons than I could ever tell you."

Rosie looked up at her mother with hesitation and uncertainty in her eyes. She scooted off her chair and crawled on Star's lap to play with her mother's curls, something she often did to soothe herself. "What's wrong, Mommy?" she asked as she twisted tendrils of curls in her tiny fingers.

"There's nothing for you to worry about, honey. I'm just mad at an adult for making bad decisions."

Rosie rested her head on Star's chest and closed her eyes. "Uncle Kory didn't want to play today," she said. "Are you mad at him?"

"No, Rosebud. I'm not mad at Uncle Kory. What I would really like to do, though, is go upstairs, give you a bath, and then read a gazillion books in my bed. Is that a good idea?"

Rosie lifted her head and put her hands on both sides of Star's cheeks and smiled. She then whispered to her mother, "Goodnight room."

And Star whispered back, "Good night moon . . . Goodnight cow . . . ."

"Jumping over the moon," Rosie giggled.

"Okay! Stop there, Silly," Star laughed. "Go on upstairs and pick out four books. We'll save *Goodnight Moon* for last."

Rosie jumped off Star's lap and scrambled up the steps yelling, "*Five Chinese Brothers* is first!"

Star then turned to Leo with foreboding. "Someone needs to lasso and muzzle Emmy Dribble before she hurts too many people."

CHAPTER 25

A pig smoker and beer bottles dressed in brown paper bags . . .

A dusting of snow glistened in the morning light as Star stepped outside to collect the newspaper. Her slippers and the hem of her pajamas gathered snow as she walked along the driveway. Bending down to pick up the paper, she paid little attention to the Channel 5 News van that rolled past her and pulled into a neighbor's driveway a few houses down. But when Star pulled the newspaper from its plastic and unfolded the front page, her heart stopped and she clutched her chest. Her head snapped up as the news van was pulling out of the neighbor's drive. "Oh, my God!" she cried and ran toward the house. "Leo!" she shouted.

Star tore into the house, slammed the front door and peeked out the front window. The van had parked in front of her house as Channel 9's van headed down the street. She ran into the kitchen and handed the paper to Leo who was making coffee in Nella's old percolator.

"Quietare! What's all this racket about? You're going to wake Rosie," he told her, but as Leo read the headlines, his face grew pale. "Love Child Saves Reverend Jan's Child from Aggressive Leukemia."

Star slumped in the kitchen chair and wept. "Why in God's name did I drag my child into this mess, Leo? Once again, you were right," she cried through the tears. "Our life was wonderful two months ago, but now I've destroyed it!"

Leo wobbled over to Star and stood behind her. He rested his hands on her shoulders and caressed her head. "Mi bella, you could never predict something like this. We have no control over someone else's revenge. You were correcto all along. I was the one who didn't listen. Emmy Dribble has a cuore di pietra, a heart of stone."

As Leo was trying to calm her, the door bell rang and she told him about the television vans parked outside. "Would you speak to them?" she pleaded.

Leo nodded bravely, grabbed his cane and hobbled down the front hall. When he dragged open the door, the reporters looked surprised when an elderly man dressed in red Santa Claus pajamas greeted them.

"May I help you," Leo asked, raising his cane in the air.

"We would like to interview Starlight Nox for a story regarding the Reverend Janus Perfidius. Is she available for comment?"

"Miss Nox lives across the street," Leo said, pointing his cane in the direction of a yellow Victorian house whose owners leave for work by seven o'clock every morning.

"But our records show that she lives here," the second reporter insisted.

"Young man, I've been living on this earth a lot longer than you. So, I think I can figure out which house is my neighbor's. Now, tell me, are you going to argue with me?" Leo snapped, raising his cane again.

The reporter took one step back.

"If you please, stay off my property," Leo added and slammed the door shut. He shuffled around the room, closing all the shades and then turned on the news. When he spotted the professor's face plastered on the television, he called Star to come out of the kitchen where she was hiding.

"Steady yourself, Stella, before you watch this. The snake has beaten you to the punch. They're going to replay his comments after the commercials."

Star grasped Leo's arm when Janus' face appeared on the screen. Standing at the pulpit with Hillary by his side, Janus' olive skin glowed from the masterful lies he was weaving. The venerable minister put his arm around his wife as she peered up at him with a tender smile and then began his statement. He explained that years ago he had a single moral deviation from his marriage but immediately admitted the transgression to his wife and pleaded for her forgiveness. He repented and, together, they worked through their problems and were now more in love than they were on their wedding day. With the last line, Star noticed that Janus pulled Hillary closer to him, and she smiled more brightly in support.

Janus went on to explain that their daughter, Katie Ann, was diagnosed with an aggressive form of leukemia in early autumn. "And when all hope was lost," he cried, "God sent from heaven this sacrificial lamb I had briefly encountered years before. The tainted woman stepped forward and revealed that she had conceived a child with me and offered to have the child's bone marrow tested to save Katie Ann. Upon learning of the fruits of my sin, I bent down on my hands and knees, kissed the feet of my fellow sinner and sang halleluiah." With those words, Janus paused, raised his arms to the sky and sang, "Praise the Lord, for all God's children are sinners. Repent and you will be rewarded by our Lord, Christ the King!"

In response, the entire congregation let out a resounding, "Praise the Lord, Our Christ the King!"

When the auditorium quieted, Janus continued with his statement and explained that "God's repentant sinner, this nefarious woman, chose to remain anonymous, though I wanted her to receive public exculpation, much like Mary of Magdala, she who Luke calls the sinful woman. I respected her right to privacy, however, until another one of God's sinners stepped forward and revealed the woman's identity." With those words, he raised his arms once again and sang, "Praise the Lord, for all God's children are sinners. Repent and you will be rewarded by our Lord, Christ the King!"

Again, the congregation let out a resounding, "Praise the Lord, Our Christ the King!" As the auditorium drew to a hush, Janus implored, "This adulteress, this tainted woman, this sinner of the flesh and body, this repentant child of God is Starlight Nox!" He raised his hands and shouted, "Our Lord, Christ the King, give this wayward woman public redemption. Embrace her sins and give absolution as you did for the seven illnesses of Mary of Magdala. Praise the Lord for Starlight Nox."

As her name rolled from his tongue, the congregation sprang to their feet and cried, "Praise the Lord for Starlight Nox." As Star listened to her name ring through the Dribble Family Auditorium, the national network cut away to the local news station that was highlighting New Year's Eve celebrations around the town. A picture of Leo's appeared on the television screen, and the local reported noted, "Ironically, the band *R. U. Sinful* is Leo's featured music for their New Year's celebration."

Star sank down into the couch and wept again. "Oh, Leo," she cried. "For how long will I have to pay for my sins?"

"Stella, these aren't your sins clogging the airwaves. You carry the weight for other people's disgrace. The serpente is right for once. You've been the sacrificial lamb for many. It's time to shake off the burden. I want you to go into battle with your guns loaded and your head held high, no retreating. And remember, I always got your back."

"Leo, when you go into battle with just your own skin to worry about, it is different. Now, I have Rosie to worry about."

"That's right," Leo said, pointing his cane at her, "But, you're a survivor, and the apple's not going to fall far from the tree. Rosie's going to be just fine. If her mamma is coraggioso, Rosie will be coraggioso."

Star sat up straight and wiped her tears and dripping nose on the sleeve of her robe. "If the Tenderloin gave me anything, it was courage," she said, trying to galvanize her strength.

"True. So, the sooner you deal with the enemy, the sooner you'll be notizia vecchia, old news . . . old news to all these people. Now, get off the couch, go on upstairs, shower and prepare to tell your side of the story."

Star stood up and embraced Leo. "What would I do without you?" she whispered.

"I don't know, but without you, my life would be damn boring!" he chuckled softy.

She went upstairs to shower, and then called Ted, Jimmy's partner, for advice, forgetting that he was Janus' lawyer, as well. When Ted's secretary came on the line, the woman explained that Ted had been trying to contact her all morning, but no one answered the calls. Star remembered that Leo had gotten into the habit of turning off the phone ringer until midmorning so Rosie could sleep.

"Is he available now?" Star asked.

"He is meeting with Reverend Perfidius at Passages, but I will have him call you as soon as possible. Sit tight for a few minutes."

When she hung up the phone, Star hurried around the house to check all the ringers. As she was turning up the volume on the unit in the kitchen, the telephone shrilled and she jumped. "My God!" she yelled and grabbed the receiver.

"Star, this is Ted. How are you?" he asked quickly.

"In shock. I heard Janus' statement on the television and want to respond."

"I've got something prepared for you already. We've been trying to contact you. I've got an associate headed to your house right now. Read over the statement and call me back," he directed.

Ted was all business and was all about protecting one of his most celebrated clients. She felt like a pawn to him at that moment, but Ted was also one of the main forces behind Leo's success. Therefore, two hours later, Star found herself walking into Ted's office to make a statement to the press. He escorted her to the far end of a conference room that was overstuffed with cameramen, photographers and reporters. At the opposite end of the table, she spotted Joan Simon, the lovely reporter who had been interviewing Janus the previous day. The woman smiled at her with a knowing expression. Star's stomach knotted up, and she wanted to shout down the center of the table, "You know nothing about me, *Bitch*." Instead, she took a deep breath, closed her eyes and slowly exhaled. Ted then tapped her on the shoulder and asked her to begin the statement set before her.

Star looked out across the crowded room then bowed her head. "All of you here today have heard the dignified and heartfelt words of Reverend Janus Perfidius, and now I would like to add my own comments," she slowly read the twisted statement as disgust clotted in her throat. "Several years ago before Reverend Janus became a minister, we did have a brief encounter, and because of the fleeting nature of the relationship, I chose to keep the paternity of my child private. Only when I learned of the news that Katie Ann was desperately ill did I reach out to the family with one goal in mind. This goal was strictly to save another child's life. I was hoping to keep the donation anonymous. However, due to circumstances beyond my control, my family's identity has now been revealed.

"Through this process, I have observed a beautiful and loving relationship between Reverend Jan and his wife, Hillary. They both care deeply for Katie Ann, and as one parent to another parent, I pray and hope for the best for their family. Due to the sensitive condition of Katie Ann's health and the age and privacy of my child, I ask that the press give us space during this challenging time. This situation where we find ourselves today is about the health of a little girl, not about a highly regrettable and unfortunate moment shared between two adults. Thank you for taking the time to meet here today," she concluded, but as soon as her voice dropped, Star was quickly bombarded with questions.

"How long have you known Reverend Jan . . . Was it only once . . . Did you love each other . . . Do the children know they're sisters?" Star's head was bouncing in all directions from the barrage of questions. Finally, Ted leaned into the microphone and explained there would be no further statements. Star stood and he escorted her back out the conference room and into his office. When she walked in, Janus was sitting in a chair, grinning broadly. He jumped to his feet and stuck out his hand to congratulate her, but she walked past him and sat down in front of Ted's desk.

"Put your hand away, Janus," she sneered.

"Why are you so angry? The plan is working like a well-oiled machine, isn't it, Ted?" Janus asked excitedly.

"Perfect. I checked with Marie. Early polls and reviews of last night's statement indicate that your followers are eating up every word. Hillary was the quintessential wife. The only thing we missed was having Katie Ann on stage in a wheel chair with Rosie at her side in bows and frilly stuff."

"Nah. That may have turned off the mothers. Using kids as a sympathy card can backfire. What do you think, Star?" asked Janus.

"What do I think?" Star asked incredulously. "Was this entire thing scripted out?"

"Hell, yeah," Janus said. "Ted advised we leak it to the press before Emmy had a chance. That way we take the fire from her flame. I'm working with *20/20* on an expanded scoop. Joan Simon is all over me."

"I bet she is," Star said, seething. "How could you do this to me, Janus? I begged you to protect my privacy."

"Star, you should be thanking Ted and me right now. Instead of looking like a conniving whore, the Catholics are going to beatify you for sainthood after all this is said and done."

"Janus is right, Star. Emmy was unpredictable. We couldn't have her running around like a chicken with her head cut off. Way too dangerous. This is orchestrated chaos that saves both of you," explained Ted. Wait a few days and another scandal will become the big story. It's the holiday season. Celebrities are always making asses of themselves this time of year."

Star quickly realized that there was nothing she could say to help them understand the violation she felt for her family and the concern that she had for her privacy. Star wondered if she would forever regret saving Katie Ann's life, for now she was doomed to an undeniable relationship with this man whom she despised. At some point, Star would have to inform Rosie that both her father and her sister live only a few miles from their home. If she didn't tell Rosie soon, her daughter would learn about her family tree underneath the playground slide by some snot-nosed kid named Billy or Emmy.

Star took the long way home that day heading up Vine Street and through Over-the-Rhine. On the street corners, groups of teenagers crowded around steel drums filled with fire, warming their hands, laughing and elbowing each other. She parked her car along the curb and cracked her window to feel the vibe and take in the smells. Diesel fumes and sweet barbecue filtered through her car. She spotted a pig smoker midway down the block commandeered by rusty old men holding grill tongs and beer bottles dressed in brown paper bags. Star rested her head against the seat and closed her eyes. Flowing from car radios was a cacophony of *Puff Daddy* and *Usher* singing about lost love and bad love, which seemed to be the story of her life.

She opened her eyes and peered at the century-old buildings that echoed the Tenderloin. All at once, she desperately missed and desperately hated the District. She missed the simplicity of life that was focused entirely on survival. She hated the life that taught her about destructive love and addiction, which were quite often indistinguishable.

Her journey back into the underworld was disrupted by a quick tap on the window. She looked over her left shoulder, and not six inches from her face was a toothless woman with leathery cheeks begging for a dime. Star opened her console, pulled out a twenty dollar bill and slipped it through a thin crack in the window. That should buy her a few smack trips for the New Year, Star thought. She started the car, pulled from the curb and headed back to Hyde Park.

A few news vans were still parked in front of her house as she drove down the street. "Let's deal with these guys head on," she mumbled to herself. Star pulled into the driveway, jumped out of the car and waited with her arms crossed. The reporters both irritated and bemused her as they raced from their vehicles to reach her first. With questions erupting all over again, she raised both her palms and told them to stop.

"Please listen," she said firmly. "There is no more scoop to be had. You can ask me how many times we kissed or if Reverend Jan has an oddly placed tattoo, but honestly, none of that stuff matters. Like I said, it was a horrible split-second decision that ended up with a strange silver lining. So, can you please leave me alone? Go home to your friends and families for New Year's Eve." With that, Star climbed back into the car and pulled into the garage.

Only silence greeted her when she walked in the back door. She headed through the kitchen and into the living room yelling, "Yoo-hoo! I'm home!" until she heard tiny feet running across the floor above. Star stood at the bottom of the steps with her arms wide open and yelled "Jump!" as Rosie raced down the steps. She flew into her mother's arms and both squeezed as tight as they could.

Leo was at the top of the steps, smiling down on them. Star looked up and noticed a soft glow framing his head. The last of the evening's light was shining through an upstairs window and was collecting in the wisps of his remaining hair, creating a halo. For no obvious reason, Star felt uncomfortable and looked away.

"It's about time you came home, Twinkles," Leo teased.

"Don't give me a hard time, mister. You shouldn't be going up and down the steps without me home," she cautioned him. Star set down Rosie and asked her to run and find Leo's cane. As Rosie scrambled up the stairs, she followed to help him maneuver the staircase.

"Well, we needed somewhere to hide out. It's been a busy day here. The phone hasn't stopped ringing, either."

"Leo, I know, I know," she repeated. "I should have listened to you six years ago *and* six weeks ago. You tried to steer me from the two worst decisions of my life, but I didn't listen. Now, for the rest of our lives, we'll all be connected to Judas Iscariot."

"Ah, forget that. Dwell on the good, not the bad. My babbo always said, 'il vino è fatto da aceto.' Wine is made from vinegar. Don't dwell on the vinegar. You saved a child's life."

As they spoke, Rosie came clopping down the hall, dragging Leo's cane behind her. "Mommy, here," she said, holding up the cane at the top steps.

"Hold onto the rail and walk it down the steps, Rosebud," Star directed as she helped Leo come down the final step.

"Another thing. The circus around here has finally called out all the clowns," Leo laughed. "Guess who called from Florida to complain that the Nox family name has been sullied all over again?"

"I'll be darned," Star said. "It's funny how people like Greer raise their ugly heads only when someone else's shamefaced news strikes. Nice of him to remind me of how I have followed in Jack's footsteps," she grumbled.

Leo took the cane from Rosie and offered his free hand to her. "Will you escort me into the kitchen for a delicious meal of meatloaf, Madame?"

Rosie grinned and tried to whisper to Leo, "Should we tell Mommy about the sweet rice I made for New Year's?"

"Sweet rice for dessert? Holy cow! Rosebud! I'm not eating anything else," Star teased as the motley trio headed into the kitchen.

Star skipped the New Year's celebration but went into Leo's early the next day to assess the damages that 1999 carried through the front door. There was a broken stool and a dozen wine glasses that needed to be replaced. One beer tap was drained empty and only a few bottles of wine were left in the racks. The total receipts for the night confirmed, however, that *R. U. Sinful* was worth every golden penny they commanded.

As she was reviewing the calendar to book the band for another date, the phone rang. "Must be the owner of the pink stiletto," she mumbled, looking at the shoe that the cleaning crew left on the counter.

When she answered the phone, a vaguely familiar voice asked for her. "This is Star Nox. May I help you?" she offered.

"Damn sure you can help! Don't you know who I am, missy?" the scratchy voice asked.

"No," Star said, but Sue's voice was echoing somewhere in her memory.

"You don't recognize your momma?" the woman charged.

"Sue Nox?"

"Yeah! Momma to you, missy."

"Oh," Star said flatly, but her heart catapulted and the room shifted. She steadied herself against the counter. *My god, what more can I take*, she thought.

"You don't sound too happy to hear from your momma," she screeched. "I miss my baby. It's been ten long years since I seen you," the scratchy voice continued.

"Actually, seventeen years," Star corrected the woman with complete contempt.

"Goddamn! Time flies when you having fun, don't it?"

"Like a bat out of hell," Star answered stiffly, slowly regaining her equilibrium. "Just tell me what you want, Sue. Why are you calling?"

Star ran her fingers through her hair, silently pleading, *Make it go away! Please, dear God, make it go away!* As the plea rang in her mind, an image of the Tenderloin's dirt and grime rose up, rolling out its filthy carpet before her. *You'll never let me be, will you?* Star cried inside.

Her mother's screechy voice pulled her back into the moment, though. "You don't talk to your momma in years and you ask why I'm callin'. What kind a' kid are you?"

"Busy."

"I seen that on TV. I seen what my grandbaby did for that preacher's daughter. She saved that little girl's life. She looks like her granny, don't she?"

"Is that why you're calling?" Star asked sharply.

"Damn right! I'm mighty proud of that little Daisy."

"Her name is Rosie, not Daisy."

"Ah, what the hell? They're both a flower."

"Sue, listen carefully. I'm hanging up. I've got nothing to say to you. Never have and never will." The room shifted once more, and her mother's pock-marked face and black teeth, all ravaged from years of drug abuse, were laughing at her, dragging her down Turk Street. "Go away! Go away!" she demanded. "Never call again."

"No, don't! Don't hang up!" Sue screeched. "I need to ask you a little favor. Sugar, I run into a little money trouble. I'm thinking that you could help me out, seeing you got yourself a sweet little thing going on."

"No! You sold me for over one hundred thousand dollars. And you want more money? No! The answer is no today and will be no forever. Lose my number and forget my name," Star almost shouted.

"Don't you go disrespecting your momma with words like that! God's going to get you. You're just an inconsiderate whore, Missy. A little hussy at ten years old. You never did change. You're still spreading your legs like a bald eagle. That shit on the TV is all an act. You're just a little whore."

"Never call me again," Star roared and hung up the phone. A frigid chill ran through her body. This was more than a circus with clowns coming out for the show. Star was certain that somewhere in the earth's surface was a deep schism releasing fiery fiends, succubi and incubi, evil spirits of every type, all working their way toward her.

CHAPTER 26

Breaded veal, risotto and peas,
but most importantly, crostata di mele, the apple tart . . .

As Ted predicted, pestering by the press quickly waned for Star as the New Year brought other more important news. By the fourth of January, her name was nowhere to be found in the *Cincinnati Enquirer.* The press had turned to a brutal snowstorm that was pounding the Midwest, leaving sixty-eight deaths in its wake. All the while, the Gallup Poll named the First Couple, Bill and Hillary Clinton, as the most admired couple in America for 1998. In spite of illicit blowjobs and unsavory cigars, President Clinton was still revered. As Star read the story, she mused over the fact that no one called him *white trash* or *whore.*

She folded the newspaper and put it away as customers began to trickle in.

Star wasn't surprised when Kory walked through the door early that evening. She was more surprised that he hadn't shown up sooner. He sat down at the very end of the bar with eyes already glassy from drink. His typical short, military hair cut had grown into a thick, even carpet covering his scalp. His dress shirt was half untucked at the waist and his tie was askew.

Star slowly walked toward him. "Where've you been hiding out?" she asked.

"Been with my loving wife," he quipped back.

She placed a napkin in front of him but did not ask if he wanted a drink. Instead, she poured him a club soda.

"How did you know about them, Star?"

"By accident," she admitted. "I wasn't snooping. I figured it out at Leo's opening-night party. I was in the bathroom with Rosie. Emmy and Janus were right outside the door, making plans to rendezvous. Very sloppy and reckless on their part. Anyone in the bathroom could have heard their conversation."

"Why didn't you tell me? You're my friend," Kory asked. His eyes and lips hung with exhaustion.

Star paused and thought about his word choice. "Friend is an interesting word, isn't it, Kory?" she finally said. "The term holds different responsibilities for different people. Emmy's relationship with Janus wasn't my business to share, whether we're friends or not. I led you down the stream with a bit of bait, but you weren't biting, so I dropped it. I don't make a habit of treading on other people's relationships."

"That's a lie!" he charged. "Look what you did to Perfidius' wife! You're no better than Emmy or him. I delivered the preacher's daughter right there on that floor!" he said, jabbing his finger in the direction where Rosie was born. You know what they say about people who live in glass houses, Star?"

"I'm no stone thrower, Kory" she whispered indignantly. "Your wife came in here and threatened to reveal Rosie's identity as the donor because she was a spurned lover, by whom, it does not matter. What matters to me is the fact that she directed her anger at my family. She forced the hand that has made me and my daughter forever connected to Janus Perfidius. Furthermore, she obliterated my sense of privacy. From this point forward, Emmy Dribble does not exist to me."

"Don't blame Emmy for your fuck up with Janus, Star."

"I don't blame Emmy for my 'fuck up.' I blame Emmy for violating my right to privacy. Six years ago Janus Perfidius rescinded all paternity rights regarding Rosie. I never had any intention of revealing his identity to Rosie or to anyone else. That is why the donation was completed with the strictest confidentiality. In one of their final romps, however, Janus told Emmy about Rosie."

"That's Janus' fault," Kory insisted. "Like I said, don't blame Emmy."

"You're right. Janus violated the confidentiality agreement we signed. He is to blame, as well. But this information was not Emmy's to share."

"She didn't share the information. *He* went to the press," Kory insisted.

"True, again, but she forced his hand," Star said. "Listen, defending your wife is admirable, but I don't have to agree with you. Marriages can survive infidelities, and I hope yours does. However, as long as Emmy and you are together, I cannot handle a relationship with you. I love you and always will, but for now, ending our friendship is best for all parties involved."

Kory looked at Star in disbelief. "Are you making me choose between my wife and you?"

"Absolutely not! *I'm* choosing not to be your friend at this juncture in our lives."

Without a word, Kory pushed the club soda back toward Star, stood up and walked out the door.

Within a week, Star's life had settled back into kindergarten pickup, shift juggling for absentee employees, and a quick bedtime story with Rosie by nine-thirty. She enjoyed the predictability at home and the managed chaos at work. Leo's eighty-ninth birthday was in two weeks, and she now had time to think about the planning. She wanted to surprise him with a band that played from the Great American Song Book, which of course would include "Don't Sit Under the Apple Tree." The menu would be breaded veal, risotto and peas, but most importantly, crostata di mele, the apple tart that Leo bought from Nella some sixty years before. Star wanted nothing outlandish, only the little things that would delight him. The guest list was the sticky part, though, as he would expect Kory to be invited. "You must love people the most, when they are the most unlovable," Leo would tell her, but she didn't know how well she could bite her tongue this time.

Leo's was crowded and loud for a Tuesday evening, but the distraction was what she needed. As she was following her finger down a list of jazz groups with vocalists who sang Big

Band standards, she noticed a young girl wander in the door. She was dressed nicely in expensive jeans, a petrol blue sweater and a choker necklace dripping with beads, something Kate Winslet would wear. Star also noticed her much-sought-after Fendi purse. But no matter how expensive the clothes, the girl didn't look a day older than seventeen. Star slid off the bar stool and headed toward her.

"Very cool necklace," Star commented, approaching the girl.

"Thank you," she said with poise. "I am looking for Mrs. Nox. Do you know where I may find her?"

Star instantly felt dated. "I'm Star Nox," she said, fluffing her curls to give them a little boost.

"Oh, you look different in person . . . not in a bad way, just younger," she explained. "I saw you on TV a few weeks ago. You were talking about Reverend Jan and his little girl." The girl's voice dropped as she finished the last few words about Katie Ann.

"Are you from a school newspaper or something? Because, if you are, I don't give interviews," Star explained.

"No, no! It's not that at all." Her lips began to tremble and her voice quivered as she spoke.

The girl made Star uncomfortable. She seemed jittery, confused or off balance somehow. "What's your name," she asked, eyeing her closely.

"Penelope, Penelope Defloro, but everybody calls me Penny," she whispered.

"Penelope is a lovely name."

"People tell me that, but I like Penny," she said, fiddling with the heavy beads on her necklace.

"Well, Penny, what can I help you with? I'm a little busy tonight," Star asked cautiously.

"Is there anywhere that we can talk privately, Mrs. Nox?" she asked nervously.

"Is it important? I'm pressed for time."

"It's very important, Mrs. Nox. Please, may I speak with you?"

As the girl spoke, Star noticed droplets of sweat balling on her forehead, and her upper lip began to twitch. She knew the signs of a desperate addict in need of a fix and wondered about the girl.

"Are you okay?" Star asked, moving closer. "If you're looking for drugs, you've come to the wrong place," she warned.

"Oh! God no!" she cried. "It's nothing like that, Mrs. Nox. I need your help with something else. It's like, like . . . I just really need to talk to you."

Star stepped away to speak with the private security that she had hired a few weeks back. She then returned to the girl and guided her up the narrow steps to Leo's old apartment that was now used for her office. She pulled out a set of keys and unlocked the door.

"Have a seat at the table, Penny," Star directed as she turned on a few lights.

She joined the girl at the cramped kitchen table and gazed around the room. Her heart tingled and her lungs constricted. Some of the happiest moments of her life were spent sitting right where she was with Leo across from her, talking about the Cincinnati Reds and Nella's apple tart.

When her eyes finally rested on the girl, Star explained that she could spare just a few minutes and that an armed security guard was standing at the bottom of the steps, prepared to intervene.

"Mrs. Nox! It's not like that!" the girl cried. "I'm just a normal teenager. And I promise to make it quick. But first . . . I need to ask . . . I need to ask if I can trust you with a secret?"

Star cleared her throat, sat back in the chair and folded her arms across her chest. "*First*, please call me Star," she began. "Second, I can't answer your question until I know what this is about. I just met you five minutes ago. So, I don't know if *I* can trust *you*."

The girl looked up with tears in her eyes and began fiddling with the beads of her necklace again.

"Penny, listen to me," Star finally said with growing frustration. "I'm not sure why you came here or what you want from me, but I'm very busy and want to get home to my family. So, if there is something stirring in your pot that you want to talk about, you're going to have to pour it out now. Otherwise, I'm going to ask you to leave."

"I'm sorry, Miss Nox. I'm so sorry for bothering you at all. I shouldn't have c-c-come," she cried as the tears crested and streamed down her face.

"What is it?" Star pressed.

"I'm in trouble!" she cried. "I saw you on the news. I thought you could help me. You seemed so honest and nice on TV."

Star swallowed hard. She wasn't comfortable being counselor or role model for some anonymous, wayward girl, especially a girl who seemed to be leaning over the edge way too far. "Penny, what kind of trouble is it?" Star reluctantly asked.

"The kind that only stupid, idiotic teenage girls get into. My parents are going to kill me," she said and began to cry harder.

"How far along are you?" Star asked, assuming that pregnancy was the problem seeming to threaten the girl's very existence.

"Almost three months. And I'm freaking out!" she cried through the tears.

"Where's your boyfriend in all this?"

"That's part of the problem."

"Why? Has he tried to hurt you or something?" Star pressed further.

"No, no. Not like hit me, if that's what you mean. He . . . he . . . he wants me to get an abortion," she sobbed.

"Do you want one?" Star asked with growing impatience. She would give the girl five more minutes and then insist that she call her parents or seek help elsewhere. She had just climbed out from under her own enormous drama. Penny's problems were the last thing she wanted or needed.

"No, but what else am I going to do with it. I'm barely eighteen. I just got accepted into Vanderbilt. I don't want the baby, but I don't want to have an abortion, either."

"What about adoption? I'm sure there are plenty of wonderful people who would love to adopt the baby."

"He said that's impossible. Then, people would find out," she sniffled.

"Honey, you're not the first teenager to get pregnant, and you won't be the last. This doesn't have to be a deal killer in the grand scheme of life. I won't say it's easy," Star conceded, "but life is manageable with a baby, and like I said, you can think about adoption."

"I told you! He won't even consider that as an option," Penny wept.

"Well, whoever this boy may be, he doesn't own your body. You need to do what's best for you. And the first thing I recommend is that you tell your parents. They'll be pissed for a while, but you're their daughter. They'll get over it."

Penny shook her head long and wide. "They might get over a baby, but they won't get over the father, Mrs. Nox."

"Why?" Star asked, narrowing her gaze.

"Because he's older."

"Like how much older?" Star asked with increasing anxiety.

"Almost thirty years," she whispered.

"What!" Star let out. "Who is this maniac? Is he married?"

Penny slowly nodded her head yes as tears streamed down her face, plopping on the threads of her sweater.

Star got up from the table and grabbed a napkin for Penny to blow her nose. Once she sat down, Star asked if that was why she came to see her, because she knew that Reverend Jan was much older than herself.

The girl again nodded yes but began to cry harder. "My parents are going to absolutely die, Mrs. Nox. The father is their close friend. He's our minister," she wailed. Penny dropped her head into her hands and continued to cry.

"Penny, look up at me," Star asked, but the girl refused. "Penny, is this man Reverend Jan?" she demanded, tilting back her head, trying to breathe. But before Penny spoke, Star already knew the answer. She stood up and went around the table and pulled the girl into her arms.

"The world isn't ending," she whispered. "This is a baby, not a monster. The good news is that you can get rid of that old monster but keep the baby."

"But I thought he really loved me," she said, lifting her head.

"We all do, honey, but the married ones never love us. They buy us gifts and whisper "I love you" in our ears, but that's part of their fantasy. Once they get their rocks off, they go back home to their wife and kids. The cheats rarely leave their wives, which is a good thing. Because, if they did leave, there would be a lot of young girls stuck with old, shriveled up dicks that don't work."

"But he gave me this necklace for Christmas," the girl said, clutching the beads.

"Penny, that's part of his game," Star said, empty of all emotion. "I may sound harsh, but you've got to deal with reality. He doesn't love you any more than he loved me, but the fact remains that you are pregnant. You've made adult decisions that landed you right where you are. Now, you've got to make some fairly quick decisions to make the best of your life. The first step is taking off that damn necklace to begin the emotional break from him. Secondly, whether you like it or not, you've got to get your parents involved."

Penny peered at Star. "He really *doesn't* love me?" she asked.

"No. Absolutely not. He likes to fuck you. That's all you are to him—a young fuck machine. Nothing more. Corruption runs through that man's veins, not warm blood. There's not a drop of love in his entire body." Star stopped and stood up. "Listen, Penny," she said, looking down at the girl. "The man is insidious. You need to believe me, accept what I have to say, and run like the devil's got your tail. Otherwise, he will destroy what little dignity you have left." Star was surprised how her advice flowed out so easily and with such little emotion, but that was the only thing that surprised her that evening.

Penny's swollen eyes and runny nose reminded Star of herself, when she sat in the same chair, revealing her similar fate to Leo. "There's a reason why you came here tonight, Penny. You wouldn't have found me if you wanted to stay with Janus. I've confirmed your worst nightmare, so what do you plan to do?" Star pressed on.

The girl slowly raised her hands and slipped her fingers around her neck. She unclasped the heavy choker and handed it to Star. Cupped in her hand, Star glanced at the necklace and noted that the piece was too mature for her, anyway. "It looks like something out of *Titanic*," Star said.

"That's funny. Reverend J and I saw the movie together over Christmas break."

"How did you pull that off without people recognizing him?" Star asked.

"I always arrived first and sat in the very back row of the theater in the left corner. He came in after the movie started and left before it ended. Then we'd hook up afterward."

"'Hooked up.' Ah, I see . . . Where?"

"Depends. In the park—in his car. It was weird, though . . . it got messy. He freaked out. So, we started going to his office."

Star shook her head in disgust. "When was that?"

"September. I'm in theater at school. I told my mom that I was building the set for *The Wizard of Oz*. She never questioned why I was out on school nights. Before Reverend Jan, I did everything right. I was the perfect child. I was the teen leader of our youth group at church. That's how I met him."

"Righteous fucker," Star mumbled. She squeezed the choker in her hand and walked to the window. She opened it and threw the necklace in the street, well past Nella's apple tree.

She returned to the table and stood with her arms crossed. "Penny, tell me something. When did you turn eighteen?"

"Last week. Reverend J gave me a Sony Walkman for my birthday."

"Didn't your parents wonder where you got a Walkman? They're expensive."

"My dad noticed it first. I told him that I won it in a school raffle," she said and paused, "It's funny how lies come so easily, once you start telling them. My mom always said that lies are like snowballs. She was right. You keep telling them, and they get bigger and bigger."

"Damn right. There's something to that snowball effect," Star agreed. "But now it's time to forget about snowballs and get straight with your parents. I want you to call them," Star said, reaching for the phone on the wall. She took the receiver, stretched out the curly cord, and handed the phone to the girl. "Here, time to call," she said decisively.

"Will you call them, Mrs. Nox—I'm mean Star? Please!" she begged.

I'm too young to be making the dreaded call to the parent, Star thought. She stood there, looking at the girl and thinking about herself when she was in Penny's shoes. Thank heaven she had Leo to turn to at the time. Otherwise, the fear and loneliness would have eaten her alive.

"Okay," she eventually conceded. "If it gets the job done. Give me the number slowly." She twirled her finger around the rotary dial nine times before a woman's voice came on the line.

"Hello, is this Mrs. Defloro?" Star asked.

"Who is this?" the woman demanded.

"My name is Star Nox. You may know my name from Reverend Janus Perfidius."

"Yes," the woman snapped with condescension.

Knowing what the woman was about to face, Star ignored the disdainful tone and continued. "Your daughter Penny came to see me tonight, Mrs. Defloro. She's with me right now."

"Why?" she demanded. "What's this all about, Miss Nox?"

"Ma'am, this is your daughter's business to share, not mine. She's safe, but your husband and you need to come and get her at Leo's. We're located on Ambrose Avenue. Ask the gentleman at the door to escort you to my office. We'll be waiting for you," she said and hung up the phone.

Star sat down next to the girl and grasped her hand. "Penny, to get through this in one piece, you've got to come clean with everything. Tell me . . . how long have you been seeing Reverend Jan?"

"Do you mean like hooking up or like friends?"

"Both."

"I've been in youth group since freshman year. We were just friends at first, but then we started, you know, hooking up in sophomore year. He gave me this ring for my sixteenth birthday," she said, holding up a garnet ring, a piece of birthstone jewelry that could be found in the makeup section of Walgreens.

Star rubbed her temples and ran her fingers through her curls. The value of the fuck to Janus must get smaller with age, she thought. But he failed to remember that the punishment for his sin was inversely related. "You realize what Reverend Jan has done with you is illegal, don't you?" she finally asked.

"Now, I do, but it didn't seem illegal then."

"Well, you need to prepare yourself for that. Your parents may want to press charges. If someone doesn't, there's no stopping this snake."

Star fell into silence, wondering if Penny's parents would have the courage to stand up against Janus to protect the dignity of their daughter and other girls whom he would surely target. With this knowledge, Star wondered if she had a moral duty to inform the police. She stepped back into the quagmire to help save Katie Ann, but she wasn't prepared to take the step again.

But two hours later, Star found herself sitting in a small room at District 1, giving a statement to Detective Schmidt. She looked at her wrist watch which already read eleven-thirty. Rosie was sound asleep without a bedtime story.

"Miss Nox would you like me to repeat the question?" the detective asked.

"No, sir," she said. "I'm just worried about my daughter. I promised to be home three hours ago."

"And she is Janus Perfidius' biological daughter, is that correct?" he asked again for the umpteenth time.

"Yes. We've gone over that and everything else I know about the man twice," she said irritably. The bright fluorescent lights were burning her eyes and her head was pounding.

"I want to make sure I have a clear picture of Reverend Perfidius. If you find me repetitive, Miss Nox, I apologize."

Star sat up straight in the steel chair and took a sip of water. "Listen, Detective Schmidt, I'm going to give you one last statement about the man. Then, I'm going home."

"Fair enough," he said.

She leaned toward him, pressing her stomach against the table. "Have you ever heard of the Tenderloin District in San Francisco, Detective?" she challenged.

"Every cop has. It's as rough as it gets."

"No shit," Star said. "I was raised on the filthy streets of the Tenderloin. I fought off pimps and pill pushers and scraped through garbage cans for half-eaten sandwiches just to get to the next day. I should have spotted Perfidius' twisted dick a mile away, because it's the same twisted dick that was shoved in my face ten times a week in the District. This wank is just packaged with a slick tongue and nice clothes, but he's still just a wank. The Tenderloin wanks aren't nearly as dangerous as Janus, though, because they don't have his power. And the more power he possesses, the younger his pussy will become. Because that's what he is driven by, power and pussy."

Detective Schmidt put down his pen and narrowed his stare at her. "That's quite an accusation, Miss Nox," he said.

"Detective, don't look at me so wide-eyed. I call a wank a wank when I see one. I've told you everything I know. Now, it's your job to get this asshole off the streets before he hurts another young girl. And don't be surprised if more panicked parents and girls come knocking at your door when this goes public."

"Why?" he said cautiously. "Are there other victims that you haven't disclosed?"

"No, that's not it. Unfortunately, I'm too familiar with too many other wanks just like the good Reverend Jan."

CHAPTER 27

Meatloaf, a delicatezza made with slow hands and the finest ingredients . . .

Thirty-six hours later Star woke to the same network frenzy in her front yard that was there the month before. This time, however, she refused to make Leo take the brunt of the media. She opened the door and headed straight down the driveway to the crowd of cameras and microphones.

"We need to stop meeting like this," she quipped to Tim Fletcher, a reporter she recognized from ABC who covered Janus' mess the first time around.

"How are you, Miss Nox?" Tim asked.

"Fine. What can I do for you and the other ladies and gentleman who have congregated on my doorstep so early in the morning?"

"What do you have to say about the statutory rape charges against Janus Perfidius?" a reporter from CNN called out.

"For the dignity of his wife and daughter, as well as the young lady involved, I would like to quell the hysteria and protect their privacy by not commenting. I only offer my prayers to both families."

"Rumors are floating that claim Penelope Defloro first came to you about the relationship with Reverend Perfidius. Is that true?" someone else called out.

"The Defloro's business and matters of the police investigation are not mine to share. As I said before, I will make no comment on the case."

"But you must have some reaction to the rape charges. This is the father of your child."

Star snapped her head around in the direction of the voice and stepped toward the reporter. "How dare you draw my daughter into this degeneracy? What? Will she have to pay for the sins of others for the rest of her life, too? Get off my property—all of you! And never trespass in my life again!" With that, she turned around and headed back into the house and closed the door.

Leo was waiting for Star in the hallway as Detective Schmidt had called to ask her a few more questions. Ted Keating had phoned, as well, but she already knew what he wanted, cooperation and corroboration. The venerable preacher had crossed into the darkest depths of the river, however. And she would no longer crouch behind her own shame, perpetuating Janus Perfidius.

Star pulled down the shades, turned off the phones and decided to remain bunkered in the house for the entire day.

Rosie and she played beauty parlor, putting on makeup and painting nails. They colored pictures and played *Candy Land* four times. Barbie married Ken twice before it was time for *Dora the Explorer.*

While Rosie was enthralled with Dora, Leo called Star into the kitchen to help with dinner. Carrots, onion, zuchinni, parsley, basil, garlic, eggs, bread, ground veal, pork and beef, and olive oil were all crowded on the countertop.

"What's all that for?" Star asked. Exhausted, she plopped down at the kitchen table.

"It's time you learned to make polpettone della nonna, my grandmother's meatloaf," he said. "I won't be around forever, and somebody's got to be able to pass the tradition on to Rosie."

"Leo," she groaned. "I'm not the cook. You are. Write down the recipe for her."

"No! Meatloaf is not just a recipe of hamburger, breadcrumbs and egg. Meatloaf is a delicatezza that is made with slow hands and the finest ingredients. Not everybody can make a meatloaf, but when it is done right, delizioso! It has depth and delicate flavors. And a meatloaf is strong, too. It should stand firm in the hottest oven," he explained with glistening eyes. "Up from the table, Stella. It's time you learned meatloaf," he demanded.

Star understood that there was no fighting Leo. He was on a mission. So, for the next hour, he taught her how to slice vegetables so thin that the carrots and zuchinni melted into the meat, leaving only a hint of color. The bread was diced into light, downy crumbs and mixed with fluffy, gently beaten eggs. All the ingredients were then kneaded together with herbs and olive oil and baked for another hour creating a succulent symphony of flavor.

After he pulled the hot dish from the oven, Leo called Star back into the kitchen and asked her to take a seat. "People who don't cook—they judge the meatloaf," he began. "They call it lowly, peasant food. But the good cook, he knows a real meatloaf when he tastes her. He knows she takes time to develope, tenderize and flavor. But when all the ingredients come together, she is a masterpiece, a da Vinci."

He wobbled from the stove and sat down next Star, taking her hands into his. "Comprendere, Stella?" he asked, looking at the meatloaf and then looking back to her.

"You're calling me a meatloaf! Aren't you?" she asked with tears welling in her eyes.

"Yes! Yes! A lovely meatloaf," he said proudly.

"Oh, Leo. Thank you. Thank you for calling me a meatloaf and for teaching me so many lessons," she said, bringing his fingers to her lips. "You've truly saved me."

After putting Rosie to bed that night, Star and Leo sat on the couch together, watching CNN's coverage of Janus' arrest. Phil Roberts, the evening anchor, was reporting that two other families had stepped forward with charges against Perfidius involving sexual relations with their teen daughters. Leo smacked his knees and laughed as he watched the clip of Perfidius being escorted to the police cruiser in handcuffs.

"Like I've said before, Stella, life is never tedioso when you're around."

Star laughed a sad laugh and grasped his hand. "I love you, Leo, damn I love you," she whispered with exhaustion.

Star woke early the next morning to wrestle Rosie out of bed. They planned to see *Hercules* that day but were going to the pancake house beforehand. Just as she reached for the door-knob of Rosie's room, the front bell chimed through the house. Star cringed with anger, turned on her heels, and stormed down the steps. When she peered through the sidelight, she was shocked by the image before her. Hillary Heisman, a disheveled mess, was standing on her step, with bleary eyes and a swollen nose.

She yanked open the door in dismay. "My God, Hillary, please come in," Star said, scanning the street for reporters.

The woman stepped through the door and threw herself in Star's arms. "Oh, dear God, Star! This is so horrible," she wailed.

Star peeled Hillary's arms from around her neck and quietly agreed. "I can't imagine what you are going through right now, Hillary. Please come in and sit down," she said, guiding her to the couch.

Hillary sat down and rested her purse on her lap. With trembling fingers, she pulled a finely embroidered handker-chief from her purse and wiped her eyes.

"You have done so much for me already, Star. But, I need you to help me once again," she began.

"What is it, Hillary?" Star asked with sincere sympathy.

"I want you to tell me everything you know about Janus. Tell me about your relationship with him, tell me about Emmy Dribble, and tell me about this new girl, who's barely twelve years older than our daughter. I need to stop creating my own fantastical reality and face the ugly, horrible truth about my husband," she cried. "And I want you to help me."

Star stared at the floor quickly comprehending what the woman was asking of her. She was in dangerous territory. If Janus was found innocent and the couple reunited, she would be forever fingered as the one with a malicious agenda. And need she remind the woman that Rosie's life was put on the line to save Katie Ann? How could Hillary ask more of her?

"I've been drawn into this web over and over again. I want to cut the strings and move on with my life," Star firmly but gently answered.

"Listen, Star. I'm begging you. I'm begging you!" she cried.

Star couldn't ignore the pain embedded on Hillary's face. A visible line was now etched across her brow and thick slants had been drawn on her forehead, pointing down toward the bridge of her nose. Star took a deep breath and slowly released the air, trying to put herself in Hillary's shoes. Star's own life had been hard, but Hillary's Chanel suits and South Sea pearls didn't make her world any easier. Life as Janus' wife must have been a true curse.

Star hesitated but then clasped her hands together and raised her eyes to Hillary. "From woman to woman and mother to mother, I'll tell you what I know, but this will be the last time we ever speak about Janus. Do you agree to that?" Star asked.

Hillary nodded her headed in agreement, so Star began with her time at Bosco University where she first met Janus as a professor. She ended the account with Tuesday's revelations regarding Penny. The only key detail that she chose to leave out was Janus' initial refusal to accept Rosie as a bone marrow donor. There was no need to dig the knife any deeper.

When Star concluded the history, Hillary thanked her. "I appreciate everything that you have done for Katie Ann and me. Please forgive me for calling you the "sacrificial lamb" along with the other horrible things I may have said. How blind and coarse of me!"

Star reached out and patted her hand. "I understand why you said those things, Hillary. At the time, you had to believe your husband for your own survival. Like I've said before, we choose ignorance at different times in our lives just to keep our heads above water."

"Thank you, Star. Sincerely, thank you. Trista would be very proud of you. When the ashes settle, I want our daughters to be a part of each other's lives, and I hope to be your friend, as well," she said with sincerity.

Star slowly stood as she heard Rosie's door creak open and her tiny feet begin to pad down the steps. "I think eventually Rosie and Katie Ann will be sisters and friends, but let's wait a while longer," Star said.

By the time Leo's birthday rolled around, Ted apologized for his misguided role in Janus' games, and Star responded with opened arms when he accompanied Jimmy to the party. Prodded by Leo's "perdonare e dimenticare," forgive and forget philosophy, Star opened the door for Kory and Emmy to attend, as well, but when Kory arrived without his wife, she was immensely relieved. As the band kicked up "Don't Sit Under the Apple Tree," Leo and Rosie held hands and wobbled around in a circle, dancing and singing. When it was time for cake and ice cream, Rosie helped Leo blow out all eighty-nine candles. And for the first time in many months, Star was relaxed and happy.

She was sitting at the bar enjoying the good spirits of the evening when the sleigh bells jingled and in stumbled an unlikely patron. The woman had a gristly face and matted hair, dense as steel wool. She wore a faded sweatshirt, jeans and ratty canvas gym shoes. Star bowed her head to the one of the managers as a sign to remove the woman and push her on down the street. While Steve spoke to the vagrant, a knot balled in Star's conscience. She could have easily become that woman if she hadn't found her way out of the Tenderloin. She went around the backside of the bar and pulled two twenties from the cash register to give to the woman. But as she approached her, Star stopped and stood as still as stone. *Breathe, just breathe*, she repeated to herself.

There, amid the disharmony of voices, Star heard, "That's Star, right there. That's my Star. Star Nox! That's my baby!" As people began to stare at the commotion, Star bolted toward Sue. "What are you doing here," she demanded through gritted teeth.

The woman grabbed her and pulled Star into a strong hug. As she sucked in her breath, the woman's stench seared her nose. Star yanked away, grasped the woman's elbow and pulled her out the front door. She dragged her down the sidewalk toward the parking lot and stopped.

"What are you doing here?!" Star roared. "Leave now and never come back!"

"I told you on the phone. I need help. I'm flat out a' money," the scratchy voice explained.

"Then how in the hell did you get here from Oregon or wherever the hell you are living?" Star demanded.

"A friend was comin' out this way. Did me real good and dropped me in Cincy. I thought you'd be glad to see me," the woman said, yanking on her sweatshirt that had inched up above her stomach.

"I told you on the phone. Forget my name. Forget my number. Forget that you ever knew me. I suggest you call your friend and tell him to get you right now, or I will have you arrested for stalking, harassment and trespassing," Star promised in a low growl.

"You kick me to the curb—I'll get you back, missy," Sue threatened as she leaned closer to Star's face. "You may be smart and pretty and rich now, but I'm mean and ugly and poor, so when I get you, it'll hurt."

Star's heart was pounding, and the street seemed to be moving under her, but she stood her ground. "Get out of here now, or I will call the police. I'm certain there's a warrant out for something you've done in the past fifteen years. As a matter of fact, I've got an undercover on duty right inside," she warned.

Sue raised her hand to slap her daughter's face, but slowed by years of drug abuse and life on the streets, Star easily caught her arm and twisted it. As the woman wriggled and yelped in pain, Star roared, "Get out of Cincinnati and stay out! Otherwise, your ass is going to be locked up forever." Star let go of Sue's arm and tossed her to the ground.

The woman scrambled to her feet, stuck her chin toward Star and screeched, "I'll be back! I'll be back, missy. And it's gonna' hurt when I do!" With that, she turned around and headed down the street, but in doing so, she raised both arms high in the air and gave Star the finger as she walked into the darkness.

Star was pale and shaken when she went back into Leo's, but only Kory seemed to notice.

"Are you okay?" he asked, coming up behind her.

"Yeah. Just a bad nickel that keeps showing up. Everything's under control, though," she simply said. Star had no desire to confide in him about Dirty-Syringe-Sue. "Where's Emmy tonight?" she asked only to change topics.

"I don't know. She moved back in with her parents for a while."

"I see," Star said coolly. She was too shaken to say much else.

"Listen, Star. I'm sorry for being such an asshole to you," he began to explain.

Star noticed that his hair was neatly trimmed and his clothes were no longer disheveled. Nonetheless, her tolerance for him had dwindled. She wondered if he really had the strength of character that she had always afforded him. "Okay" was the only energy she had left to give.

He looked into Star's eyes with a sense of urgency, like what he had to say was life-altering. "You were right," he began again. "I married her for all the wrong reasons. I thought I was her hero, but I never really was."

"You're a proud man, Kory, who needs his ego stroked. Pride is good when the dignity comes from within, but when you rely on others to determine your importance, you are certain to fall. You abandoned our relationship because I treated you like a friend but not a hero. The pain you left stays with me."

Kory winced and shrugged his shoulders. "I am sorry, Star. What else can I say?"

"I'm not asking for anything more. I'm tired, though. I need to get my little crew home. Stop in sometime and we'll chat again."

Kory hung his head and then slowly raised it. "Thank you for the honesty, Star. I needed it."

"I've always had your back, Kory," she said, patting him on the shoulder. "Like I said, stop in and we'll talk," she assured him and walked back into the thick of the crowded bar.

Neither Rosie nor Leo put up a fight when she said that it was time to go home, and both nodded off in the car. Though Leo's was only ten minutes from their home, Star felt uncomfortable for most of the drive. Sue's grisly stench was still in her nose and on her clothes. She tried to push the woman's face out of her mind, but she couldn't. Star sensed that Sue was following her, but she didn't know if the feeling was her imagination or reality. A car a few lengths back seemed to be changing lanes when she changed. When she slowed to let the car pass, the driver slowed, as well. She took a right on a side street and looped back around to the main thoroughfare with the same car on her tail. As she turned down her street, however, the car passed on, but her heart was still pounding in her chest.

She kept a sharp eye while she unloaded her crew. As she carried Rosie into the house, she reminded Leo to deadbolt the door and to activate the security system. Her little party girl was sound asleep before Star hung up her dress and tucked her under the covers. Leo was rustling around in his room as she went back downstairs to double check the windows and doors.

Sue was probably harmless, but she really was 'awfully mean and ugly.'

She stuck her head in Leo's room to say goodnight. The light was still on, but he was under the covers. "Did you have a good time, Birthday Boy?" she asked.

"The evening was bravissimo!" Leo said with delight. "But tell me something. Who was that old strega who came through the door? She acted like she was your long, lost friend," he said with his wise eyes.

He never missed anything, she thought. "I'll tell you in the morning. I'm too tired to go into it," she said, leaning against the door frame.

"No, Stella. Tell me now," he demanded.

"It was Sue, Leo, my mother. She came to town begging for money from me. I told her to get lost for good." As she told him, Star watched a dark shadow cross Leo's brow.

"Leo, that's exactly why I didn't tell you. I don't want you to worry. She's a broken-down drug addict with one foot in jail and the other in her grave."

"I'm not so sure about that, Star. She has a dangerous look to her," he said.

"I know. I'm not stupido. I beefed up security at the shop. There's an undercover on duty every night. I'll give him a call. And you need to start using that outrageously expensive security system that I had installed here. Even when you are in the house, I want the system on. Did you put it on alert tonight like I asked?"

"I forgot the damn code," he said sheepishly.

"Leo, it's Rosie's birth date," she said, shaking her head. "I'm changing the code to your birthday right now, 2-8-10. If you forget that, then I'll be worried," she said with a teasing smile.

Star moved to the bed and kissed him on the forehead. "Happy eighty-ninth, Leo! Long live my precious king!" she said gently.

Star stepped out and closed the door behind her. She went directly to the front door and triple checked the locks and then tested the living room windows. Dead leaves crackled outside as she walked through the dining room, checking each window. Maybe the raccoons were shuffling around in the bushes, preparing an assault on her garbage cans, she thought or hoped. Cold air rushed in as one of the windows slipped open with a slight tug. "Damn. He's got to be more careful," she whispered. When she turned from the window, Star thought she saw something black gleam in the moonlight. She stood still and stared out the window, waiting for movement. Sue was wearing a blue sweatshirt and jeans earlier that evening, she reassured herself.

As she walked into the kitchen to change the security code, Star felt like she was being watched. She stood in the doorway and listened. She was certain she heard the back steps creak. A few loose boards on the bottom steps always moaned with the slightest pressure. Her heart was pounding, and she felt like she was in one of those horrific dreams where she was so scared that she couldn't move or scream for help. She yanked herself into motion and flew at the door, reaching for the deadbolt, but pushing against the door was him, Leather Jacket, laughing at her futile attempt to keep him out. He slammed against the door and easily broke through the frame on the old house.

Star flung back and slammed into the kitchen table. She caught her balance and reached for the drawer holding the knives, but Leather Jacket snatched her by the leg and dragged her to the floor. She kicked him in the gut with her free leg and screamed for help, but he lunged forward and grabbed her by the throat. "I told you that I'd be back," he snarled, with his face inches from hers. He pressed Star to the floor with his own body weight while she flailed under him. "You castrated me. Now, it's your turn," he said, pulling a switch blade from his pocket. He snapped it open and jammed his knee between her legs. "Here it comes, baby. Just like I promised!" he sneered as he cocked back his arm. He then rammed the knife straight into her crotch. The blade struck her pubic bone, and her body jolted in agony. He cocked back his elbow once more and came forward with greater force, but just as he did so, a powerful blow knocked the knife out of his hand. Star raised her head and saw Leo standing behind him, holding his baseball bat, cranked again for a full swing at the monster's head. He swung hard, but Leather Jacket caught the bat in mid air and pushed Leo against the wall with the force of the bat. Star managed to kick herself away and scrambled for the knife. She stole it from under the table but not in time to prevent Leather Jacket from swinging the bat across Leo's head, sounding a horrible crack through the kitchen. In utter rage, she leaped toward him, and with all her force, slammed the knife deep into his back. Leather Jacket gasped for air a few times and then fell to the floor. The entire fight lasted no more than sixty seconds, but a man was dead and she saw blood streaming from Leo's ear.

She crawled to Leo and cried, "Can you hear me? Talk to me, Leo! Talk to me!"

He opened his eyes and tried to talk. "I'm here Stella, but I'm leaving now. Nella's calling me. She says it's time for me to come home," he whispered. "Tell Rosebud, I'll always be with her."

"Don't leave me, Leo! Please don't leave me! You're all I got," she cried. Star heard sirens in the distance.

"I called them," he whispered. "You're safe now."

"Leo, please don't go!" she wailed, "I'm begging you!"

Leo closed his eyes and let out a heavy breath. "I love you, Stella. I love you," he whispered and released his final breath. Star fell on his chest and wept until she felt hands tugging on her shoulders. She screamed and jerked her head up to find a police officer standing over her.

"Miss Nox," he said gently. "We're here to help." Star shook her head and leaned back down to Leo. She pulled him into her arms and rocked softly, humming his favorite apple tree song, while officers poured into her kitchen.

"Ma'am, I know this is hard, but is your little girl safe?' one of the female officers bent down and asked. Star turned chalk white but then remembered that Rosie was safe and sound, fast asleep in her room. "She's upstairs in bed," Star whispered With that, one of the female officers rushed from the room and headed up the steps.

"Ma'am, you're bleeding all over the front of your dress. You need to go to the hospital. Is there someone who we can call to take care of your child?" another officer asked.

Star nodded her head yes and looked down. "He's in my arms," she cried.

The officer looked away and quickly wiped a tear from her eye.

By the time the paramedics came through the door, Star's wound was bleeding profusely, and she was growing weak. They cleared the room and drew up her dress to find a deep gouge in her groin. Her blood pressure was dropping and her pulse was weak.

"We've got to pump up her volume. Fast! Get the plasma and saline. I'll start the line," the paramedic told his partner who was already heading out the door.

"Am I going to be okay?" Star whispered to the paramedic. "My baby's upstairs."

"You'll be fine," he said, establishing the IV port with precision.

His partner came in the door with two bags, one clear and one straw color. They moved her to a stretcher and started the IV. The liquid gushed through the line while they went to work on the wound site. Star closed her eyes but tried to stay focused on the paramedics. She listened to the one who seemed to be in command as he radioed the hospital. "Caucasian female, late twenties, approximately one hundred fifteen pounds, medium, height. Excessive bleeding from wound at pubic bone, likely internal. Blood plasma and saline drip started. Prep for surgery."

Tear drops streamed from the corners of Star's closed eyes and collected in the wells of her ears.

"Officer!" Star tried to shout.

The paramedic called over an officer who squatted down next to the gurney. "Yes ma'am."

"Call Kory Huber to take Rosie. He's her godfather. Call Ted and Jimmy, too," she added, but her strength began fading and her eyes closed.

CHAPTER 28

The Tenderloin . . .

"Stop! Stop! I'll kill y—Leo! No!" Star tried to yell, but the tubes stuck up her nose and down her throat were in the way. The beeping grew louder and louder. She thrashed her arms to pull the apparatus from her mouth. "Leo!" she cried, but no words were coming out to warn him. "Stop!" she yelled, but the only sound she could hear was the horrible beeping that was ringing in her ears.

"Star, quiet! Calm down. It's an IV machine. You're in the hospital," the vaguely familiar voice was saying.

What hospital? I've got to stop him. He's going to kill Leo! With her last bit of strength, Star yanked her arms free from the pressure holding her back, and the beeping exploded into wild pandemonium.

"Star! It's Kory! Stop! Stop! You're going to hurt yourself!" she heard somewhere in the distance. Hands were all over her body, holding her arms and legs down. She tried desperately to break free, but their force was too strong. She thrashed a few more times, but like a dying animal, her body soon gave up and went limp. Her breathing slowed and became shallow. But the poking and the piercing seemed relentless. Voices were clamoring about blood pressure and oxygen levels. But she didn't care anymore, for reality was slowly setting in. She needn't open her eyes to understand that Leo wouldn't be sitting before her with his crystal-clear blue eyes and sturdy smile. He was gone. Her courage. Her moral compass. Her guardian. Her best friend. Her hero was gone.

When the room quieted and her body was left alone, Star slowly opened her eyes. She peered around and spotted Kory who was sitting in a chair next to the window. He was leaning forward with his head hung and hands clasped together. Sharp sun rays shining through the window were caught in his grip, making his knuckles stark white.

Star stared at him for a few minutes, trying to regain her consciousness. "Where's Rosie?" she finally whispered through the oxygen tube pried down her nose.

Kory's head shot up in surprise. "Star . . . she's okay. She's okay," he said, jumping up and coming to her bedside. "Ted and Jimmy are taking good care of her."

"Thank heaven . . . There's nothing else . . . to care about," she whispered more to herself than to Kory.

He took her hand in his and squeezed tightly. "Leo loved you so much, Star."

"Please don't say his name, not yet," she said and fell silent. She eventually dropped into a restless slumber with her body jerking, fighting for peace.

That next morning there was a soft knock on Star's hospital room door followed by the charge nurse who came into explain that a detective was in the hall, waiting to speak with her. Kory was half asleep in a chair but quickly rose to wake Star.

He approached the bed and stared for a moment before waking her. Star's black curls seemed frozen in motion about her shoulders. Her face was motionless, something he had never witnessed. From the first day Kory saw her on Bosco's campus until now, he marveled at how her mouth, her eyes, her cheeks danced with energy. And her thick lashes were every bit as long as they were six years ago. He still fought the burning desire to touch the black fringe with his lips, to press his lips against her temples, feeling and absorbing her thoughts. But so much life had been lived in the past six years, a time that could not be changed. He closed his eyes and gripped the steel bed railing until his fingers grew numb. Star must have sensed his presence as she awakened and found him standing over her. He let go of the railing and tried to smile.

"How are you feeling?" he asked.

"Okay," she whispered.

"Strong enough to talk to the police? There is a detective in the hall waiting to speak with you."

Star tugged on the railing to test her strength and managed to pull herself to a sitting position. She looked around the room, trying to gain a sense of balance. When she steadied her gaze back on Kory, she was silent for a moment but finally agreed to see the police. "This won't get any easier. Might as well let him in."

Kory bent down and kissed her forehead and then turned to find the detective. Star rubbed her eyes and pulled the blankets up over her chest. When the two returned, she immediately recognized Detective Schmidt whom she had met during the Penny Defloro calamity.

"We meet again, Detective Schmidt. Guess I can't keep myself out of trouble's way," she whispered.

"I hope we will meet under better terms in the future, Miss Nox," Detective Schmidt said solemnly.

"Please call me Star. Pull up a seat. I imagine this will take awhile," she said sadly.

Detective Schmidt was an astute professional who was very familiar with the drill that was to follow. He knew his time with Star would be limited, so he grabbed a chair and began to unravel the sordid details that he had pieced together in just thirty-six hours. Ira Black was indeed dead and her mother, Sue Nox, had been taken into custody and charged as an accomplice to a felony-murder and attempted murder. The police arrested her as she was trying to drive out of Star's street but ended up slammed into a parked car. Events began to unfold earlier that day, however, when Officer Tony Martinelli contacted the Cincinnati Police Department from San Francisco, alerting them to the fact that Ira Black, a convicted felon, had missed a parole meeting. Detectives found a similar message from Officer Martinelli on Star's answering machine, which was also left just hours before the attack.

Detective Schmidt went on to explain that he had spoken to Tony Martinelli who was able to shed light on the convoluted statement that Sue had given. By Tony Martinelli's account, Sue had turned up on the streets of Tenderloin the year before, prostituting and breaking into cars to support her smack habit. In the past few months, Tony had spotted Ira Black and Sue hanging on the street corners together, one too many times. When he got word that Black missed a meeting with his parole officer a few days back and that Sue had disappeared from the streets, he became concerned and contacted the Cincinnati Police Department.

"Based on Sue's pathetic statement to the police . . . acting as the distraught mother and devoted grandmother . . . looks like Black and she had a twisted plan to kill you then take off with Rosie and your money." After he finished, Detective Schmidt hung his head, shaking it in dismay.

"Detective Schmidt, no need to shake your head in confusion. None of this surprises me. I predicted something like this would happen a long time ago," Star said flatly. "And when my involvement with Perfidius went public, I knew that it was only a matter of time."

"Star, I know what you're saying, but I still find it shocking when a mother tries to kill her own child. I don't' think women are wired to kill, especially mothers."

"I told you when we met the first time around that I'm from the Tenderloin. Nothing is wired right in the District . . . nothing, including Sue Nox. A woman who'd sell her daughter to support her heroin habit would as quickly kill her off."

"What do you mean?" the detective asked.

Kory had been sitting quietly in the corner listening, gathering details about Star's life that she had never revealed. But now, silently, he moved his chair closer to her bed to hear more of the lurid facts. He had always sensed that she had a tough childhood. He read the hard knocks in her stories and saw the calloused scars in her character, but he completely underestimated the hell that she had gone through to become the woman now before him, battered and bruised all over again.

The detective scooted his chair closer to the bed, as well. "Star, tell me about your life with Sue. It's important to the case."

Star looked at Kory and then at the detective. "There's nothing pretty about my life, gentleman. When I was ten, Sue began prostituting me to support her smack habit. I had a back-alley abortion by the time I was eleven. Ira Black showed up in the picture because Jack and Sue owed him money. He polluted me to pay off their debt. I stuck a knife through his balls when he came after me the second time. Black ended up in jail for twelve years for attempted murder and rape. When Jack overdosed and died, Sue sold me to my grandparents for one hundred grand. That's it in a nutshell. Typical life down in the Tenderloin. Fun, wouldn't you say?"

Kory sat stunned in the corner. Though the detective already knew some of the information, he still seemed shocked. He closed his notebook and raised his eyebrows. "You're tough as nails, aren't you?"

Star shook her head. "No, Detective . . . I'm salty . . . made from the grit and grime of Tenderloin salt blown in from the bay," she said with a sad smile. "But none of that matters now. The only thing that matters is that I've lost my precious Leo." Star held back the tears until Leo's name formed on her lips. She began to weep silently, trying to keep the pain just between Leo and her. "I'm tired now," she finally said. "Do you mind if we call it a day?"

Detective Schmidt stood and thanked her. Kory followed him out of the room while Star fell into a private reverie with Leo. His spirit was lingering about, shuffling around the bed, soothing and protecting her. She needed time alone to absorb his strength and to lock his memory into her heart and soul forever.

Later that day, Star was awakened by the phone. Kory had left earlier, so she scrambled to reach the receiver. "Hello," she said in a crackly voice.

"Star! It's Tony. Officer Tony," he said in repressed panic.

"Tony . . . it's you," she answered, still drowsy.

"Star, I am so sorry," he began.

"Everything's going to be okay," she said weakly.

"But I promised that it would be okay, that he never would find you. But then . . . then all that goddamn publicity about the preacher and you. . . . I'm just so sorry. Julie and I were visiting the grandkids over the weekend, and I missed the parole officer's report about Black going AWOL. If I had just gotten to you a day sooner, none of this would have happened," Tony rambled in stream of words washed together with apology and regret.

"Tony, slow down," Star said, sitting up in bed. "None of this is your fault. Ira Black was going to find me somehow, no matter what. He promised. I knew it. I've known it in my heart since the day he shouted at me in the courtroom. Please don't carry any of this in your conscience. Black and Sue's lives were out of your control. Addiction and pure evilness drove them crazy. You couldn't control them. You know that as well as I."

"I know what you're saying, Star, but you've always been special to me, special since the night I found you, freezing underneath that bench at four in the morning."

"Tony, listen to me. I'm safe now. We're safe, Rosie and me. And Leo's with me. I can feel him," she explained.

CHAPTER 29

Fearless capo cuoco . . .

February's misery hung in the sky with dark, heavy clouds and a bitter wind that whipped through the trees, rattling their bony branches. The funeral party climbed out of the limousines as a full Military Honors Detail accepted Leo's coffin from the hearse. A bugler, a firing party and a full color guard stood at attention several yards beyond the grave while the mourners slowly made their way behind the coffin. Ted accompanied Jimmy who was carrying Rosie nestled in his neck. Kory pushed Star's wheel chair across the icy grass and halted in front of the gravesite as the rest of the cortege gathered around.

Father Marco stepped forward and began the committal service, but Rosie's cries interrupted his prayers. Jimmy caressed her head, but the cries grew stronger. She wriggled down from his arms and threw herself at her mother. Despite the pain shooting through her body, Star pulled her close and held tight. "I'm here, Rosie. I'm here . . . Leo's with us, too," she whispered, trying to console her daughter as well as herself. Rosie wrapped her arms tightly around Star's neck and, together, they wept as the coffin was lowered into the grave.

A fierce wind picked up, swirling about the small crowd, swallowing Father's final words of prayer. When the time came for Star's tribute, she tried desperately to stand up, but the pain in her abdomen was too strong, forcing her back into the wheelchair. Sorrow and grief were threatening her strength, as well. She looked across the crowd and down into the coffin, searching for Leo's courage. Willed by his audacity and honor, she sat up straight, took a deep breath and began her farewell.

"My dear Leo, we were a motley pair in the kitchen, were we not? You with your wispy grey hairs and me with my wild curls—but we were a great team, my tireless capo cuoco, my master chef. The lessons were frequent and the recipes were complicated. But look what was cooking in the oven. You taught me that no one is born with courage. Corragio is found in the burns and cuts you get from cooking with fire and handling knives. You taught me that anger is best pounded out by making potato dumplings, not by pounding out other people. And about respect, it's not always about what you demand from others. Respect is about how you handle the onion. You slice it thin, delicate-like, to earn that velvety flavor. Now dignity, that was a tough beast to tame, but you had a recipe for that, too. You taught me that dignity is found inside the pie, by the way you cultivate and care for the apples—not by the way others judge the looks of your crust. And yes, yes. I remember the *stupidos*. Scorch the milk once—ignorant. Scorch the milk twice—stupido! And Leo, you taught me that Happiness is really out there within reach, but you have to create it yourself by what's already in the cupboard. And it's not impossible to make, either. You just have to be patient and follow the recipe. Combine together a bushel of love, several pounds of strength, a couple quarts of kindness, a few cups of tears, some sprigs of faith, a dash of disappointment and a pinch of heartache. Mix all the ingredients together and bake for Eighty-nine years. And there you have it—puro, delizioso Happiness." With her last words, Star caught her breath and a single teardrop slide down her cheek.

Kory bent down and kissed the top of her head. "That was beautiful, Stella," he choked.

Jimmy stepped forward and lifted Rosie into his arms. He whispered into the little girl's ear while Ted handed her a single red rose, and then the three moved forward as Rosie dropped the first blossom into the grave. Determined to stand, Kory helped Star rise and take a step forward. She tossed the rose and whispered, "Goodbye, my Leo." She turned and leaned against Kory for support. The clouds billowed over head and snowflakes began to fall, dusting the coffin with a blanket of perfect ice crystals.

"Present arms!" echoed through the air, commencing the rendering of honors. Rifles were raised and the ringing of three volleys of musketry ricocheted off the hillsides. When the sounds of gunfire quieted, the mournful cry of "Taps" enveloped the funeral party, reminding them of Leo's honor and service to the country. With just a few final notes flowing from the bugle, two soldiers stepped forward to fold the American flag. They then passed the 'Stars and Stripes' to the leader who presented it to Star. She clutched the flag to her chest and closed her eyes.

"He was my hero," she told the small crowd.

The End

ACKNOWLEDGEMENT

I thank my husband, Michael, who is my most ardent supporter and candid critic. I thank my daughters, Grace and Margo, for their sassy laughter while *"Salty"* was being crafted. I thank my many manuscript readers including Norma Huber, Terri Middleton, Julie Martina, David Reid, Nancy Malas and Susan Fitzgerald for their editorial direction. I would like to acknowledge the spirit of my grandmother Alma Amorini Swarts who, much like Leo, showed her love and support through meatloaf, gnocchi, mostaccioli, breaded veal chops, and soups. Also, I hope the truly great writers, Thomas Hardy and Nathaniel Hawthorne, hear their stories of the human condition ringing through these pages.

I would like to give special acknowledgement to my dear friend Nancy Castellini Hecht who passed away while the final edit of the book was being drawn. Nancy was a "salty" woman with an amazing personality and a generous heart. She gave voice to people when they struggled to find their own strength. Nancy leaves a beautiful legacy with her husband, Mike, and children, Erin, Nicholas, Kevin and Jeffrey.

READING GROUP QUESTIONS
AND TOPICS OF DISCUSSION

1. Most every female dreams of meeting "Prince Charm-ing," the handsome hero who swoops her up and saves her from an ill-starred life of drudgery! This fantasy is founded in the Pygmalion myth, a story about a Cyprus king who sculpts a beautiful statue and begs the goddess Aphrodite to breathe life into the life-less girl. Aphrodite abides by his wishes, permitting Pygmalion to marry the image he shaped and molded. This "Prince Charming" theme continues to endure, even in contemporary tales. *Cinderella*, *My Fair Lady* and *Pretty Woman* are just a few of the modern ver-sions of the classic Pygmalion story. What role does Pygmalion play in the Tenderloin? Does Star believe in the Pygmalion ideal? Is she searching for her "Prince Charming"? Does she discover her Pygmalion? If so, in whom?

2. Oftentimes, women are attracted to men who pos-sess traits that seem familiar to them, regardless if the traits are good or bad. Subconsciously, what does Star find familiar in Janus Perfidius that allows her to fall for him? How does this relate to the Pygmalion theme?

3. Though Kory Huber is a superior character, why does Star hold back from developing a romantic relationship

with him? What does she believe a friend will accept but a lover will not? Is she correct in this assumption? Would Kory have accepted her dark history early in the story?

4. When and why is Star compelled to clean?

5. Naming characters is an important literary tool for Jacki Lyon. Hester and Stella are both forms of "Star." *Salty Miss Tenderloin* has loose connections to the *Scarlet Letter,* Nathaniel Hawthorne's novel about secret sins and hypocrites. His central character, Hester Prynne, is condemned to wear a scarlet letter **A** on her breast, as punishment for adultery with a minister whose identity is concealed until the final pages of the tale. In her isolation, Hester must also deal with a society of well-oiled moralists whom Jacki Lyon refers to as "stone throwers." What is Star's badge of disgrace that she wears? Who are the primary "stone throwers" in Star's life? Is she ever able to escape her badge of disgrace and judgment by these people?

6. Stella is the Italian and Latin term for Star. Stella Maris is a title for the Blessed Virgin Mary as well as Polaris, commonly known as the North Star. Do you find Leo's endearing term of Stella ironic?

7. Leo is one of the earliest recognized constellations, dating back to as early as 4,000 B.C. From an astrological perspective, Leo ("The Great Lion") governs will and authority. As a fire sign, Leo people are confident and generous. Does Leo Bartatello characterize this great constellation by governing will and authority in the story?

8. Fate and destiny are significant themes in the story. With a name like Starlight Nox, how does destiny or fate play a role in Star's life? Is she able to escape the stigma of "white trash"? Without the great wisdom of Leo, would her fate have taken a different course?

9. Star frequently refers to Thomas Hardy's *The Mayor of Casterbridge*, clinging to Elizabeth Jane's belief that "happiness was but the occasional episode in a general drama of pain." Similar to Elizabeth Jane, Star was sold by her father [and mother] as was Rosie. Is Star ever able to move beyond the scarring from these events and embrace happiness?

10. Related to the above question, Michael Henchard of *The Mayor of Casterbridge* along with Janus Perfidius and Jack and Sue Nox sold their own children. Michael Henchard spent twenty years trying to repent for his sin. Is this one of those sins against mankind that can never be forgiven? Is Janus the kind of man who would repent?

11. Janus Perfidius' name has mythological origins. The term Janus refers to an old Roman god who is represented as having two faces, one looking forward and one looking backward. The term Perfidious means treacherous. Is the name fitting for the venerable minister? How is he related to Arthur Dimmesdale, the minister in the *Scarlet Letter*?

12. Koros (Kory) Huber's name also has mythological origins. Koros (Kouros) was the name of a fallen Greek warrior who came to represent the idealized, archetypical warrior. Koros was also the son of the Greek deity,

Hybris (Excessive Pride). How does Kory's name relate to his role in the novel?

13. What has changed in Star that finally allows her to embrace her inner "Salty Miss Tenderloin"?

14. The theme of battle, military or otherwise, plays a significant role in the novel. Identify the different battles and battlefields that are developed within and among the characters. Who ultimately wins their internal/external battle? Who loses the fight?

15. Both food and the need for love are at the top of Maslow's Hierarchy of Needs. How does Leo intertwine these basic needs to help Star evolve into a complete person? What roadblocks within herself does he help her defeat?

16. What inner and external conflicts keep Star and Kory apart? By the end of the novel, have they both evolved enough to finally come together as a couple? Have they come together as a couple?

17. The Seven Deadly Sins are:

Lust	Greed	Gluttony	Sloth/Sadness
Envy	Pride	Wrath	

In the novel, who best represents each of the Seven Deadly Sins? Some of their names provide clues.

CPSIA information can be obtained
at www.ICGtesting.com
Printed in the USA
LVHW080013291020
670138LV00013B/232